CRUNCHY ORANGE CHICKEN

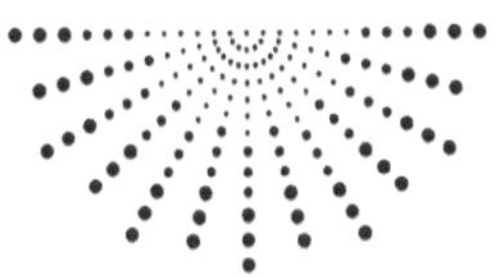

TREY LARI

Oclari Publishing
USA
oclari.com

Cover Illustration by Angga Jaya

ISBN: 979-8-9906303-0-7 (Oclari ebook)
ISBN: 979-8-9906303-1-4 (Oclari paperback)
ISBN: 979-8-9906303-4-5 (Oclari hardback)

To Drew

CRUNCHY ORANGE CHICKEN

For trigger warnings, bonus content and the latest news and updates from the author, visit:

TreyLari.com/books

Or scan the code:

1

KADEN

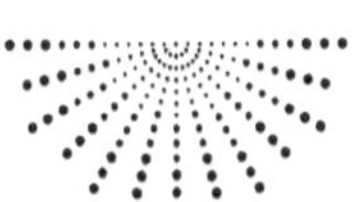

Aldenbrook Academy's cafeteria buzzed with conversation and clanking dishes. The aromas of lunch blended with the stench of teens who should have showered after gym class but didn't. Kaden twisted his fork in a gloopy pile of angel hair pasta, wondering if he could force another mouthful down, when Hunter Gan slid into a chair next to him, his gray lunch tray landing lightly on the table.

Kaden stared at him, wide-eyed. He'd never seen someone as smooth and graceful. The cubes of gelatin in his dessert dish hadn't even jiggled. It was as if he'd teleported here.

His white school uniform shirt was unwrinkled and flawless, as always. How Hunter kept it so immaculate ranked as one of the greatest mysteries of the universe. Kaden's own shirt had creased on the ride to school and was freshly stained from the tomato sauce he wiped away a minute earlier.

Jacob, Kaden's half-brother, was on the other side of the table. Before Hunter's seeming materialization, Kaden and Jacob had been conversing in Filipino, with Jacob chastising him once more for still drinking from a juice box at age fifteen.

"Secretly planning world domination again?" Hunter asked, continuing a long-running joke, repeated whenever they were speaking a foreign language. He grinned at Jacob, then Kaden, his teeth as bright as his shirt, and equally pristine.

Kaden smiled slightly, keeping his mouth closed while running his tongue over the braces on his teeth, trying to dislodge a stuck bit of pasta.

"It's so weird hearing a white guy speak Filipino," Hunter said to Kaden.

Admittedly, there was a certain irony. Hunter's ancestry was Korean, but he only spoke English. Meanwhile, Kaden and Jacob spoke fluent Filipino. Jacob's biological mother, Angie, was Filipina and had taught the half-brothers from infancy.

"Dude. What's up?" Jacob said, as the best friends gave each other fist bumps in that manner jock boys do.

Kaden nodded in greeting, sipping from his juice box, still working at that stuck bit of pasta. "Hey," he said after swallowing. He inhaled. Why did Hunter have to smell so nice? Because he was perfect, obviously. Perfect in every way, except one.

"The *EoOO* update notes are posted." Jacob held his phone screen toward Hunter. It displayed a web page for a video game called *Elves of Ora Online* and listed numerous updates to the game that were released that morning.

The trio had spent far more hours playing *EoOO* than they should have, especially during the pandemic lockdown. It's not like it was their fault. The developers had made the game way too addictive.

"Did you read them yet?" Jacob asked Hunter.

"Not yet. Anything good?"

"*Only* a brand new dungeon!" Jacob said, barely containing his enthusiasm.

A spark of excitement flickered in Hunter's eyes. "What?" He put on his glasses as he studied the screen. It was like he'd transformed from Superman into Clark Kent. Kaden melted a little more. How could he look even cuter with glasses?

"It's a surprise from the devs. They didn't even put it on the beta server," Jacob said.

Kaden made a scoffing sound. "No beta testing. Bet it's buggy as hell."

"So, same as everything else in *EoOO*," Jacob said. "I say we try it. That is, if we can find a third person to join us." Widening his eyes, he looked at Hunter.

"Can I come to your house?" Hunter passed the phone back. "Downloading patches takes forever on our internet. We only have twenty meg down."

Jacob shook his head. "Dude, how do you *even* survive? Why don't your parents upgrade? Not like they can't afford it."

"It's a long story."

"Of course you can come over." Jacob continued in a haughty voice, mimicking a character from the game. "It is our honor and duty to help those wretched souls less fortunate than ourselves."

Kaden's chest tightened. Hunter's looks distracted him enough in his school uniform, but if he changed into his typical attire of a tight tank top and athletic shorts, it would challenge Kaden to focus on anything other than Hunter's arms and legs. This new dungeon adventure might end in calamity. Kaden was the healer of their gaming group, restoring their characters' hit points to keep them alive. Jacob's recklessness made that task difficult enough, but with Hunter's limbs exposed, begging to be gawked at. Disaster! He twisted his lips before taking another sip of juice.

Hunter and Jacob chattered on about swim team stuff, and Kaden tuned it out to avoid conjuring visions of Hunter in his competition swimsuit, which would doubtless provoke his brain to explode... again!

He took out his phone to send a message to Gabby. If there was one person who had a bigger crush on Hunter than Kaden, it was Gabby.

Even though Hunter had never shown an interest in her—probably because she was only fourteen, and he was sixteen—Kaden still had to try to be a good wingman for her. They texted each other in Spanish, another language Kaden spoke fluently.

KADEN RIVERA-WATSON:

Hey, Gabs. What's happening? How's yucky public school today?

GABRIELA RUIZ:

🙄 Yucky. How's snooty private school today?

KADEN RIVERA-WATSON:

Snooty

GABRIELA RUIZ:

Geometry is kicking my ass again. Don't think I can play EoOO today

KADEN RIVERA-WATSON:

Too bad, cause H is coming over

GABRIELA RUIZ:

OMG! Maybe I can just study in the evening

KADEN RIVERA-WATSON:

😏 That's what I figured LMAO

GABBY WAS SO PREDICTABLE, and Kaden knew her better than he knew himself. They'd been friends and neighbors as long as he could remember. She was practically a sister.

The remainder of the school day dragged, like it invariably did when he craved to try out something new in *Elves of Ora Online.*

THE BROTHERS, along with their moms—Angie and Roz—occupied a typical Port St. Lucie, Florida residence. One story, cinder-block and

stucco exterior, with a backyard barely large enough for a lanai, an in-ground pool, and a few palm trees around the perimeter.

Inside, the floors were all tile and the heart of the house was a huge great room, with an open kitchen and dining area.

Seated on a sofa, game controller in hand, Kaden stared at the television screen, watching the painfully slow game software update on the Xbox, when he glimpsed movement through the sliding doors adjacent to the lanai. Gabby entered through their pool screen enclosure. She never bothered coming to the front door.

Gabby waved as she approached, let herself in through a slider, and kicked off her sandals. She wore a red blouse and skimpy white shorts, showing off her long, tan legs, which Kaden expected, but her makeup was a gaudy shock, with too much foundation and overly made-up eyes.

Kaden stared at her face, his eyes wide, jaw agape. "Oh, dear."

Gabby pouted. "Too much?"

At that, Jacob whirled around. He'd been watching the screen of their archaic PC, downloading the *Elves of Ora Online* updates onto it. "¡Dios mío!"

Gabby groaned and collapsed onto the sofa. "What have I done? I should just go home." She almost ran her hands through her hair, but caught herself before she made a wreck of that too.

Jacob turned to Kaden. "Bro, can you fix it?"

"Why do you think *I* could fix it?"

"Aren't your kind supposed to be great at doing makeovers and shit?"

"My *kind*?" Kaden asked.

Jacob rolled his eyes. "Not this again. Listen, whether you label yourself or not, we all know you're gay, bro. It's okay."

"Why do you just assume—"

"Browser history, bro! Browser history." Jacob turned back to the computer and launched the web browser. "If I type the letter S into this search box, we both know the first autocomplete suggestion is gonna be 'Shawn Mendes shirtless.' That's not from any searches I've ever done. And I'm pretty sure our lesbian moms aren't searching for that either."

"Would you two stop this!" Gabby said. "We've got a crisis here. Hunter might get here any second."

As if on cue, the doorbell's silly tune echoed across the cavernous room. Through the obscuring glass of the double front doors, Kaden saw the outline of the most beautiful boy in the world, silhouetted by the bright South Florida sun blazing upon him, looking like some mystical creature shrouded in fire.

Kaden's heart skipped, but only for a moment. He flew into action, hopping off the sofa, grabbing Gabby's hand and launching her toward the kitchen. A torrent of words gushed from Kaden's mouth. "Cabinet left of the stove. Coconut oil. Take it to the bathroom. In the vanity, bottom shelf, cotton balls. Dab oil on your cheeks with cotton balls, then gently massage and rinse."

As Gabby dashed through the house, Jacob rose from the computer chair, smirked at Kaden, and headed to the front door. "I knew you'd fix it, bro. Your kind are great at that shit."

Kaden growled as his brother gave his shoulder a condescending pat on the way past.

When the door swung open, sure enough, Hunter had on one of his tight tank tops, the legendary, ribbed white one, making him look even more tan, and black athletic shorts, cut well above the knee, showing off his shiny, smooth legs. Kaden pulled his tongue back into his mouth, hoping no one saw it.

Hunter and Jacob exchanged fist bumps, followed by a bro-hug. Jacob was a hugger. Kaden was not, so instead, he fist-bumped Hunter. The fist-bump was awkward, leaving Kaden's knuckles stinging. Surely, he must be doing it wrong. He would have to get Jacob to tell him the secret.

"Can we put my bike in the garage?" Hunter asked.

"Sure." Jacob headed outside. Hunter handed his laptop bag to Kaden and followed Jacob. It was a Tumi backpack, expensive, elegant, and fitting for the almost perfect owner.

Kaden glanced toward the short hallway off of the dining area, wondering if Gabby was making progress in the bathroom.

The bag strained his shoulder, so Kaden set it on a side chair before it completely ripped his arm off. He sat back down on the middle of the sofa, resting his bare toes on the edge of the cocktail table's glass top.

The progress bar on the download had only moved three or four pixel points along the screen. He let out a deep, frustrated groan. So slow! Everyone on the planet must be downloading it at the same time.

After the familiar clunk of the garage door hitting bottom, the boys came in.

Angie, Kaden's non-biological mom, was Filipina. And following tradition, she made everyone remove their shoes at the door. Hunter had been over enough times that he kicked off his swim sandals without being asked. Since he was of Korean descent, he probably did that at home too.

Hunter glanced curiously toward the bathroom, as the sound of running water emanated from it. "Are Roz and Angie here?"

"No," Kaden said. "Mom's playing golf and Nanay's at work." The brothers referred to Roz as Mom, and called Angie, Nanay, Filipino for mother. "That's Gabby in the bathroom."

Hunter nodded and moved to the side chair to fetch his laptop.

The door to the bath opened and Gabby timidly peeked out from the hallway. Her face looked much better, though it was slightly red from wiping off the makeup. Kaden gave her an approving thumbs up while Hunter wasn't looking.

Gabby made her entrance. "Oh, Hunter. I didn't know you were coming over."

Kaden cringed. She was such a poor liar.

"Gabs. Wassup?" Hunter nodded to her, then turned back to his bag to get his power cord.

"Going great, Huns... ah, Hunter," Gabby said.

Huns? Kaden glared at her. It was way too premature for her to be attempting a nickname for him. And *Huns?* This was not going well at all.

Hunter pulled his laptop out. It was a top-of-the-line Bazooka Stealth Z16 ProMax Ultra with all the upgrades. The brothers' Xbox performed decently, but the graphics and speed of Hunter's gaming laptop blew it away.

Gabby approached Kaden on the sofa, and after making sure Hunter couldn't see them, she motioned to Kaden to move over. At first, he didn't understand why, then he realized, if he was sitting in the middle, he'd be between her and Hunter. He slid to the left and Gabby sat down on the far right, leaving the center available.

Hunter, computer in hand, headed for the sofa, and halted mid-step, eyebrows raised. "I'll need to plug this in."

"No problem." Kaden routed the power cord behind his own back. It was awkward, and Hunter no doubt wondered why Kaden had moved, causing the predicament. Not ideal. But soon enough, Hunter sat down and seemed satisfied.

Hunter had his glasses on again. His bare legs, with those ripped thighs and calves, stretched out onto the cocktail table. How was a gay boy supposed to concentrate with this sexy-legged Clark Kent sitting next to him? Kaden closed his eyes and took a breath.

"You okay?" Hunter asked.

Kaden's reply was short and clipped. "Yep. Great."

"You seem stressed."

"Nope. Fine."

Kaden gazed at his own legs, skinny and pale by comparison, and covered in thin, dark hair. He wondered if his biological father might be an ape-man of some sort. That would explain a lot, as Jacob was naturally hairy too.

Kaden typically would have changed into long pajama bottoms to hang out around the house with visitors over, hiding his toothpick legs. But Hunter had become enough of a fixture lately that he decided to be more casual.

"You're wearing shorts." Smiling, Hunter reached over and squeezed Kaden's knee for a second before flipping his laptop open.

Kaden gulped and stared at the exact spot on his leg, where a moment ago, Hunter's fingers, in the flesh, had rested. He'd probably even left DNA evidence behind on Kaden's skin, his actual cells commingling with Kaden's. "Yeah," he finally said.

Gabby scooted closer to Hunter. "You guys exploring the new dungeon?" She drew her legs up onto the sofa, where Hunter couldn't miss them.

"We're gonna try," Hunter said. "I'm surprised you aren't joining us. Having your wizard along would be helpful."

Kaden knew the reason Gabby wasn't joining them. She'd have to be home and logged in from her Xbox. However, given the fiasco with the makeup, along with her bad acting performance, perhaps that would have been a better way to impress Hunter. Gabby was the best gamer of the four of them.

"Mom says I've been playing too much," she said.

Another lie, but this one sounded more convincing.

Hunter launched the game on his laptop, and the updates began downloading. The progress bar moved quicker on his computer than on the Xbox. "This is so much faster than at home."

"So, Hunter," Gabby said, "my quinceañera is coming up soon. I wondered if you wanted—"

"Soon?" Jacob snorted from across the room. "Ten months!"

Gabby glared at Jacob.

"You were saying, Gabs?" Kaden's mouth smiled while his eyes hurled daggers at his brother.

"Yeah. Um. Hunter, would you like to come to it?"

"Oh, I'm busy that day," Hunter said, his face stern.

"But I didn't..." Gabby's eyes widened, her eyebrows furrowed.

Hunter burst into laughter. "I'm messing with you, but yeah, text me the date and time so I can put it on my calendar."

Was Hunter being flirty with Gabby? He might be, but Kaden

couldn't tell for sure. Flirting was a mystery to him, and at least for now, seemed like an irrelevant skill to learn.

He only knew one openly gay boy at school, and he wasn't Kaden's type. Besides that, Kaden's obsessive crush on Hunter didn't leave room in his heart for anyone else. Best to ignore romance all together for now. Maybe when he went off to college, and away from Hunter, he would get over him and crush on some hot college boy, who also wouldn't like a skinny boy like him back.

"So, you're on the Xbox today," Hunter said, turning to Kaden.

"Yep. My lucky day." The brothers hated the desktop PC that was so old it had a CD-ROM drive. It barely even ran *Elves of Ora Online*. While the Xbox couldn't hold a candle to Hunter's Bazooka Stealth Z16 ProMax Ultra laptop, it ran circles around their desktop PC. So, after many rounds of negotiation, the brothers reached an accord to take turns, with Kaden getting the Xbox on odd-numbered days, except on the 31st of any month, or February 29th, when a best two-out-of-three coin toss would determine who got to use it.

Meanwhile, every birthday and Christmas, the brothers conspired to convince their moms to get them a new computer. Each time, their requests were rejected. For some reason, they prioritized paying for their sons' tuitions at "nationally recognized" Aldenbrook Academy over a new gaming computer. No wonder adults always seemed so miserable.

Gabby kept asking Hunter annoying questions. About his computer. Was he still taking driving lessons? Had he gotten his learner's permit yet? How were his sisters doing? And so on.

Kaden wanted to shake her, because Gabby was trying way too hard. Hunter fidgeted and eased a few inches away from her. Kaden hoped she picked up on that body language and chilled some. However, she started another line of interrogation.

As Kaden tried to figure out how to signal her to ease off, something happened. In moving away from Gabby, Hunter edged closer to Kaden. Then Hunter removed his feet from the cocktail table and set them on the floor. As he did so, he spread his legs slightly, and his left knee rested against Kaden's leg.

All further attempts to maintain a conscious train of thought failed Kaden utterly. He stared blankly at the television screen and the snail-like progress bar, while the skin on the back of his neck tingled.

His brain wasn't going to work now. He needed to move his leg away, but he didn't want to seem obvious about it, lest Hunter think he was offended. Kaden coerced a few synapses into producing a coherent idea for an escape.

"Anyone want something to drink?" Kaden moved like he was going to get up and pulled his leg away as he did so.

"I'm fine," Gabby said.

Kaden looked at Hunter. "You?"

"I'm good." Hunter squinted, then gave a short laugh. "I didn't notice that before."

"What?"

Hunter reached toward Kaden's left ear. "That earring. It's on point."

Kaden had on a cheap knockoff of something Korean pop stars would wear. He owned an entire collection of them. This one had multiple fine chains with various charms hanging on each. Given how admittedly ostentatious it was, why was Hunter only just now seeing it?

"It's not too much?" Kaden asked.

"No. It looks wicked good on you." Hunter fingered the dangling charms. As he retracted his hand, his fingers brushed the side of Kaden's cheek. Kaden's skin tingled again. "I've been thinking about getting an ear piercing."

"Oh," Kaden said, realizing that it was all Hunter would need to look exactly like a K-Pop star, the image of him on a stage, in a sexy outfit, dancing and singing, painting itself in his mind.

"I'll take some water, bro," Jacob said.

"Well, you can get it yourself," Kaden said, startled out of his fantasy, and raising his voice.

"Wow," Jacob said. "Your kind can be so testy."

"Your kind?" Hunter asked.

"Nothing," Kaden said. He eased back onto the sofa, leaving extra room for Hunter, in case he needed to move further away from Gabby. More importantly, his flesh no longer contacted Hunter's. He let out a breath and relaxed.

Hunter's computer finished the download first. Then his avatar appeared on the screen, resplendent in glowing green armor, carrying two swords, a bow, and a golden quiver. He was a ranger named Sanyangkkun. Hunter had customized the avatar to resemble himself as much as possible, and it took little imagination on Kaden's part to visualize Hunter and Sanyangkkun as one and the same.

Eventually, the Xbox and the desktop PC finished their downloads. Kaden's avatar was a cleric with mismatched leather armor and a holy hammer for a weapon. But his crucial role in the group was to heal the others. Jacob's avatar was a warrior with metallic plate armor. His job was to lure their enemies into hitting him, since his armor was the hardiest.

The trio entered the new dungeon together, taking on never-before-seen foes. They got lost a few times, but Gabby gave them solid advice now and then. Finally, they reached the first elite dungeon boss, Vineth, Goddess of Chaos.

Their first attempt at battling her ended with the deaths of all the boys' characters.

"Great effort, guys," Hunter said. "I thought we'd pull through with your expert healing." He momentarily rested a hand on Kaden's arm.

"Sorry," Kaden said. "I ran out of power at the end."

"Not your fault," Hunter said. "And I have to say, I really appreciate you playing a healer. I know that's the least fun type of character to play."

"Oh. Thanks."

"You're welcome." Hunter's knee drifted toward Kaden's again and he rested it against his leg, exactly like earlier.

This time, Kaden got out of it by going to the bathroom. When he came back, he sat further away than before.

Later, it happened again. There was no escaping this time. Gabby was practically on top of Hunter, explaining a strategy to try in the next attempt. Hunter had no choice but to nudge closer to Kaden, who was now pressed against the left arm of the sofa.

It took eight tries for the boys to kill Vineth. Several of the failed attempts were the fault of Hunter's luscious legs. That was the alliterative phrase Kaden had selected to refer to the limbs in his head: luscious legs. He was still undecided on what to call Hunter's arms, but he had it narrowed down to awesome, amazing or astounding.

Despite the sexy distraction, Kaden finally mustered enough concentration to keep them all alive through the battle, and they won at last. When their foe's body fell into death spasms, they all jumped up, including Gabby. Jacob and Hunter bear-hugged. Then Hunter turned to Kaden, grabbed him, and gave him a hug too.

Kaden tried to play it cool, but when Hunter backed away, Kaden frowned.

"Oh, damn," Hunter said. "Sorry. I forgot you don't hug. My bad." His cheeks reddened, and he held his hands tightly to his body.

"It's okay."

"You sure?" Hunter asked.

"Yes."

"Okay," Hunter said, relaxing.

"You can hug me, Hunter," Gabby said. "I don't mind."

Hunter laughed nervously and mussed her hair. He turned away and checked his watch as Gabby's smile melted away. "Shit. Look at the time. I gotta run," he said.

Hunter was soon gone, leaving behind only the fresh smell of his cologne on the sofa cushions and perhaps some skin cells on Kaden's leg.

"So," Gabby said. "How do you think it went?"

Jacob shook his head. "Not bad for our first time there."

"Not the stupid game, you lunkhead," Gabby said.

"Oh," Jacob said. "You mean your love quest with Hunter? That was a disaster. You tried way too hard, girl. For Kaden, on the other hand, also a disaster, but in a different way."

"What are you talking about?" Kaden asked.

"Bro, are you playing hard to get or something? Props if you are. Pretty ballsy."

"Huh?"

Jacob rolled his eyes. "So clueless. Dude, he was throwing himself at you with all his might, and you rejected him *every* single time. That takes guts."

"Shit," Gabby said. "I thought I was just imagining it, but yeah, he was flirting with you."

"Have you both gone loco? He wasn't flirting with me. What are you even talking about?"

"I counted about twelve times he touched you," Jacob said. "It was so obvious I could see it across the room. And you rejected him *and* rejected him. It was like watching the world's slowest train wreck."

Kaden looked at Gabby. "He's crazy. Right?"

She tilted her head and raised her eyebrows.

"Bro, why did you keep moving away from him when his leg touched yours?"

Kaden's jaw dropped. "That? That's what you call flirting? He was getting away from grabby-Gabby, and man-spreading. That's all."

Jacob shook his head. "So clueless, bro. So clueless."

"Listen," Kaden said. "Have you ever seen any sign that Hunter has even the slightest interest in guys? I mean romantically?"

"Not until today," Jacob said.

Kaden stared at the ceiling and exhaled. "Okay, let's say hypothetically—just for fun—that Hunter is the gayest boy in the entire world. There's no way in hell he'd ever give someone like me a second look. He's fire, and I'm so basic. We are not in the same league. Not even close."

"I know what my eyes saw," Jacob said. "The boy was super into you, and you flat out rejected him."

"Yep," Gabby said. "Totally. I'm giving up. I know when I've been defeated. He's yours."

"Defeated? Gabby, I'm not even competing. I'm trying to help you."

"I dunno. That earring and those shorts..." She raised her eyebrows.

"I have to wear an earring to keep the hole from closing up since I can't wear it at school. And I only wear shorts when I'm *not* trying to impress anyone. Look at these hairy toothpicks."

"Some people like hairy, slender guys," she said.

"She's got a point, bro," Jacob said, a hand on his chin. "I mean, you don't have much muscle, but you got, like, zero body fat, so it shows off what you have."

"You are both nuts." Kaden stood and glared at both of them.

Gabby stepped closer, resting her palms on his shoulders as she fixed a pleading gaze on him. "Would you at least keep an open mind? I can't figure out why you're your own worst critic, but you're the whole package—kind, adorable, and brainy. You know three languages, whip up culinary magic, and most importantly, you're a gaming genius. Hunter would be lucky to have you. I wish you could see that." Her voice wavered, betraying her emotion, as she pressed a soft kiss to his cheek before stepping back.

Kaden held back a tear or two as his throat tightened. They were insane. His brother and Gabby were certifiably insane.

Right?

2

DUNCAN

Duncan Valentyn loathed exercise and detested the idea of leaving his warm bed at the ungodly hour of dawn. He was still in shock that he had even agreed to meet his boyfriend, Chip—the human cheetah—at the greenway for a dreaded run at this preposterous time of day. Even more absurd, it seemed he had done this out of love. Why had he given up the single life?

Ever since Chip had learned that Duncan's father had heart disease, he'd subtly and not-so-subtly hinted about lifestyle improvements Duncan could make to avoid the same fate. Chip was giving him the loving kick in the butt that he needed. Still, Duncan reserved the right to grumble about it, even if just to himself.

The parking lot was full, and it took Duncan a few tries to find a space. It seemed everyone in Charlotte decided to go to the greenway for exercise this morning. Why were there so many people here? Was the entire city populated with masochists? He debated whether he should give up and go home. But the thought of disappointing his boyfriend was too much for him to bear, so he persisted until a spot opened up.

He pulled on his jogging shoes, ran—or what he thought of as running—for a quarter of a mile, and spotted Chip waiting for him at an overlook, his sandy-brown hair fluttering in the breeze. When Duncan saw him, a surge of energy pushed him to pick up his pace. Chip flashed a dimpled smile at him from across the way and Duncan sped up again. Five months into their relationship, Chip made him feel more like a teenager than a man in his early forties. He couldn't help but smile back as he ran over to meet him.

"Hey, babe." Chip wrapped his arms around him in a tight embrace as others passed along the greenway, some strolling, others running.

"Hi, sweetie," Duncan said, catching his breath.

"I'm glad to see you. I thought you might change your mind."

"No way. I wouldn't want to disappoint you."

Chip smiled and pulled him close again. "You never have to worry about that."

As they stood in each other's arms, Duncan realized how much he loved Chip. He couldn't help but wonder where this love would take them. It seemed like it could last forever.

It wasn't the first time he'd felt this way about a lover. In his twenties, he'd experienced this same euphoria with Robert. The two of them had spent over a decade together. However, there had been warning signs early in that relationship that he'd glossed over. Robert never met a bottle of wine he didn't finish in one sitting, and if they opened another, that one would be gone too.

It had pleased Duncan the first time he visited Chip's apartment, and saw a half full bottle with a vacuum stopper on the counter.

"Ready for a run?" Chip asked.

"Wasn't that what I just did?"

Chip laughed. "That was the warmup."

Duncan shook his head. "I am not cut out for this. You realize I sit in front of a computer screen all day, clicking a mouse, right?" He flexed his index finger.

"That reminds me, did you put in the request for that standing desk yet?" Chip asked.

"Not yet." Duncan didn't want to mention the bank was doing some belt-tightening. First, it was confidential, and second, he didn't want Chip to worry. It wasn't just Duncan whose fortunes were tied to Xeler National Bank. Chip's employer did a lot of business with the bank as well. That's how they'd met.

"Well, get that shirt off, and let's run," Chip said, pulling his own tank top off, revealing a body that had no business looking so fit for his age.

"I'm too much of a dad-bod type to go sans shirt, I'm afraid."

Chip snorted. "Don't be ridiculous. It takes years of practice and dedication to truly have a dad-bod. And even then, you actually have to be a dad to officially have one."

Duncan widened his eyes. "Well, I've got a Systems Analyst-bod."

"You're great just the way you are."

"Really?" Duncan's eyebrows arched with disbelief. "I get the feeling I'm not. And maybe that's why you got my fat ass out here in the first place."

The hurt in Chip's eyes was unmistakable. "You know that's not true. Did I ever bug you about fitness before I found out about your dad's heart attack?"

"No."

"Exactly. Despite your feeble attempts to hide it from everyone in the world, I know you have a heart of gold in there." Chip tapped Duncan's chest. "I just want to make sure it keeps ticking for a long time, for your sake, and for mine."

Duncan smiled at him. "Sorry. You know me. I'm not the most secure guy in the world, especially in the looks department."

"Babe, you look better than eighty percent of the guys out here."

He glanced away shyly, his eyes meeting the ground. "I doubt that," he muttered.

"I'm not going to twist your arm, but you don't have any reason to be ashamed of your body."

Unable to resist Chip's dimpled grin, Duncan gave a slight smile and took off his T-shirt, tucking it into his waistband. About that time, a pack of twenty or so young men, probably some high school cross-country team, ran past them, each one of them shirtless, slim and fit, none with an ounce of body fat.

Duncan looked down at his own squishy chest, slight man-boobs and pooched out belly. "You said eighty percent?"

Chip placed a reassuring hand on Duncan's shoulder. "Ignore them. Come on. We're going the other way anyhow."

Duncan grinned.

The two of them spent the morning running along the greenway, pausing from time to time, resting on benches, enjoying each other's company. They laughed and joked and talked about everything and nothing. By the time they were done, both of them were panting and out of breath. But utterly content.

As Duncan jogged beside Chip, he wondered what he'd done to win the heart of a guy like him. Chip was a person who clipped coupons and dug through flyers for sales to scrimp and save money, then turned around and left oversized tips at restaurants, and donated to the food bank. Even now, as they traversed the greenway, Chip was picking up empty cups and candy wrappers, and depositing them in the trash cans they passed.

Duncan felt so lucky to have Chip in his life. Yet, he'd felt this way before and was so wrong. Not that Robert had been a bad person. That was part of the problem though. If Robert had been a jerk, life would have been so much simpler. Duncan could have simply walked away when Robert went down the rabbit hole of alcoholism and then drug addiction.

However, on those increasingly rare occasions when Robert had managed a little sobriety, the same man Duncan had fallen in love with was still there, deep down inside, trying to escape his own personal hell. Then, he slipped further and further away, like a drowning man, and try as he might, Duncan couldn't get a lifeline to him.

Duncan eventually had a breakdown of his own. Months of counseling gave him the confidence to do what he had to: walk away. Save himself. No sense in both of them sinking to the bottom, his therapist had convinced him. Still, the guilt ate him up. Even after two years, he had nightmares, though he was sure now that it had been the right decision.

As great as this felt with Chip, there was hesitation, partly born from his experience with Robert, and partly from his own disbelief that someone like Chip would be interested in him in the first place. He was too good. There must be some hidden flaw that he'd yet to uncover.

They finished their run and returned to the parking lot. Chip, glistening and beautiful, unlocked his car and handed Duncan a steel, insulated water bottle, while taking one for himself.

"I got this for you, babe," Chip said. "I hate single use plastics."

"Thanks." Duncan peered down at the waterfall of sweat cascading down his own body. "Why do I look like I just went swimming, while you look like you've been sitting in an air-conditioned room?"

"Don't worry. Once you get into shape, you'll be less drenched. I'll bet you handle it much better next time."

"So, you mean we get the pleasure of repeating this torture once again?" Duncan said, mocking disbelief.

They laughed.

Chip took a swig of water, then wiped the excess off his lips. "You know, my lease is up soon, on the apartment."

"Um, yeah. So, you can go month-to-month?"

Chip's face contorted. "I suppose, but you know…"

A half-smile tugged at Duncan's cheeks as he gazed at him. "Chip, I know you can barely restrain yourself. It's like you haven't seen a dad-bod in years and you're itching to wake up next to it every morning. But we've talked about this before. I don't want to jinx this by going too fast. Five months in, we're still getting to know each other. You know I love you, but there's a big difference between dating and living with each other."

Chip heaved a reluctant sigh, the corners of his lips forming an anxious smile. "You're right. You're right. I let my heart get ahead of logic sometimes. Feel free to keep me in line though." He mock-punched Duncan's ribcage with his fingertips.

"You know I want it as much as you. I don't want to mess it up." And there were things Duncan needed to tell Chip, some of which would probably be quite shocking. He just had to find the right time. "Now, can I put my shirt back on? Everyone in South Charlotte has seen enough of these man-boobs."

They chuckled.

3

ROZ

SIXTEEN YEARS EARLIER...

Rosalyn "Roz" Watson pulled her Saturn Vue rental car into the parking lot of Roxbury Apartments and attempted to follow the bewildering directions Duncan had emailed her. All the stupid buildings looked the same. How did anyone ever find a specific unit in this place? The leasing agency's motto must be "Apartments for Introverts," because living here, no one could find you to visit.

She parked the car, released the seatbelt and took a moment to inhale a few deep, slow breaths, pulling dark auburn strands of hair off her face. *This will all be worth it.*

That morning, she'd finished visiting her widower father in the mountains just outside Boone, North Carolina. She'd listened to him grumble for three days that Pluto was probably being downgraded from a planet to a dwarf planet—the pitfalls of being the daughter of a retired astronomy professor.

She had driven to Charlotte for her evening flight back to her home in Port St. Lucie, Florida. First, she had a mission to accomplish.

Still stubbornly refusing to get an actual purse, she took the BlackBerry phone out of her jeans pocket and called Duncan.

"Roz! Where the hell are you?" he said instead of "Hello."

"The question is, where the hell are you? Queen, your direction writing skills suck. Which building are you in? Don't you dare tell me it's the beige one or I'll slap the shit out of you, assuming I ever find you."

"Wait," Duncan said. "I see a bitchy looking dyke in a Saturn Vue? Is that you?"

"Yes."

Roz loved that even though they hadn't seen each other in person for a couple of years, they still instantly fell into their familiar banter.

A few seconds later, she spotted him coming out of a door, waving, clad in cargo shorts and an Abercrombie and Fitch muscle shirt, which he truly didn't have the body for, but she wouldn't be the one to break that news to him. Or would she?

"You're still trying to rock the college boy next door look, I see," Roz said as she entered his apartment. "Isn't twenty-six too old for that?"

"What? I've never tried to be a college boy next door. I'm a one hundred and ten percent, All-American muscle jock."

They both burst into laughter and hugged. Roz glanced over Duncan's shoulder at his apartment. It was all as disgustingly tidy and well-appointed as she expected from him. She resolved that before she left today, she'd find a way to spill a few crumbs on the floor some place he wouldn't discover them for months.

"How've you been, darling?" Roz said. "You look like shit."

"Hangover." Duncan rubbed his eyes. "My new beau can seriously drink. I mean, I'm half Irish and half Ukrainian, so you know I'm no slouch, but Robert... geez."

Roz folded her lips into a thin line and tried to hide her disappointment. She'd known Duncan since their first day of kindergarten and had long ago learned that once he was infatuated with some guy, no matter how many red flags waved at him, there was no point wasting her energy trying to point them out. He would always learn lessons the hard way.

"How about you? Doing well? Wait! I almost forgot." Duncan stepped back and studied her chest. It was the first time they'd seen each other since her full mastectomy and reconstruction. "Nice. Can I touch them?"

"No, silly queen! Why is it gay men always want to play with tits?"

"Really? Is that a thing? I was just joking. Besides, I only want to touch them because they're fake."

"Why? You want a pair too?"

"No way. I'm sure I'll have some man-boobs one day. No need to rush that." Duncan's face turned serious. "So, everything's okay?"

"Yep. I just didn't want to take any chances with my family history."

Duncan glowered. "I still miss her."

"I think about her every day," Roz said.

Roz's mother got her first bout with cancer at the age of twenty-eight. Two more followed, but she resisted a total mastectomy. The fourth one, though, escaped the barn, and was stage four before they discovered it. Eight-year-old Roz lost her thirty-three-year-old mother.

When Roz was diagnosed with her first tumor, she determined it would be her last as well.

They shared a smile before Duncan eventually broke the silence.

He sighed. "So, what's Angie think of the twins here?"

"She loves them. She also loves that I won't follow in my mother's footsteps."

"Me, too," Duncan said. "How's Professor Bill?"

"Dad's run off another girlfriend, doubtless by talking about that damn Pluto shit too much. I swear. Oh, he says 'hi,' by the way. Wants you to come up and visit his cabin in the mountains."

"The next ninety-five degree day, I'll have to take him up on that." Duncan gestured to the sofa so they could sit down and talk.

The childhood friends sat and laughed as they talked about mutual friends from their grade school and college years, family, lovers, and even enemies.

"Listen," Roz said, "one reason I dropped by is I've got this absurd idea. Hear me out before you poop all over it, like I know you will."

"Why do you think I'll poop on it?"

"Because it is truly crazy." Roz took a deep breath. "Angie and I want children."

"Children? Wow! More than one, even?"

"Yep. Two. Here's the thing. We're thinking, one each. She'll carry one, I'll carry one."

Duncan leaned back with his eyes wide, saying nothing.

"What?" Roz asked, narrowing her eyes.

"I'm just trying to picture you and Angie as moms," Duncan replied, a smirk on his mouth. "I don't even think of us as adults yet. But you, as a mom?"

"It's not as preposterous as the notion of you being a father."

"That's for sure. One hundred and ten percent."

"By the way," Roz said, "we want you to be the father. That is, we need your sperm."

Duncan erupted into laughter and doubled over. Roz simply leaned back, her expression deadpan and serious. As Duncan sat back up and saw Roz's face, his brows knit together in confusion. "You're serious?"

Roz nodded.

"Holy shit. Why me?"

"One reason is because the idea of you being a father *is* so unbelievable. I'm a fan of irony, as you well know."

They both grinned.

She continued. "The thing is, Angie and I don't want anyone to interfere with how we raise our kids. And you *have* to be the least paternal man I've ever met."

"Ouch."

"Need I remind you of Goldie? Or Mertle? Or—" Roz said, naming a small sampling of his childhood pets that met their demise in his not-so-nurturing care.

Duncan raised a halting hand. "I'm not denying it. It just stings to hear it out loud."

"Sorry. There's also the fact that Charlotte is about six hundred miles from Port St. Lucie, so you won't be all up in our business."

Duncan tilted his head. "Yeah. That makes sense. But is that the only reason you want *my* DNA?"

"You're gonna make me say it, aren't you?" she asked.

"Come on. You know you can," he said, grinning.

She groaned. "Okay, you might have a pretty decent brain in that noggin' of yours."

Duncan gave her knee a mock patronizing pat. "See, that didn't hurt too much, did it?"

Roz rolled her eyes.

Duncan gazed past her, lost in thought for a moment. "So, assuming I'm foolish enough to join you in this scheme, what role would I play in their lives? Any?"

"Well, I'll keep you in the loop about how they're doing. You can see photos of them on my MySpace page."

"Oh. Just photos then." Duncan frowned and stared at the floor.

"Listen, I know it sounds harsh, but we have our reasons. Some friends of ours did something similar, and it's been nothing but drama."

"And you think I'd be dramatic?" Duncan paused half a second, then added, "Don't answer that."

"Here's what we're thinking. If you want, you can come down for the births. That's up to you. And when the kids are mature enough to understand how babies are made, we'd explain it all to them and if everyone is open to it, you could meet them and have some part in their lives. However, you would have no obligation to."

He shifted in his seat. "No obligation. I see."

"We've got a friend who's a family attorney. We'd get everything in writing, so you have no responsibilities of any kind, including financial. All we require is your man juice and nothing further from you, ever, unless, like I said, you want to meet them at the proper time."

Duncan raised an eyebrow. "Speaking of my man juice, how are we... We're not making a baby the old-fashioned, disgusting way, are we?"

Roz's eyes widened. "Oh, hell no! You will hand it over in a beaker, thank you very much."

A look of relief washed over Duncan's face. He scratched his chin. "Logistically, how will that work with me being six hundred miles away? Fedex?"

"We would prefer you to visit us in Florida to present your, uh, contribution. We'll pay for your airfare."

"So, I presume multiple trips then, for each of you?" Duncan asked.

"Well, and here's the part you'll poop on. We're wanting to carry our babies concurrently."

"Shit," Duncan said. "What?"

"Here's the thing"—Roz cupped her silicone implants in her palms—"these puppies aren't nursing any baby. The only liquid in them is saline solution, so Angie will nurse both of the babies."

"At the same time?" Duncan asked.

"Well, she's got two boobs last time I checked. She'll take maternity leave and nurse them. Meanwhile, I return to work as soon as I can so we don't go broke, lose the house, and have to wheel around town in a shopping cart eating cold refried beans from a Taco Bell dumpster."

He slowly shook his head. "This entire plan is wild. Just wild."

"I know, but we've mulled this over and over, and it's the best plan."

"You want me to be the baby-daddy for both?"

"Yep. That way, they'll be related by blood, half-sisters."

Duncan tilted his head. "Sisters? What if they're boys?"

"Oh god, please don't give us two boys. I don't think we could handle that. At least one has to be a girl, so Angie can doll her up in girlie clothes."

Duncan leaned forward, pressing hands to his knees. "If you used a clinic, couldn't they make certain you receive the genders you prefer?"

Roz made a scoffing noise. "If we were rich, queen, sure! But we're doing this on a budget. Besides, this way is easier. And bonus, we don't have to worry about being discriminated against. So, no clinic. Just two lesbians, and a beaker full of your... contribution. There's a seventy-five percent chance we'll have at least one girl, so we'll take those odds."

Duncan raised his eyebrows. "With your record on basketball betting?"

Roz waved a dismissive hand. "Yeah, yeah, yeah. Anyway, what do you think?"

"Maybe I should speak with Robert about it."

"Oh, no. I forgot to mention you can't tell anyone."

Duncan pouted. "What?"

"If you tell someone, word will spread. If your mom finds out, she'll be on the first jet to Florida to see her grand-babies."

"Oh geez. You're right. You're so right. I need to figure this out on my own, then." He shook his head. "You want to have two hormonally imbalanced, pregnant lesbians in the same house, with golf clubs and softball bats? You'll murder each other."

"Admittedly, it is a calculated risk, but we're willing to chance it. And if we survive that, we'll be tighter than ever. So, you in?"

Exhaling, Duncan leaned back, placing his hands behind his head and staring at the ceiling. "Let me think about it. I absolutely am the least paternal guy in the world. One hundred and ten percent."

After a week of consideration, Duncan finally agreed. Roz's gambling luck had not changed though. Almost a year later, Angie gave birth to a boy they named Jacob. Fifteen days after that, Roz had a boy they named Kaden.

4

KADEN

The Aldenbrook Academy gym echoed with the sounds of sneakers screeching on the floor, boys grunting, and basketballs boinging. Fortunately for Kaden, the teacher was happy to have those who were less athletic stay out of the way. So, he lounged on the bleachers, chatting with Aaliyah, a girl who despised P.E. class as much as he did, admiring her ability to look engrossed in her phone when she was really just ogling the shirtless boys playing on the "skins" team. Meanwhile, the popular girls in the class sat on the opposing bleachers in their clique, being less discrete in their gawking at the same guys.

Even as she pretended to read from her phone, Aaliyah seemed to have her sights set on one particular boy. Kaden couldn't blame her —the boy looked like a Greek god. Kaden liked Aaliyah because even when she caught him staring at the godly boy, she politely acted like she didn't notice.

"What'cha reading?" Kaden asked her.

Caught off guard, she gave him a side-eye glare. "It's called 'Happily Ever Afters.'" Focusing back on her phone screen, she pushed her glasses back up onto her nose and uttered in a flat tone, "You?"

"Guess!"

Aaliyah made a big show of rolling her eyes. "Um, a cookbook of some sort, maybe?"

Kaden beamed. Ever since he could remember, he'd been obsessed with baking and cooking. By the time he could hold a spoon, he was helping Angie in the kitchen. With over a decade of experience, he was already an accomplished cook, but to his chagrin, there was another student in the school who was better.

"You're still obsessed with her, aren't you?" Aaliyah asked.

"She's not invincible, you know?"

They both cast a quick glance across the gym, past the sweaty boys zooming up and down the court, and onto the third row of bleachers where a blondish girl named Unique Mills-Foy sat, chattering away like a parrot, hands gesturing, cackling with laughter, probably at her own jokes.

As if she sensed they were talking about her, Unique pursed her lips, puckered her cheeks, then gazed toward him and Aaliyah for a moment, before resuming her conversation.

"Isn't she invincible, though? Three to zero," Aaliyah said.

Kaden gave a dismissive grunt. "Last year was a fluke. I was soooo close."

"As my grandfather says, close only counts in horseshoes, hand grenades, and making love."

"Thanks," Kaden said, his eyes shooting daggers. "So encouraging."

"Sorry, but you're the one who keeps saying second-place isn't good enough."

Kaden scrunched his face and groaned. She was right. Every year for the past three years, he'd entered a junior cake-baking competition at a baking-themed trade show held in the city. On a shelf in his room, he displayed the three red ribbons he'd taken home for coming in second each time. Unique had three blue first-place ribbons, which she flaunted like a peacock in mating season whenever she was within earshot.

"I'm going to beat her this year. I know it. I've got a new recipe I'm going to try today."

Aaliyah shrugged. "Just bring me a slice tomorrow; that is, if it isn't a complete disaster."

"Of course."

They returned to their gawking.

AFTER SCHOOL, Sophia, the mother of one of their classmates and this week's designated carpool driver, dropped the brothers off. Kaden smiled when he saw Angie's car in the driveway. She was going to help him practice his recipe today since she was off work.

"Nanay! We're home!" Jacob exclaimed as he bounded through the front door, with Kaden trailing. Jacob had his book bag over one shoulder, and all of his clothes except his boxers were stripped off his body and crumpled under his arm. He usually couldn't wait to get out of his school uniform when he got home, but today, he'd gotten a head start, removing it in the car on the way.

"Oh my god," Angie said, standing at the kitchen sink. "Why are you practically naked?"

"You know Sophia's AC doesn't work for shit."

Angie shook her head. "Language young man! And your brother still has his clothes on."

"He's skinny. He's more heat resistant. Besides, you know Sophia digs my booty."

Rubbing her forehead and closing her eyes, Angie let out a long sigh. "You have got to stop trying to seduce grown women. You're only fifteen!"

"That's exactly why I need to seduce them. Older women could teach me so much."

"*Any* woman could teach you so much," Kaden said.

Jacob gave him an evil eye and started to speak, but stopped. "You know what, even though you're being mean to me, bro, I'm not going to say what I was about to. You're lucky I'm feeling monogamous today."

"*Monogamous?* Really?" Kaden asked.

"Whatever, Mr. Dictionary! I'm hoping y'all let me lick the mixing bowl."

"With raw egg in it?"

"It hasn't killed me yet." Jacob dropped his clothes and book bag in the middle of the great room floor. "Y'all bake. I'm going for a swim." He headed out the door to the pool.

Angie stared after him. "I gave birth to that." She shook her head, jostling her pink-tinted locks.

"Am I really related to him? Maybe the clinic mixed up the... um... you know... the baby batter." Kaden's cheeks flushed.

"No mix-ups, I'm sorry to report." They smiled at each other, then she mussed his curly hair. "Get changed, and let's bake a cake, bunnaboo. You're gonna beat that little bitch this year."

"Nanay! Language!"

She giggled.

The new layer cake recipe was an improvement, but Kaden still wanted it to be better. They tweaked the recipe again the next day after school, and neither of them liked the result. The day after that, Angie was back at work. He was determined to keep trying though. He had to get that blue ribbon this year. Even if he didn't, maybe he'd put a few pounds onto his skinny body in the process.

KADEN PARKED himself in front of the family's ancient, dinosaur-era desktop computer. He growled impatiently as the decrepit machine wheezed to life. He couldn't remember how old he was when they got it, but it must be long ago. When was the last time any company made a beige computer?

Over the last two weeks, the brothers, along with Hunter and Gabby, had played *Elves of Ora Online*, working their way through the new dungeon. However, since that first day, they'd all participated from the comfort of their own homes. Today was different. Having given up on any romance with Hunter, Gabby stayed home and logged into the game. However, Hunter was at the brothers' house to play because he'd broken his headset.

"Much obliged for the crash invite, amigos." Lounging on the sofa in his go-to tank top and gym shorts, Hunter popped his laptop open like a party trick. "Typing to talk is such a buzzkill."

"No probs," Jacob said, sitting on the other end of the couch, with the Xbox controller in his hands. "Bro, you in yet?"

"Still loading Windows."

"Damn, I hate that piece of shit," Jacob said. "We'll start clearing the low-level guards until you get online."

"Don't get yourselves killed," Kaden said. He watched their avatars on the television screen as his brother, with Gabby and Hunter following, entered the dungeon and, once inside the first corridor, attacked some low-level creatures.

They should survive without Kaden healing them provided Jacob didn't get cocky and take on too many at once. Gabby's wizard had a couple of weak healing spells she could use in a pinch.

Kaden rolled his eyes and groaned as Jacob charged into a mob.

"Whoa!" Hunter said. "That's a lot of guards."

"No probs," Jacob said. "I can take them on. Just... aww... damn!" His health bar plummeted to zero percent. A few seconds later, Hunter and Gabby died too.

"You lunkhead," Gabby's voice blasted out of the television speakers. "You pulled too many."

"Sorry, but don't act shocked. You know me," Jacob said into his headset.

Hunter glanced at Kaden and laughed. Kaden shrugged at him and rolled his eyes.

"I'm on the load screen now," Kaden said. "Tell Gabs I'll resurrect you all once I'm in."

In a few minutes, Kaden had logged in and teleported to the

dungeon. He brought the fallen characters back to life, and they resumed working their way into the tougher parts of the dungeon.

Almost immediately after he was online, Gabby was shooting him direct text messages through the game's chat system.

GABBY THE GREY:

So, H is there today?

KADENATOR:

Yes.

GABBY THE GREY:

Is he half naked, as usual?

KADENATOR:

I hadn't noticed.

GABBY THE GREY:

Right. LMAO. You still don't believe he was flirting?

KADENATOR:

No. Why are you even obsessed with this?

GABBY THE GREY:

Oh! I'm obsessed? 😕 Like you aren't obsessed too

KADENATOR:

Wouldn't matter either way. He was not flirting!

GABBY THE GREY:

He's on the sofa with J, yes?

KADENATOR:

Yes.

GABBY THE GREY:

See if he gets all touchy with J like he was with you

Kaden hated to admit it, but that wasn't a bad idea. He looked at the boys. They weren't even near each other. The center sofa cushion was vacant.

A few times during the afternoon, they reached to each other for fist bumps, but that was something they regularly did. Of course, without Gabby on the sofa being annoying, Hunter had no reason to scoot over.

Why was he agonizing over this? Jacob and Gabby were just imagining the whole flirtation. Neither one of them had any sense. Jacob was no authority on romance. The longest he'd had a girlfriend was barely a few weeks. Kaden had lost count of how many times Jacob had been dumped.

And Gabby had even less dating experience. No. He was sure they had no idea what they were talking about.

"What time is it?" Jacob blurted in the midst of assaulting three cavern trolls.

"Five 'til four," Hunter said, glancing at his watch.

"Crap! I've gotta log out after this battle," Jacob said. "Conference call with Middleton."

"Again?" Hunter said. "What now? Another fight?"

"Yep," Jacob said. "How did you ever guess?"

"Gee, I don't know. Who this time?" Hunter said.

"The usual suspects. Racist white boys."

"Damn, white boys," Hunter said. Then he turned to Kaden, his face reddened. "No offense intended."

"None taken. I don't like them either."

"They're such morons," Jacob said. "They don't even use the right slurs. I'm not Mexican, dammit, I'm half Filipino. Is it asking too much that they get the slurs right? I feel like I should hand them a list."

They concluded the battle and Gabby said her goodbyes then logged out. Jacob went to his bedroom, iPhone in hand, ready to talk with the school principal and Angie.

Hunter was still on the sofa. "Sorry about that crack about white boys earlier. You're nothing like them."

"No problem."

"Those assholes piss me off."

"I know what you mean."

"Hey," Hunter said. "Would you help me with something in the game?"

"What?"

"You know the Port Master quest in Evonweld?" Hunter asked.

"Yeah."

"I keep getting slaughtered by the palace guards when I try to solo it. Could you tag along and heal me? I really want those horseshoes for my mount."

"Sure," Kaden said.

"Cool. First, I need to use the washroom. Maybe you should log onto the Xbox so you don't have to use that old PC."

"Good idea."

Kaden sat where Jacob had been. When Hunter returned, instead of the far left cushion, he took the middle one. Why had he sat there? Kaden's heart beat harder.

The pair completed the quest in a few minutes. After their triumph, Kaden anticipated a shoulder squeeze or a pat on the leg, but Hunter offered neither. Kaden received only the same fist-bump that Jacob had earlier.

He knew it! Jacob and Gabby were so wrong.

"Thanks for healing me," Hunter said. They logged out of the game and Hunter shut his laptop lid, then stared at Kaden. "So, those guys at school..."

"Yeah."

"I'm curious," Hunter said. "Do they ever mess with you? I mean, there's a rumor going around about you, and I wonder if they pick on you about it."

Kaden knew the gossip was that he was gay. "Yeah, sometimes."

"They're dicks. Do you ever get into fights about it?"

"No. I ignore them. Besides, I'm sure they'd kick my skinny ass."

"You're not skinny."

Kaden gazed at his thin arms and legs. "Well, I kinda am."

"You're fine." Hunter looked away, then back at Kaden. "And I just want to say, I mean, I'm not asking you about the rumor, like if it's true or not. That's your business, but if it is true, I'm totally chill with that." Though Hunter claimed he wasn't asking about the gossip, his unblinking gaze fixed on Kaden, eyebrows lifted, as if awaiting an answer.

"I'm not ready to label myself yet," Kaden said.

"That's cool. I'm sure you'll get it figured out in time, eh?"

"It's not that. I know who I am and who I like. I just..." Kaden sighed and gazed into Hunter's warm eyes. "People keep making assumptions, and it pisses me off. I'm so... powerless. I have no control over my life. Everyone tells me what to do. Even when we play *EoOO*, Jacob is the one who calls the shots. I wish I could control just one thing in my life." Kaden rubbed his eyes. He hadn't meant to pour his heart out, but something compelled him. He'd looked deep into Hunter's expressive eyes and felt like he would actually listen to him, so he'd opened up.

Kaden turned away as he struggled to hold back tears. Then he felt a tender squeeze on his shoulder and Hunter's leg pressed against his.

"Hey, I get it," Hunter said. "I get it." He stood and cleared his throat. "I should go home. I've got homework."

"Same."

"Thanks again for helping with the quest. It was fun, just the two of us."

"Yeah."

As he was about to leave, Hunter stepped close, like he might give Kaden a hug, but then he withdrew. Perhaps he remembered Kaden wasn't a hugger. They waved, their gazes lingering on each other, while Hunter slipped his swim sandals on and departed.

~

AFTER JACOB FINISHED his conference call, he came back into the great room.

"Hunter's gone?" Jacob asked.

Kaden sniffed and wiped his nose. "Yep. Homework." He was slouched on the sofa, the game controller hanging limply in his hand. The TV had switched to the screen saver.

"What's wrong with you?" Jacob said as he passed by on the way to the kitchen.

"I think I really embarrassed myself in front of Hunter."

"Not shocking. You're basically a walking embarrassment." Jacob rubbed his belly with one hand while opening and closing cabinets with the other. "What did you do? Rip a big fart? I told you not to eat that—"

"Stop it. I'm serious," Kaden interrupted.

"Sorry." Jacob exhaled. "So, tell me what happened."

"I like, spilled my guts out to him, and almost cried."

"What'd you say to him?" Jacob turned to the fridge and opened it.

"I vented about how I don't have control over anything in my life. Apparently, that also includes not being able to control my mouth and my emotions around Hunter."

"Listen, Hunter's an understanding and chill guy. I've never seen him be mean. He jokes around, but he's not nearly as bad about it as I am. I'm sure it's okay. When you melted down, did he seem upset?"

"No."

"Told ya. He's a great guy. I'm sure he won't blab to anyone about it." Jacob opened a milk jug and sniffed it.

"I'm just scared I freaked him out. What if he won't want to hang out anymore?"

"I doubt that. Hell, he puts up with me. Your brooding is easy to deal with compared to my bullshit." Jacob walked to the sofa, milk jug in hand.

Kaden looked at Jacob. "I brood?"

"Um, well, yeah. That's what Nanay says."

"What? Why is she talking to you about me?"

Jacob smiled. "Well, she wasn't. She was talking to Mom. I just overheard. The cool thing about being as loud as I usually am, when I'm quiet, people don't even realize I'm in the room."

"Yeah. I can see that."

"So, yeah. She told Mom you brood, and overthink things sometimes. And Mom was like, yep." Jacob gulped milk directly from the jug.

Kaden plopped over onto a pillow and buried his face in it. "Oh, god. They're right," he said, his words muffled by the pillow.

5

KADEN

Kaden stared at himself in the bathroom mirror. Pimples covered his face like stars across a night sky. His skin was so oily, he lived in perpetual fear of open flames. And for some reason, his nose had decided it should proudly lead the march toward manhood by being the first, and so far, only facial feature to reach adult size. Despite all that, and a mouth full of braces, Gabby said he was cute. If it hadn't been for the fact that she had a massive crush on Hunter, he would question her taste in boys. But if she was on point with Hunter, could there be any truth to her judgment about him?

He'd updated his hair style during the lockdown, letting it grow out like wild vines, into a long, curly brown mop on top with buzzed sides. Many classmates sported the same style, so he figured he may as well dive in with the rest of the school of fish. But there was still so much else that was wrong with him. Gabby was just being kind.

Despite the differences in appearance because of Jacob being half Filipino, the brothers bore a resemblance, and Jacob was popular enough with the girls in school. Still, Kaden couldn't see himself as desirable.

Jacob was athletic, outgoing, funny; all the things he wasn't. He even had a sizable number of TikTok followers, despite being a lousy dancer, or perhaps because he was a hilariously awful one.

The very notion of recording himself dancing induced nausea in Kaden. He was content being a nerd into baking and cooking, reading, and gaming. Sure, he wished he wasn't so skinny, but Nanay insisted he'd fill out.

Kaden's daydreams revolved around him meeting a gay boy who was desperate enough to settle for him. It seemed a million times more likely that he might find the lost city of Atlantis than Hunter turning out to be that guy. In a completely farfetched alternate universe where Hunter even liked guys, he would never go for Kaden. He'd surely have eyes for an attractive, popular jock, a gay version of Jacob. Never mind Kaden's impressive range of *Stranger Things* quotes and knowledge of the best cat videos online.

Kaden flashed a brittle grin at the mirror, his braces glinting like a prison fence. He stared for a moment, as it might be the final time he would see them.

"You ready, bunbun?" Mom called from the great room.

"Coming!" Kaden exited the bathroom. Mom and Nanay awaited him, both beaming.

"You excited?" Nanay asked, pinching his cheek.

"Yep."

"We have a surprise for you," Nanay said. "After we get your braces off, we're heading to the bakery to celebrate."

Whenever anyone in the Rivera-Watson household referred to *the bakery*, they meant their favorite French bakery in a strip shopping center. Kaden licked his lips.

"You can get the stickiest, crunchiest stuff in the shop," Mom said.

"What about school?" Kaden asked.

"Well," Mom said. "It won't hurt you to miss a few classes. Besides, we told Jacob to take notes for you."

Kaden grimaced. "You know that's a bad idea."

Mom shrugged. "Probably, but it's not every day you get your braces off, bunbun. So, enjoy it. Don't look a gift horse in the *mouth*. No pun intended. Or was it?" She wiggled her eyebrows.

Kaden groaned. "Is that supposed to be your version of a dad-joke?"

"Maybe, bunbun. Of course, it could have been acci-*dental*. But who knows if that's the *tooth* or not? That's something you'll just have to *chew* on."

"Oh, god. Nanay, make her stop!"

"You know there's no hope when she starts *drilling* down on puns. So, you better *brace* yourself. I got a *filling* more teeth puns are coming like a root canal."

"Not you too," Kaden said.

"Quit overreacting," Mom said. "It's not a *cavity*-tastrophe."

"Okay, that one... I'm not even... it was the worst. Straight teeth are not worth this torture," Kaden said, holding his hands over his ears as he walked out the front door.

With the taste of peanut brittle lingering in his mouth, Kaden unbuckled his seatbelt as the Rivera-Watson's SUV came to a stop in front of Aldenbrook Academy.

"Mahal kita, Nanay," he said.

"Mahal din kita," she replied.

"I love you, Mom." He grabbed his book bag and opened the door.

"Love you too, bunbun."

Kaden heaved his bag over one shoulder and brushed crumbs off his school uniform. Before he reached the building, the bell sounded through the front courtyard. He glanced at his phone to check the time. The halls would be filling with students, including the bullies. He scowled.

He made it to English class with only two anti-gay slurs hurled at him and being "accidentally" bumped into only once. Not too bad.

Why couldn't he have continued with home schooling? It was so much better in the safety of his own house, comfortable in his pajamas. But no, the damned scientists just had to invent vaccines.

Jacob had been elated when they went back to school. Between soccer, swim meets and flirting with the girls, he was thriving.

For Kaden though, it meant the return of the gossip, the incessant presumptions, the name-calling. It picked up right where it had left off in 2020, only worse. It seemed his classmates had stored up their venom, waiting to strike him at the first opportunity. And to make it worse still, his brother stuck his nose into things.

That was one of the many drawbacks of having a brother fifteen days older, in the same grade. Kaden loved his brother and appreciated that his heart was in the right place, but he didn't need or want Jacob to stand up for him. However, they attended many of the same classes, so there was no escaping his interference. Jacob also felt obliged to tell their moms about the harassment too. That just magnified his shame.

KADEN RAN his tongue over his teeth, still struggling to get used to not having them covered in sharp metal bits. The sensation was peculiar after two years.

He gazed out the window, staring at nothing, while his science teacher droned on about genetic mutations in fruit flies. At the desk next to him, Aaliyah stealthily gazed at her phone, tucked in her lap.

Mr. Jackson's monotone lecture came to a sudden halt in mid-sentence. Kaden looked up to see why. A gray-haired lady from the school offices had entered and passed Mr. Jackson a note.

"Kaden," he said, glancing at the note.

"Which one?" another student said. Three boys in the class had that first name with various spellings.

Mr. Jackson squinted at the paper. "Um, Kaden Rivera-Watson. Report to Principal Middleton's office immediately."

"Me?" Kaden said. His pencil dangled from his hand.

"Apparently."

He exchanged glances with Aaliyah, her eyebrows raised high above her glasses, like she was looking at someone who'd just been given a prison sentence.

As he shuffled through the corridors, Kaden struggled to figure out why he was called to the office. Unlike Jacob, Kaden never got sent to the principal, but maybe this had to do with Jacob. That must be it!

Two days earlier, Jacob had gotten into a scuffle in the lunchroom with an eleventh-grader who'd launched into a slur-laced, anti-gay tirade against Kaden. Perhaps the principal needed Kaden to recount what happened. He grumbled under his breath. The last thing he wanted to do was talk about it. He'd relived it enough in his mind the last two nights.

When he reached the office, an administrative assistant with a grave countenance directed him to a conference room.

There were four people in the room. None of them were at the large table in the center. Instead, they were clustered at the far end of the room. The principal herself was seated there, as expected.

Next to her was Tamika James, an attorney who was a close friend of his moms. She had assisted them in making the arrangements for their adoptions once Mom and Nanay had been able to legally marry. The brothers had known her their whole lives. Tamika's eyes were red, as if she'd been weeping.

Jacob was there too. And he was crying. No! Not just crying, but hunched over, sobbing, with his face buried in his hands, hair disheveled, like he'd run his fingers through it and pulled at it. Kaden would cry at anything, but it had been years since he'd seen Jacob weep. Kaden's stomach tightened.

Standing in a corner was a police officer, face buried in his phone, coldly oblivious to the blubbering teen.

What had Jacob done now?

Kaden froze. Should he ask Jacob what was happening here? In front of the officer? He could speak to his brother in Filipino. It was a given no one else here would understand. But Jacob was such a mess, Kaden doubted he could even hear him, let alone respond.

"Kaden," Tamika said, her voice shaky. "Sit down." She pointed to a chair next to Jacob. Kaden cast nervous glances at his brother and Tamika while he sat.

Tamika got up, then kneeled in front of Kaden, placing a hand on his knee. "I need to tell you something, sweetie." She closed her eyes as tears ran down her cheeks.

"What's going on?" Kaden's throat was so tight the words were barely audible.

"Dear," Tamika said, "there's been an accident. Your moms were in a traffic accident, a hit-and-run."

"Are they okay?" Kaden whispered, but his gut told him the answer would not be yes.

"Sweetie, I'm afraid Angie didn't make it."

Kaden's breath caught. Every muscle in his body tensed as a torrent of tears burst forth. "Nanay! No."

Angie was Jacob's biological mother. And Roz was Kaden's. Not that it mattered to him. They were equal in Kaden's heart. Certainly, Jacob felt the same.

"Roz is in the hospital, but her condition is grave. The officer is going to drive us there."

Kaden was barely cognizant as Tamika and the police officer led the boys out of the conference room to his cruiser. He was in a daze as he and his brother sat in the backseat, huddled in each other's arms. Tamika sat with them, stroking Kaden's neck from time to time.

Angie didn't make it.

The words echoed in Kaden's mind as the car rushed through the city toward the hospital. Even while the words floated around in his head, he didn't accept this. There must have been a mistake. Nanay couldn't really be gone. Could she? No.

And Mom was gravely injured. What did that mean? Was there any hope?

Kaden lost all sense of time. He couldn't remember arriving at the hospital and being led to the waiting room. He was only vaguely aware when the nurse came to say that Roz was still in surgery to try to stop some internal bleeding.

At some point, Angie's parents arrived from West Palm. Cesar and Maya Rivera rushed to Jacob, their biological grandson, and hugged him while completely snubbing Kaden. Then, after getting an update from Tamika, they sat one on each side of Jacob, with their arms on his shoulders. Jacob hadn't spoken a word. Still, not one since he'd been in Ms. Middleton's office. Occasionally, he'd stop sobbing for a while, stare into space, or cast forlorn glances at Kaden, then break into another round of sobbing.

Cesar and Maya continued to spurn Kaden. When they first came in, they glanced at him, murmured something to each other, then ignored him. They were conservative Catholics and had no use for gay and lesbian people. There were times Angie was completely estranged from her parents. In fact, it was Jacob's birth that had brought them back together, though it was still a strained relationship. However, Kaden recalled a time when Cesar and Maya were at least friendly with him. They would greet him with the same hugs as their biological grandson, give him gifts and cards on special occasions.

Then, one day, years earlier, they were visiting, and Kaden was in the kitchen, cooking as he did many times, twirling around happily, wearing his pink apron with a picture of Hello Kitty on it, and Cesar concluded Kaden wasn't masculine enough. He must be queer. After that, it was like Kaden didn't even exist to them. Jacob got hugs and holiday gifts; Kaden was ignored or scorned. That's when Kaden resolved he didn't enjoy hugging anyway.

Tamika now sat next to Kaden, holding his hands in hers. She threw an icy glare at Cesar and Maya. From the shade she was throwing, Tamika must have been told what had happened that day so many years ago, must have heard about Angie's rage at her father.

It was almost sundown when a doctor escorted the whole family to a conference room. Kaden didn't comprehend the doctor's words, but later, Tamika explained it in plain English.

"Roz has a severe head injury. There's internal bleeding causing the brain to swell. The doctor operated to alleviate it, but it's going to take time to see if it worked."

"Can we see her?" Kaden asked.

"No, dear. She's in the ICU. She can't have visitors now."

That night, despite attempts to make them go home, the boys insisted on staying. Some time after midnight, as Kaden dozed in a chair, Grandpa Bill arrived.

Bill Watson was Roz's father. He lived in the mountains of North Carolina. The family had visited him a few times, usually in the summer, to escape the South Florida heat.

Kaden roused at the sound of his grandfather's voice. It was odd seeing the man's craggy face and gray beard without his pipe hanging out of his mouth. He shook Jacob awake, and the two ran up and hugged Grandpa Bill. Jacob hugged him because he was a hugger. Kaden did, too, because in a time like this, it was okay to break the no-hugging rule, especially with Grandpa Bill.

"Grandpa!" Jacob said, finally breaking his silence.

"When did you get here?" Kaden asked.

"Just a few minutes ago." Grandpa Bill's face drooped, but he seemed to try to be cheerful.

"Have you heard the latest from the doctors?" Kaden said.

"Yes. I've been on the phone with Tamika several times on the drive down."

Kaden nodded and glanced toward Tamika, who had promised to stay at least until Grandpa Bill arrived. She was across the room talking with a man he'd never seen before. "Who's that?" Kaden nodded in their direction.

Grandpa Bill turned around. "Mr. Valentyn. Um. He lives in

Charlotte and volunteered to drive me down. He's an old childhood friend of Rosalyn." Grandpa Bill always called Roz by her full name.

It seemed odd that the man didn't speak to them. Then again, under the circumstances, Kaden didn't feel like talking to strangers. Maybe the man understood that.

Grandpa Bill approached Cesar and Maya Rivera. "I'm so sorry."

Kaden didn't want to be near the Riveras. "I'm heading to the restroom," he said to Jacob while all the grandparents chatted.

A few minutes later, the sorrow built up so much that Kaden was sobbing over the bathroom sink while the water ran. He wiped the tears away and went back to the family waiting room, then wedged himself between Jacob and Grandpa Bill, who were sitting on a couch.

"You took a while," Grandpa Bill said. "I was about to send out a search party."

"Sorry."

"You okay?" Jacob asked, searching Kaden's eyes.

"No. You?"

"No."

Exhaustion consumed Kaden, and he drifted off again, yet he found no respite in sleep. His dreams were plagued with the image of him, Angie, and Roz driving to the bakery after Kaden's braces were removed. Suddenly, it all changed as another car careened into them, sending their SUV tumbling violently and smashing into a tree. Mercifully, Kaden was unharmed, but his moms lay motionless in his arms after he bravely dragged them out of the inferno. He could only sit helplessly while the last breaths escaped their bloody, limp bodies.

He jolted from the nightmare, but the cruel reality of the present was no less daunting than the dream. Intense rays of light poured through the towering windows of the sterile waiting room, his unwelcome wake-up call. He rubbed his eyes with a trembling hand, trying to erase the nightmarish images now imprinted on his mind.

Grandpa Bill and Jacob were still asleep, with Jacob snoring.

Cesar and Maya must have left while he slept. Tamika was gone too, but Mr. Valentyn still sat there alone, staring out the window.

He had yet to speak with Kaden or Jacob, but he must care deeply for Mom to stay the whole night. Once in a while, he peeked at them, but looked away when caught. His eyes were bloodshot, blinking slowly. There was something more in his face that Kaden couldn't read.

Kaden felt wetness on his shirt and realized Jacob had drooled on him. He shoved his brother's face away from his chest. Jacob awoke with a start.

"What?" Jacob gazed around. "Shit," he said, apparently recognizing where they were. Jacob squeezed his eyes closed for a moment.

"Yeah," Kaden said. "Shit."

Grandpa Bill stirred too. "Boys. Any news?"

"We just woke up," Kaden said.

Grandpa Bill glanced at Mr. Valentyn, eyebrows raised.

Mr. Valentyn shook his head.

Grandpa Bill beckoned the man over. He hesitated before approaching and standing near them.

"These are my grandsons, Jacob, and Kaden."

"Pleased to meet you, but..." Mr. Valentyn's voice broke.

"Not the best circumstances," Grandpa Bill finished for him. "Not at all."

Mr. Valentyn nodded, chewing on his lips, not speaking. His eyes became glassy, and he wiped them. Was he crying? A grown man crying?

Kaden didn't understand what compelled him, but he stood up. He walked to the man, and broke his no-hugging rule again, wrapping his thin arms around the man's torso.

Mr. Valentyn wailed then. Kaden felt the man's whole body shaking. Jacob stood and joined in, encasing his arms around both of them. Kaden closed his eyes. He didn't know why the three of them embraced, two brothers and this stranger, some long-time friend of

Mom's. But seeing the man's eyes, whatever was in them, compelled Kaden to hug him.

Kaden didn't know how long they had stood that way, when Mr. Valentyn said he needed to leave for now. He would bring them some breakfast when he came back.

"So, he was a childhood friend of Mom?" Kaden asked Grandpa Bill.

"They were inseparable from kindergarten and on into college. Then Angie came along and stole Rosalyn from him. When I told him what happened, the wreck and all, he insisted on driving me down here. He figured I was in no condition to drive. He's a good man and even now, a friend Rosalyn can count on. More like a brother than a friend."

Like Gabby was to Jacob and himself, Kaden reckoned.

6

DUNCAN

Sitting in the basement of Xeler National Bank, Tower One, Duncan blew on a cup of hot Earl Grey tea, hoping to thwart his usual after lunch lethargy. The bank ordered some of the staff to come into the office now that the latest wave of the pandemic had subsided.

It made no sense. Just when the medical workers were catching a break, why had society decided it was okay to tempt fate again? The only motive was the bank had made too many loans to hospitals, and they wanted to make sure there was enough revenue coming in to make the payments.

He was about to take the first tentative sip of his tea, trying to avoid a repeat of the tongue scorching incident from this morning's cup, when his personal phone rang. The caller was Bill Watson. He hadn't talked to Roz's father in a year, at least.

"Bill, what's up?"

"Duncan. Thank god! I didn't know if this number was still good." There was road noise in the background.

"What's going on?"

Bill's voice cracked as he spoke. "There's been a traffic accident with Rosalyn and Angie. And uh, Angie, she's dead. Rosalyn is probably not going to make it."

"Holy hell." The cup shook in Duncan's trembling hand. He set it down and exhaled. "What happened?"

"Not sure of the details. Hit-and-run."

"Fuck." Duncan closed his eyes to hold back tears. "Bill, I don't know what to say."

"I know. It hasn't sunken in yet. I'm running on adrenaline at this point."

"Was it in Port St. Lucie?"

"Yes. I'm driving there now. Anyway, I just thought you should know."

Duncan shook his head. What could he do? "Bill, that's a long drive for you, especially under duress. Have you passed Charlotte yet?"

"No."

"Come here. I'll drive you down at the very least. Sit vigil with you."

"You sure?"

"It won't be a problem to take off from work."

"Well, I mean, the boys, they'll be at the hospital."

Duncan raised his head and exhaled. "We'll figure that out on the way."

Two hours later, Duncan was behind the wheel of Bill's rusty 1998 Suburban, rattling down the highway toward Port St. Lucie, breathing in the lingering smell of pipe tobacco, with an undertone of decaying foam seat cushions and old plastic.

"I appreciate this," Bill said as they merged onto the interstate.

"The least I can do. So, how's Roz? Any details?"

"She smacked her head pretty hard, apparently. Her brain is swelling. They're operating to relieve the pressure. Tamika says the prognosis is not good."

"Tamika?"

"James. The family attorney."

"Right. I remember her." Duncan hadn't seen her since they signed the legal documents for the sperm donation.

"About that, with the boys and all," Bill said. "I presume they still don't know about you."

"Correct."

How long had it been? Four, maybe five years earlier, Roz had called Duncan one night out of the blue. They'd been in touch on social media from time to time, but hadn't spoken in a while.

Roz had asked him if he wanted to meet the boys, to become a part of their lives. Unfortunately, it was at the height of the crisis in his relationship with Robert. Duncan had been straddling the edge of a complete breakdown as Robert sank lower into addiction. They were getting into shouting matches. Duncan was missing a lot of work. It hadn't been the time for Duncan to add the emotion of meeting the boys with everything else. By the time he'd broken up with Robert and distanced himself from that chapter of his life, the pandemic lockdown had arrived.

When the worst of that was over, Duncan thought about reaching out, but he was gripped by fear. Would the boys be resentful that he'd delayed the meeting? Would they even like him? The longer he put it off, the more guilt he had about the delay. The whole thing fed on itself.

"I don't think today is the time to spring this on the boys," Bill said. "We can just tell them you're a friend of Rosalyn's."

"Agreed, one hundred and ten percent."

There was still something nagging at the back of Duncan's mind. What if the boys were complete assholes? It was a possibility he'd long suppressed. But Bill had gone quiet now, and Duncan was stuck with nothing but his own thoughts to pass the time. Even with everything else going on, this thought bubbled to the top.

When Roz had first approached him about being the biological father of their children, Duncan spent several nights contemplating if he wanted to go through with it or not. And in those hours spent staring at a dark ceiling, his greatest fear was that one, or worse, both of the children would be monsters. If they were, then who would be to blame?

Neither Roz nor Angie seemed like parenting material at that time. But he'd based that on their college days. He'd quickly realized that wasn't a fair judgment. Or was it?

Duncan didn't miraculously transform the day he picked up his diploma. Other than showing up to the office on time and doing enough work to keep from getting fired, his twenties had still been filled with spending too much time in dance clubs, getting shit-faced, and, until he met Robert, playing the field. Were Roz and Angie the same? If he gave them his DNA, and they weren't ready to be responsible parents, wouldn't he share in the blame, since he'd ignored the lingering doubts?

Or worse, what if they were first-place and runner-up in the mom-of-the-year competition, and their children were still little shit-heads? If that turned out to be the case, there was one person to blame, and he could see that guy's face if he opened the cover on the vanity mirror of the sun visor.

However the boys had turned out, he should know the answer soon.

Many hours later, he walked with Bill into the waiting room and there they were, Kaden and Jacob, in the flesh, clad in rumpled school uniforms. He'd seen photos of them. Roz provided pictures and details about their lives all along. He knew Jacob enjoyed swimming and soccer. Kaden was into baking and Roz was certain he was gay; she'd seen his browser history. However, it was only the second time in his life he'd seen Jacob in person, and the first time ever seeing Kaden. They both bore a resemblance, but Kaden could have been his clone at that age.

Duncan had intended to be present for Jacob's birth, but the fellow arrived a few days earlier than the due date and Duncan missed it. He came down for Kaden's birth fifteen days later. Angie had brought little Jacob to the hospital for Duncan to meet.

That had been a mistake. A huge mistake. As soon as he held the infant, he fell in love. He broke down crying, realizing that he wouldn't see his son again for at least a decade. Duncan didn't even look at Kaden. He couldn't handle a second newborn to instantly love, and a second breakdown. He waited long enough to hear that mother and child were healthy, then left the hospital. Roz had been angry at him for leaving early until he got the courage to call her and confess why.

Now, here he was, some fifteen years later, in the same hospital no less, seeing his nearly grown sons, but he couldn't reveal who he was, so he stared at them throughout the night. They looked like angels as they slept huddled together next to Bill. Wounded little angels.

Duncan didn't sleep a wink.

He sat there all night in awe that he, with a little help from Angie and Roz, had made these two human beings. And his first real time spent in the same room with them, he was seeing them in the worst hours of their lives.

Duncan yearned to reach out to them, tell them everything would be all right, hug and hold them, but he couldn't. Bill was right. Now wasn't the time to spring their biological father on the boys. They had enough to deal with. He was nothing but a stranger to them. And there was no one to blame but himself. How could he have been such a coward not to meet them when he had the chance years earlier?

He was still staring when Kaden, bathed in golden light streaking through the windows, awoke. Duncan turned away. Surely, he must be creeping him out, gawking all the time.

Jacob and Bill woke as well. They were murmuring, and Duncan could barely hear them.

"Boys. Any news?" Bill asked.

"We just woke up," Kaden said.

Bill looked at Duncan with raised eyebrows.

Duncan hadn't seen doctors or nurses in the waiting room all night. He shook his head and shrugged. Bill waved, beckoning him over.

Duncan's heart skipped. He took a deep breath, then crossed the room.

"These are my grandsons, Jacob, and Kaden."

Standing closer to the boys, they seemed even more real, and the experience became more surreal. For the first time, he would speak to his sons.

"Pleased to meet you, but..." Duncan's voice cracked. There were too many emotions swirling inside him. The long-delayed meeting with his sons, not being able to tell them who he was. Angie dead. Roz, whom he loved like a sister, clinging to life. Hours of interstate driving. And no sleep. His throat felt like a boa constrictor was squeezing it. He lost the ability to speak another word.

"Not the best circumstances," Bill said. "Not at all."

Duncan's eyes filled with tears. He closed and wiped them. Suddenly, arms wrapped around him. He looked down to see Kaden hugging him. It was too much. He turned into a quivering, sobbing mess. Then Jacob joined in.

Some minutes passed before Duncan composed himself. "Listen, I need to run an errand, but I'll bring you some breakfast biscuits or something back. Okay?"

The boys let him go.

"That would be great," Jacob said.

Kaden nodded. "Thanks, sir."

Duncan left. He maintained composure long enough to get to Bill's car, closed the door, and broke down again. Of all the wrong turns he'd taken in his life, the worst had to be delaying meeting his sons.

7

ROZ

Roz couldn't believe that their sons were eleven. Well, Jacob was. Two more days until Kaden's birthday. It seemed like only yesterday she'd hatched the crazy idea of having two kids at once. Since they'd been born only fifteen days apart, she figured they would combine birthday parties and save some hassle and money.

Angie had bristled at the very notion of it. She insisted the boys always have individual parties. One of Angie's siblings shared her birth month, and she never had a birthday party dedicated only to her. She would not subject her sons to the same "inhumane cruelty."

Roz walked to Jacob's room, knocked on the closed door, and waited for permission to enter. She'd learned the hard way not to barge into Jacob's room, and she didn't need to see him doing *that* again.

"Come in," came his immediate response. His voice cracked when he spoke. It did that more and more now.

The odor of sweaty socks and sneakers, combined with what

must be an old pizza box, wrinkled Roz's nose. She smiled. It reminded her of her own room growing up.

The blinds were closed, blocking the heat of the afternoon sun. Jacob was lying in bed, listening to music, blissfully singing along, not caring that he was off key. His iPad cast a blue glow across his tanned face.

He took his earbuds out of his ears when she came in. "Wassup, Mom?"

Roz closed the door and sat on the edge of the bed. "How's my dumpling today?" she asked, stroking his leg.

Jacob glared and folded his arms. "Mom, we've had this discussion before. No food-based nicknames. If you refuse to use my preferred nickname of *Badass*, you may choose from fierce animals or royal titles."

Roz rolled her eyes. "Sorry. How's my wildcat today?"

"Oh. Wildcat." Jacob smiled and continued in a voice imitating a robot. "That name is acceptable. And I'm fine. Thank you very much, human."

She spoke in a low voice. "So, your brother's birthday is in two days. He's going to bake his own cake. Just so you know, we bought him an extra present."

"What? Why?" Jacob looked like he'd just been told he was going to be executed at dawn.

"We got him an apron."

"Why does he get an extra present? That's not fair."

The boys had decided that they would get just one gift between them to share this year, but it was a big one, an Xbox.

"We got you a store-bought cake. He's baking his own, and we decided that with the money we save from that, we'd get him an apron. If you want to make your own cake next year, we'll get you an extra present."

"You know I can't cook. That's so unfair."

"How is that unfair? We're spending the same money on each of you."

Jacob stuck out his lower lip. "Well, it still seems unfair."

Roz shook her head and laughed. "Now, there's one thing I need to tell you. This apron, it's a pink Hello Kitty apron."

Jacob erupted into laughter. He nearly fell out of the bed.

Kaden had been instantly enamored with the cute Hello Kitty merchandise at five or six when he saw Gabby's pajamas. Jacob had poked fun at Kaden's interest in such a "girly" character regularly until Roz and Angie had put a stop to it.

"Go ahead and get that out of your system, because this is the last time you're allowed to laugh at it. And you are not to make fun of him or say anything negative about it. We've had this conversation before. I'm serious as a heart attack. Understand?"

"But... but... really?" He sighed and rolled his eyes. "Dios mío."

"I mean it, young man. He gets enough abuse at school. He's not getting it at home too."

Jacob's smile vanished. "Sí, Señora."

She figured that would register with him. Already this school year, Jacob had gotten into three fights with boys who were picking on Kaden. Jacob's disciplinary problems notwithstanding, his heart was in the right place.

It was so paradoxical that the boy she'd given birth to was the well-behaved one. She hadn't seen that one coming. At one point, she swore they'd handed over the wrong baby at the hospital, but when Kaden was five, his face was one she knew. He was nearly the spitting image of Duncan at that age and what parts of him didn't look like Duncan resembled her.

"Thank you, your highness." She mussed his hair, then left him to his music.

Roz went to the great room, where Angie was sitting on the sofa, book in one hand, twirling strands of her purple-tinted hair with the other. Her feet were bare, toenails painted the same shade as her hair.

"How did it go?" Angie asked, looking up.

Roz flashed a thumbs up. "The expected amount of whining. No more, no less. Ready?"

"Yep." Angie set aside her book and picked up a box festooned in Hello Kitty wrapping paper.

Roz plopped onto the sofa next to Angie and caught a whiff of her perfume, a light floral bouquet with a hint of spice.

"Kaden!"

He bounded down the short hallway from his room, eyes wide. "Yes?"

Angie held up the box. "Surprise."

"Nanay, for me?" he asked, taking the box.

"Bunbun, with this wrapping?" Roz said. "Who else would it be for?"

"What is this?" He held his ear to the box while shaking it.

"We got you something extra," Angie said.

"Open it," Roz said.

Kaden sat on the floor in front of them. He carefully untaped the paper. He *must* get that from Duncan. Roz would've shredded it in seconds.

Opening the lid, Kaden took out the apron. His eyes grew wide, his mouth hung open, a grin stretched across his face. He held the apron up like a treasure and draped it over his head.

The pure joy on his face filled Roz's heart. She looked at Angie and they smiled at each other. It was moments like this that made it all worth it.

Kaden stood and tied it behind his back. "It's a bit big."

"Sprout, you don't want to outgrow it too quickly," Roz said. She didn't mention that this size was several dollars cheaper than the smaller one. There must be a lower demand for Hello Kitty aprons that fit teens, she figured.

"Oh, good point. How does it look?" Kaden marched past them with one hand on his hip, chin up, imitating that stompy walk of high fashion runway models.

"Spectacular," Angie said.

"Thank you." He leaned down and kissed Roz's cheek.

"You're welcome, bunbun."

"Salamat po." He repeated in Filipino as he kissed Angie.

"Walang anuman."

"I'm going to start my cake now." He trotted to the kitchen, beaming from ear-to-ear.

"I think he likes it," Roz said. "Good choice."

"Self-interest played a part too. The more he's excited and encouraged to bake, the less we have to."

"I thought you liked baking?"

"I do," Angie said. "And I love Kaden's interest in it. It's great bonding time when we can do it together. But sometimes, I'm just too tired and it's nice to have someone else do it."

"There is that." Roz laughed. "But I swear, if that boy keeps binge-watching *The Great British Bake Off* or *Baking Show*, whatever it's called, over and over, he's going to start speaking the Queen's English."

"Is that a problem?"

"It'll be one more language he speaks that this North Carolina girl can't understand," Roz said.

Angie giggled and pinched her knee.

8

KADEN

The television in the waiting room was showing ESPN. Jacob had turned it on to distract himself and kill time. Kaden would have rather had silence, but he tuned it out and stared through the window at the grounds of the hospital, its palm trees jostling in the breeze.

The air in the room was dry, sterile. It had no smell, either good or bad. The leather armrests beneath his fingers were worn and caressed by thousands of hands before him—hands that had sweated nervously, like his did now.

Kaden's phone dinged. He took it out of his pocket. A notification from Gabby appeared, overlaying his Hello Kitty wallpaper.

GABRIELA RUIZ:

Aww. Hugs! H was wondering why you guys weren't online last night. Should I tell him?

KADEN RIVERA-WATSON:

If you want

GABRIELA RUIZ:

Okay. Do you need anything? My mom is making a huge pot of chicken tortilla soup for you guys

KADEN RIVERA-WATSON:

People have been bringing us food. But thanks. Battery 8% so I may have to power off

GABRIELA RUIZ:

Okay. Let me know if I can do anything. I love you. 🤍 xoxoxo ttyl

He could have used a change of clothes. The school uniform was never comfortable and now that he'd been wearing it for a day and a half, it was rank. But he didn't want to bother Gabby's family. If he stayed here much longer, he might have to. Gabby knew where they hid the spare key, so she could bring them whatever they might want.

Across the room, all three grandparents and Tamika James were having a quiet conversation, when suddenly, voices grew heated.

"What are you saying, Cesar?" Grandpa Bill said.

"Jacob's mother is gone. We just feel like it's better to get him out of here and get him some rest at our house."

Jacob switched off the TV and spun around, his face scrunched in confusion. "What's going on?"

"Son," Cesar said, "wouldn't you like to come home with us? You can get some sleep and relax."

"I'm staying here." Jacob walked toward them.

Kaden got up and stood next to his brother.

Cesar fixed Jacob with a stern gaze. "You can't keep staying here."

Jacob crossed his arms. "Well, what about Kaden?"

"Grandpa Bill can look after him," Maya said.

Jacob shook his head. "I'm not leaving. We need to stay here with Mom. And I'm definitely not leaving without my brother." He placed an arm over Kaden's shoulder.

Cesar's face grew darker, his scowl intensifying with each word. "Excuse me! Young man, you will do as you're told," he bellowed. "We're your grandparents."

Jacob didn't flinch, his expression a mask of defiance. "I'm not going. I don't care who you are."

"Cesar, this is ridiculous," Grandpa Bill said. "I can take the boys back to their house and stay with them. It's a ten-minute drive. We can rush back if anything changes in Rosalyn's status."

Cesar's eyes flashed with anger and his lips pulled into a tight line as he shot back, "Don't tell me what's ridiculous. Jacob is *our* grandson. *Our* blood. Not yours."

"Whoa," Tamika said, inserting herself between the two men. "Blood or not, from a legal standpoint, Bill is just as much Jacob's grandfather as you are. Need I remind you they were both jointly adopted after their moms legally married?"

Cesar turned to Tamika, nostrils flaring. "Why are you even in this conversation?"

Tamika responded coolly. "It just so happens that not only am I the boys' legal representative, I'm also who Roz and Angie chose as a temporary guardian in case they were both incapacitated."

Cesar glared at her, but didn't have a response.

"Young sirs," Grandpa Bill said, his tone calm, "I think it might be a good idea for us to go to the house tonight, so you can sleep in your own beds, change clothes, shower and such. But what do you young men think?"

Kaden and Jacob exchanged glances and nodded.

"That sounds good to me," Jacob said.

"Me too."

"Excellent. We can come back first thing, or even sooner if events warrant. Any objections?" Bill glanced at Cesar and Maya. Cesar's muddled eyebrows curved downwards, while Maya's lips pursed in disapproval, but neither spoke. "Good. It's settled then."

It was nice to shower and eat a meal that didn't come from a fast-food drive through or a hospital cafeteria. Gabby's mom's savory chicken soup hit the spot. At first, with his nerves on edge, Kaden had no appetite, but after forcing himself to down a spoonful, his stomach yearned for more.

It was better still for Kaden to be in his own bed, wearing his sea turtle pajama bottoms, snuggled with his stuffed manatee he'd had since he was four. He even fell asleep.

About two in the morning, that ended.

"Kaden," Jacob said, shaking him awake. "Get up. Put on a shirt and flips. We have to go. Now."

Kaden shook his head to wake himself. "What's going on? Is she out of the coma?"

Jacob didn't answer, but his stern expression was answer enough. "Hurry."

THEY WERE LET into Roz's room. The ICU's gray walls closed in on Kaden. It was like being buried in a casket. With the lamps turned so low, the only light that cut through the black was from the monitors. Those electronic devices, blinking like red eyes, seemed to be waiting for someone to press the death button.

Roz's head was bandaged, and various tubes all around her were running who knows where. Her swollen face was unrecognizable. Kaden wished he hadn't looked at her. He knew her spirit was already gone, even before the doctor told them there was no chance she'd ever regain consciousness.

The monitors made a beeping sound, each one tracking a

different function of her body. The only other sound was the whirring of the air conditioning that sent a chill through Kaden's body.

Jacob took one of her hands in his.

With his own clammy fingers, Kaden touched his mother's other hand. It was cool and limp, with a slight twitch, like she was moving it in a dream she wanted to wake from.

Kaden wiped a tear and choked back a lump in his throat as he stared at her blank face.

Grandpa Bill sniffed and patted Roz's shoulder as the machines were cut off and the rest of her body soon followed her brain into death.

The family remained there for a few minutes, each one trying to acclimate to the fact she was no more. Kaden remembered what the doctor had said about the last few moments, wondering if Roz had heard any of it. Was there some voice in her subconscious that understood? Had she known what was going on?

Another tear fell from Kaden's eyes, as he realized that, whatever that voice had been, it was now silent. He bent his head and put a hand over his face, sniffing, not caring if the others heard him sobbing.

9

DUNCAN

Duncan stared blankly at the shoulder of the highway as the smelly cab hauled him home from Charlotte Douglas International Airport. He would have rolled down the window, but he had a feeling the outside air would be even more putrid than that inside the car.

He was thankful he didn't have to look at the driver, as he'd seen cleaner creatures in slaughterhouses. His body reeked of sweat, cigarette smoke, fried food, and alcohol. Not that Duncan looked or smelled any better himself.

"You okay, buddy?" the cabbie asked. He had a miniature Ukraine flag mounted on his dash and spoke with a heavy accent. Maybe he was a distant cousin of Duncan's, for all he knew.

"Nothing three or four days of sleep won't fix."

"I hear ya, man."

In Florida, Duncan had sensed he was in the way. There were too many emotions for him to have to negotiate at once, and with no sleep on top of everything else. He'd wept until his tears wouldn't flow any longer, then his eyes had merely burned. He was always the one to wear his feelings on his sleeve.

Not like Roz. She was adept at compartmentalizing, perhaps because she'd lost her mother at such a young age. Duncan had bawled more than Roz did when her mom died, at least as far as Duncan knew. Well, that wasn't entirely true. She admitted she cried, but she did it in private, letting no one see her vulnerability. Duncan was jealous of that skill.

After Duncan had delivered Bill to the hospital and spent the night in the waiting room, gazing at his sons, he couldn't stay any longer. Bill assured him he had things in hand and so Duncan took a ride share to the Palm Beach airport and flew home.

But Duncan left a changed man. The guilt of not meeting the boys earlier when he'd had the chance was now tenfold worse. For four years, he missed out on being part of their lives. Time he would never get back. Precious time.

Shortly after he got home, his phone rang from an unknown number. He almost didn't answer, figuring it was another one of those damned car warranty people, but he thought he recognized the area code being a Florida one, so he hit the answer button.

It was Tamika with the news that Roz had passed.

"Should I come back down?" Duncan asked.

"No. Not right now. Bill and I have things under control. And the funeral is going to be a small, family-only affair. However, there's going to be a Celebration of Life in a few weeks. Why don't you come down then?"

"Ah, okay. Can you get me the details so I can send something, flowers, or make a donation or whatever it is they wish?"

"Yes. I'll do that."

A couple of days later, Tamika called him back and gave him the funeral home name and address.

"Is there one of those donation web page things for the boys or something?" Duncan asked.

"Yes. I'll text you the link. And Duncan, listen, I know you've been—how shall I put it—looking for the right time to come meet the boys, to properly meet them, that is. Yes?"

Duncan suppressed a groan. "Sure. You might put it that way, in an abundance of politeness that I don't deserve."

"Well, maybe this Celebration of Life is the opportunity to do that. Or even before then."

"Yeah. I'll think about it."

"One more point to consider, since the boys already met you in a way, how would you feel about either Bill or me telling them that, maybe in a little while, after they've had some time to grieve?"

"Okay. That would be good. Just one thing though, promise me you'll let me know how that goes? How they react to it?"

"Certainly," Tamika said. "I'll do that for sure."

After he hung up, Duncan realized there was another difficult conversation he needed to have. If he did go ahead with this meeting, he'd need emotional support, and the best person to provide that support would be the man he loved. But first, he'd have to tell Chip his secret.

Again, he put that off. But Father's Day was coming up, and he decided that would be the time. He psyched himself up for it. *I can do this.*

When Father's Day came, he hoped he was ready. Early in the day, Duncan visited his parents' home, which was also in Charlotte. His sister showed up too. Neither of his brothers made it, but they did FaceTime. Maybe all this family bonding would be the lift he needed to get him a burst of courage, push him over the top.

Chip was with his family, too, but came to Duncan's house afterward, and joined him for dinner.

Duncan wanted to bring up the subject while they ate, but put it off. He downed a second glass of wine to muster more courage. This was almost as stressful as when he'd come out to his parents.

"Let's sit on the couch," Duncan said to Chip.

"Should we clear off the table first?"

"No, I'll get it later."

Chip raised an eyebrow, as that was out of character. "Okay, something's going on. You've been a little off all evening. Did something happen at your parents' house?"

They sat on the couch sideways, facing each other, legs stretched out, and touching. "No, not there, but well, you know Roz's father, Bill, and some of her friends are planning to have a Celebration of Life for her and Angie?"

"Yeah, you mentioned that. Did they pick a date?"

"Not yet. Anyway, I realize you can't commit without knowing the date, but I was wondering if you wanted to go there with me."

Chip smiled. "I was waiting for you to ask me. Certainly, dear."

"I need to tell you something. It's about their sons."

"Oh, okay. How are they holding up, anyway?"

"They're doing as well as expected under the circumstances. Roz's father, Bill, is staying with them for now. Have I ever shown you their pictures?" Duncan grabbed his phone off the side table in one last-ditch effort to stall further.

"No."

Duncan pulled up an album and handed the phone to Chip.

"They're handsome young men," Chip said. He held the phone closer and zoomed into one photo, then smiled. "You know, this one looks like he could be your son."

Duncan cleared his throat and forced out a barely audible, "Um. Yeah."

Chip narrowed his eyes and locked his gaze on Duncan.

Duncan's heart beat faster, and he swallowed through a tight throat.

Chip positioned the phone to view the screen and Duncan's face at the same time. His jaw dropped. "Oh... my... god."

Duncan's gaze sank to the floor, fearful of the judgment that would come. "So, surprise, sweetie. I really do officially have a dad-bod."

"Fuck," Chip said. "Why didn't you tell me, babe?"

"Well, I was under a confidentiality agreement for one. And also, I guess I was afraid of what you might think."

Chip set the phone down and grasped Duncan's hand. "I think it's great." He leaned over and placed an encouraging kiss on his lips. He picked up the phone again and scrolled through the photos, eyes widening in realization. "Oh man. Now I see the resemblance in the other one. They're both yours?"

"Yep."

"This is so cool."

"Really?" He raised an eyebrow in disbelief.

"Absolutely, babe." He reassured him with a gentle smile and a loving touch to the arm.

"So, here's the thing. They don't know yet. They think their biological father is just some random anonymous donor."

"Oh, wow. Wait. Didn't you see them when you went down with Bill?"

"Yes, but we didn't tell them who I am." Duncan explained the entire story, including the fact he'd postponed the meeting for years. "You must think I'm some kind of coward."

He set Duncan's phone down, then took his hand in his. "No, babe. I get it. It's understandable."

"Well, you're more forgiving of me than I am of myself."

"Isn't that one of the reasons you love me?" Chip smiled.

"One of the many reasons, sweetie."

"So, when are the boys going to find out the truth? Before we get there? Or are you planning to surprise them and video the whole thing to put on YouTube?" Chip winked.

Duncan's eyebrows raised. "Um, no video. Bill will tell them soon. They're just finishing the school year."

"Still in school this late?"

"Yes. It's a private school, and the schedule is off because of COVID. Anyway, we figured we should wait until summer break some time. They're overwhelmed enough as it is. So if I give him the word, Bill will tell them then. But I wanted to talk to you first. Assuming they even want to meet me, I'd like you by my side if you're willing."

"Of course, dear. Of course. And I'm sure they'll want to meet you. Why wouldn't they?" Chip squeezed his hand.

"I guess I just feel like I've been horrible by not contacting them earlier."

"Well, I bet they'll understand," Chip said. "Who else knows about them? Does your family know?"

"Oh no. I haven't told them yet. My mom will flip out in a good way, I'm sure. But now is not the time."

"Yeah. That makes sense." Chip grinned. "Babe, I'm so happy that you helped Roz and Angie have kids. You surprise me more every day. I..." He stopped himself and let out a deep breath. "No. Not going to rush things." He squeezed Duncan's knee. "Happy Father's Day, baby."

"Thanks, sweetie."

10

KADEN

A week after Roz died, the boys resumed attending classes for a slight return to normality. Kaden shuffled through the corridors, his heart so heavy even his feet felt weighed down. At least school provided a distraction from worrying about what would transpire now that he and Jacob were officially orphans.

In the hallway, there was the usual banging of lockers; boys and girls talking, laughing, and conversing, just like normal.

But it wasn't normal. Kaden walked with his arms drawn close, clenching them against his body to keep them from trembling.

While a few classmates offered condolences, most avoided speaking to him or making eye contact. It was like he was a ghost roaming the corridors. In P.E. today, Aaliyah had actually participated in volleyball to get out of having to hang with him on the bleachers like they usually did. Even the boys who frequently picked on him were staying clear. At least there was that small mercy.

Kaden was so preoccupied, the silent treatment didn't upset him. Because of his school absences, he'd missed many assignments and end-of-year exams that he had to make up now. Jacob was equally consumed. They couldn't even hang out with their friends at lunch.

Instead, they grabbed some chocolate milk and crackers, then headed to the math teacher's room for some makeup lessons.

As he and Jacob walked to the classroom, Jacob kept his head down and his shoulders bent, eyes fixed on the murky gray-brown terrazzo floor. Normally, Jacob would stand tall, flirt with girls, strut down the corridor like he owned the place, larger than life. Today, he just looked small.

"What's wrong?" Kaden asked. "The usual?"

"I think Hunter's avoiding me."

"Well, everyone's avoiding me. It's like we have a disease or something."

"Yeah. They're all being weird." Jacob twisted his lips, then sipped milk from his straw.

Kaden missed Hunter too. Even if they didn't see him in person, they usually interacted with him in *Elves of Ora Online*, but neither of the brothers had been playing since the car wreck.

That afternoon, when he arrived home from school, Kaden logged into the game, not because he felt like playing, but because he yearned for some sort of connection with Hunter.

As Kaden loaded the game and his avatar entered the virtual fantasy world of Ora, he checked to see if any of his friends were online. He scrolled through the alphabetical list until he got to Hunter's character: Sanyangkkun. A green dot next to the name meant he was online. Kaden grinned, then began typing a message to him. Before he could finish and hit enter, the dot turned red. Hunter had logged off. Coincidence? Or?

Jacob walked past, munching on a granola bar. "You're playing the game?"

"Kinda. I was gonna see if Hunter was on and say hi. He logged out a few seconds after I came online."

Jacob halted mid-step. "He *is* avoiding us." After finishing the last bite of granola, he wadded the plastic wrapper and tossed it toward a trash can, almost landing the shot. "Dammit!" he shouted as it hit the floor. "That's it. Let's grab our bikes and go to his house."

"Really?"

"Yep. Come on, let's tell Gramps."

Grandpa Bill was watching television in bed, drinking a beer. Neil deGrasse Tyson was being interviewed about the James Webb Space Telescope on a news channel and Grandpa was muttering something under his breath. Grandpa Bill referred to Tyson as a 'Pluto hater' because he kept saying Pluto was a 'dwarf' planet. Kaden had learned many new cuss words from listening to Grandpa Bill complain about this topic.

"Gramps, we're going to visit our friend Hunter," Jacob said.

"What? Oh, okay. Be back in time for dinner. The Chinese carry out is dreadful enough in this town as it is, but worse if it's cold and soggy."

"Will do."

Grandpa Bill belched, and it reverberated through the house as the boys headed to the garage.

It was a ten-minute bike ride to Hunter's house. The neighborhood was more upscale than Kaden's. At least it looked that way. There were fewer cars parked on the street, prettier houses. It wasn't a gated community though. The edges of the yard were neat, and well-kept junipers and flowering shrubs dominated the landscaping.

"Should we have texted him first?" Kaden asked Jacob as they dismounted their bikes in the driveway and removed their helmets.

"In a ghosting situation? Nope."

"Maybe he's not even home."

"You said he was online. He's probably home. We'll find out." Jacob punched the doorbell.

Shortly, the door opened. A girl answered. She must be Hunter's sister, Emma, who was almost eighteen. She stood in the doorway, keys in hand, purse strapped over a shoulder. "Hi Jacob."

"Yo, Emma."

"And who's this?" Emma asked.

"I'm Kaden."

"Ah. Interesting." She looked him up and down, one eyebrow raised. "*The* Kaden."

What did she mean by that?

"In the flesh," Jacob said.

"I'm very sorry for your loss. You guys doing okay?" She stared at Kaden while placing a comforting hand on his shoulder.

"We're fine." Kaden realized he didn't sound particularly convincing, but that was the easiest answer to give when your whole life was falling apart.

"Is Hunter here?" Jacob asked.

"Yeah. Come in." She focused on Kaden. "Shoes off, and beware of toys. They're everywhere. We're even still finding Hunter's old Legos on occasion." Muttering, she added, "Of course the goof only stopped playing with them last year."

Kaden glanced warily at the floor as Emma let them into the foyer.

"I'll get Hunter for you." She held her free hand to the side of her mouth and let out an ear curdling call. "Huuuuuuunter!"

Kaden was positive he'd just lost most of the hearing in his right ear with that yell.

"I'm sure he'll be here in a minute," Emma said. "I've got to go pick up Zoey from daycare." That was Hunter's little sister. She was almost three.

Emma left, and the brothers were alone. It seemed strange to be in someone's house with no one around.

"Maybe he's in the pool," Jacob said. He wandered down a hallway to the great room, motioning Kaden to follow. One wall was sliding glass doors that looked out onto the pool deck, similar to their own house. A submerged figure swam the length of the pool, his head popping out of the water as he reached one end.

Jacob opened one slider and Kaden stepped through after him. "There you are!" Jacob yelled.

Hunter glanced up, and Kaden couldn't read his reaction. He had on swim goggles and was shaking water from his hair, like a wet puppy. Was there any situation where he didn't look adorable?

"Oh. Hey."

Kaden was trying to figure out a polite way to broach the subject of Hunter avoiding them when Jacob shouted to Hunter while he was still in the pool. "Dude, why are you ghosting us?"

Kaden's eyes grew wide and he bit his lower lip.

"What?" Hunter swam to the edge near the steps and emerged from the pool, his wet board shorts clinging to every contour of his body, causing Kaden to flush. Hunter removed his goggles and grabbed a towel. "I'm not ghosting you."

"Come on, dude," Jacob said. "You can't bullshit a bullshitter."

"Jacob, maging mabait ka," Kaden said. *Be nice.*

Hunter stared at the concrete deck and heaved a couple of deep breaths as water puddled beneath him. "You're right. I'm sorry."

"Why?" Jacob asked.

Hunter joined them under the shade of the lanai, wiping water out of his ears. He frowned as the gaze of his brown eyes shifted between the brothers. "I don't know what to say or how to behave around you. I've never had friends who, you know, lost your..." Perhaps it was because of the harshness of the pool water that ran down his face, but Kaden thought Hunter was on the brink of tears.

"Oh," Jacob said.

"I've been afraid I might say the wrong thing. Or, if I talk about my family, you might get upset."

"Dude. You don't have to worry," Jacob said. "I'm not gonna lie. We're both a mess right now." He looked at Kaden for corroboration.

"Yep."

Jacob turned back to Hunter. "But you're one of my best friends. Honestly, you are my best friend, because I don't count Gabby. She's more like a sister and majorly annoying, usually. Anyway, we miss you, dude. Right, bro?"

"Yeah."

"We just want to hang with you. And don't worry about saying something that upsets us. I mean, sure, sometimes Kaden breaks down crying, but it's not anyone's fault."

Jacob wasn't lying. Kaden had even cried today before he got out of bed, then again in the restroom after third period. But Jacob withheld that he occasionally broke down as well.

Hunter looked at Kaden with compassionate eyes. "I'm sorry, guys. I'm just stupid."

"It's okay, dude." Jacob hugged Hunter, getting himself wet in the process.

After the hug, Hunter turned to Kaden. "I'm sorry." He extended his hand and Kaden shook it, realizing only afterwards that Hunter had probably meant to give him a fist-bump.

"No problem," Kaden said.

Hunter sighed. "Thanks for coming over, guys. I don't know why I'm such an idiot."

"Same reason I am," Jacob said. "Bad genes."

The boys all chuckled. When the laughter quieted, they stood awkwardly. Kaden stole glances at Hunter.

Hunter fidgeted. "You guys wanna hop in the pool or something?"

"I wish," Jacob said. "I'm still trying to catch up on the assignments we missed. I've got to study today."

"Okay." Hunter dried himself off more and turned to Kaden. "How about you? You busy with school stuff, too?"

"Um." Kaden's brain filled with conflicting thoughts. He was both elated and terrified by the prospect of spending time alone with Hunter. Not just Hunter, but *Swimsuit Edition Hunter*. However, if they swam, he'd have to take his own shirt off!

Worse, what if Hunter wanted to make conversation? To actually talk to him about, well... who knows what? It was one thing to play the game together and chat with each other, having the game itself be the main subject, but what would they say to each other outside of that? His mind flashed back to the last time they actually talked to each other, when Kaden had spilled his guts and brought himself to tears. No. He didn't need a repeat of that disaster.

Kaden exhaled. "I'm mostly caught up, but I'm kind of tired. I'm just going to play *EoOO*."

"Cool. If you want, we can run some quests together when you get home."

Kaden smiled slightly. "Yeah."

"See you online then."

The brothers said their goodbyes and let themselves out.

"Dude," Jacob said, shaking his head. "Why didn't you stay?"

"What?"

Jacob hopped onto his bike and frowned. "You know what. Even you can't be that clueless," he said, adjusting his helmet chin strap.

Kaden looked back at the door of the house, wondering if the boy inside was as disappointed in Kaden as he was at himself. Then he got onto his bike and caught up with Jacob.

When Kaden got home, he logged into the game and spent the afternoon with Hunter. For a couple of hours, it was like old times. Kaden hadn't realized how much he needed that. He slept better that night than he had in two weeks.

11

ROZ

The sun beating down on Roz would have been uncomfortable but for the light, tempering sea breeze. She strolled arm-in-arm with her father along the sands of Jensen Beach, just a half hour drive from her house. There were few clouds in the sky, and the ocean seemed to glow with a light of its own.

A shift in the wind whisked the familiar scent of Bill's pipe tobacco past her nose.

The ocean waves crashing against the shore drowned out all other sounds of the world except for the chirping cranes and the two rambunctious boys zipping around them.

Bill had driven from North Carolina to spend Thanksgiving with them. Angie was at work, but Roz took Wednesday off.

Her six-year-old sons flitted about, chasing each other into the shallow water, giggling and yelling as chilly waves splashed over them. Birds skittered away as the boys got too close for comfort.

"Don't scare the shit out of the birds, boys," Roz scolded. "I mean poop. Don't scare the poop out of them." She turned to her father and spoke in a lower voice. "Angie is gonna kill me."

The boys, dripping wet, gave squealing shrieks as they darted between their grandfather's legs, sand flying in their wake.

"Careful, boys! Don't knock the old man down and break his hip."

As the brothers sprinted off into the distance, paying their mother no heed, Bill chuckled. "It's funny how even at this age, their personalities are already showing through. If you hadn't told me, I'd know that Jacob is a handful, and I imagine he's just going to be more so in a few years."

"Yep," Roz said. "And Kaden, poor thing, he tries to tame his brother, but it's a lost cause. Like trying to herd a cat."

Suddenly, Bill halted, the smile on his face vanished. He took his pipe out of his mouth. "Fuck!"

"Wow," Roz said. "Don't let Angie hear you talking like that, or you'll be putting money in the swear jar too."

She stared at her father, but it was like he didn't even hear her. He stood still like a statue, his eyes wide and darting between the two boys, his jaw agape.

"You gonna tell me what's going on, old man? You're not having a stroke, are you?"

He faced her, one side of his mouth lifting. "I just figured something out."

"Does it have to do with Pluto? Because if so, I don't want to hear it."

"I worked out why both of your sons' middle names are Duncan." He raised an eyebrow and studied her face, like he was waiting for a reaction. The wind tugged at the strands of his beard, making it waver in the ocean breeze.

Roz exhaled. "I told you at the time, we just liked that name. I've always liked that name since I was a kid." Would he buy that?

Her father's face was creased with wrinkles, his gray beard and hair had streaks of silver, his blue eyes studied her behind his aviator sunglasses.

The other parents and kids on the beach were blurry figures in the background. His withered lips parted slightly, and Bill let out a skeptical laugh. "Bullshit," came his deep, raspy reply.

Her face was already flush with shame, and she'd never been able to succeed at lying to him. Despite that, she tried. "What do you mean?"

He rolled his eyes. "Daughter of mine, I still remember what Duncan looked like at that age. Kaden is the spitting image, and Jacob bears a strong resemblance too."

Roz groaned. "Listen, don't tell another soul. You got that? No one at all."

"Why the secrecy?"

"We have our reasons. Now promise me you won't breathe a word. If you tell someone, it might spread. And if Duncan's mom finds out, she'll be down here getting all into our business."

Bill nodded. "Yeah. I can see Olivia doing that. Don't worry." He zipped his fingers across his lips. "And all this time, I thought you used an anonymous donor."

"This way was cheaper. And we Watsons know how to do things on the cheap, eh, old man?"

"Truly. I'm amazed you got Duncan to agree to it though. He doesn't seem... what's the word I'm looking for? Nurturing?"

"Paternal."

Bill's eyes brightened. "Yes. Paternal."

"That's why we chose him. Well, that and he's got a good brain. I can already see that Kaden's going to be a nerd, just like him."

"Well, I wasn't intending to say anything, but now that you mention it, I think Kaden might be like him in another way."

"Oh," Roz giggled. "Yeah, he's not the most boyish boy."

"Not that there's anything wrong with that."

"Nope. Nothing at all. By the way, if you want to know what to get him for Christmas, try to find the Hello Kitty edition of the Easy Bake Oven. You'll be his favorite grandparent forever."

"Where could I find one of those?"

Roz shrugged. "eBay? I dunno."

Bill never found that edition of the Easy Bake Oven, but that didn't stop him from getting a regular one and hiring an artist friend to paint it into one. Roz had been right. A boy never loved his grandfather more than Kaden did that Christmas morning.

12

KADEN

The morning sun cast a golden glow into Kaden's room as it streamed through the sliding door that led out onto the concrete pool deck. A gentle wind rippled the pool's water, creating a shimmering light across his ceiling. A fan spun over his head while he lay in bed. It should be calming. *He* should be calm.

After all, it was the beginning of summer break. Ninth grade was done. No more homework or tests. No more snide comments in the halls. No more name-calling. He should be cheerful.

Instead, Kaden struggled and failed to catch his breath. His chest felt like it was gripped in a vise. It was happening again. He was paralyzed, powerless to do anything but watch from inside his own head as nightmare scenarios of his future unfolded in his brain.

His heart beat twice with each tick of the Hello Kitty wall clock across the room. The sound of it only made him more anxious. He glared at its face. The black dots in its eyes seemed to pulsate with each tick. He couldn't look at it. Like the therapist had taught him years ago, he needed something else to focus on. Anything.

The ceiling fan? Perhaps. As beads of sweat ran down his face, he stared at it, willing his heart to stop racing. He drew a deep breath into his tense chest, then slowly exhaled. Yes!

Another deep breath. And another. In his left hand, he held a seashell he'd had since he was six, concentrated on the texture of it, smooth inside, rougher outside. He recalled the day he found it on the beach with his brother, Mom, and Grandpa Bill.

Focus on that day. Breathe. Go there. Hear the ocean waves. The soothing sounds. The birds. Remember the feel of the sand between toes, the water rushing over bare feet. Breathe.

Gradually, his heart slowed its pounding. Breathe. Breathe.

The panic attack retreated, leaving him chilled and shivering in a pool of perspiration. He ran a hand through his wet hair.

When his mop of hair was nearly dry, he donned a shirt and athletic shorts. If Grandpa Bill suspected he had another attack, he'd wind up at the therapist again. Not that he minded visiting the therapist. After all, that's who taught him the techniques to help him cope with them. But having to see the therapist was one more reminder that Kaden didn't have control of, well... anything.

There was another reason too. Hunter was coming over today. The last thing Kaden needed was for Hunter to see how much of a wreck he was.

The previous evening, while they were playing *EoOO*, they discussed Hunter coming over today to hang out with them. Kaden didn't want Hunter to witness one of his panic attacks, nor did he want Grandpa Bill to bring up the subject in his presence.

Kaden steeled himself and crept from his bedroom, putting on his finest brave face. Jacob was stretched out on the great room sofa, watching *Avatar: The Last Airbender* on TV.

"Hey you," Kaden said.

"Lazybones finally got up." Jacob squinted and looked him over. "Did you sleep?"

Kaden shrugged. "I dunno. I guess so. Where's Grandpa?"

"Grocery store."

By the time Grandpa Bill got home, Kaden was confident he had beaten down the panic enough that no one could tell this was one of his rough days.

~

WHEN HUNTER ARRIVED in the afternoon, Kaden's mood was bordering on jovial, perhaps buoyed by the anticipation of seeing him. Also, to Kaden's relief, Grandpa Bill had left again, so there was no danger of him mentioning the attacks. He just had to worry about Jacob's loud, unfiltered mouth.

They played for several hours, running quests. But later in the day, Jacob and Hunter decided to enter a battle arena where players fight other players.

Kaden hated that part of the game. The enemy players always targeted healers first. It was an excellent strategy, but totally frustrating for Kaden to get killed, respawn a minute later, then die again in a few seconds.

At Jacob's and Hunter's insistence, Kaden tried to play. Even with both of them to protect him, Kaden's avatar still died a quick death. Worse, his heart raced, stoking fears that the panic attack would return.

"That's rough, buddy," Jacob said as Kaden's character shrieked and fell to the ground with a sickening thud.

"I'm gonna log out," Kaden said. "I need to start dinner, anyway."

Hunter took off his headset. "Your grandpa isn't getting you dinner tonight?"

"No."

"That guy cracks me up with his Pluto rants." Hunter smiled. "Where is he, anyway?"

"He's meeting with a lawyer."

"Wow, he's taking this Pluto thing seriously," Hunter said.

Kaden smiled faintly. "No, it's the family attorney. Something to do with estate stuff and figuring out what to do with us, I guess."

Hunter frowned. "What do you mean? Isn't your grandpa taking care of you?"

"I wish," Jacob said. "You know, the old man hasn't even gotten mad once when I drop the F-bomb. In fact, he even made us teach him some Filipino cuss words."

"I feel something is wrong," Kaden said. "Just a gut instinct, like he's worried about something. He doesn't talk about it though. He changes the subject if we even hint at it."

"That sucks."

"Yep," Kaden said. "Well, you guys have fun. I'm starting dinner."

"So, you cook? Like for real?" Hunter asked.

"Yeah."

"Get him to make you his legendary Crunchy Orange Chicken," Jacob said, smirking.

"Crunchy?" Hunter raised an eyebrow. "You mean crispy, eh?"

Kaden groaned. "One time, when I was like twelve, I sorta overcooked it and he's never let me live it down."

A dimpled grin tugged at Hunter's cheeks.

"Honestly," Jacob said, "he's a bomb chef. He'll make someone a sick wife one day."

Hunter's eyes grew wide and his mouth dropped in shock.

"Wow," Kaden said. "Good one, bro. Are you trying to see how many groups of people you can outrage in a single sentence?"

Jacob snorted. "You know I'm joking."

Kaden thrust his arms in the air and stormed across the room to the kitchen. He wished the kitchen was a separate room so he could slam the door and hide his embarrassment from Hunter. Normally, Kaden took Jacob's ribbing in stride, but not this time with Hunter as a witness.

He was annoyed with himself for caring about that because it shouldn't matter. His massive crush aside, Hunter was just a friend, and that's all he would ever be. But he couldn't help caring. Just like he hid his panic attack and the fact that he was seeing a therapist.

He exhaled to calm himself, then opened a cabinet and took out some pots. As he turned to set them on the counter, he found Hunter sitting on a barstool next to the kitchen island.

"Oh," Kaden said. How did he get there so fast and silently? Did he materialize again? He had to be part ninja.

Hunter cocked his head to one side and smiled. "Can I watch?"

"Don't you want to do the arena combat thing more?"

"Nah. I'm bored with that."

"Okay." But it wasn't okay. Even under normal circumstances, Kaden found it distracting with someone watching him cook, although he used to pretend he was hosting his own cooking show, and sometimes still fantasized about that.

But how could he concentrate now? Looking at Hunter's smooth skin, the dips and curves of his muscles stretching his tank top. All Kaden could think about was how it would feel to run his hand down Hunter's chest. Kaden turned away, heat rising to his cheeks.

"I didn't realize you could cook."

Kaden shrugged. "Well, my moms' work schedules meant they didn't get home in time to make dinner much. And I really enjoy cooking and baking."

"That's wicked."

"Really?"

"Yeah. Do you ever like to watch baking shows?"

"All the time," Kaden said.

"What's your favorite?"

"*The Great British Bake Off.*"

Hunter's eyes widened and a grin spread across his face. "I love that show."

Kaden's brow lifted. He set the pots down and turned back to Hunter. "Seriously?"

"Yeah. I keep watching it over and over, even though I remember who wins."

"Me too."

"Okay." Hunter rubbed his hands together. "In your opinion, what's the best season?"

"¡Dios mío!" Jacob yelled. "You're both cooking nerds?"

"Baking!" Kaden and Hunter said almost in unison. They turned to each other and smiled.

"I can't take it," Jacob said. "Thank god these are noise-canceling." He clicked a button on his headset. "Okay nerds! Geek out all you want, dudes!" His voice was raised even louder, as he couldn't hear himself.

"For the record," Kaden said to Hunter, "I'm a cooking nerd too."

"So, you didn't answer my question. Best season?"

"Twenty nineteen. No doubt."

Hunter smiled. "Mine too. And your favorite contestant of all time?"

"Henry."

Hunter's face lit up. "No way! Mine too."

"Really?"

"Yeah. I can't believe we never talked about this before. You remember when Henry got that handshake from Paul? What he said to him?"

"Oh my god. I think that was the funniest ever," Kaden said. "So, do you cook or bake?"

Hunter got up from the stool, walked around the island, and stood near Kaden. "Me? Oh, no. I can barely microwave popcorn without burning it. But I like watching British people bake things for some stupid reason."

"I know, right?" Kaden gave a short laugh. He turned his attention to the iPad he kept on the kitchen counter, opening his favorite recipe app.

Hunter sidled closer, rested a bent arm on Kaden's shoulder and looked at the screen. "What ya' making?"

The weight of Hunter's arm pressed on Kaden, making the back of his neck tingle. He flipped through recipes, but his mind was elsewhere. "I dunno."

"Wait. What's that? Looks yummy."

"Beef carnitas."

"You ever make that?"

"Yeah. Mom loves that..." Kaden's voice trailed off. Visions of the family, sitting at the table, sharing a meal. Jacob digging in like a wolf. His moms savoring every bite, giving him that proud smile, and a pat on the hand for a job well done.

Never again. He tried to escape it, but there was no use. Like a wave crashing on the beach, the stark, cold reality hit him. His moms were gone. It was a mystery who would take care of him and Jacob. Would they have to move? Change schools? Or worse?

His head drooped as his eyes filled with tears.

"You okay?" Hunter stepped back and bent down to look Kaden in the face.

Kaden closed his eyes, squeezing out tears that ran down his cheeks. He stopped breathing, but that only made it worse. His body tensed and quivered. This was a nightmare. The last thing he wanted was to break down in front of Hunter. Why now? The fear of triggering him had been why Hunter had ghosted them. And now it had happened. Hunter would surely start avoiding him again.

"Kaden. I know you don't like to hug, but I kinda really low-key wanna hug you right now. Can I?"

Kaden's throat was too tight to speak, but he nodded, eyes still closed. Hunter's firm arms wrapped around him, pulled him tight, cradled him.

Moments passed, or minutes. He wasn't sure. Hunter's solid chest against his was comforting, a rock that held him up.

"It'll be okay, Kaden. Just relax and let it out." Hunter's voice in his ear was soothing.

Kaden sniffed and choked a little, but he found his anxiety receding. "I... I dunno what's wrong with me."

"What's wrong? Nothing's wrong. Of course you can cry. Geez. There's nothing wrong with that. It's normal. Perfectly normal." Hunter's hand cupped the nape of Kaden's neck.

Kaden clutched the back of Hunter's shirt. He clung until his whole body went limp, until he couldn't think at all. And for that moment, Kaden forgot about everything.

"It's okay, buddy," Hunter said, his hand stroking his neck.

He wanted to thank Hunter, but he couldn't speak. Part of him wanted to run away out of embarrassment, and another part wanted this embrace to last forever.

Finally, a deep breath filled Kaden's lungs. He blinked his eyes to push the tears away, swallowed the lump in his throat. "I'm better now."

"You sure?" Hunter released the hug and stepped back.

Kaden bobbed his head in a hesitant nod. "Yeah."

"Did the hug help, or just make it worse?"

"It helped... a lot."

"You're not just saying that?"

"Honest. It helped," Kaden said, crossing his heart.

Hunter thumbed the corner of his mouth and widened his gaze with a satisfied expression. "If you ever want one again, they're free."

They shared a smile.

In the great room, Jacob clicked away on his game controller and cussed from time to time, oblivious to Kaden's emotional crisis, thankfully.

Hunter glanced down at the spot where Kaden's tears had wet the front of his shirt. "Perhaps I should head home."

"Hunter, you're not... you're not going to avoid us again? Or avoid me? Are you?"

He looked Kaden in the eye. "No. I promise you, I'm not. I should let you cook in peace. Yeah? You don't need a repeat of the Crunchy Orange Chicken."

A slight grin crossed Kaden's face. "I guess."

Hunter said his goodbyes and left.

Afterward, Jacob popped over to the kitchen. "So?"

"So, what?"

"You guys hugged."

"You saw that?"

"Saw it and heard it, the whole thing."

Kaden's forehead furrowed. "But you had the noise-canceling turned on."

"Or did I?" Jacob smiled slyly, then smugly rubbed a hand through his spray of hair.

Heat rose to Kaden's forehead, and his eyes narrowed. "Shit."

Jacob chuckled. "When you were nerding out over this cooking show, who was that guy you both liked?"

"What? Henry."

"Henry. Okay. I'm gonna go out on a limb here, because I've known you for, like, I dunno, fifteen years, and I'm going to make a wild guess that Henry is a cutie. Yes?"

"Maybe."

"Maybe?" Jacob rolled his eyes. "Obviously, he's cute, probably in some super nerdy way, and you and Hunter coincidentally happen to like him."

"So?"

Jacob pushed the headset microphone to his lips, and launched into his snooty maitre d' voice. "We have a table for gay, party of two!"

"You don't know that."

"I admit, he's not a five-bar gay like you obviously are, but still..."

"Five-bar? What the hell are you talking about?"

"Gaydar, bro. Gaydar." Jacob shook his head. "Dios mío. You have much to learn, young padawan. See, when you walk into the room, my gaydar gets a full five bars of 5G high-speed gayness. Most of the time, Hunter is zero bars, No Service. But sometimes, like today, he's one bar of LTE."

"That's not much, is it?"

Jacob tilted his head. "It's something. Of course, you could just ask him?"

"Yeah, right," Kaden said, rolling his eyes. "You've known me for fifteen years, so you know I won't do that."

"Okay, you could post a thirst-trappy selfie on Instagram and see if he hearts it. You can even borrow one of my competition swimsuits."

A wave of warmth rushed into Kaden's cheeks at the very idea of wearing one of those tiny suits. "Again, you know I won't do anything like that. If you were actually a kind and loving brother, you would ask him if he's gay."

"Yawn. That's way too basic for me. Plus, the answer is pretty obvious to anyone who's paying attention."

"Obvious how?"

"That hug, bro."

"What about it?" Kaden asked.

"It was a full-on romantic PDA, like the kind someone gives when they get asked to be someone's bae. So, what's the tea? When are y'all tying the knot? And don't forget, I gotta be your best man."

Kaden gave a dismissive grunt. "If you were paying attention when you were eavesdropping, Mr. Sneaky, you heard no marriage proposal! That wasn't a romantic moment. It was just a friend comforting a friend."

"It looked like way more than that to me. I think you should grow a hairy pair and ask him if it was."

Kaden closed his eyes and drooped his head as he let out a breath. He opened his eyes and looked back at Jacob, his expression somewhere between an angry frown and an annoyed pout. "I don't need him rejecting me like everyone else does."

The smile melted from Jacob's face. "Bro..." Jacob choked up. "Bro..." He clenched his hands into fists. "I can't control anyone else, but I will never reject you. Even if everyone else on the planet does, you're still stuck with me. Okay?"

Kaden nodded. "I know. I love you."

"I love you too." Jacob squeezed Kaden's hand, but his smile wavered. Kaden searched Jacob's face for any indication of his feelings, finding the same dread that had taken root in his own heart.

"Are we going to be all right?" Kaden whispered.

Jacob's eyes glistened with unshed tears. "We are, bro. We just take it one day at a time, and we've always got each other's backs, no matter what."

"No matter what." Kaden took comfort in Jacob's words. Despite that, anxiety bubbled in his gut, ready to boil over at the least provocation.

13

DUNCAN

Duncan reclined on a chaise in his backyard, the afternoon sunlight dappling his skin through a canopy of oak leaves. Spring had given way to summer, but at least it wasn't scorching hot in Charlotte today. He held his iPhone at the ready, awaiting a FaceTime call any minute.

Tamika James had messaged him earlier and said she needed to speak to him about an item from Roz's will. When the phone lit up, it surprised him to see Bill Watson with Tamika.

"Duncan," Bill said. "You look like you're living the good life."

"Trying to. How goes it in the Sunshine State?"

Bill gave a noncommittal shrug. "It's going."

"So," Tamika said, "do you recognize this?" She held up a silver locket with small diamonds.

Duncan's eyes widened. It had belonged to Roz's mother and had been inherited by Roz. One day, when they were teens, he'd seen it while they were hanging out in her room. She'd never worn it, or any other jewelry. "If you're not going to wear it, you should give it to me," he'd said at the time.

Her response had been, "Over my dead body." He hadn't seen it after that and suspected she hid it somewhere. And that may have been wise, because he really coveted it. Duncan wasn't a thief, but that one was tempting to borrow, especially since she never wore it.

"I remember it. Roz's mom left her that," Duncan said.

"Well, apparently, it's yours now," Tamika said. "And there's a note with it. It says, 'I told you that you would only get this over my dead body. Looks like you win, queen! I'm sure it will look great with at least one of your diamond tiaras. Wear it in good health.'"

Duncan tried to suppress a grin, but he couldn't help it. Even in death, Roz was still Roz. Bill was beaming too.

"I appreciate her thinking of me," Duncan said, "but that's easily worth three or four thousand dollars. I'd rather the boys have it."

"They'd just sell it and buy video games and shit with it," Bill said. "If it has sentimental value to you, I would really like you to take it."

It was more than just an object to Duncan. "Okay, but I'm going to contribute some more money to their fund thingy on that web page."

The corners of Bill's eyes narrowed as he nodded. "That would be helpful." He averted Duncan's gaze with an expression betraying a mix of fear and heartbreak.

"What's wrong?" Duncan asked.

Bill was silent. Tamika looked at him expectantly. Bill nodded at her and she turned to the camera. "We're having a challenging time with the custody situation."

"I thought Bill was just gonna stay with them."

"I would love that," Bill said. "It's just that I can't afford to. Between their mortgages, the homeowner's insurance, and other expenses, no wonder the girls worked so much. There's no way my pension and social security will come close to covering it. My only option would be for them to come live in the mountains at my cabin."

Duncan had visited the two-bedroom cabin a few times. It was in the middle of nowhere and no place for two teenage boys, especially when one was presumably gay and the other mixed race. Duncan knew the kind of people the boys would have to contend with up there.

"Wow," Duncan said. "That would be culture shock."

"And then there's the other issue," Tamika said. "Angie's parents are seeking custody of Jacob."

"Jacob? Only Jacob?" Duncan asked.

"Yes, and they've lawyered up," Tamika said. "Some high-priced firm in West Palm."

"But why only Jacob?"

"I assume you know they're homophobic as hell?" Bill said. Duncan was well aware of that. "And they have it in their thick heads that Jacob being around his 'sissy' brother, will turn him gay too. Never mind that the bigger fear is that Jacob is gonna wind up getting some girl pregnant before he can even drive."

"The Riveras have got a good law firm," Tamika said, "one with a lot of ties to some of the judges down here. We've got a proper battle on our hands to keep the boys together."

Duncan swept his fingers through his hair in disbelief. His mind drifted to the boys embracing him in the hospital, showing him—a stranger—compassion, even while one of their moms had just died and the other was near death.

His grip on the phone weakened, and it slipped from his grasp and skidded across the deck.

"Shit." Duncan picked it back up. "Sorry. Uh, sweaty fingers," he said, hoping they'd buy the lie.

"No problem," Tamika said. "Anyway, we're considering our options."

"Could I ask you to please keep me in the loop?" Duncan asked.

"Sure," Bill said.

After the call ended, Duncan leaned back in his chair, the sun beating down on his face. He had always tried to respect people's deeply held beliefs, even when he disagreed with them. That didn't mean he'd keep silent when someone made a factually false statement, like saying that gay people choose to be gay. He would invariably challenge falsehoods, but otherwise, he granted them space.

However, the Riveras were using their faith to actively destroy what was left of the boys' family. All they had now was each other, and through this foolish and horribly misinterpreted idea of what their savior would want them to do, that's exactly where this was headed.

What could he do? Try to talk some sense into them? Angie, their own daughter, had tried for two decades to break through to her parents, and had failed. They'd never listen to some stranger.

The last time he'd felt this powerless was when he was dealing with Robert's alcoholism and drug addiction. He couldn't stop Robert then, and he doubted he could stop the Riveras now.

"Fuck," he muttered.

14

KADEN

The first days of summer vacation, Grandpa Bill allowed the brothers to play *Elves of Ora Online* from daybreak until nearly midnight and didn't make them do any chores. But today, he wanted some bonding time.

In the morning, Grandpa and Jacob roused Kaden out of bed for a trip to Kaden's favorite bakery, where they bought several treats to take home. It sometimes triggered him going to the bakery now, since it had been the last place he went with his moms. Today, he'd held his composure, perhaps because he was still half asleep.

After returning home with their bounty, they relaxed at the table on their lanai, sipping coffee and hot tea while ceiling fans spun overhead. Their swimming pool had a waterfall that flowed from the adjacent spa, its sounds soothing Kaden.

Jacob stripped off his tank top, and jumped into the pool to cool off before returning to the table to munch on biscotti, which he dunked into his tea.

Kaden sat wearing a T-shirt and pajama bottoms, his toes curled over the cool metal base of the table, while savoring strawberry cheesecake. "This is nice," he said. He knew his grandfather enjoyed these moments, but Kaden hadn't said that to humor him. The time they were spending together this morning was strangely calming. Only at this moment, he recognized how much he needed that.

"You deserve it." Grandpa Bill sipped coffee, wetting his mustache. "So, a couple of weeks ago, you boys mentioned something about doing a DNA test to see if you could find out who your biological father is. You remember that?"

"Yes," Kaden said. Grandpa Bill said he would look into it, but then never discussed it again until now. Perhaps he realized it was just a foolish, long-shot wish by his grandsons to find some missing piece of their shattered lives.

"Well, see, the thing is, that's not necessary."

"What?" Jacob said. "Why not?"

"Grandpa, I know it's expensive, so we can wait until they have a sale and—"

Grandpa Bill held up a hand. "You don't understand. I already know who he is."

Jacob and Kaden stared at each other with raised eyebrows.

Kaden's heart thumped hard. "You do? Seriously?"

Grandpa Bill nodded and took another drink of coffee, slurping it.

"Dios mío." Jacob anxiously tapped his foot against the table base.

"Can you tell us?" Kaden asked.

"I can now. I couldn't before."

"Why not?" Jacob asked.

"Sworn to secrecy."

Jacob's eyes widened. "He's a spy for the CIA. I knew it!"

"No. No." Grandpa Bill shook his head and grinned. "Just a guy."

Kaden exhaled. "So, he's not an anonymous donor then?"

"Nope. He and Rosalyn were childhood friends."

"What's his name?" Kaden asked.

"Duncan."

"Dios mío," Jacob said, almost in a whisper. "Our middle names. Damn."

"Yep," Grandpa Bill said. "And you may not remember it, but you've met him."

The brothers looked at one another, then back at their grandfather.

"No shit?" Jacob said.

"No shit," Grandpa Bill replied.

Kaden looked down at his chest, his heart thumping visibly. "When we were little or something?"

Grandpa Bill shook his head. "No. Remember when we were at the hospital? There was a man there."

Kaden recalled many people had visited. Angie had worked at a clinic near the hospital, so a steady stream of visitors checked on them. "Which one?"

"The one who drove me from North Carolina. Mr. Valentyn."

Kaden's breath stopped. The man who had been staring at them. The man he'd hugged. Kaden had broken his no-hugging rule and hugged a complete stranger, and it was, in fact, the man who'd fathered him. His own flesh and blood. He sat in stunned silence as tears formed at the edges of his eyes. He closed them, turned his face up, and hoped the ceiling fans would dry his eyes before they noticed.

Jacob was also quiet.

"With everything that was going on then," Grandpa Bill said, "we didn't think it was the time to drop that on you. You had enough to deal with."

Kaden nodded slowly.

In the hospital, Kaden had been aware the man was watching, but he hadn't made a point of paying much attention to his face, and now he couldn't even remember anything except his dark hair and angular features.

He took out his phone and searched 'Duncan Valentyn North Carolina.' The first result was a LinkedIn profile. He held the phone up to Grandpa Bill. "Is this him?"

Bill squinted. "Yep. How did you do that so quickly?"

Kaden read the profile. Jacob scooted around the table, rested his chin on Kaden's shoulder, and peered at the screen.

"Xeler National Bank, Information Technology Department," Jacob said. "Is he a nerd?"

Grandpa Bill licked the coffee off his lips and stared into the distance for a moment. "Yeah. Pretty much, I suppose."

"So that's where Kaden gets it from."

Kaden ignored the jibe. "Is he married? Any other kids?"

"No, and no. He's gay, by the way."

"So that's where Kaden gets it from," Jacob said once more.

"There you go assuming again." Kaden lightly bopped his brother's nose with his knuckles.

"Browser history, bro."

Kaden raised his middle finger at Jacob, then looked at the picture again. "I kinda look like him."

"You do," Grandpa Bill said. "Very much like him when he was a teen."

"You knew him that young?" Jacob asked.

"Younger even. He and Rosalyn became friends in kindergarten."

"Did you know he was our biological father from the beginning?" Kaden asked.

"No. I figured it out when you boys were about six, I think. The resemblance was indisputable by then. But your mom made me swear not to reveal it to anyone."

"Why?" Jacob asked.

Grandpa Bill scratched his head. "They didn't want Duncan's mom to know. She would've wanted to come meet you."

"So, what's wrong with that?" Jacob said, pulling away from Kaden and sliding back around the table.

"Your moms didn't want interference from her or the rest of Duncan's family. Some of them are, um, let's just say, opinionated. And your moms had enough of that to deal with from Angie's family."

Jacob stared into his tea. "Yeah. I suppose so."

"Here's the thing, guys. If you want, we can invite Duncan down and you can spend some time with him. It's up to you though. It's your decision and he'll respect it either way. Any thoughts?"

Kaden and Jacob looked at each other and nodded.

"We'd like that," Jacob said.

"He'll be pleased to hear that. He was afraid you might not want to."

"Why would we not want to?" Jacob asked.

Bill took a moment to answer. "Well, it's probably going to be very emotional, you see. And you boys have been through a lot." He took another sip from his mug.

Kaden felt like there was something Grandpa Bill wasn't saying, but he let it go for now. Instead, he stared at the profile photo on his phone. Duncan's shoulders appeared broad. It gave Kaden hope he would fill out himself.

He shared the web page link in a message to Gabby with the caption, "My biological father." She replied with a gasp emoji and "WTF?" He messaged back he would explain later.

The brothers pestered their grandfather with question after question the rest of the morning. He told them stories about the shenanigans that Roz and Duncan got into growing up.

"They loved each other, didn't they?" Kaden asked. "I mean, as friends."

"Certainly," Grandpa Bill said. "They were as different as two kids could be, but he was the closest Rosalyn had to a sibling."

As he studied the portrait on his phone, Kaden took a certain comfort in knowing that his mother and his biological father had such a deep bond. He wasn't sure why, but he felt more complete. He took a breath and allowed this feeling to settle into his being, to take root. *I am your son.*

15

ROZ

THREE YEARS EARLIER...

Roz gazed at the pool, steeped in the relentless summer sun. Kaden was chilling alone on an inflatable tube, merrily sipping away at a juice box. His skin had already caught a light rosy hue. She rolled her eyes and sprang towards a patio table, grabbing a bottle of sunblock and clenching it in her fist.

"Young man," she yelled over the roar of the water cascading through the waterfalls that flowed from the spa into the pool. He didn't hear her. Louder, "Kaden Duncan Rivera-Watson!"

He glanced up, and she beckoned him to get out.

"What?" Kaden said.

"Did you put sunblock on?"

He scowled. "Maybe."

"Get over here this minute." Roz sat on the corner of a chaise.

Kaden met her in the lanai, huffing with his arms crossed, glowering. "Is this the purple stuff?"

"Yes. Turn around." She slathered some on his back.

"Yuck. I hate that stuff."

"You used to like it."

"When I was six. It's for babies."

"No, it's not," she said.

Kaden slowly pivoted his head toward her and sighed heavily, as if he carried the weight of the world on his shoulders. "Mom, it literally says 'water babies' on the bottle."

He was still a year from being a teenager and he was already this surly? Heaven help her.

"Well, no one's going to see you. You can't go out there without this on. You've got too much of my Irish skin. Why are you even out here this time of day? Have you decided you finally want to get some color?"

"Maybe. But not purple!"

"It dries clear... -ish. Hold up your arms," she ordered him, as she smeared on more. "What's this?" Roz tugged on an underarm hair.

He yelped. "Why'd you do that?"

"Come on. It didn't hurt that bad, you big baby. I hadn't noticed you had pit hair. I suppose you're at that age. Hair sprouting everywhere."

Kaden looked further perturbed and his cheeks reddened. "Apparently, my biological father is a gorilla."

"I'm sure he's not a gorilla. We specifically requested a chimpanzee donor. Turn around. Let me get your chest."

"If you tickle me again, I'm running away from home."

"That's tempting. Is that a promise?" She concluded with his legs and feet. "You can hop back in once this dries."

Kaden gazed at his purple skin. "The sun will be down by then. Or possibly even burned out."

Roz rolled her eyes and moaned. "So, is there someone in particular you're trying to seduce with a tan?"

"What?"

"Just curious," Roz said. "Perhaps that Alexei boy you always ogle at Jacob's swim meets?"

Beneath the purple sunblock, Kaden's skin turned redder. "His name's Sasha, not Alexei. And I don't ogle him."

"Really? Then how did you know who I was talking about?" A sly smile crossed Roz's face.

Kaden's chin and lips tensed. "You're evil."

"Evil? No. Tricky, sure, but not evil."

Kaden growled. "Same difference."

"Bunbun, sit here." Roz pointed to an empty spot on the chaise.

Face in full pout mode, Kaden plunked down.

Roz rubbed at a glob of sunblock on his cheek. "Listen, I know this is stating the obvious, but occasionally it's useful to say something, even if it is obvious. It doesn't matter to me, Nanay or your brother if you're gay, straight, in-between, none of the above. And if you want us to use different pronouns, tell us."

"He and him are good, and I already know all that."

"All right. Just making sure. And also, I realize that some of your classmates pick on you. I understand sometimes it's better to just ignore it, but if it gets bad, you tell someone. Okay?"

Kaden cast his gaze downward and nodded.

"Just remember, in a few years, you'll graduate and you'll probably never see those assholes again. I'm not trying to force you to come out or anything, but at the same time, I don't want you to let anyone make you feel awful about who you are and who you like. Okay?"

"Okay." Kaden looked up at her. "It's not like they make me feel awful. It's just... I don't know..." His eyes became glassy, and he looked away.

She saw the hurt in his eyes. But more, there was determination. Something in him pushing back. It was a feeling she remembered; being the target of name-calling, words filled with judgment. That deep down fear, that maybe you deserved what they were dishing out, because you were what they said. So, you refuse to give in.

"You don't want them to get the satisfaction of saying they were right," Roz said.

Kaden swallowed hard, but didn't speak.

"Bunbun, I get that. Trust me, been there," Roz said, stroking his shoulder. "But don't let your damned Watson stubbornness make you hesitate to do something that you want to do."

"Watson stubbornness?"

"You know you have a stubborn streak, right?"

Kaden shrugged.

"You do. Trust me, you do. You get that from Grandpa Bill. It skipped a generation, bypassed me and went straight to you."

Kaden tilted his head and shot her a skeptical gaze. "Um, right."

Roz winked at him and mussed his mop of hair. "Okay purple boy. You can get back in the pool and work on your tan for Alexei."

"I told you it's Sasha." Kaden closed his eyes a moment as he groaned. "Evil!" He hopped up and plunged into the water.

16

KADEN

In the week since Grandpa Bill had revealed the identity of their biological father, Kaden and Jacob had devoted a considerable amount of time each day to pestering the old man so they could learn more about Duncan.

The brothers had agreed amongst themselves that they would not tell their friends about Duncan, except for Gabby. Jacob hadn't wanted to share with her either, but Kaden broke the news to him he'd already texted her about it.

Their secrecy included keeping Hunter in the dark for now. "Before we tell our friends about him, I think we should properly meet Duncan first and make sure he isn't an asshole. Or at least, not more of an asshole than I am," Jacob had said. Kaden agreed to keep it quiet for now.

Today, Hunter was visiting for the first time since the brothers had found out, and Kaden worried he couldn't contain his excitement enough to keep Hunter from suspecting something.

He sat on the couch with a game controller in hand, and loaded *EoOO* on the Xbox while listening to music on his AirPods. Jacob was in his room.

Kaden pulled one of the AirPods out of his ear. "You want me to boot up the PC for you?" he shouted to his brother.

Jacob popped out, and he was wearing a shirt. Not only was it a legitimate shirt with sleeves and no holes or tears, but it had a collar. He also had on some nice shorts, not athletic shorts, or just briefs, which is usually all he wore around the house these days. What was going on?

"Oh, I forgot to tell you, I'm going over to Amanda Pérez's house," Jacob said.

Kaden's eyebrows raised. "Amanda? Seriously?"

Amanda was a girl Jacob had been struggling to impress all year at school. Typically, she ignored him.

"I know, right? I guess she was playing hard to get, or maybe she's feeling sorry for me. Either way, I can't pass up this chance even if it's just pity sex." Jacob shoved a breath mint into his mouth, thought for a moment, then took another.

"I guess I'll play by myself then."

"Oh, Hunter's still coming over."

"What? Didn't you tell him you won't be here?"

"Yeah." Jacob slid on his sneakers. "He said he was coming over, anyway."

Grandpa Bill was at the attorney's office again. That meant Kaden would be alone with Hunter. He'd never been truly alone with him before. There had always been at least someone else in the house.

His chest tightened. He exhaled gradually. The last thing he needed now was another panic attack. He placed the AirPod back into his ear and the music started playing again. The song was Shawn Mendes's "Nervous." That wasn't encouraging.

Gabby! She could come over. She had to. He messaged her.

KADEN RIVERA-WATSON:

I'll be alone with H and I'm low-key freaking out. Help!

GABRIELA RUIZ:

Oh no! I'm in West Palm shopping
with mom!

KADEN RIVERA-WATSON:

Shit! What can I do?

GABRIELA RUIZ:

Whatever you do, don't panic!

KADEN RIVERA-WATSON:

Not helpful! Too late!

GABRIELA RUIZ:

Sorry. Just keep H occupied playing EoOO.
Run the twins vs pirates quest. That'll keep
you busy

KADEN RIVERA-WATSON:

Excellent idea!

GABRIELA RUIZ:

Good luck! You got this! xoxoxox

KADEN RIVERA-WATSON:

I hope so! xoxox

Jacob was already gone by the time Hunter rang the bell. Kaden answered the door.

"Hi," Hunter said, smiling.

"Hey. How's it going? I figured we could run the twins versus pirates quest, that is, if you want to?" Kaden said.

"Señor. I don't speak Español."

Kaden closed his eyes after realizing he was still in Spanish mode after texting Gabby. "Sorry." He restated his greeting in English.

"That sounds cool."

After they sat on the couch, Hunter opened the lid on his laptop and the familiar boot-up melody chimed.

Kaden kept peeking over at Hunter, sitting so close. Even though Kaden had sat on the far right end, Hunter was just a foot away, if that.

Hunter wore the perfect amount of cologne, enough to entice but not overwhelm. His feet rested on the cocktail table, his legs angled such that his athletic shorts slid up his thigh.

This was too much. Kaden could never concentrate enough on the game to prevent them from dying a thousand deaths once they commenced the quest. *Focus on the TV screen*, he told himself repeatedly, like a mantra.

Soon, they were logged in and started the quest. Neither had spoken much. Hunter fidgeted. Kaden wondered if he was noticing how awkward this was. Could he sense Kaden was on the edge of losing it? Once they started playing the game, Kaden felt himself gaining control of his nerves.

But then, for some unknown reason, a stream of words involuntarily gushed from Kaden's mouth. "You didn't have to come over here, you know? I mean, like, the last time, I cried and you're probably only here because you're afraid I'd assume you're ghosting me. So, it would've been okay to not come since Jacob is gone."

Hunter turned to him and laid a hand on his knee. "I wanted to come over."

Kaden's eyes shot to the hand, then to Hunter's face. "You're not just saying that out of Canadian politeness?"

"No. Really," Hunter said, chuckling. He squeezed Kaden's knee a second, then removed his hand from flesh that had every hair standing on end.

"Oh." Kaden's heart throbbed.

Hunter turned his attention back to his computer screen, away from Kaden's gaze that lingered on his face too long. "You think Jacob will get lucky? Seemed like Amanda ignored him all the time."

"I dunno."

Hunter laughed. "Jacob is such a mess, constantly flirting with one girl or another."

"Yeah." Kaden gulped, struggling to ease the tension in his throat. "He's such an idiot. Like, one time, he thought..." Kaden's voice trailed off. No. He couldn't say it. He couldn't bring up the notion that Hunter had possibly flirted with him.

No good could come from it. The vision of Hunter's reaction formed in his head. The very idea of it was so ridiculous that Hunter would start giggling, a little at first, then growing as the full preposterousness of the situation struck him. He'd literally roll off the sofa in uproarious, uncontrolled laughter. His Bazooka Stealth Z16 ProMax Ultra laptop would crash to the floor, smacking into the tile, cracking the screen, and half the keys on the keyboard would pop off and scatter everywhere.

The whole incident would then spread throughout school. It would haunt Kaden for months, then just as he had put it all behind himself and moved on, he'd be moving the sofa to vacuum under it, and there, amongst all the dust bunnies, he'd find the Enter key from the laptop, and all the horrors of it would come rushing back to torture him all over again.

"Thought what?"

"Nothing." Kaden faked a grin. "Not worth repeating."

"Oh, come on. I always love a good Jacob story."

What could he say? His brain went into overdrive. He needed a plausible alternative tale to tell. Almost immediately, three different ones flooded into his brain. Any of them would work. The one where Jacob was texting the totally wrong girl was the most hilarious one.

As he was about to open his mouth to start that story, Jacob's voice replayed in his head: *I think you should grow a hairy pair and ask him...*

His brother was right. Kaden swallowed again, cleared his dry throat, and steeled himself, ready to catch the laptop if Hunter started to laugh. "Remember the first time we tried to play that new dungeon zone? You, me and Jacob and Gabby were here."

"Yeah."

"Well, Jacob, he's so stupid. He thought that you—this is so ludicrous, like you're literally gonna die—he thought you were, like, um, flirting with me." After the words left Kaden's tongue, he could hardly believe he'd uttered them.

Hunter looked away and said nothing.

Kaden's stomach stirred uneasily. "I mean, that's absurd. Right? I mean, like, even if you liked boys, and I don't even think that, but like even if you did like boys, like, we're not even in the same league..."

Hunter peered at him sideways, his expression indecipherable, then his gaze drifted away. "Oh. Okay." Slumping his shoulders and crossing his arms, he stared at his computer screen with a stern expression on his face.

Why did he look that way?

"Hunter."

Hunter continued to stare at the screen, jaw set firm.

Kaden's heart thumped even harder, his faced flushed. "When I said we're not in the same league, you know, I mean that I'm not... I don't... Fuck. I can't even make sentences." He took in a deep breath and let it out haltingly. "What I mean is, I'm not good enough to be in your league."

Hunter turned to him, eyes wide, jaw dropped. "What? Really?"

"Of course."

"Oh, man. That's not what I thought you meant." Hunter's face relaxed.

"What did you think?"

"I figured you didn't like me because I'm Korean."

"No. No. I really like Korean guys." After the words left his lips, Kaden's mouth hung open. There it was. The echo of the words lingered in the air, almost palpable. A confession. A confirmation. A coming out!

For the first time in his life, he'd admitted that he liked boys. Years of not labeling himself had come to an abrupt and unintentional end. Even the closest members of his family had never heard him confirm this. He lay awake some nights lamenting that he would never be able to come out to Mom and Nanay now.

But here he was, sitting on the couch with the most beautiful boy in the world, and in a moment of sheer panic, he'd inadvertently shared this part of himself.

"You okay, Kaden?" The hand returned to his knee.

"I think I just officially came out to someone for the first time ever."

"Oh, dude. That's right. You said you never labeled yourself before. I feel honored." With his right hand still on Kaden's knee, Hunter set his laptop aside with his other hand and turned to face Kaden, but then averted his eyes as he spoke. "By the way, um, Jacob was right."

"Right? Right about what?"

"About me flirting. I don't seem to be any good at it, but I was trying to flirt."

Kaden's eyes grew wide. "When you say you were trying to flirt, like, you mean in a friend way, right?"

"Uh, no," Hunter said, blushing.

"So, you were flirting ironically, then?"

Hunter tilted his head. "Ironically flirting? I'm not sure what that even is."

"I'm not sure either."

They laughed.

"Why then?" Kaden asked.

"The normal reason."

"The normal reason?"

Hunter looked into Kaden's eyes. "Kaden, I *like* you more than just friendship. A lot more." Hunter's ears were bright red. He turned his face aside.

"Oh." Kaden took a deep breath. He looked at the hand still on his left knee, set his own atop it, feeling the warm flesh under his fingers, hoping that touching his hand would make this moment seem less surreal. "I'm sorry I'm so quiet. I'm not sure... I'm just... Is this actually happening?"

Hunter laughed. "Pretty positive it is. I guess this is a bit of a surprise, eh?"

"Yeah."

"A pleasant surprise?"

"Yes. I don't think anyone has ever liked me as more than a friend before. I'm plainly having difficulty believing it. So, just to make sure," Kaden said, squeezing his eyes closed, "are you saying you like boys romantically?" He partly opened one eye, peeking at Hunter sideways, awaiting his response.

Hunter laughed nervously and nodded. "Yes. I'm gay."

Kaden's eyes grew wide. He couldn't count how many times he'd imagined hearing Hunter utter those words. "Shit."

"Wow, you're cussing like Jacob today."

"Sorry," Kaden said. "This is too much."

Hunter let out a brief chuckle. "It's okay."

Kaden paused a moment to process. "Are you out to anybody, I mean, besides me?"

"Only my immediate family."

"Oh," Kaden said. "And they're okay with it?"

"Yeah."

"When did you come out to them?"

"Well, I didn't literally come out. My mom figured it out when I was like ten. Stupid me, I didn't realize she could track my internet usage."

Kaden groaned. "Yeah. I had the same issue with Jacob searching my browser history."

"It was so embarrassing." Hunter stared at him, looking like he was wrestling with some decision. Then a slight smile crossed his face. "I came home from school one day, and as soon as I walk in, Mom's in my face, yelling in Korean. I've got no idea what she's saying, but she's waving my laptop in the air. At first, I couldn't see what was on the screen. Then she flips it around and there's a video looping of two guys going at it." Hunter raised his face to the ceiling.

"Oh my god. I would have died. Literally, died."

"She was okay with me being gay, but I got in trouble for looking at porn."

Kaden laughed. "Well, I'm glad she's fine with the gay thing. I'm kinda surprised. I've heard horror stories about Asian parents being very strict and controlling."

"Fortunately, mine aren't like that, at least most of the time. *They* had the stereotypical Korean parents and try not to be like them. They succeed most of the time, though I got some shit for the C-minus in history. I probably deserved that."

Kaden half smiled. "Everyone figured me out early on. And I refused to acknowledge it because I'm too stubborn." *And brooding, overthinking and prone to panic attacks. But Hunter doesn't need to know all of that.*

"So, am I truly the first person you officially told?"

"Yep." And yet, Kaden still hadn't said the actual words. He squeezed Hunter's hand tight and placed his other hand on top of it. "Hunter, I'm gay. Now, I'm officially official."

"So, when you said you, quote, 'really like Korean guys,' is that just a general statement, or is there anyone in particular?"

"I like you a lot, but I don't know why in the world you like me."

Hunter closed his eyes as a tranquil smile stretched across his face. He flipped his hand over, so his palm was facing Kaden's palm, then intertwined their fingers. "What's there not to like? You're so cool?"

Cool? No one had ever, in his fifteen years on this planet, used that word to describe Kaden. Surely 'cool' meant something else in Canada, and Hunter still didn't understand how Americans used the word. "I'm cool? Honestly?"

"Absolutely. You're also, like, really cute."

Gabby had called him cute before. Kaden hadn't believed it, but could she have been right? "I am?"

"Of course. You're so cool and cute," Hunter said. "But it's more than that."

"Like what?"

"It's hard to explain," Hunter said, scratching his head. "You remember when we'd barely even met in person, and we first started playing *EoOO* together?"

"Sure."

"Well, every time I'd log in, you were always the first person to greet me. And if I ever needed help with a quest, you'd drop everything and join me. You're always so kind. That means a lot to me."

"Oh."

"Do you remember one time, when Jacob and I had a swim meet, and Angie drove us, and you came along?"

"I remember a few times," Kaden said, flushing a little as his primary motivation for going to the meets was to see Hunter in his skimpy swimsuit.

"Remember the gopher tortoise in the road?"

"Kinda," Kaden said.

"We were coming home, and you swore you saw one heading toward the road from the grass. You begged Angie to go back to it, but she hadn't seen it. Jacob was all grouchy and tired, so I think she seriously just wanted to get him home. But you insisted there was a turtle there and it might get hit."

"Yep," Kaden said, smiling. "Thank goodness you saw it too. Otherwise, she wouldn't have gone back."

Hunter grinned. "Here's the thing, I didn't see it."

"What? You didn't?"

"Nope. I could tell you really wanted to go back though, and I trusted you knew what you saw. Sure enough, it was exactly where you said, just coming into the lane. You were practically out of the car before it stopped, and you blocked off traffic in the other lane. People started honking their horns, but you stood your ground until that tortoise made it safely across the road."

"That wasn't anything special," Kaden said, looking away.

"Yes, it was. I was so in awe of you, and this light bulb went on in my head. That was the moment I realized I liked you as more than just a friend."

Kaden swallowed through his tight throat.

Hunter leaned in close, pushed back some of Kaden's hair that was in front of his eyes. The unruly strands dropped back down. Hunter grinned at him.

"I never knew you even paid that much attention to me." Kaden stared at Hunter, mesmerized. He ran a tentative hand down the side of Hunter's perfectly handsome face, his white teeth gleaming. The indentation of his dimples became ever-so-visible when he smiled.

Kaden blushed and turned away, astonishing himself at his own boldness for touching Hunter's face.

"Are you sure you like me?" Hunter asked.

"Positive."

"Okay. I didn't get a feeling you did when I had flirted with you. Maybe I was just bad at it, eh?"

"No. I was just an idiot. I didn't think you could possibly like me."

"Oh," Hunter said. "So, can I ask you then, what do you like about me?"

Kaden wasn't sure what to say. He stared at the floor for a moment as he tried to collect himself. "I've always thought you're really cute too," Kaden said softly, cheeks burning. "And I like how kind you are, so patient and understanding with everyone, even when they don't deserve it. I like your smile and your laugh too." *And your sexy legs and arms and everything.*

Hunter reached out to caress Kaden's cheek. Kaden smiled back, his heart trembling in his chest. Hunter scooted closer and leaned in, their mouths almost touching. His lips brushed against Kaden's, filling him with an excitement he'd never felt before. He'd dreamed so long for a moment like this, and it had come.

Kaden's eyes shut, savoring the feel of Hunter's lips grazing against his own. Hunter pulled back, took a deep breath, and leaned in again. As their lips pressed together, Kaden gasped into his mouth and his whole body shuddered and tingled.

Startled, Hunter backed off. "You okay?" he asked, his voice barely above a whisper.

"Yes."

"Should I stop?"

"No."

Their lips locked into a long, tender kiss. Kaden felt something deep inside him open up and make room for Hunter, like a part of himself finally coming alive. His heart warmed in a new and wondrous way for the very first time, and as Hunter kissed him softly, Kaden thought that this might be his first taste of love.

Hunter withdrew, easing the tense grip he had on Kaden's arms. He exhaled deeply and gazed at Kaden with a shy, longing expression. "I've been wanting to do that for so long," he said, his voice barely audible.

Kaden's eyes widened in surprise, and his face began to flush. "Really?"

"Yes," Hunter replied, glancing at the floor and blushing. "And you're my first."

The words hung in the air, heavy with anticipation, as Kaden's expression shifted from surprise to relief. "I am?"

Hunter looked away. "I can't believe I just said that."

"Why?"

"It's kinda embarrassing—I'm sixteen and never even kissed anyone before."

Kaden smiled bashfully. "I've never kissed anyone before either."

The tension in Hunter's face melted away, and a grin pulled at his cheeks.

There was a clunk, the garage door closing. That meant either Grandpa Bill was home, or Jacob was and had put his bike away.

"Someone's here?" Hunter asked, sliding away, putting some distance between them.

"Yep."

The door to the garage opened and Jacob came in. "Well, that was a bust." He paused and stared at them. "Why are you both blood red?"

"What?" Kaden said.

Jacob smirked slyly. "Um hm."

Kaden threw a pillow at his brother, but it slipped from his grip as he hurled it, and it missed Jacob.

"Butterfingers," Jacob teased. "By now, I would have thought you could hurl a pillow at me with much more accuracy." He took off his polo shirt, balled it up and tossed it toward the basket outside the laundry room. It unfurled in flight and fell well short of its target.

Kaden and Hunter looked at each other and burst into laughter.

Jacob looked at the TV screen. "You laugh now, but did you notice you're dead?"

Kaden checked the screen. Jacob was right. Laughing pirates were dancing around his and Hunter's characters' bloody corpses. Kaden let loose a string of cuss words in Filipino.

"I wonder what could have been so distracting?" Jacob said, wiggling his eyebrows. He sighed. "At least somebody got some booty." He went to the bathroom and Kaden was alone again with Hunter.

Thankfully, the bathroom door was closed. With Jacob, that was not a given. Nonetheless, certain unpleasant sounds from the bathroom were still audible through the door.

"Well, this is awkward." Hunter's grin seemed to get smaller with each second he stared at Kaden.

Kaden would have suggested they go to his room, except it was adjacent to the bathroom. He stood up, grabbed Hunter's hand and dragged him out onto the lanai. The air was humid, but the waterfall sounds calmed Kaden, and brought his thoughts into focus.

They faced each other, staring and holding hands.

"So, what do we do now?" Kaden asked.

Hunter looked skyward, as if searching for an answer. "I dunno. I'd like to hug you, though, if that's okay? But if you're not comfortable with that, I understand—"

Kaden interrupted Hunter by embracing him so hard that he squeezed all his breath out. Hunter gasped and wrapped his arms around Kaden, lifting him off the ground. Kaden bent his knees.

"You can hug me any time you want," Kaden whispered into his ear. He lost track of time, Hunter's firm grasp unwavering, holding Kaden as easily as he would a stuffed animal. The hug could have been a few seconds, or an hour.

Kaden moved his head back and stared into Hunter's eyes, wishing he could read them, but he couldn't, at least not yet.

Kaden searched his mind for what he wanted to say. In the end, he simply voiced his feelings. "I really like you."

Hunter's eyes softened, and he gripped Kaden tighter. "I really like you too."

Jacob called out from inside the house. "Hey you two, get a room."

"We won't get any privacy now," Kaden said to Hunter.

Hunter eased Kaden down, then checked the time. "I guess I should head home, anyway. I've got to watch Zoey this afternoon."

"Okay. Can you text me later?"

"Count on it."

After they got Hunter's bike out of the garage, Kaden gave him a goodbye kiss on the cheek.

Hunter shook his head. "That won't do." He took Kaden into his arms once more and their lips met. He backed off after a while with a wide grin across his face. "I'll message you." Hunter put on his helmet and rode off.

"Bye." Kaden stared at him until the bike and its rider were out of sight. He went back inside.

Jacob was standing in the great room waiting for him, with a grin like a Cheshire Cat. "Next time I tell you a guy is flirting with you, maybe you'll listen to me."

"Maybe." Kaden's head felt like it was floating, and the rest of his body didn't even exist. He flopped onto a chair, one leg lying across the arm. "I can't believe that really happened."

"You mean that Hunter kissed you? Because he did. I peeked through the window. He looks like a good kisser for a dude. Is he?"

"I don't have anyone to compare him to."

"Well, did it feel good? Or did it feel all slobbery?"

"Good. Not slobbery."

"Tongue?" Jacob asked, wiggling his eyebrows.

"What? No."

Jacob frowned with disappointment. "Oh well. Maybe next time. Or you can stick your tongue into his mouth." He scratched his chin. "But I dunno. I see him as the more dominant one." He waved his index finger at Kaden. "Am I right? You come across as a bottom."

"Oh my god. Shut up!" Kaden felt his cheeks flush. "All we did was kiss, and you've gone off on this wild sex thing."

"You can't blame me. Look at you, you're all breathless, and it's absolutely adorable."

"I am not adorable."

Jacob insisted, "Yes, you are. So damn innocent, a babe going into his first ever sexual encounter." He grinned again. "Does he know how inexperienced you are? It's okay if he doesn't. I'm sure Hunter will be gentle."

"Can we stop talking about sex?"

"Wow. You can be such a prude."

"I am not." Kaden said, but he wasn't sure he believed it himself. "I need..." He exhaled. "I need to process what happened. It hasn't sunken in yet."

"Okay. Okay. I'll stop picking on you." Jacob turned serious. "I do want to say I'm happy for you guys. And I'm kinda jealous, because I feel like the two of you have a stronger bond already than I've had with any girl yet. Hunter's special. You got a good one. And you know what else?"

"What?"

"He's got a good one too. I hope you know that, bro."

Kaden's jaw hung limply. Jacob had surprised him. He was such a loose cannon, so unfiltered, and joking all the time. Sometimes, Kaden forgot how empathetic Jacob was. "Thanks, but I'm not sure that's true."

"You're welcome and it is absolutely true."

"Can I ask you something?"

Jacob sat on the sofa across from him and looked at him attentively. "Sure, bro. What?"

"What drew you to Hunter, to become friends?"

"Well, at first I suppose it was that he was the only other Asian on the swim team."

"That's it?" Kaden frowned.

"Only at first, kinda like an icebreaker, you know. Like I said, he's a good guy."

"So, how would you describe him?"

"Well, you want to know about his..." Jacob grabbed his crotch. "Because you know, I see him naked a lot in the locker room."

"Oh my god. You're doing it again!"

"Sorry. I'm all horned up and Amanda was just a tease. That girl, damn. The shit she messages me... but when it comes to actually doing any of it, she gets all shy," Jacob looked lost in thought. "Anyway, you already know what Hunter's like. He's a very caring guy, doesn't especially like confrontations or arguments, so he does a lot of things to keep the peace. He's from Toronto, you know?"

"Yes."

"So, it's probably that famous Canadian politeness, *eh*? And he's always doing favors for people expecting nothing in return."

"Yeah," Kaden said. "I've kinda seen that when we play the game."

Jacob leaned back and put his hands behind his head, then rested his legs on the cocktail table. "I think he spends a lot of time alone reading or listening to music. You know, quiet guy, but when you get him talking about something he's passionate about, like swimming, he opens up. Why are you asking me this, anyway? I'd think you guys can get to know each other better yourselves."

Kaden let out an exasperated breath. "I'm afraid I'll be too boring for him. He'll figure it out and dump my skinny ass."

"Bro, just nerd out over that baking show thing. And remember, if you run out of things to talk about, that's when you get some booty."

They laughed.

"Christ, Jacob. You're impossible!"

"I try," Jacob said with a shrug. "It's pretty much my brand."

The garage door clunked again and the boys perked up. Grandpa Bill came in a minute later, his pipe hanging from his mouth, the lines on his face looking deeper.

"Boys, in a few days, we're going to have to go down to the courthouse."

17

DUNCAN

Duncan was dining at Chip's apartment one evening when his phone chimed. He put down chopsticks and checked the notification; an event invite from Tamika James.

"Ah," Duncan said, after swallowing a bite of sushi. "The date for the Celebration of Life is set." He shared the event to Chip's phone.

Chip glanced at it when it dinged and ran a hand over his chin. "Oh sweet. I'm available then. Actually, what would you say to taking the entire week off, and staying in Miami or Fort Lauderdale first?"

"Yeah. That might be good. I haven't had a whole week of vacation since before the pandemic."

"Me either."

Though he didn't mention it to Chip, Duncan also liked that it would give him more time to emotionally unpack. He hadn't liked the idea of just dropping in on the boys a day before the celebration, anyway.

"You know," Chip said, "there's a small gay hotel I used to stay at in Fort Lauderdale years ago."

"The hotel is gay?" Duncan raised his eyebrows.

"The owners are, and the guests. The hotel itself is just bi-curious."

Duncan chuckled.

"Seriously," Chip said, "it's quaint and relaxing, assuming it's still in business."

It turned out that it was still around, and after they got their vacation time approved, Chip booked a room.

Even before the pandemic, flying was not one of Duncan's favorite activities. Half the time, he'd catch a cold or worse on those airborne Petri dishes. Not to mention the hassle of the TSA screening. Plus, booking anything out of Charlotte was always overpriced. So he and Chip drove, taking turns behind the wheel.

Under a gray sky, the interstate was a ribbon of concrete stretching into the horizon. Cars, trucks, and motorcycles all zipped along the highway. Apparently, the angry gods of Interstate-95 had been recently appeased by prior sacrifices because they smiled upon Duncan and Chip today. The nine-hour drive took nine hours.

Chip had been right about the resort, an old Art Deco era place, but well-kept, with a few modernizations. The rooms were simple, and there were only about a dozen of them. As was his nature, Chip made quick friends with the staff and some of the guests.

On their second full day there, having spent the morning on the beach, they planned to relax at the pool. Chip was already out on a chaise, wearing a too skimpy swimsuit. Well, too skimpy for Duncan, but Chip could still pull it off.

After finishing a talk with Bill to discuss details of meeting the boys, Duncan put on his baggy board shorts and headed out to the pool. The scent of a salty sea carried by the light breeze blowing in from the ocean blended with chlorine and sunscreen.

"There's my sexy man," Chip said, grinning ear-to-ear.

Duncan sat in an adjacent chaise that Chip had already reserved for him by placing a towel over it. "Hey, sweetie. How's the water?" Duncan tried to sound casual and upbeat, but after the conversation with Bill, he was anything but.

"Great! This trip is delightful. Here with my man. You realize this is our first real vacation together."

Duncan tilted his head and looked at Chip sideways. "I'm not convinced a vacation that includes a funeral could be considered *real*."

"Aw, babe. We've got an entire week here before that. Besides, it's not a funeral, it's a Celebration of Life. And you're going to properly meet the boys." Chip curled his lips. "Are you okay?"

Duncan leaned back in his chair and exhaled, gazing skyward and smiling slightly. "Sorry. I guess I'm in a mood. I just got off the phone with Bill."

"Yeah? Is he being an ass or something?"

"No, no. Bill's great. It's just that the meeting with the boys is delayed by a day."

"What? Why?"

"They've got some kind of hearing in family court."

"What's that about?"

Duncan passed his hands through his hair. "There's this whole custody issue."

"Oh yeah. You alluded to something before, but I didn't want to pry."

"It's not a pretty situation. Angie's parents want custody of Jacob, but only Jacob."

Chip's jaw gaped. "You're kidding? They can't do that!"

"I know, right?" Duncan said. "Cesar and Maya are massively homophobic."

"Huh? What's that got to do with anything?"

"They don't want Jacob to be near Kaden."

"Is Kaden gay? I thought you said he hadn't labeled himself."

"Last I heard, he still hasn't, but it's not really a secret. Roz figured him out long ago. And Bill said Cesar and Maya have been complete asses toward Kaden for years because in Cesar's words, he's 'nothing but a big sissy.'"

"For the love of..." Chip shook his head.

"So anyway, Cesar and Maya are actively trying to get the boys apart. And they've got expensive lawyers. They want to take Jacob to live with them in West Palm and they don't give two shits what happens to Kaden."

"Damn," Chip muttered. "Poor guys. I can't believe the ignorance and cruelty of some people. I mean, just wow. I have no words. No wonder you're in a bad mood, babe." He grabbed Duncan's hand and gently massaged it.

Despite Chip's soothing attention, Duncan's gut churned the rest of the day.

18

KADEN

Kaden hadn't even had time to process the fact that earlier today, Hunter had kissed him and they were now in some sort of relationship, when Grandpa Bill had dropped the bomb about the family court hearing.

He and Jacob had asked him why in unison, and Bill told them it was just some formalities, not to worry. He had spoken with such aplomb that Kaden believed him, even though a knot in his stomach told him not to.

With the afternoon he'd experienced with Hunter coming out, kissing him and all of that, Kaden needed to ground himself, and his go-to for that was cooking. He sent Grandpa Bill and Jacob to the grocery store to get vegetables and chicken thighs while he prepared some sauce. An hour and a half later, they were devouring Filipino style chicken adobo.

As they were eating, Kaden spoke to Jacob in Filipino. "Did you tell Grandpa about Hunter?"

"No. Not a word, bro."

"I think I'm going to tell him."

Jacob smiled. "You can do it!"

"Are you boys making fun of me again?" Grandpa Bill asked.

Jacob's lips pressed into a hard line. His shoulders tensed. "Grandpa, we never make fun of you. You're the most lit boomer dude we know. Kaden has something he wants to talk about, is all."

"Ah. What is it, young man?"

A sliver of doubt wiggled its way into Kaden's mind, but Jacob had already committed him to talking, probably on purpose. "Grandpa, you know how I like, haven't labeled myself. Well, I'm finally ready."

Grandpa Bill set his fork down and looked at him. "Okay, then. Am I going to be shocked?"

Kaden rolled his eyes. "Doubtful." He took a deep breath. "I'm gay." Considering how long Kaden had fretted over saying those words to someone, anyone, it surprised him how easily they rolled off his tongue.

Grandpa Bill smiled and rested his hand on Kaden's. "Congratulations. I'm so proud of you. We'll have to find some way to celebrate that."

"You going to tell him the rest?" Jacob said in Filipino.

"I'm getting to it." Kaden's voice was showing agitation. "So, there's something else, Grandpa. You remember Hunter?"

"Well, of course, I remember him. I'm not that senile yet."

"Um. Sorry. Anyway, like, he and I, we're kinda like, I guess we're going out."

"Going out where?" Grandpa Bill said.

"Like dating."

Grandpa Bill laughed and winked. "I knew what you meant." He gripped Kaden's hand tight. "I'm not surprised, the way he always looks at you. And he seems like a fine young man."

Even Grandpa Bill had noticed Hunter's interest in him? Maybe Kaden really was as clueless as Jacob insisted.

"He's a dope guy," Jacob said.

"Dope?" Grandpa Bill said, raising an eyebrow.

"Not that, Gramps," Kaden said. "He just means... um... what's the Boomer word? Coolio?"

"Nah, bro. Way off. That's Millennial."

"It's not gnarly. That's what Mom and Nanay would say," Kaden said.

"Yeah, that's Gen X," Jacob said. "I think in Boomer it's *groovy?*"

"Ah. Okay then," Grandpa Bill said. "Right on, man."

"It's so cool that my best friend is now your boyfriend. I ship you guys," Jacob said.

"I ship you, too, whatever that means," Grandpa Bill said. "It's a good thing, right?"

"Yep," Kaden said.

"But bro, just remember, y'all can't ghost me. Unless I get a girl-friend. Then I'll be ghosting you guys."

"Don't worry," Kaden said. "I think I want to tell Hunter about the whole Duncan thing, but I know you kinda wanted to keep it quiet."

Jacob nodded. "It's okay. Kaya mo yan." *You can do it.*

The rest of the evening, Kaden felt like he was floating. Hunter texted him. Every time his phoned dinged with another notification, his heart soared. Hunter was still on babysitting duty with Zoey. He and his little sister made silly-faced selfies and sent them to Kaden. Hunter begged Kaden to make the same faces and send him pictures. He said Zoey was demanding the photos, which Kaden found highly dubious. Only after Hunter swore he wouldn't share them on any social media *ever* did Kaden take a few and send them.

HUNTER GAN:

😍 You're too cute. Next time I have to babysit, maybe you can come over and hang out

KADEN RIVERA-WATSON:

Yeah. And I could cook for you

HUNTER GAN:

That would be awesome, but Zoey doesn't have a very sophisticated palate, I'm afraid. Can you make mac and cheese?

KADEN RIVERA-WATSON:

LMAO. Of course!

HUNTER GAN:

Yeet! She'll be so happy

KADEN RIVERA-WATSON:

So, I hope it's okay, but I kinda told grandpa about us

HUNTER GAN:

Yep. Besides, J couldn't keep it a secret for long if we wanted him to. Was grandpa cool with it? I hope he likes me

KADEN RIVERA-WATSON:

Yep. Totally cool. And he likes you. And J ships us

Kaden went on to tell Hunter about their biological father and the upcoming meeting. He was elated for them and wished them the best.

They texted until after midnight. Kaden would have stayed up all night, but Hunter was sleepy.

It took Kaden hours to fall asleep, and then it was an unsettled sleep. During the night, nagging doubts regarding the family court hearing invaded his thoughts. Anxiety knotted his stomach again.

Kaden tossed and turned, his mind swimming with uncertainty. His gaze darted across the room, focusing on the cracks in the ceiling that illuminated every time a car passed on the street outside. The thump of every heartbeat pounded hard and loud in his ears, so it drowned everything else out.

Splotches of sweat formed on his forehead, running down over his eyes and nose and dripping on to his pillow case. He sighed, clenching his fists. The anxiety was choking him.

He struggled to his feet. The room spun, but he held onto the bedpost, then the wall as he staggered to the bathroom, ran the faucet, and splashed cold water onto his face. The water stung and when he shut his eyelids, he lost all sense of balance, collapsing onto the floor with a thud. His left kneecap smashed into the tile and he yelped.

He lay sprawled there for some moments, clutching his stinging knee. Then sturdy hands rolled him over.

Kaden strained to open his eyes. A figure in a dark robe loomed over him. His heart thudded harder.

Seconds later, the room lit up. Jacob had flipped on a light, then he kneeled next to him, clad in his black bathrobe. Kaden opened his mouth, but he couldn't speak.

"Shit! Bro, you okay?" The words resonated as if echoing through a long tunnel. "Breathe. Breathe, Kaden. Come on. Breathe." Jacob took his hand, caressed it.

With a gasp, Kaden sucked in a gulp of air. His tongue seemed thick, like it was covered with a layer of fur.

"That's it, buddy." Jacob stroked his cheek. "Now, let it out if you can."

Kaden exhaled, took in another breath. Between each gasping breath, he felt like he was either going to implode or dissolve. He clenched tight to Jacob's hand.

"Okay. Hold it in, bro. You got this." His brother's voice reverberated through the bathroom like a chorus of a million whispers.

Kaden held the breath, then let it go. Each breath was a hollow, gulping sound. Jacob coached him along for several minutes. With every breath, Kaden sensed a little of the tension dissolving. His brother's voice and encouragement were like a blanket, coddling an infant. Kaden kept his eyes closed and found a rhythm in Jacob's words and a peace in the sound of his voice.

Eventually, Kaden's breathing returned to a regular cadence. His heart no longer pounded. He was left in a puddle of cold sweat on the tile floor.

"You did it, bro. You're back."

But he didn't feel like he was back. He was more out of control than ever. Weak. Powerless. Lost. He lifted his head and tears spilled from his eyes. He sobbed, a long, low wail that came from deep within.

Jacob cradled him and kissed his forehead. Kaden lost track of time as his brother hugged him tight. "It's okay, Kaden. We're gonna be okay. We got each other's backs. We got each other."

When Kaden could finally speak again, he murmured to his brother. "Don't tell Grandpa about this. Or Hunter. Don't tell anyone. Please."

"I won't, bro. I won't. Don't worry."

Jacob tucked Kaden back into bed, gave him a few more reassuring words, then left. Spent, Kaden plunged into a deep slumber. He awoke to voices coming from the great room. One was a female.

"Kaden! Got company!" Jacob yelled through the door.

"Coming." He threw on a T-shirt and left his pajama bottoms on, then cracked open the door and peeked out.

"There he is," Jacob said.

Standing with Jacob and Grandpa Bill was Hunter and a woman who bore a strong resemblance to him.

"Hi Kaden," Hunter said. "This is my mom."

Kaden ran his fingers through his messy hair, attempting to straighten it, then came into the room. He extended his hand. "Pleased to meet you, Ms. Gan."

"And you as well. Hunter told me you guys have a big day today, so we wanted to bring you something. He said you like the bakery on Bayshore." She pointed to some boxes sitting on the dining table. "Hope you men like what we selected."

"I'm sure we will," Grandpa Bill said. "You're so kind to think of us."

"Well, I'm glad to finally get to meet Kaden. Hunter's been talking about him for months."

"Mom!" Hunter said.

"Oh, I guess I wasn't supposed to say that." Ms. Gan pinched Hunter's cheek, which was already red. She glanced around the great room. "This is a lovely home." Turning to Grandpa Bill, "Perhaps you and Jacob could give me a tour of the lanai?"

Hunter rolled his eyes. "Wow. Really Mom? That was subtle."

Ms. Gan giggled. However, they all went outside, leaving Hunter and Kaden alone.

"Sorry," Hunter said. "I tried texting you but you're on Do Not Disturb. Hope you're not feeling too ambushed."

"It's okay. Ambushing is probably the best way anyhow. At least I didn't have time to get nervous."

"Yeah. She insisted on coming over. I tried to talk her out of it." Hunter peeked outside to make sure no one was looking in on them. He planted a quick kiss on Kaden's cheek.

"I wish I didn't have morning breath."

"I don't care if you do." Hunter kissed him on the lips and then drew him into a hug. "I'm not sure what this court hearing thing is about, but I hope it goes well. Can you text or call me and let me know?"

"Sure."

LATER THAT MORNING, the brothers rode with their grandfather to Tamika James's office. As they sat across from her desk, Jacob fidgeted, tapping his foot endlessly. Kaden sat still, his chest tight, arms and legs tense, but he was breathing, paying attention to the breaths, counting them.

"So, here's what we have to do today, gentlemen," Tamika said. "Bill and I will go to talk to the judge assigned to your case. Meanwhile, you will individually have a chat with a social worker."

"What about?" Jacob asked.

"She's probably going to ask you how you're coping. Making sure you're being well looked after, things like that." She glanced at each of the boys. "Speaking of which, how are you holding up?"

The brothers exchanged nervous, knowing glances.

"Fine," Kaden said, perhaps too quickly.

"He's doing great," Jacob said. "I am, too, but especially Kaden. He's even got a boyfriend."

"Oh. That's great." She let out a breath. "However, I think maybe... maybe it's best not to mention that to the social worker."

"Seriously?" Jacob let rip a string of curse words and insults in Filipino, all directed at Cesar and Maya.

"Do we want a translation of what he just said?" Tamika asked Kaden.

"Not really."

Jacob took Grandpa Bill's hand. "At least I have one grandparent whose guts I don't hate."

"Listen," Grandpa Bill said. "I know this is rough on you guys. Tamika and I are fighting for you. I don't give up easily. And from what I've seen so far, Tamika doesn't either. Give us time and be patient. We'll figure this out."

"I'm not leaving my brother," Jacob said. "I don't care if we wind up living in a cardboard box. He's not getting left behind."

Kaden held back tears and sniffed. He turned to Jacob and spoke in Filipino. "Brother, I love you, but you can't ruin your life for me. If it comes to it, you have to look out for yourself."

"Nope. I'm not leaving you behind. I swear it, bro. I swear it."

THE SOCIAL WORKER interviews were uneventful. Kaden concluded that the woman was just going through the motions, filling out her paperwork, without thought or care.

Thankfully, she didn't ask him any questions about his sexuality or dating, so Kaden didn't have to deceive her.

Afterward, the only thing Grandpa Bill said was that they had bought some time. And he and Tamika planned to use the time well.

"Don't worry, boys. She's a smart cookie. She'll figure this out."

Kaden knew Tamika was smart. But he had also learned that his grandfather was a good liar.

19

DUNCAN

Duncan and Chip headed up the coast for the ninety-minute drive to Port St. Lucie the following day.

"Sweetie," Duncan said on the way, "one thing I need to mention. Whatever you do, when we're around Bill, never broach the subject of Pluto."

"Pluto? The Disney dog or the dwarf planet?" Chip asked.

Duncan winced. "The celestial body, and you must never refer to it as a dwarf planet. Please, try to avoid the subject all together, but if it comes up, don't call it a dwarf planet under any circumstances."

"That's random. Is there a reason?"

"It's a sore spot with Bill."

"Okay. Noted."

They met Bill at a coffee shop prior to seeing the boys. It was a quaint mom-and-pop operation with mismatched tables and chairs. The coffee was mediocre, but the pastries were delectable.

They sat outside under an umbrella that kept the Florida sun at bay. Bill puffed away on his pipe. Duncan caught the occasional whiff of the familiar smell he knew from his childhood visits to the Watson house.

"So, professor," Duncan said to Bill, "you mentioned wanting to brief me about the boys first?"

"Yes," Bill replied, his voice dampened by the pipe hanging from his lips. He set it down and tapped his fingernails on the metal table. "They've obviously been through the wringer. I've taken them to a grief counselor a few times, but grief seems to be the least of their worries at this point."

"Why is that?" Chip asked.

"They don't know what's going to happen to them," Bill said.

"What is going to happen?" Duncan asked.

Bill shrugged. "Beats me. I'm working with Tamika to figure out a plan."

"Tamika?" Chip said.

"She's the family attorney," Duncan said, "and the trustee for the estate."

"Also, she is, for now, their legal guardian," Bill added. "I would love to take care of the boys, but from a financial standpoint, I just can't afford it. Between the mortgage payments on that house and the other expenses. Geez, that snobby private school charges an arm and a leg."

"Isn't there life insurance money?" Duncan asked.

"Well, yes, but it can only be used for educational purposes. We're trying to preserve that for college, though we could use it to help with the private school tuition. Problem is, even without the tuition expenses, it's beyond what I can afford. Then there's the matter of Angie's parents."

"Her homophobic parents, you mean?" Chip asked. "Duncan told me about them."

Bill's lips tightened, and he let out a deep growl. "Yes. They never really came to terms with the whole gay thing. For a while, Angie was completely estranged from them. It was only when Jacob was born that they tried to reconnect so they could see their grandson."

"Grandson? Not grandsons?" Chip asked.

"They don't consider Kaden to be their grandson since he's not their blood. They used to at least be sociable with him, but they grew colder because, well, Kaden's not the stereotypical boy."

"As in gay?" Duncan asked.

"Yep, that and... how can I put it? He's never been one to conform to societal expectations when it comes to gender roles," Bill said. "Oh, I forgot to mention, he's now *officially* labeled himself as gay."

"Really?" Duncan said. "What brought that on?"

"He's got a boyfriend."

"Wow," Chip said. "That's exciting."

Bill nodded. "Even though they aren't aware that he is now officially out, just like the rest of us, Cesar and Maya figured it out long ago, and that made things worse. They were already worried about the boys being '*exposed*' to homosexuality through their moms' relationship. Then when they saw Kaden leaning that way, they figured it was proof he was brainwashed, and worried Jacob would be the next to succumb to the '*recruitment*,' if you will."

"Duncan was telling me about that. The ignorance of some people is astounding," Chip said.

"That brings me to something else about Kaden. He's not a hugger."

"What?" Duncan asked. "He hugged me at the hospital."

"Yeah." Bill scratched his beard. "I'm still trying to figure that one out. Now Jacob will hug anyone and everyone. He's very affectionate. Kaden is the opposite. I'm not sure why, but... well... I suspect he might have either some mild form of autism or social anxiety disorder, but Rosalyn balked at that, told me to stop playing doctor. Kaden used to be more like Jacob. When they were little, they both expressed a lot of playful affection with each other and with me when I visited. However, Rosalyn said that at some point, Kaden changed."

"Interesting." Duncan stared into the distance. There was a ring of familiarity about this. As a youngster, Duncan had been acutely shy himself, and he'd often wondered what caused him to be that way. He had either outgrown it, or gotten better at coping with it, he wasn't sure which.

"Anyway, don't take it personally if you don't get hugs from Kaden."

"Good to know," Duncan said.

"As for Jacob, he's kind of a loose cannon, speaks before he thinks."

"Jacob is the one who's a loose cannon?" Duncan raised his eyebrows. Bill had just described Roz to a 'T.' He would have expected Roz's offspring to be the loose cannon.

"I can tell what you're thinking," Bill said, grinning. "But Angie was like that too. You just didn't notice it because Rosalyn was so much wilder." The smile soon dissipated and his brow furrowed as he appeared lost in reminiscent thoughts.

"How are you doing, Bill?" Duncan asked.

"Hanging in there—barely. I've lost the four most lovely women in my life: my mother, my wife, my daughter, and her wife. However, life must go on." He inhaled from his pipe, then exhaled a long breath before finally continuing. "How about you?" Bill asked Duncan.

"I'm nervous as a long-tailed cat in a... Shit!" He turned to Chip. "We forgot the presents. Dammit! They're sitting on the bed."

Chip slapped his forehead.

Bill laughed. "Don't worry, guys, I got you covered."

"So, are the boys excited?" Chip asked. "I bet they couldn't sleep."

Bill let out a big belly laugh. "I only told them five minutes before I left the house to come here."

"What? Why?" Duncan asked.

"Well, Chip nailed it. They wouldn't have slept. Jacob will probably be bouncing off the walls as it is. Kaden will be a mess too, I'm sure. However, I'm certain you guys are all going to hit it off. Don't worry about that."

The three men finished their coffee and pastries in relative quiet, then Duncan and Chip followed Bill's car as they traveled to the house.

A bead of sweat rolled down Duncan's forehead. He wiped it with a napkin, but another bead came to replace it. His fingers massaged his temple, and his tongue darted over his dry lips. It felt like an undulating serpent had coiled around his torso, making it difficult to breathe.

"Nervous?" Chip glanced at Duncan a moment as he drove.

"I've put this off for so long."

"But you've already met them, dear."

Duncan appreciated what Chip was trying to do, but it wasn't helping. "It's not the same thing. I'm just glad you're with me." He rested a hand on Chip's knee.

"This is such a pretty city," Chip said.

Duncan humored him and gazed at the wide avenue they were on, swaying palms in a grassy median, sidewalks, bike lanes, and set back from the road, subdivisions filled with houses. Eventually, they pulled into the driveway of one of them. The last time Duncan had seen this house was when he visited for Kaden's birth.

Chip got out and came around to Duncan's side. He opened the car door and took Duncan's hand. They approached the entryway and Chip cupped Duncan's cheeks, kissed his lips. "It's going to go great. They'll love you as much as I do."

Bill had gone to the back of his SUV and gotten out a gift bag. He handed it to Duncan. "This is from their favorite bakery. Tell them it's from you." He winked.

They entered the double doors of the house, and Duncan expected the boys to be waiting there. Instead, he saw them outside, through big sliding doors. They were sitting at the edge of the pool, their feet dangling in the water. Jacob had an arm over Kaden's shoulders and appeared to be talking to him. The boys hadn't noticed them.

"You want to go out there and see them while Chip and I stay in here?" Bill asked.

Duncan had really wanted Chip by his side, but perhaps it was for the best that he go alone. "Okay." He turned to Chip. "If I look like I'm floundering, come rescue me."

"I will, babe, but you'll do great." He kissed Duncan and patted his back. "Go meet your boys."

Duncan took a deep breath and let it out slowly. His feet felt like lead as he stepped toward the door. He wiped his brow again and slid the door open.

The boys looked around, their eyes lit up, and in an instant, they were standing in front of Duncan, each clad in white button-down shirts and khakis with the legs rolled up, their feet and calves dripping on the pool deck.

Though Jacob's was cut shorter, both boys sported dark brown mops of unruly hair on their heads. The trio stood staring at each other. It was Jacob who broke the stalemate, stepping forward and pressing himself against Duncan's chest, arms wrapping around him.

Tears started to stream down Duncan's face. Jacob convulsed in sobs. Kaden stood his ground, wiping at his eyes. Duncan reached out a hand toward Kaden and they shook hands, but Duncan didn't let go. He held on as if his life depended on it.

"Forgive me, please," Duncan said. "Forgive me."

"For what?" Kaden asked, sniffing.

"I should have been here before now. Way before now."

Jacob broke off the hug, stepped back and looked at Duncan, his face drawn, his brow furrowed in concern. "You're here now. That's all that matters. Besides, you brought us chicken biscuits at the hospital. That makes up for it. Chicken biscuits fix everything."

Duncan grinned. He swallowed, his throat tense. "Should we go inside? I brought you a gift."

Jacob looked inside. "Well, if the gift is that man, Kaden's already got one, and I'm not into that."

Kaden's eyes grew and his mouth hung open until Duncan laughed.

"No, that man is mine. I got you boys something else."

They went inside. Bill and Chip were all smiles.

"Boys, this is Chip. He's my boyfriend."

"I'm Jacob." He shook Chip's hand but pulled him into a hug. "Nice to meet you."

"You too."

"I'm Kaden." He extended a hand, and they shook.

"Snacks are up," Bill said, as he pointed to pastries on the dining table. "Thanks for bringing these, Duncan. Looks like you even got my favorite."

"Fancy that," Duncan said.

"Eat up, gentlemen." Bill tucked into a chocolate eclair.

"I'm too nervous to eat," Duncan said. "This is absolutely the most nervous I've been in my life."

"Even more than the first time you did anal?" Jacob deadpanned.

Duncan's eyes widened. "Wow. That's... quite something."

Kaden's face turned a fiery crimson color as he began his verbal assault on his brother, speaking in a language that Duncan couldn't understand, but he was pretty sure he heard the words 'no filter.'

"Um," Jacob said, facing Duncan, "I have been informed that my joke may have been inappropriate and in poor taste. Sorry if that was offensive."

"Well, I thought it was funny," Chip said. He mussed Jacob's hair, then mock-punched him.

"Not really offensive, I guess," Duncan said. "Just unexpected."

"I warned you about that one," Bill said, his mouth full. "Don't say I didn't warn you." He took another bite as chocolate and cream oozed onto his fingers. "If you guys aren't going to eat, why don't you sit down?" He nodded to the sofa and side chairs.

Duncan and Chip sat beside each other on the sofa, Chip resting a reassuring arm over Duncan's shoulders. The brothers then sat opposite in separate chairs, sitting on the edge of their seats.

After an awkward silence, Chip broke the ice. "So, you guys finished ninth grade, yes?"

"Yes sir," Kaden said.

"Nice," Chip said. "I have to say, you boys are so charming in your matching outfits there."

"Kaden made me dress this way," Jacob said.

"Well, it's very cute," Chip said. "We need to make a portrait of you with Duncan later."

"So, Duncan," Jacob said, "can I call you Duncan?" The intonation and tenor of his voice had changed, and it seemed he was intentionally trying to sound like a game show host interviewing a contestant.

"Sure," Duncan said hesitantly.

"So, Duncan, we cyber-stalked you and apparently, you're some kind of computer nerd? Or is that your cover story for being a secret agent?"

"Yeah. I mean, about the computer nerd thing."

"Tell us about that, if you would be so gracious," Jacob said.

"Oh. Okay. Well, I work for Xeler National Bank as a Disaster Recovery Analyst II."

"Mmmkay. I've still got no clue what you do," Jacob said.

"Well, let's see. How to describe it? I write detailed plans for how to restore computer systems and services in the event that a disaster hits one of our data centers."

Jacob's eyes brightened. "Disaster? Oh, man. Like the zombie apocalypse?"

"Not exactly. More like a storm or flood hitting a facility."

"Oh. I see. And how long have you been doing this?" Jacob asked.

"Twelve years in this role, next month."

"Twelve years? And you're not done yet? You must be a slow typist. You do look like a hunt and peck kind of keyboarder," Jacob said. "Am I right?" He glanced at Kaden, who shrugged.

"No," Duncan said, examining his fingers. "I'm a good typist. It's not that the plans take that long to make, they just have to be updated every few months as we swap out computer systems and upgrade. Things are always evolving."

"I see. So, how many disasters have you guys had?" Jacob asked.

"Well, none so far."

Jacob tilted his head and scratched his chin. "So, Duncan, let me see if I understand. You've been updating these plans, like every couple of months for over a decade, and none of them have ever been used, because you've never had any disasters?"

Duncan sighed. "Correct."

"So, in reality, you have no idea if any of your plans are even good," Jacob said. "Am I right, or am I right?"

"Well. Um."

"And they pay you for this? Like real money?"

"They do." Duncan stared at the tile floor. "At least for the moment, though now I'm beginning to wonder why."

"That's rough, buddy. And people laugh at me when I say I want to be a rodeo clown." Jacob turned to Chip. "Mmmkay. Chip, how about you? We didn't cyber-stalk you yet. We didn't have your last name."

"Masterson."

"Chip Masterson," Jacob said. "Sounds like a gay porn star name. Though Rod Masterson would be better. Or Rod Rammington. Not that I'm into that."

Kaden buried his face in his hands, but then peeked out between his fingers, glancing at him and Chip.

"Oh my," Chip said.

"Anyway, Rod," Jacob said, "what do you do?"

"After you eviscerated Duncan's career? Hard pass."

Kaden stared at his brother, looking like he was about to throw knives at him. He spoke in that foreign language again, still sounding angry. This time, Duncan didn't understand any words.

"Dios mío. You know I can't help it," Jacob said to Kaden.

"What language was that?" Duncan asked Kaden.

"Mostly Filipino," Kaden said. "I mix in a few Spanish or English words for things I don't know in Filipino."

"Oh, right. Angie taught you," Duncan said.

"Yes sir." Kaden's jaw was set firm as he glared at Jacob.

"Pretty sure they make fun of me all the time in Filipino," Bill called out from the dining area.

"No, we don't, Grandpa," Jacob said.

"So, that's cool," Chip said to Kaden, "I wish I were multilingual, but I have a hard enough time with English. And a little birdie told us you just came out and have a romance going on, yes?"

Kaden's expression softened, and his body relaxed. "Yes sir."

"That's so exciting," Chip said. "Congratulations on coming out. What's the lucky fellow's name?"

"Hunter Gan."

"So, how do the young gays meet these days?" Chip asked.

Kaden shrugged. "Well, he's Jacob's best friend, and I got to know him while we played *Elves of Ora Online* during the lockdown."

"Oh my god." Chip's eyes lit up. "You play *EoOO*, too?"

"Yes sir."

"I play a level three forty-two cleric," Chip said.

"I play a cleric, too," Kaden said.

Duncan cringed.

Chip must have felt it, with his arm still on Duncan's shoulders. "But I guess we shouldn't get started on that subject. I bet we could talk all day about it."

"Thank you," Duncan said, flashing a smile at Chip.

"Well," Jacob said, "even though he has a porn star name, I officially approve of Chip Masterson. You have my blessing to marry him as long as he games with us some. We can always use another healer."

"With your reckless attacks," Kaden said to his brother.

"Speaking of health," Jacob said, "so in real life, Duncan, any hereditary diseases on your side?"

"My father had a mild heart attack a couple of years ago. So, a good diet and exercise would be advisable."

Chip gently patted Duncan's knee. "Good advice that I hope you will take more seriously yourself, dear."

"I'm working on it."

Chip nodded to Jacob. "He is. We've been going running."

"Hear that, lazybones?" Jacob said to Kaden. "You need to come out biking with me." He turned to Duncan and Chip. "I bike in the mornings a lot to train for swimming. Meanwhile, he sleeps until the crack of noon. I bet you'd go biking if Hunter asked you."

"Maybe," Kaden said.

Jacob laughed.

There was another awkward silence. This time, Duncan broke it. "So, guys, when I was outside there with you, and had my embarrassing emotional outburst, I didn't say everything I wanted to."

"Oh," Jacob said. "Is this going to be cringy?"

"I hope not."

"Okay. You may proceed for now, Duncan, but I will put my hands over my ears if I detect cringe-worthy shit," Jacob said.

Duncan exhaled and looked at Chip for reassurance and support before he gazed back at the boys. "I just want to tell you that I'm genuinely sorry I wasn't here for you earlier. When you were about ten or eleven, Roz invited me to get to know you. At the time, I was in the middle of a mental breakdown because I was dating a guy who had become a drug addict. I've always told myself that was the reason I put off the meeting. But if I'm being honest, that was only part of it. I was scared. I was afraid you wouldn't like me. And I didn't know if I could take that, especially then, but even now. I don't deal well with rejection."

Kaden lowered his head and stared at the floor.

Jacob had a look of concern. "I know I've been kind of an ass today—"

"Every day!" Bill interrupted, wiping crumbs off the table.

"Well, more than usual today. It's just how I deal with this touchy-feely stuff. A straight guy thing. Am I right, or am I right? But I like you, Duncan."

"Thanks, Jacob."

Kaden looked up. "Me too," he said, but there was a sadness in his eyes.

Duncan smiled uneasily. "Thanks."

"So, is this thing between you two serious?" Jacob said, looking at Duncan and Chip.

"Yep," Duncan said. "Almost six months. And going strong."

"Nice. My longest relationship is about two or three weeks," Jacob said. "But I still got Kaden beat, for now."

"Kaden, your guy's name is Hunter, you said?" Chip said.

"Yes sir."

"Pictures?" Chip asked.

Kaden brought out his phone. He smiled. "These are him with his baby sister making silly faces."

"Absolute cutie pies, both of them," Chip said, beaming.

They talked for a couple of more hours. Voices overlapped, and the laughter filled the space. Duncan began to feel more at ease, even tolerating it when they started talking about that elf game they all played. For a while anyway.

They also reminisced about the two women who weren't in the room with them in body, but always present in spirit. Duncan recounted tales from his childhood with Roz, as well as Angie from their college days.

Duncan's stomach settled enough that he got hungry. "I think I'd like to try some pastries now."

"We've got a leftover casserole if you want something less sugary," Bill said.

"That would be great. Right, babe?" Chip said, widening his eyes at Duncan.

Soon, the room was filled with the sounds of eating, forks scraping against plates, muffled chewing, and the occasional groan of pleasure. Between them, they wiped out the casserole and the baked goods.

It was getting late, and Duncan and Chip had a ninety-minute drive ahead of them. They said their goodbyes.

Jacob gave Chip a quick hug, then a longer one to Duncan. When Jacob finally backed away, he looked up at Duncan with a contented smile.

Kaden approached and shook hands with Chip and Duncan. But before they left, Kaden spoke. "I was wondering if maybe you guys would come back tomorrow?"

The request caught Duncan by surprise. The whole afternoon, Kaden had been much more reticent than his brother. Duncan looked at Chip, who instantly gave an approving nod.

"We would be glad to. Assuming it's all right with Bill."

"Of course," Bill said, picking a crumb out of his beard.

"Do you guys like Chinese food?" Kaden asked.

"Love it," Duncan said.

"I'll make Crispy Orange Chicken."

"Crispy?" Jacob said. "Or?"

Kaden's lower jaw jutted out at his brother and he glared.

"Just kidding," Jacob said, mock punching his brother's shoulder. To Duncan and Chip, "Kaden's a really wonderful cook."

As he and Chip headed back to their resort, Duncan thought it couldn't have gone better.

"Sweetie," Duncan said. "I can't put into words how much it meant to me that you came with me. I don't think I could have done that without you and your help."

Duncan held Chip's stare as long as he could, then had to turn his attention back to the road.

"I think you could have, but I'm glad to have been there to support you. And I feel privileged you allowed me to share such a special event in your life. When we get to our room, I am going to cuddle you so hard."

Duncan laughed. "Then I better step on it."

"You know, I hadn't realized how much I'd learn about you, listening to you and Bill talking about old times."

"There were stories I really wish Bill hadn't brought up, especially in front of the boys. I hope you don't think too much less of me."

Chip chuckled. "No. Not at all. It makes me more appreciative of the man you've become."

After some minutes of silence, Duncan spoke again. "I was surprised Kaden invited us to come back."

"Yeah."

"He was so quiet and hard to read."

"Well, I can't imagine what he's been through," Chip said, exhaling. "Both of them, losing their moms. Then Kaden's dealing with coming out and his first boyfriend. When I was that age, I stressed out over what shirt to wear. He's burdened with so much, poor guy."

"I just hope he doesn't get completely overwhelmed and melt down," Duncan said. Like he would have at that age if he were in Kaden's shoes.

20

KADEN

The door had barely shut as Duncan and Chip left, when Kaden turned to ask his brother how he felt it went, but he was too late. Jacob had already stripped his khakis off right there in the great room and was unbuttoning his shirt.

"I'm hitting the pool," he said, walking out the sliding door in nothing but his underwear.

Grandpa Bill grabbed his pipe and headed in the same direction.

"Grandpa, can I invite Hunter over?" he said just before the man closed the door.

"Sure. Why not?"

Twenty minutes later, the pair were in Kaden's bedroom. Kaden had changed into his pajamas and a tee. Hunter was in his usual distracting shorts and tank, lying on his back on a rug, his luscious legs propped against the wall, arms behind his head.

Hunter's shorts had slid to reveal more thigh than usual, and Kaden wanted to personally thank whoever invented gravity.

"You sure it's okay with your grandpa that we're in your room, alone?"

"I guess so, given the things Jacob has done in his room with girls.

Besides, the door's open." Kaden sat crossed-legged near Hunter, casting glances at him, trying not to get caught.

"Speaking of Jacob, why was he just in underwear?"

"Cause Grandpa won't let him run around naked."

Hunter chuckled. "Really?"

"Yeah. I guess wearing the swimsuits you guys do, in front of millions of people at your swim meets, he overcame his body shyness."

"Millions of people?" Hunter's eyebrows raised.

Kaden shrugged. "Looks like that many." It would feel like that many to him if he were caught in the nightmare of having to wear one of those in public.

Hunter turned his head and gazed up at him. "How come you keep turning away when I look over at you?"

"Am I?"

Hunter laughed. "Yes." He popped up and sat cross-legged in front of Kaden. "You know you can look at me if you want, eh?"

"Oh. I didn't want to seem like I was gawking."

"We're going out. You don't have to sneak a peek. You can gawk all you want."

Kaden half smiled. "Old habits, I guess."

Hunter touched Kaden's cheek and looked deep into his eyes. "You're so adorkable."

"Adorkable? Is that a good thing?"

"Absolutely."

"I honestly still can't believe this is happening," Kaden said. "I'm trying to get used to the idea that a jock boy like you is even gay, not to mention that you like *me*."

Hunter let out a dismissive moan. "Not that jocks can't be gay, but I don't even think of myself as a jock boy."

"Why not?"

"Well, the actual jocks say swimming isn't a real sport, because we don't have balls."

They laughed.

"But you play soccer too. That's got balls." Kaden's face flushed with all the talk about balls.

Hunter tilted his head. "I'm just a bench warmer. I probably won't even play next year."

"Seriously?"

"Yeah. It takes too much time, and I'd rather have more free time to spend with you, assuming you want to hang out."

"Of course, I do!"

"Speaking of hanging out, you haven't mentioned anything about how it went today. I'm not trying to pry, but... okay, I am trying to pry. The suspense is killing me here. However, I understand if you don't want to chat about it."

"Oh. I just thought it would be boring to talk about," Kaden said.

Hunter rolled his eyes. "Boring? Like the most important thing that happened to you today, and you think it's boring?" He laughed and launched himself at Kaden, grabbing him playfully and laying him flat onto the floor as he crawled on top of him and planted a kiss on his lips. "I figured you might need a reminder that I'm gay and I like you. To help it all sink in. Did that help?"

Kaden looked up at him, ran a hand through Hunter's hair. "Maybe."

Hunter hopped up, extended a hand to Kaden, and dragged him up to the bed. "More comfortable up here," he said as they lay on their sides on a pile of pillows at the headboard, their bodies facing each other. "Seriously, if you don't want to talk about how the meeting went, that's fine, but I want to hear about it." He held Kaden's hand, massaging it gently.

"It was fine, I guess. It was kind of weird. I didn't know what to say, and then Jacob was being an ass and messing with them."

"So, a typical day for Jacob." Hunter grinned.

"Yeah. Duncan seems nice though, and, oh, his boyfriend plays *EoOO*."

Hunter's eyebrows raised. "Cool. Class?"

"He's a cleric. He said he'd join us some."

Hunter balled his free hand into a fist and raised it into the air, as if he'd just won a swimming heat. "Yay! Another healer. Not that you aren't great at it, but the way Jacob plays..."

"Tell me about it," Kaden said, rolling his eyes.

"Are you gonna see Duncan again? Like, is he going to spend more time with you guys?"

"Well, I invited him and Chip to come again tomorrow and they said yes. I'm gonna cook for them."

Hunter smiled and squeezed his hand. "That's great."

"Do you want to come over and meet them?"

Hunter squinted. "Um. I dunno. That seems kinda scary."

"Scary?" Kaden looked at him sideways. "Like when your mom ambushed me into meeting her?"

"I tried to stop her. I swear, and I'll make it up to you."

"Yeah? How?"

Hunter scooted closer, placed a hand behind Kaden's head, and leaned in for a kiss. It was deep and long, and for a brief second, Hunter's tongue slipped between his lips and flicked into Kaden's mouth, sending a tingle through his whole body.

Hunter backed away, a bashful grin on his face, cheeks rosy.

"That was nice," Kaden said between rapid breaths.

"Yeah?"

"Yeah."

"There you are." Jacob's voice boomed from across the room. He came in and sat at the foot of the bed, still clad in boxer briefs.

"Did I say you could come in here and invade our privacy?" Kaden said.

"Bro, you left the door open. You guys wanna get all sexy up in here, you need to close the door, otherwise, this happens." Jacob held his arms stretched, palms in the air.

Kaden let out a low growl. "Those briefs better not be getting my sheets wet."

"I can take them off, bro," Jacob said.

"Oh hell, no!"

Jacob laughed. "So, did Kaden tell you all about us meeting the bio-dad?"

"Bio-dad?" Hunter said. "Is that what you're calling him?"

"Mmm. I dunno. I just came up with it. What do you think?"

"I'm going to stick with calling him Duncan," Kaden said, sitting up now that he realized Jacob would not leave them alone.

"Gabby's coming over," Jacob said. "She wants all the deets on the whole bio-dad meeting."

Gabby arrived a few minutes later.

"Shouldn't you put some clothes on?" Hunter asked Jacob when Gabby walked in.

He made a dismissive sound, blowing through his lips.

"At least he's got underwear on. This time!" Gabby said.

"She's seen it all, bruh," Jacob said. "And I'm sure she loved it."

Gabby rolled her eyes. "How did meeting Duncan and Chip go? I may have happened to be next door, behind some shrubs when they arrived. Duncan's boyfriend is cute. So is Duncan, mind you. They're the second cutest gay couple I know." She winked at Kaden.

"It was strange," Jacob said. "The whole time I kept looking at Duncan and I'm like, this is exactly how Kaden is gonna look when he's an old man."

"Really?" Hunter said. "Perhaps I should meet him."

"Yep," Jacob said. "See if you'll still like Kaden when you're an old married couple."

"Well, he still has a full head of hair," Kaden said. "I'll take that."

Gabby grinned. "I can't even imagine you without that enormous blob of hair on your head."

Jacob put a hand on Gabby's knee. "Hey Gabs, you should come over tomorrow. The bio-dad and his boyfriend are coming back and Kaden's cooking for us."

"Really? They're coming back?"

"Yep," Jacob said. "Kaden invited them. I think he wants to get gay lessons from them or something."

Kaden grabbed a pillow and whacked his brother's head with it.

They spent hours talking. It was like old times when Hunter was only a friend. Except now Kaden stared at the luscious legs, or looked deep into the warm brown eyes, without looking away, and he held Hunter's hand. When Kaden felt tired, he rested his head on Hunter's lap.

Gabby had to leave at ten, but the other three continued on.

"Almost eleven," Hunter said later on. "I wish I could stay longer, but I gotta go."

They all got up and Jacob bro-hugged Hunter.

"I don't know if I like you hugging him in your underwear," Kaden said.

"Bro, this underwear covers more than my swimsuit, and we hug in those all the time. Don't worry. I'm not gonna steal your man. You know I don't roll that way. Anyway, I'm gonna let you two do some smoochie-smoochie." Jacob wiggled his eyebrows at them as he walked out and closed the door.

They were alone again, finally. Hunter stood close, really close, and leaned in, touching his forehead to Kaden's. The sweet scent of Hunter's cologne wafted into his nose. Hunter placed his hands on Kaden's face and kissed him. Kaden closed his eyes, pushed his lips against Hunter's, trying to put all the emotion he couldn't say into that kiss.

Hunter moaned and pulled back. "Sorry. I'd better not get too... um... excited."

"Oh." A sudden rush of warmth flooded into Kaden's face. "Did you get... well, excited before?" Kaden averted Hunter's eyes.

"Yep. You?"

"Maybe."

Hunter laughed. "Bye, Kaden. Sleep well."

"You too."

But Kaden didn't sleep. The idea that Hunter could become excited by kissing him? How could he sleep now, thinking about that? And then his mind just wouldn't shut the hell up!

He replayed the entire meeting with Duncan and Chip in his

head. Next, he thought about all the ingredients he needed to cook Crispy Orange Chicken and vegetables the next day.

Eventually, his mind even revisited the dark places. What was going to happen to him and Jacob? Would they have to move? Would they be separated? In different cities? Would he have to leave Hunter just as he was... he was... maybe... falling in love?

A few times during the night, his breathing became short and rapid, but he fought off the panic attacks, then finally dozed off.

21

DUNCAN

When Duncan and Chip returned to Port St. Lucie the next morning, they found the house more crowded. They met Gabby, who had come over ostensibly to assist Kaden in the kitchen, though Duncan wasn't sure how much help she was since she was paying more attention to them than the cooking.

Tamika James was there too. The reason for her presence only became apparent in the afternoon.

They'd finished eating, and Duncan helped Kaden clean up. Then Chip, Gabby, and the boys gathered around the Xbox to play that elf game. It was then that Bill and Tamika took Duncan outside onto the lanai.

To Duncan's surprise, there were three lowball whiskey glasses on the table already. After they sat, he fixed Bill with an appraising, one-eyebrow-raised glare. His voice was accusatory when he spoke. "Have you and the boys been out here drinking?"

Bill slowly packed his pipe with tobacco and looked up, the corners of his mouth turning up into a knowing smirk. "You didn't used to object to teenage drinking."

Duncan rolled his eyes and shifted back into the comfortable chair. He knew exactly what Bill was referring to—those countless occasions when he and Roz had raided Bill's liquor cabinet in their youth. "If you're willingly letting teens drink, that's a change."

Bill chuckled. "Nothing like that. These are for us."

Tamika reached into her purse and pulled out a slender bottle of bourbon; the label advertised that it had been aged twelve years. She poured into each glass.

Duncan sized up the beverage, his eyes glinting with curiosity as he took a sip, his lips curling in satisfaction. "Nice."

They were all quiet for a while, but Duncan noticed Bill's and Tamika's eyes locked in a meaningful exchange. It occurred to him the drink might have been some sort of offering. "I feel like there's a hidden agenda here."

Bill laughed and looked at Tamika. "I told you."

Tamika shrugged.

"So, it's convenient that Kaden invited you guys over today," Bill said. "Saves us from having to do another one of those video call things that makes people's noses look disturbingly huge."

"Uh. Okay. Good to know, I suppose." Duncan ran an index finger over the bridge of his nose.

"Duncan," Tamika said, "let me be candid. The prospects for the boys' future don't look great. The Riveras have a lot of money. In fact, it turns out they've been paying most of Jacob's tuition at Aldenbrook Academy."

"But not Kaden's?"

"Correct. I talked to the family court judge, and he confided he's going to have a tough time justifying placing Jacob anywhere but with them, even as much as he hates breaking up the brothers. The only shot we have is to present a better option, something that's a slam-dunk."

"I have a feeling I know where this is going," Duncan said.

She tilted her head and stared at him with compassionate eyes. "I appreciate that you never signed up to be anything more than a biological father, but you could be the best hope for these boys."

"You realize that one reason Roz and Angie asked me in the first place was because I'm the least paternal guy there is? I wouldn't have any idea how to raise kids."

Bill gave a dismissive grunt. "I helped raise a baby girl, dealt with diapers and potty training. And from age eight on, I was flying solo. Hell, I had to deal with the whole 'where do babies come from' thing and tampons! These boys—not boys, young men—they're pretty self-sufficient. Kaden does most of the cooking and much of the cleaning."

"Cooking and cleaning is the one area I'd feel competent about," Duncan said.

"You could learn the rest," Bill said. "Another reason Rosalyn chose you is you're smart as a whip. Always have been. Just watch some YouTube videos."

"This isn't like figuring out how to fix a lamp switch or giving someone a makeover. I screw up, and these guys are in therapy." Duncan took a healthy swig of bourbon, then reached for the flask to refill his glass.

"They're already in therapy," Bill said.

Duncan laughed while pouring, spilling a few drops. "That's not helping you win the argument."

"Well, it should," Bill said.

Duncan let out a breath as he set the flask back down. "You're right. I, of all people, should know the value of a good therapist. It's just this whole idea is freaking me out. I don't have the best track record when it comes to nurturing things. Need I remind you of the 'goldfish incident' or the 'turtle incident?' And you can't just flush teenage boys down the toilet when they go belly up, nor bury them in the backyard. The local authorities take a really dim view of that sort of thing."

Left unsaid was that twinge that shot through his gut whenever he thought about Robert's decline into alcohol and drug addiction. To this day, Duncan wondered if he bore at least some of the blame.

Could he have done more? Or worse, was he the cause of Robert's drinking in the first place? His therapist told him repeatedly not to blame himself. But that might have just been some bullshit therapists say whether it's true or not.

These teenage boys might already be into things they shouldn't be. If they weren't before the tragedy, they might be now. He wasn't any more equipped to deal with that today than he was with Robert, not really.

Tamika set her glass down and opened her purse again. She pulled out a paper and slid it to Duncan before picking the glass back up.

"What's this?"

"Read it." She sipped her bourbon.

"I don't have my reading glasses. Can you summarize, please?"

"Okay," Tamika said, "It's a letter that Roz and Angie wrote, one of those 'To Whom It May Concern' things. Basically, it says that in the event anything happens to them, they want you to have the option of getting parental rights. Now, it doesn't hold any legal force, but it could help sway a judge."

"See?" Bill rested his weathered hand on Duncan's. "Rosalyn and Angie believed in you. And I believe in you too."

Duncan stared at the sky, its wispy white clouds in the deep blue. "Just for shits and giggles, what exactly are you proposing here?"

"Okay," Tamika said. "The ideal would be that you move here, into this house, and take care of the boys. They continue to live in the only home they've ever known, keeping all their friends and classmates. We can legally use the trust funds to pay for the private school tuition and should have plenty left over for college. You'd pay the mortgages, taxes, utilities, food, clothes, etc."

"But it's not just the money. I'd have to be a parent to them." Duncan slowly shook his head.

"Duncan," Bill said, "they'll be eighteen in three years. Just three years! Then they'll be off to college. I mean, they're already practically adults. Rosalyn and Angie did a great job getting them this far.

We want you to consider stepping in and bringing them across the finish line."

"If you don't," Tamika said, "then I don't know what will happen to Kaden. Foster care? Group home? He could wind up a runaway."

"Wow, that's sticking the knife in me and twisting it," Duncan said.

Bill exhaled. "I'd bring him to the mountains to live with me if it came to it, but geez, you know that's no place for a fifteen-year-old gay boy."

Duncan glanced inside the great room. Chip was holding an Xbox controller while the kids all watched him playing that elf game. They were all smiling, and occasional bursts of laughter filtered outside. Chip was a natural at this. But himself? He sighed.

"I'm not sure how this would work," Duncan said. "I mean, job-wise, could I even do it? And Chip too."

"You've been working from home a lot, right?" Bill said.

"Yes."

"Well, see if they'll let you do it permanently, in another state."

"Yeah," Duncan said. "That's the first hurdle. If we can't do that, then there's no sense in even stressing over it further. I know the job market down here isn't like Charlotte. Roz complained about that from the outset."

Tamika pointed to the papers she'd gotten out earlier. "Take these and look them over. Besides the letter, I've put together a spreadsheet of the household expenses and the figures on the trust account."

"A spreadsheet? You know the way to a nerd's heart," Duncan said.

"She's good," Bill said, laughing over his pipe.

"THAT WAS SO MUCH FUN," Chip said on the drive back. "Kaden can really cook. I thought he was just going to cheat with some takeout thrown onto plates, but damn if he didn't make it all."

"Yeah, it was yummy," Duncan said, mindlessly.

"And it was a riot playing 'that elf game,' as you call it. I felt like a kid again hanging out with them."

"Glad you liked it."

Chip glanced at him with a look of concern. "I feel like you're not here. What's up?"

Duncan let out a breath. "How would you feel about making it a regular thing? Hanging with them, that is?"

"What?"

Duncan shared his conversation with Bill and Tamika, though he left out some of the more dire sounding scenarios regarding Kaden.

"We can't even begin to consider it before finding out if it would be possible from a job relocation perspective," Duncan said. "And it's just a lot to have sprung on me. So, what do you think, or do you need some time before you can form coherent thoughts?"

"It's a lot to absorb. How about you? Like, if the employment stuff worked out, what would you think?"

Duncan noticed the redirect and tapped his fingers on the armrest. He wasn't sure what he thought. "Before the pandemic, and before I met you, I wouldn't have considered moving from a city the size of Charlotte to Port St. Lucie. But when we were locked down and couldn't go anywhere, I realized that at this point in my life, I don't need a big social scene. I never enjoyed clubbing anyway. Less so at my age. Honestly, so much of my life revolves around you now, I need less of the outside social stuff."

Chip glanced at him and smiled. "I feel the same."

"I'd be far from my parents, but I'm forty-two. I don't need to live near them. Dad's recovered from the heart attack. And it's a trade-off anyway, being near my parents or being near the boys. And for now, it seems the boys need me more."

"You know," Chip said, "both of them seem like good kids. Jacob wasn't quite as unhinged today. And Kaden was in his element in the kitchen, as well as playing *EoOO*."

"Yeah, I noticed that. However, the idea of trying to be a parent still scares the shit out of me."

"Do the boys know about this idea?"

"No. Bill didn't want to get their hopes up if we can't make it work." Duncan let out a breath. "So, now I've shared my thoughts. What about you?"

Chip glanced at him, then looked back at the road, remaining silent. Duncan couldn't read his expression, and that worried him.

"I mean," Duncan said, "I know this is a huge ask. A few weeks ago, you thought you were just dating some typical gay guy with no kids. Now I'm kinda asking you not only to co-parent, but to move to another state."

"It's a big change, for sure. But honestly, I've considered moving to Florida one day. I like to vacation here. And that's a gorgeous house, with a pool no less. Kinda like a permanent vacation. I could get used to that."

"But we'd have to raise the boys."

"True," Chip said. "However, they'll be off to college soon enough."

"And then I might miss them!" Duncan laughed. "I'll be just like my mom. Part of me is a little excited by the idea. The other part is scared shitless. And I feel like I'm worrying myself to death when I don't even know if the bank will let me move."

Chip made a noise, blowing through his lips. "That's going to be... *interesting*."

"I know. I was on a call with management the other day, and some of the higher-ups want everyone back in the office five days a week. They're like, 'some of our best ideas come from those chats around the coffee pot.'" Duncan pinched the bridge of his nose, trying to ward off a headache. "And I'm listening to this bullshit thinking, are they really saying an important part of our business success is centered around the caffeine addicts randomly bumping into each other? Heaven forbid they actually fix a broken corporate culture. But I guess that would require, you know, management that actually manages, instead of just patting each other on their backs and giving themselves bonuses. So, I dunno if I can do the remote thing or not."

"Well," Chip said. "I guess we're going to have to call our bosses and see about that part of it, anyway."

"Really? You want to make that call?"

"I do babe. I love you. And I want to see if we can do it."

"Damn, sweetie. I won the lottery when I met you."

Duncan had a restless night back at the resort. It didn't help that there were loud people in the hot tub drinking and laughing at 3AM just outside their window. But mainly, his mind kept him awake, conjuring images of him on chat shows, being booed by audiences because his boys turned into serial killers, or he was being lambasted on social media when they'd published tell-all books about how horrible he was to them.

However, he also kept imagining Kaden in tattered clothes, face covered in grime, digging through a dumpster, sleeping in an alley. Then he remembered a moment he and Kaden shared from the previous day. They'd been in the kitchen, cleaning up after the meal, both reaching for the same dirty plate, their hands touching. "Sorry," they'd said at the same time. Kaden had looked up at him, smiled. Warmth welled up in the pit of his stomach. In that moment, his mind had flashed to his childhood, to time spent with his own father. It wasn't a trigger to a specific memory, but an overall feeling of contentment.

Duncan had already known before then that he wanted to be part of the boys' lives. Deep down, he longed for more of these moments since the first second he held tiny Jacob in his arms fifteen years earlier. But being a full-time parent? Living in a house with them, a house where he also would work? Could he spend that much time with them without going nuts? Could they stand him being there all the time?

Another concern was he'd be competing with the ghosts of Roz and Angie. Duncan was awed by the job they'd done raising these young men, and at the same time, intimidated by the sacrifices they'd made. Those two women had devoted their lives to the boys, working long hours to give them a gorgeous home, and a first-class education. How could he measure up to that?

In the morning, Chip and Duncan ate breakfast at the resort, sitting at a poolside table.

Duncan yawned between sips of coffee.

"Someone's a sleepyhead this morning," Chip said, spreading cream cheese onto a bagel.

"I tossed and turned a bit."

"I know."

"Oh, sorry."

Chip smiled. "It's okay. I didn't sleep great either. I guess we both had a lot on our minds."

"Truly. Sweetie, are you sure you even want to consider uprooting and moving to Florida? I'm asking a lot. The move itself is a big enough deal, but also having to help raise two boys? That's not something most gay men even think about."

"Actually, I have," Chip said. "I've considered fostering if I met the right man who was of a similar mindset."

Duncan raised an eyebrow. "Really? You never mentioned that before."

"I guess it never came up, and it's not that my heart is set on it. It's just something I'd be open to. Yes, this is an unexpected turn, but I'm fine with that."

"And how about the moving part? You've been in Charlotte your whole adult life. I've been there my whole life except for college."

"I want to do some research for sure, but South Florida is not a bad place to live. I mean, look at this." Chip waved toward the blue sky.

Duncan felt a warm glow come over him. As much as his stomach churned over this whole situation, he couldn't have asked for someone better to be with him in the thick of it. Chip seemed not only to be willing to uproot his life, but even excited about it. Duncan wasn't sure he'd feel the same if it were the other way around.

After they finished eating, Duncan went to their room to call his boss, while Chip sat by the pool to talk to his.

Duncan plopped onto the bed and dialed his manager.

"You're on vacation. Why the hell are you calling me?" Cindy said to Duncan before he even said hello.

"Good morning to you too. Something's come up and I need to ask you a question." He explained the situation, starting with the fact that he had fathered two boys.

"Wow. I'm still trying to get over the shock of this. You've never seemed at all like the fatherly type."

"I know, right?"

"Well, I've got no problem with you being remote. Unfortunately, we work for a huge-ass bureaucratic corporation, so it's not up to me alone. Let me run this up the chain and see if I can get it officially signed off."

"Don't commit me to anything yet," Duncan said. "This isn't a certainty. And I've got to see what Chip's situation is. The judge might nix the whole idea."

"Gotcha. Well, for my part of the puzzle, I'll get back to you ASAP."

"Thanks, Cindy. You're the best."

Chip returned shortly, smiling. He laid down on the bed next to him. "So, what's the word on your end?" Chip asked.

"Cindy is fine with it, but I'm waiting for her to get the boss's boss's boss to approve it. You?"

"We're good to go on my end." Chip squeezed his shoulder.

"Really? That's great. Okay. Wow, this is getting real. I mean, now it looks like I must actually decide if I can do this. No easy outs."

Chip sat up. "Babe, listen, I can't make this decision for you, but I want to make clear that I will support whatever choice you make. Either way, you have my one hundred and ten percent support. If you stay in Charlotte, that's okay. If you move here, then we can figure out an appropriate timeframe for me to come down. I think it would be best if you got settled in and acclimated first."

"Agreed. I know we'd talked about waiting one year before moving in together, and I'm not quite ready to shack up yet, but if I relocate here, I think we could accelerate things some. But yeah, the boys will have enough to get used to with just one of us at first."

"Any inkling of which way you're leaning, assuming you get the okay from corporate?" Chip asked.

"I dunno. I go back and forth. And when I think, yes, I'll relocate, I have to suppress the urge to vomit. And when I think, no, I can't do it, it's like I'm letting the universe down, and I also want to vomit."

Chip snuggled next to him, wrapped him in his arms. "Search your soul, babe. You have a good heart. Let it be your guide. And think about 'Future Duncan' and make certain he won't regret anything."

It was already too late for that; "Present Day Duncan" was already full of regrets.

Later that morning, Cindy texted Duncan a thumbs up. "I pulled strings," she messaged. "You owe me. Hope there's a spare room for me to visit when I'm freezing my ass off up here."

"You got it. And thanks!" Duncan sent back.

He exhaled and stared at the trashcan squatting next to the bed. He set it closer, in case he needed to grab it in a hurry if the nausea came on abruptly. *This is real. I must decide my fate, and the fate of the boys—my boys. What will "Future Duncan" wish I'd done?*

22

ROZ

TWENTY-THREE YEARS AGO...

The frat house was a quintessential frat house. Roz imagined it was always a wreck, but now that it was full of partying college kids, spilling food and sloshing drinks everywhere, the place would need to be blasted with a firehose in the morning.

A keg stand bar was set up in the corner, inundated by a sea of people. Shirtless boys stood on top of tables with girls in skimpy shorts and halter-tops, all hooting and hollering.

Roz took another swig from a red solo cup. Her tongue and throat burned, a shiver went through her body. "Wow, that's some nasty shit," she said to Duncan, raising her voice over the thumping music blasting from a monstrous pile of speakers in front of the DJ stand.

"It might be paint thinner," Duncan said. He was standing next to his boyfriend, Paul. They'd been dating since the beginning of the semester. Duncan had found another gay boy who was as skinny as he was.

Roz kidded Duncan about that all the time, saying they both looked like sticks and to be careful when they rubbed up against each other, because they were likely to start a fire. And if they drank much more of this... this... whatever it was, all three of them were likely to burst into flames spontaneously.

"You look preoccupied," Roz said.

Duncan nodded at some people across the room. "I think that big frat boy is harassing the girl with the blue hair."

Roz gazed at them. The frat boy was so drunk he could barely stand, head wobbling back and forth.

The girl's arm was tense, with the frat boy clenching her wrist in his hand so tightly that his fingers turned white with pressure. The girl's face was flushed, her blue hair strands fell haphazardly around her shoulders. Her eyes were locked on the frat boy's; her mouth contorted into a look of disgust.

The frat boy's face didn't seem to register that he was hurting the girl. There was only one thing on his mind.

"We have to do something," Duncan said.

"Agreed," Roz said.

"You realize that guy is twice our size," Paul said to Duncan. "I mean literally, both of us together barely weigh more than him."

"We just need a good plan," Duncan said.

"I dunno," Paul said. "He's in my English class. He's a jerk even when sober. I can only imagine how much worse he is in this state."

"We don't have to imagine it," Roz said. "We're looking at it."

"I'm gonna go over and pretend I'm her boyfriend," Duncan said.

Roz burst into laughter. "There is no way you could butch it up enough to pull that off. Even as drunk as that boy is, he would see through that."

"I'm not that obvious. Am I?"

Roz and Paul stared at each other with a knowing glance.

"Any other bright ideas?" Paul asked.

"I've got an idea," Roz said. "I'll pretend to be the girl's date."

"Well," Paul said, "that's more plausible than Duncan's plan."

Duncan stood with his jaw hanging open. Paul probably didn't realize how thin the ice was beneath his feet. Roz and Duncan had chatted at length about Paul's shortcomings. Duncan was on the brink of dumping him already, and this wasn't helping.

The only reason he hadn't already broken things off was Duncan had this fear the world would enter some post-apocalyptic age because of this stupid Year-2000 crisis thing happening in a couple of months. He told Roz he was going to have as much sex as possible until the world ended. Roz tried to convince him the world would be fine come January 1st, 2000, but all his computer science professors had him brainwashed.

"You boys be ready to back me up." Roz headed across the room, checking behind her to see if the guys were coming. They weren't. She glared at them, and Duncan caught up, dragging Paul along.

"Darling," Roz said to the blue-haired girl. "Who's this boy? Is he bugging you, sweetie?" She turned to the frat boy. "Why are you holding my girlfriend's wrist?" Roz turned back to the girl, and saw relief in her face, then she smiled at Roz.

"What?" the boy said, spit flying from his mouth. "Fucking dykes." He let go of the girl's hand and walked away, muttering.

"Oh my god," the girl said. "Thank you!"

Another boy approached, carrying two solo cups. "What's going on?" He handed the girl one of the cups. "Who are you all?"

The girl took the new boy's hand. "They're my saviors, babe. While you were gone, some dumb jock was hitting on me. He wouldn't go away until they helped me." The girl looked into Roz's eyes. "Thank you so much." She patted Roz on the shoulder and her heart skipped and a tingle ran through her body.

Roz knew she should reply with words, or something—anything. Instead, she stood speechless with her mouth agape.

"Glad to help," Duncan said.

The girl and her boyfriend wandered away, but the girl glanced back at Roz once more, her eyes full of warmth, another grin crossing her face.

Roz exhaled as the girl disappeared into the crowd, then turned to Duncan. "She hasn't figured it out yet, but that girl has no business being with that boy. And I mean, she has no business being with any boy."

"What? Her? You wish." Duncan gave a dismissive grunt. "You need to get your gaydar fixed."

"Well, if nothing else, at least we did our good deed for the day," Roz said.

23

KADEN

After struggling to sleep for most of the night, Kaden finally drifted off. Then, just as he'd gone deep enough into slumber to begin dreaming, he awoke with a start.

"Lazybones! It's after ten." Jacob was inches from Kaden's ears. He ripped the covers off Kaden and snatched the stuffed manatee that Kaden was snuggling, tossing it to the floor. Then he grasped Kaden's ankles and started dragging him off the bed.

"God! I'm awake!" Kaden shook his legs to escape his brother's clutches.

The day for the Celebration of Life had arrived. Kaden's nerves had been on edge all week, mostly because he figured it was a given that he'd have to give some sort of eulogy. Then, Kaden and Jacob had attended therapy sessions to make sure they understood what to expect. When he'd confided his fear of public speaking, especially about something so emotional, to his shock, the therapist informed him he wouldn't be expected to speak.

As the date approached, Kaden kept himself active, baking and decorating three cakes for the ceremony. He was in his element in the kitchen. And even better, Hunter had come over to help. He kept calling Kaden "chef" and each time Kaden heard that, he wanted to grab Hunter and press a kiss to his smiling lips.

It had been almost two months since the funeral. The heartache had been overwhelming then. He was used to the grieving now. It was just a part of his daily life, and he carried on. But there were two aspects of the event that caused him to toss and turn the night before the big day.

One was that Hunter's family would be there. Kaden had assured him that it wasn't necessary, but his mom insisted they show their support of him and Jacob.

Kaden had previously met them all except for Mr. Gan. According to Hunter, his dad was "super chill" and Kaden had no reason to fret. Even so, meeting the father of the perfect boy? Getting judged by him? *Breathe*, he reminded himself.

The other unnerving detail was that at the last minute, Duncan had paid to fly his parents to the celebration and they still didn't know that he was the boys' biological father.

Grandpa Bill drove the boys to the clubhouse that had been booked for the event. A loving group of Roz and Angie's long-time friends and coworkers made most of the arrangements, calling in favors to get the venue, decorations and they pitched in for a caterer too.

"Kaden," Grandpa Bill said as they walked into the building carrying the cakes. "Listen, I hate to bring this up, but just in case. We don't think Grandpa Cesar and Grandma Maya are attending... something about this not being a tradition to have the Celebration of Life this long after the funeral...whatever." He rolled his eyes.

Kaden didn't mind at all. He suspected Jacob didn't, either.

Bill continued. "However, if they change their minds and show up, it would be best if you and Hunter keep things on the lowdown."

Jacob snorted. "You mean the down-low, Grandpa."

"Okay. Whatever you cool kids call it."

"No problem." Kaden wasn't certain he was ready for a public display, anyway.

As expected, when the guests arrived, they expressed condolences and said how sorry they were for their losses. Some people's faces were wet with tears.

Aaliyah from school was there, surprising Kaden. She'd been mostly avoiding him since the accident. "It's good to see you," Kaden said.

"Likewise."

"Did you just come because of the cake?" He smiled at her.

"You know me too well." There was a glow in her eyes that she hadn't shown him in ages. "You okay, Kaden?" She touched his shoulder.

"As okay as I can be. A little better each week."

Duncan and Chip sat at a table, along with a man and woman Kaden had never met.

When Duncan saw the boys, he excused himself from the others and approached, speaking to them out of earshot of those at his table. "Guys, as you may have guessed, that older couple at my table are my parents. They still don't know about our relationship. Are you okay with me telling them later today?"

"Sure. Can we meet them?" Jacob said.

"Yes. How about you?" Duncan asked Kaden. "You both have to agree."

Kaden was surprised Duncan hadn't already told his family. He knew that many of Roz and Angie's friends were already in on the long-kept secret. It didn't seem like it should even be an issue anymore. "Sure, sir."

"All right then. First, let's introduce you, but don't tell them the big secret yet. Okay?"

They approached the table. Kaden studied their faces, seeing the resemblance to Duncan.

"Mom, Dad, these are Roz and Angie's sons. This is Jacob and this is Kaden."

"Oh, boys. I'm so sorry about your loss," his mom said.

"Thank you, Ms. Valentyn," Jacob said.

"Please call me Olivia. And this is Eric."

"My condolences," Eric said, shaking their hands.

"You boys holding up, okay?" Olivia said.

"Yes ma'am," Jacob said.

Kaden nodded.

Olivia beamed suddenly. "You know, Kaden looks a bit like you, son."

"Really?" Duncan said. "Several people have mentioned that, but I don't see it." Duncan gave Kaden a slight wink. "Well, thanks for stopping by, boys. I'm sure you have other folks you need to mingle with."

Several minutes later, Kaden spotted Hunter, and his eyes nearly popped out of his head. If he thought Hunter looked stunningly handsome in his school uniform, then there were no words in Kaden's vocabulary to describe him in the navy blue designer suit that draped his body beautifully. He couldn't help but gawk at the outline of Hunter's perfectly shaped calves and thighs, which were hugged by the fabric. His black hair hung low over his brow, covering half of his eyes.

Kaden didn't even notice the rest of his family until Mr. Gan approached, palm outstretched. "You must be Kaden. I've heard so much about you." He was dressed in a gray suit, not one wrinkle in his white shirt, and dress shoes that were polished so well that the light bounced from them. Perfection must run in the family.

It took a moment for Kaden to collect himself sufficiently to speak. "Hello sir," he said, shaking hands.

They continued with pleasantries and expressions of condolence. Mr. Gan was just as polite as Hunter had promised, though Kaden wondered if he might talk about him behind his back later, tell his perfect son that this skinny, pimply orphan wasn't good enough for his only son.

Hunter's little sister, Zoey, was too precious for words. Hunter carried her around on his shoulders and she was the star of the event, a reminder that the cycle of life continues, even after our deepest losses. She bubbled with laughter and Hunter grinned from ear-to-ear showing her off. Kaden thought that as charming as Hunter always was, with little Zoey, he had reached peak adorableness. He wondered if Hunter might want to be a father one day. For a moment, he imagined himself with Hunter, and kids of their own.

After a proper amount of mingling, Grandpa Bill went to the lectern. He stood there like he owned the room. Kaden wished he could have seen his grandfather teaching astronomy to college students back in the day. First, Grandpa Bill thanked all those who had put so much effort into the event, as well as everyone who had assembled. He spoke some words about Roz, bringing up childhood stories that melted Kaden's heart. Grandpa Bill choked up several times, moving the gathered friends and family as well.

One of his moms' college classmates read a poem, and another gave a toast.

Next, Grandpa Bill introduced numerous friends of Roz and Angie, who shared anecdotes and reminiscences of happier times.

Then Duncan stood. He paused by the boys' table and whispered a request to them. "Would you guys please go sit at my table with Chip and my parents for a bit?"

"Sure," Jacob said.

The boys moved, sitting on either side of Chip, and Duncan picked up a wireless microphone instead of using the lectern.

"Hi everyone. For those of you who don't know me, I'm Duncan Valentyn. I met Roz on the first day of kindergarten and she immediately drafted me into being her best friend. When it came time for college, we both went to Chapel Hill."

Duncan recounted a time that he and Roz were at a frat party and how they liberated a girl from the clutches of a drunken frat boy. When he had first started talking, his voice had been tentative, but at a certain point, as Duncan got into the story, it seemed like he left this crowded room and transported back to that moment. His fidgeting stopped, and he transformed into a seasoned storyteller at ease on a stage.

"And that's how we rescued this poor girl. As the girl walked away with her actual boyfriend, Roz turned to me, and said that girl doesn't realize it yet, but she has no business being with boys at all. I told her that was wishful thinking and she needed to get her gaydar fixed."

The room erupted into laughter.

"Of course, Roz was right and a couple of months later, sure enough, that girl broke it off with her boyfriend. And for those of you who haven't guessed by now, that blue-haired girl's name was Angie Rivera."

A buzz went through the crowd and laughter and applause filled the room again.

By now, Kaden was beaming at Duncan in amazement.

After the rumble quieted, Duncan continued. "So, there's another story I want to share. About sixteen years ago, Roz was visiting North Carolina, and she stopped by to see me. She told me about a ridiculous plan she and Angie had concocted. They wished to have children, one each. And she explained to me that they wanted to get pregnant at about the same time, if they could. They had a good reason for it, but I thought they were nuts."

Duncan had been moving around the room as he spoke, and he was getting closer to the table where the boys and the Valentyns were sitting.

"And there's another, even more ridiculous part of the idea she told me about." Duncan turned to his father. "Um, but first, Dad, did you take your heart medicine today?"

Eric appeared baffled, but nodded.

"Great. You see, the most ludicrous part of Roz and Angie's diabolical plan was that they had decided to ask a friend to be the biological father of both of their children." Duncan paused for dramatic effect. "That friend was me. And I told her it was insanity."

He hesitated again. "Yet, I agreed to do it, anyway. So, yeah, Mom and Dad, meet your grandsons."

The room was silent for a moment, then as realization set in, people started oohing and aahing. Kaden watched the expressions on his grandparents' faces. He could see that first it sank in with Eric, and moments later, it registered with Olivia. Jacob hopped up and hugged Olivia before she could even take a breath.

The room burst into applause. Kaden shook hands with them, and he allowed Olivia to pinch, then kiss his cheek, but no hugs. Chip interceded on Kaden's behalf regarding the no-hugging rule.

Other guests shared stories, but Kaden felt sorry for them, because nobody came close to topping Duncan's. Story time ended, and the caterers scrambled to put the finishing touches on the buffet tables.

Kaden and Jacob spent a while with the new set of grandparents before Chip convinced Olivia to let them mingle with others. "You can see them at the house later and have them all to yourselves," Chip told her and Eric.

Hunter had been waiting in the wings and swooped in as soon as Kaden was free.

Jacob grabbed Hunter first. "Hunter!" He pulled Hunter in for a hug.

Then Hunter turned to Kaden. "Hey chef. Can I give you a hug?"

"If you insist," Kaden replied, mocking indifference and smiling slyly. Hunter wasn't carrying Zoey around now, but his level of adorableness had only slipped by three percentage points. Maybe less.

After the embrace, Hunter nodded toward a girl across the room. "Who's that girl who keeps staring at you?"

Kaden and Jacob looked. At first, Kaden didn't recognize her as she was in a catering uniform. When he figured out who she was, his jaw dropped.

"Dios mío. What's she doing here?" Jacob asked.

"Oh my god," Kaden said.

"Who is she?"

"Her name is Unique," Jacob said.

"What is it?" Hunter asked.

"No," Kaden said. "It's literally, Unique. That's her name."

"Oh."

"Unique Mills-Foy," Jacob said, a scowl on his face.

"Don't let her hear you pronounce it like that," Kaden said. "She insists the *s* is silent."

"Whatever," Jacob said. "Pretentious much?"

"How do you guys know her?"

"She's Kaden's archenemy," Jacob said.

Hunter raised his eyebrows. "Wow. You have an archenemy already, and you're only fifteen? I don't know whether to be impressed or terrified of you."

Gabby came bounding up. "Kaden, did you see? Unique is here."

"Okay, what's the story with her?" Hunter asked.

"So, Unique is in our grade," Jacob said. "There's this junior cake cooking—"

"Baking!" Kaden and Gabby said in unison.

"Whatever, nerds. Cake-*baking* competition each year at the MF Event Center." The 'MF,' stood for MidFlorida, and Jacob always took a perverse pleasure in referring to it by its initials. "And each year, Unique comes in first, and Kaden comes in second."

"It's not fair," Gabby said. "Her parents own a catering company and her mom's been on that *Foodtastic* show on Disney Plus and her dad is a Swiss-trained pastry chef."

"And if you're ever unfortunate enough to talk to her," Jacob said, "she will let you know that she wins the competition every year, then tell you everything Gabby just said. And the next time you see her, she'll remind you of all that again, just in case you forgot."

"About the cakes," Gabby said to Kaden, "Unique tried a piece of one of yours. She said it was meh, but I could tell by the look in her eyes, it stunned her how great it was. I think she's scared you'll crush her this time." She turned to Hunter. "Kaden edges her on decorating, but she beats him on the flavor and gets the blue ribbon. However, with this new recipe, I think he's gonna win."

"Unless she ups her game now," Kaden said.

"Oh," Gabby said.

"Yeah, oh." This was a disaster. Of all the companies to cater the event, why did it have to be Unique's parents? And now she knew precisely what she'd be up against at the competition. His new recipe was exposed. Kaden forced these thoughts out of his mind. Of all the things to even concern himself about today, this didn't deserve a second of his time.

"Speaking of cake, I'm gonna absolutely devour some," Jacob said.

"Me too," Gabby said, following Jacob, leaving Kaden alone with Hunter.

"Hey you," Hunter said.

"Hey you. You're so adorable today. I mean, you are every day, but today, extra." Kaden reached over and straightened Hunter's tie, even though it wasn't crooked. "I still can't believe I'm saying that out loud instead of just thinking it like I used to, all the time."

"You're adorable, too, chef."

Kaden felt his cheeks flush.

"So, that was some speech Duncan gave," Hunter said, a hint of awe in his voice. "And you have more grandparents now."

"Yeah. This has been quite the day."

After the speeches had ended, a DJ had started playing music that had been relevant to Roz and Angie's lives, mostly pop love ballads from the early 2000s. However, at the insistence of one of Angie's college roommates, there was some Lithuanian Death Metal thrown into the mix. Kaden had never heard his moms listen to this... this... whatever it was. He was dubious that this ex-roommate knew what he was talking about. As one of the "songs" started, Kaden scrunched his face and groaned.

Hunter raised his eyebrows and looked at Kaden. Grabbing his hand, he led them out of the main room, down a hallway, and out into a shaded courtyard.

Kaden exhaled when they were alone outside, soaking in the quiet, glad to be away from so many people—loving, caring people, certainly—but nonetheless, pressing in on him, draining him. A smile tugged at one cheek as he looked at Hunter. "Thank you."

"You're quite welcome."

Even in the shade, the heat would not be tolerable for long with both of them in full suits and ties. Kaden hoped they could stand it at least until the next song came on.

Hunter shifted and cleared his throat. "I kinda met Duncan."

Kaden smiled and raised a single eyebrow. "You did?"

"Yep, and Chip too. Mom made me talk to them." Hunter glowered.

"And?"

Hunter exhaled. "They were nice. I didn't feel like they were judging me... too much."

"That's cool." Kaden wished he felt the same way about meeting Hunter's father. But his stomach coiled in tight knots of anxiety whenever he thought back on it.

"Did they mention anything about it to you?" Hunter asked.

"Not yet."

"You would tell me if they said something negative about me, eh?" Hunter fidgeted with the hem of his suit jacket.

"I'm sure the only thing they were thinking was, how did someone like Kaden get such a handsome boyfriend?"

Hunter cupped Kaden's cheeks, leaned in close and looked him in the eye. "Kaden, don't say that. Don't even think anything like that."

Kaden closed his eyes a moment. "Sorry. I wish I could stop, but I can't. At least not yet."

Hunter smiled sadly. "I know. I just wish you could see how special you are. Because you are, even if you don't believe it."

Kaden felt warmth fill his chest and rise to his cheeks. Hunter was always so supportive and understanding of him. He leaned in and kissed Hunter softly on the lips. "Thank you," he whispered.

~

WHEN KADEN GOT HOME, he longed for a nap, but he'd barely had time to change into comfortable clothes when guests arrived. Chip and Duncan showed up with Duncan's parents. They all gathered in the great room.

"Now, Mom," Duncan said, "before you start doting on your grandsons, I need to talk to them about something." Duncan stood and Chip did too, putting an arm over his shoulders. "Bill, would you and Chip mind entertaining my parents while I speak to the boys out by the pool?"

"It would be my pleasure. We've got a lot of catching up," Bill said.

Duncan escorted the brothers outside, and they all sat at the edge of the pool, dangling their feet and legs in the water, with Duncan in the middle, an arm over each of them.

"Boys, I was wondering something."

"What, Duncan?" Jacob said.

"Grandpa Bill and Tamika thought it might be a good idea if I were to petition the family court to get custody of you both, then move down here and into the house and take care of you. And at some point, have Chip come down and join us."

Jacob's face lit up. "For real? Are you serious?"

"Yes. So, what do you think?"

Duncan barely got the question out of his mouth before Jacob yelled, "Yes" so loudly it pierced Kaden's eardrum.

Kaden gazed up into Duncan's deep, warm eyes and tried to speak, to say something, anything, but his throat narrowed, and then his chest tightened. Breath caught in his windpipe. He exhaled, long and slow. "You would do that for us?"

"I will try, Kaden. Now, I need to make sure you understand that it's not up to me. We have to persuade a judge. But Tamika thinks we have a decent chance. So, you want me to give it a try?"

Kaden's eyes brimmed with tears. He bobbed his head in agreement and buried his face in Duncan's chest. The tension that he had been carrying for over two months leaked out of his body as if it were squeezed from a sponge.

That night, Kaden slept better than he had at any time since before the traffic accident.

24

KADEN

Kaden had spent most of Saturday afternoon in the kitchen, making beef Wellington, fingerling potatoes, and salad with balsamic-honey dressing. Everyone had loved it—his brother and Grandpa Bill—and they had been joined by Hunter and Tamika.

In the two weeks since Duncan had told him and Jacob that he'd try to become their legal guardian, Tamika busied herself working to make it happen. And Kaden wanted to show her how much he appreciated her efforts.

The cooking had exhausted him, so when Grandpa Bill suggested heading to the bakery to get dessert, Kaden told them to pick up something for him. "You know what to get me," he said to Jacob.

"Cheesecake it is."

"Can you get me cheesecake, too?" Hunter asked Jacob. "I'll pay you back."

"Dude, you're not going?" Jacob asked.

"I'll stay here and keep the chef company."

Jacob nodded and winked. "Mmm hmm."

"You don't have to stay," Kaden said to Hunter as he pushed himself back from the dining table.

Jacob gave Kaden a playful jab on the arm. "Bro, you need to shut up and let your man hang with you while the rest of us are gone. I'll text you when we cross the Cashmere intersection, so y'all have time to get your clothes back on."

Grandpa Bill and Tamika chortled as they stood from the table. Heat rushed to Kaden's cheeks, and he saw Hunter's face redden as their eyes met.

A few minutes later, Kaden and Hunter were the only two left in the house, and Kaden hastily began clearing the dinner dishes from the table.

"Let me do that for you," Hunter said.

"No, you're my guest."

Hunter made a scoffing sound. "You did all the work. You shouldn't have to clean up too."

"Well, we'll save it for Jacob," he said, though he could already imagine his brother's inevitable griping.

"Okay. Want to sit on the couch... or something? Get off your feet?"

"Sure."

They sat next to each other, resting their feet on the cocktail table.

"You look tired," Hunter said as Kaden yawned.

He shrugged. "Just my legs ache. I really need some of those squishy foam mats in the kitchen."

Hunter slid away from him. "Put your feet here." He pointed to the space on the sofa between them.

"Why?"

"Just do it. You'll see."

Kaden stared at Hunter, trying to determine what he had in mind, but saw only a mysterious smirk. Hesitantly, Kaden turned sideways and rested his legs on the cushion. Hunter took each one and stretched them out over his lap.

"You ever had a sports massage?" Hunter asked.

"I've never had *any* massage."

Hunter began kneading one of his calf muscles. "I sometimes get them during soccer season. Does this feel good?"

Every hair on his body was standing straight up, and his skin tingled. "Yes. But you don't have to do that if you don't want to."

"I want to." Hunter beamed. Looking away, he continued. "I'm kind of obsessed with your hairy legs."

"Oh?"

One of Hunter's hands edged toward Kaden's feet and squeezed one. "And I'm low-key obsessed with your feet too."

Kaden giggled. "Do you have a foot fetish?"

Hunter's cheeks took on a rosy hue. "Possibly. Is that weird?"

"No, because I'm pretty much obsessed with your entire body. And also, this feels really nice, so I don't care if it is weird." Kaden relaxed his head on a pillow and closed his eyes as Hunter's strong hands kneaded the soles of his feet. "I could get used to this."

"So, the bakery, that's like, a fifteen-minute drive?"

"Ten each way. Why?"

Hunter frowned. "Nothing. That's just not much time."

"Time for what?"

Hunter's jaw clenched, and he shrugged one shoulder. "I dunno." One of his hands slid up Kaden's leg to the upper thigh, his fingertips brushing over the leg hair, going an inch or two above the hem line of his athletic shorts. Under the fabric!

Kaden tensed, feeling surprisingly vulnerable. His heart thumped harder, and he shifted. "Uh."

Hunter's hand retreated and he smiled. "Not much time for you to rest up, I guess."

"Oh." Even as Hunter went back to massaging the lower leg, Kaden's heart still thumped hard, his stomach twisted. What had Hunter wanted to do? It was obviously something more. Was he tired of just making out? Kaden wasn't sure he was ready for too much more. What if he did something wrong and embarrassed himself, or disappointed Hunter? He spent the next several minutes worrying, no longer able to enjoy the feel of Hunter's hands on his skin.

Too soon, the others returned, and they were all at the table again, having dessert.

"Young men," Grandpa said after swallowing a bite of chocolate eclair and wiping his mouth. "We've got to have a very serious family discussion here." His brow furrowed.

"Should I leave?" Hunter asked, as he shifted uncomfortably and avoided eye contact.

Grandpa Bill raised an eyebrow in thought. "Well, I have no problem with you staying. And since it concerns the guardianship of the boys, you might want to know what's going on. But I'll leave that up to my grandsons to decide."

"He's pretty nosy," Jacob said. "I'm sure he'll ask Kaden to tell him, anyway. And Kaden will melt in his hands and spill it all. So, he may as well just stay."

"I'm not nosy... too much. Seriously, I understand if I should leave."

"Nah, bruh," Jacob said. "You know I'm just messing. Stay. You're practically fam now."

Grandpa Bill extended an open hand to Tamika. "Young lady, the floor is yours."

She rummaged through her purse, producing a notepad and her phone. Her meticulously painted nails tapped away on the screen. "Let me get Duncan on the video call."

A minute later, Duncan's face lit up the screen with a broad smile. "Hello everyone," he said with enthusiasm as he waved at them.

After some pleasantries, Tamika began. "We've had a development. After we filed Duncan's petition, the Riveras' attorneys have offered a compromise. I think they're legitimately scared for the first time that they might not win."

"Really?" Duncan asked, raising his eyebrows.

"Deets," Jacob said to Tamika.

"Here's what they're offering. They will stand down for now, if the following conditions are met. First, they've asked for a generous visitation arrangement with Jacob."

Jacob sneered and dropped his fork onto his plate as he leaned back. "Gah! They always gotta fuck up my weekends. And I don't even like them anymore. At least not Grandpa Cesar. Can I just hang with Grandma?"

"I'm sorry, sweetie. It's probably going to be both of them," Tamika said, resting a hand on Jacob's.

"Dios mío. They're gonna try to set me up with their neighbor's daughter again. I know they are. And the only thing I have in common with her is that I hate her as much as she hates me. And we both hate being fixed up."

"You might have to take one for the team," Hunter said.

Jacob made a face at him.

Tamika continued. "There's more. They want you to have full mental health evaluations periodically too."

"I'm already seeing a therapist. Isn't that enough?"

"I'm afraid not. They've stipulated that they get to select the practitioner who does the evaluation." She squinted at her notepad. "It's a man named Harry J. Billings. He's in West Palm and, well... he's a bit of a quack." She spat the words out with disgust as she continued. "He runs one of those damned gay conversion therapy practices. They passed a law to ban that in West Palm. But Billings and some others sued to block it. The Federal judges were appointed by you know who, so of course, the law was struck down."

Jacob made a scoffing sound. "This is so stupid. How many times do I have to tell them? I'm not gay, I'm not turning gay. And obviously, this Billings nut job can't convert me to anything, anyway."

"He can't convert anyone," Duncan said through gritted teeth. "Only ruin people's mental health trying."

"The problem is," Tamika said, "he's completely outside of mainstream mental health practices, and he's got an agenda. So, who knows what kind of crap he'll try to pull during these evaluations.

And the Riveras could use him to come back at us later and present some sort of unfavorable report about Jacob to strengthen their case. It's possible this is a trap."

"Okay," Duncan said. "We reject it. And take our chances in the courtroom."

Tamika raised her eyebrows skeptically. "We have a strong case, and under normal circumstances, I'd recommend that. However, these are not normal times. We've got a governor who's obviously gunning for the White House, and he's decided that attacking the LGBTQ+ community is a great bit of assholery to win points with his base."

"How does that affect us?" Grandpa Bill asked.

"It's the judge in our case," Tamika said, her tone heavy. "Word is, he's ambitious, wanting to move up to bigger and better things. If he makes a gay man a legal guardian—a gay man who is going to have another gay man living with him—and the judge wants to get an appointment from the governor, how's all this gay-friendly stuff going to look on his record?"

"Career limiting," Grandpa Bill said.

Tamika nodded. "Especially if Cesar Rivera shines a spotlight on it, which we all know he will threaten to do to get his way."

"Would this judge literally do that?" Jacob asked. "Doesn't anyone actually care about kids and what we want and what's good for us?"

"Sweetie," Tamika said, "you have many folks who care about you and love you. Unfortunately, there are corrupt people who wind up in positions of power. So, you get judges who overturn laws designed to protect kids, and other judges who aspire to get into a position where *they* can overturn laws to protect kids. It's all political."

"So, what're you recommending, Tamika?" Duncan asked.

"Neither option is great, but I think we should take the compromise and hope for the best."

Jacob looked Kaden in the eye. "I agree. I'll do whatever I have to. I'll go see my grandparents. I'll go see this Harry Balls guy."

"Billings," Tamika said.

"Whatever."

"Jacob, you don't have to do this," Kaden said in Filipino. "This is too much."

Jacob responded in Filipino. "I know I don't have to. But I am, because I love you more than anyone in the world, and I don't want anything bad to happen to you. And don't you dare tell anyone how mushy I'm being right now. I've got a reputation to keep."

"I won't. I love you." Just saying he loved him wasn't enough to express how he felt about Jacob. Despite how annoying he could be sometimes—well, most times—Kaden couldn't have asked for a better brother. But he worried. This conversion therapy guy might truly be ready to pounce on Jacob if he even came close to saying the wrong thing in an evaluation.

"And I owe you for this," Kaden added.

"No, you don't, bro. But I won't refuse part of that strawberry cheesecake if you offer it." Jacob smiled as Kaden slid his plate to him.

25

DUNCAN

Sitting across from Duncan on the sofa were two actual, living, breathing creatures that, as of today, he was responsible for. Images of dead goldfish, turtles, and worst of all, Robert, completely strung out, haunted his mind as he sat on the edge of his chair.

Kaden perched on his hands with his legs held tight against each other, toes flexing in the pile of an area rug. Jacob sat beside Kaden, munching on a peanut butter and jelly sandwich.

Both stared at Duncan expectantly. Even as Jacob took another bite and licked oozing grape jelly from his lower lip, his gaze remained fixed, eyes unblinking. It was like they were watching a horror movie, awaiting the next "jump scare."

Duncan took a deep, steadying breath. His hands trembled as he ran his fingers through his hair.

As ridiculous as Grandpa Bill's suggestion about watching YouTube videos to learn how to parent teens had sounded at the time, Duncan had spent two dozen evenings watching old TED Talks on parenting.

Some nights, he picked up great advice, but other evenings, he got distracted as the YouTube algorithms suggested unrelated videos. One night, he wound up watching a whole series of videos about a gay couple rearing a herd of buffalos. What was even more disturbing was that those videos, from a metaphorical perspective, were perhaps as helpful as the TED Talks on raising teenage boys. Sometimes, it wasn't only the metaphorical perspective either.

Unaware of his sad history with pets, and his possible culpability in Robert's plunge into addiction, the court had seen fit to grant Duncan guardianship of the boys thanks to the compromise agreement with Cesar and Maya Rivera. At least for now. Tamika had said it might be a trap. Maybe they knew Duncan would be a disaster of a guardian and had set him up. But if it was a trap, he was in it now. He had to make the best of it.

So, here he was, a month after starting the journey in family court, against all odds, and against his better judgment, sitting in the great room of this house in Port St. Lucie, sweating in a chair as the boys awaited his first profound words of fatherly wisdom.

"So, here we are," Duncan said.

Cruelly, Grandpa Bill had departed only minutes after Duncan's arrival. It wasn't Bill's fault though. Duncan's nine-hour drive from Charlotte had taken twelve thanks to the evil Interstate-95 gods. It still felt like Duncan was being set up, even though Bill had offered up some flimsy excuse about having to get to a doctor's appointment back in North Carolina. Probably, he was just missing his poker buddies, or had a date with some Tinder match, or whatever app old people used to hook up.

Jacob finished the last bite of his sandwich and licked grape jelly off his fingers. "Duncan," he said, his voice in that quiz show host mocking tone that Duncan found so disconcerting, "as you may have noticed immediately the first time you visited us, there's no ESPN in this house."

"Actually, I had not noticed that."

Jacob's eyebrows raised. "You're not another one of those gays who don't watch sports?"

Duncan tilted his head. "Well, sorry, but I never cared for—"

"¡Dios mío! Is Hunter the only gay who likes sports?" Jacob dramatically flung himself back into his chair.

"Um, I think Chip likes some kind of sports. I'll look into subscription options this evening."

"Excellent!" Jacob said, with an eager glimmer in his eyes. "Make sure it has ESPN3 on it, because I don't want to miss the hot dog eating contest again. That was a tragedy."

"Okay. Will do."

Jacob turned to Kaden. "I think I like this guy." He whipped his head back around. "Wait! Duncan, did you bring us any gifts?"

"Gifts?"

"Well, Duncan, you've got fifteen birthdays and Christmases to catch up on, and I reckon a few Easter baskets too." Jacob's eyes narrowed and he appeared sincere, then he broke into a grin. "I'm kidding."

"Oh."

"You look so tense. Am I right, or am I right?" Jacob said. "Anyway, on a more serious note, Duncan, we should work out schedules. For example, when school starts back, are you gonna be able to drop us off on your way to work, or we gotta ride the bus like commoners or whatever?"

"Uh, you realize I don't go to work."

"What?" Jacob said, eyes widening.

"I'm working from home. Xeler has no office to go to here."

"But there's a branch like a mile away." Jacob pointed. "They're everywhere, actually."

"That's the retail side. Remember, I work on disaster recovery plans that don't make any difference whatsoever to anything?"

Jacob leaned back and crossed his arms. "Dios mío. You mean, you're going to be here twenty-four seven?"

"Pretty much."

Jacob exhaled. "Well, there's no way to hide this. Just so you know, I'm sexually active."

"Wow, we're diving right into the deep end," Duncan said. "What have I gotten myself into?"

Kaden yelled at his brother in Filipino, his arms outstretched, palms up, face red and tense.

"Okay. I'm sorry," Jacob said to both, "but listen, I'm not used to adult supervision all the time. It was tolerable with Gramps because he was hard of hearing and went outside to smoke a lot. Even that was getting to be a bit much. I don't need someone even more up in my shit."

Exasperated, Kaden spoke to his brother in Filipino again.

Jacob snorted at him. "I'm a teenage boy! Of course, I brought up sex in the first five minutes. Other than food and sports, and the all-important food-sports like hot dog eating, that's pretty much the only thing on my mind. Besides, we're all guys here. We all have... sexual needs."

"You don't even have a girlfriend now," Kaden said, switching to English.

"A temporary situation, my man. She'll soon realize how much she misses my booty and come crawling back." He grabbed his crotch when he said 'booty.'

"Oh my," Duncan said, scratching his forehead. "Jacob, I'm not a grandfather yet, am I? Or imminently about to be?"

"No, Duncan. I use protection."

Duncan sighed. "Okay. I need a second to process this." He closed his eyes and took a couple of breaths. There must be something from a video he could draw upon. He searched his mind. Nope. Nothing. Improvisation time.

"Okay. You know what, sure. Jacob, thank you for being honest and open about this sensitive subject. I was your age once myself. As you said, we're all guys here, so we should be able to speak frankly. Right? My concerns are that I want you to avoid pregnancy and diseases. I'm overjoyed to hear you use protection. Let me know what particular product or products you use if you run low and need more."

"That would be the extra, extra-large, Duncan."

Kaden burst into laughter again.

"I'm a growing boy. I don't need my growth down there stunted by something too tight."

"That's not how that works," Duncan said.

Jacob slowly shook his head. "Not gonna risk it."

"Also, I'm pretty sure that 'extra, extra-large' is not an actual size," Duncan said.

"I'll get you a pic of the box for what I use."

"Kaden, um…" Duncan said, "I don't know if you and Hunter are needing protection yet, but if so—"

Kaden's face turned bright red. "No. Not necessary."

"Okay. Well, when you need something, let me know, and if you find it too uncomfortable to talk about it out loud, text me instead." *Please, just text me. Please, please, please!*

Kaden's face calmed and his shoulders relaxed. "Oh. Yes sir."

"Now, Jacob. Can I call you Jacob?" Duncan mimicked the quiz show host voice.

"Certainly, Duncan." Jacob echoed the mimicking voice.

"Jacob, when it comes to heterosexual romance advice, I'm not sure I can help much there. I will try though if need be."

"That's okay, Duncan. I'm pretty much a Crasanova."

"Um." Duncan was about to let him know that it was actually *Casanova,* but he halted when Kaden subtly shook his head, and put a finger to his lips. Apparently, that was not the first time Jacob had misspoken. Sibling rivalry. Duncan was all too familiar with that. He decided to play along. "Really?"

"Yep. The chicas all love me." Jacob grinned and ran his hands over his pecs.

"Okay," Duncan said, raising one brow.

Kaden tilted his head and rolled his eyes at his brother.

Duncan turned his attention to Kaden. "Obviously, I have experience with guys. I want you to feel free to talk to me about anything, both of you. Kaden, you seem more shy and reserved, so if it's easier, you're welcome to simply text me. I'll be glad to find resources for you."

The tension in Kaden's brow eased. "Oh. Okay. Thanks."

The smell of something scorching hit Duncan's nose. "Is something burning?"

"Oh no!" Kaden hopped up and ran to the kitchen.

Jacob crossed his arms. "Duncan, I hope you like your baked chicken blackened."

"It's okay," Kaden called from the kitchen seconds later. "It's just some broth that oozed out and burned. The chicken is fine."

"Well, perhaps that's enough real talk for our first family meeting," Duncan said.

Kaden returned from the kitchen. "Oh."

Jacob gave Duncan a patronizing shoulder squeeze. "Good job, Duncan. Good job. I'm gonna hop into the pool for a bit and practice my turns, if that's okay?"

"Sure."

Kaden uttered something to Jacob in Filipino. Jacob reacted with an eye roll and headed outside.

"That's so unnerving," Duncan said.

"What?"

"Filipino."

"Sorry, sir. I was just telling him not to take his board shorts off."

"Is that a thing he does?" Duncan asked.

"Yes sir. He says they take too long to dry out and the chlorine ruins them."

"So, he just swims in... um... what does he wear under the shorts?"

"Under those? Nothing."

Duncan closed his eyes. "Seriously? Don't the neighbors see?"

"Not since Mom and Nanay built the privacy fence."

"You have my official permission to remind him that he is not to take them off, at least when I'm here or anyone else who might object."

"Yes sir." Kaden sat on the sofa, one leg tucked under the other, his back straight. "Can I ask you something?"

"Sure."

"At the Celebration of Life, you talked about that frat party and how you were going to rescue Nanay from that drunk boy."

"Yes."

"And you were genuinely skinny? Kinda like me?"

"Yep. I was about a hundred and ten pounds."

"And you would've confronted that guy?"

"Well, I think so. It might've been the alcohol talking. I should add I don't condone underage drinking." *Not now, anyway.*

"That was still pretty brave," Kaden said, the lines in his brow drawn tight.

Duncan smiled. "Thanks. I may have been skinny, but I was scrappier than I looked. I grew up with two older brothers. That will toughen a guy up."

"Grandpa said you have a sister, too?"

"Yep. I'm the baby. Hopefully, you'll get to meet everyone soon. Mom has already told them all about you guys and sent photos."

"Cool." Kaden leaned back on the sofa, crossing one ankle over the other.

"Can I ask *you* something? And if you feel it's betraying your brother's confidence, you don't have to answer. But is he really sexually active? Or is that all just bluster?"

Kaden scrunched his face. "Honestly, I don't know how much he's really done with girls, but I would advise that you don't barge into his room without knocking when the door's closed, if you know what I mean."

"Ah." Duncan grabbed a stack of papers off a side table. "So, your grandpa left me these. One is titled *Jacob User Manual,* and the other says *Kaden User Manual.* Nice to see he's still got his dry wit and sense of humor after all these years."

"He tried to do those on the computer, but it was extremely slow." Kaden pointed to a desktop computer across the room.

"Good God. A beige computer with a CD-ROM drive? How old is that?"

Kaden shrugged.

"We need to replace that thing. That explains why he wrote this stuff out by hand. Unfortunately, I can't read it. What the hell does this say? 'Jacob is like wild geese.'"

Kaden got up and sat on the arm of the chair, looking over Duncan's shoulder. "Maybe 'Jacob is like wildebeest' or 'Jacob is like milk toast.'"

Duncan snickered and shook his head. "I doubt Bill can even read this. It's pretty useless. I suppose I'll just have to wing it."

"You're doing a solid job so far."

Duncan glanced up at Kaden. "Really? I think you're just being polite."

Kaden plunked back onto the sofa. "No. I like your idea of texting stuff." He gazed downward. "Sometimes, I don't like to talk about things."

"Do you talk about things with your therapist pretty easily?"

"Occasionally," Kaden said. "But that's different."

"How?"

"I'm not trying to get him to like me." Kaden's shoulders drooped.

"Kaden, I already like you."

"You do?" His head still low, he lifted his eyes to peek at Duncan.

"Absolutely. Both you and Jacob. Hell, I wouldn't be here if I didn't. So don't fret about that."

Kaden smiled weakly. "I'd better check on the chicken."

As Kaden hopped up and walked away, something about his facial expression gave Duncan a feeling of unease. Or was he imagining it? It was so hard to read that kid.

26

KADEN

Kaden stood outside in the driveway, clad in board shorts, flips and a tee that was covered with a sea of yellow smiley face emojis. Over one shoulder hung a colorful beach towel. On the other, a bag filled with water bottles, snacks and other accouterments for a day at the beach.

He shifted his weight from one foot to the other, while sipping from his water bottle, the liquid trickling down his chin.

A navy blue SUV soon stopped in front of the house, its tinted windows masking the occupants. Bright sunlight reflected off the smooth metal and glass. Kaden squinted to see inside as the window lowered with a whir. In the driver's seat, Hunter smiled proudly, his mother beside him in the passenger seat.

"You called a cab, mister?" Hunter yelled out the window as it rolled down. "Okay, Mom. Move to the backseat now, so Kaden can sit here."

"Hunter, you know we can't do that. You have to have a licensed driver up front."

Hunter whined. "That's no fun."

Kaden got in the back. "Hi Ms. Gan."

"Hi Kaden. And just call me Soo."

"Where to, mister?" Hunter said, gazing at him through the rearview mirror.

"The beach, fine sir."

Soo-jin Gan worked at St. Lucie Nuclear Power Plant, but Kaden didn't know precisely what she did there. He would have asked, except Hunter cranked up the stereo. Was he intentionally trying to prevent conversation, keeping his mother from saying something embarrassing as he drove to Hutchinson Island, where the power plant was located?

Practically across the road from the plant was Walton Rocks Beach, a dog-friendly stretch where the boys planned to spend the day, despite neither having a dog.

"Okay guys. Have a good day. I'll see you at quitting time," Soo said, sliding into the driver's seat. As the SUV shifted into gear and accelerated on the dirt road, gravel crunched and popped under the tires.

Kaden and Hunter sauntered along a short, sandy path from the unpaved parking lot to the beach. Hunter stopped halfway and turned to Kaden, pulled him into a hug and kissed him. His face beamed with a contented smile when he pulled aside, like he'd just gotten away with something.

The shore was empty, and they soon found a spot to set up their blanket. "I don't think I've ever been on such a deserted beach," Kaden said.

The salty scents of the ocean were all about them. Waves crashed along the beach, piling up and sending spray into the air.

"That's what I love about it. On a weekday in the summer, it's pretty empty. Once in a while, someone might walk dogs out here, but that's cool too. They usually will let you pet them."

As they settled, Hunter stripped off his shirt, exposing a tan and strong chest, and arms that were hard and smooth.

Kaden decided he wouldn't remove his own shirt.

"Aren't you hot with that on?" Hunter asked.

"I don't wanna get sunburned."

"I have sunblock. So, feel free to take it off."

"I'm fine."

"You sure?"

Kaden shrugged and glanced away.

"You remember I've seen you shirtless before, eh?" Hunter asked.

"You have?"

"Swimming in your pool several times."

"Oh." Kaden had figured his body was unmemorable enough that Hunter would have forgotten ever seeing it.

"And there's no one else out here right now. We're all alone. You don't have to be shy."

Kaden stared at the sand. "It's just you're so ripped, and I'm so unmuscly."

Hunter laughed. "I'm not ripped."

"Yes, you are, especially compared to me."

"There's no reason for you to be modest or embarrassed. You're really cute just the way you are." He playfully tapped his index finger on Kaden's nose. "I don't want to pressure you, babe, but I don't want you to feel like you have to hide, either."

Kaden stared into Hunter's longing eyes. Possibly it was only because Hunter had just called him "babe," but he took his tee off.

Hunter smiled and looked up and down his torso.

"You're looking at me." Kaden's cheeks flushed.

"Of course, I am. Why do you think I wanted your shirt off?" He giggled, pushed Kaden down onto the beach blanket, and kissed him again. After a few kisses, he released Kaden and sat back up. "Okay, we better get some sunblock on if we're gonna survive all day out here."

They each put lotion on.

"Can you get my back?" Hunter asked.

Kaden's mouth became dry and he swallowed. "Okay." He spread the sunblock over Hunter's tan skin.

"So, how are things at home?" Hunter asked.

Kaden found it difficult to think of anything but the feel of the skin under his fingers. "Fine."

Hunter then covered Kaden's back as well. Hunter seemed to be taking his time, being very meticulous. Kaden closed his eyes, letting nothing distract him from the sensation of his touch on his bare skin.

"Thanks," Kaden said when Hunter finally stopped.

Hunter wiped his hands off on the blanket. "So, it's just fine, at home?"

"Um. Is that what I said?"

Hunter laughed. "I guess you were distracted."

Kaden's cheeks flushed again. "Maybe."

As they sat serenely gazing out to sea, Hunter leaned over and whispered, "Can I kiss you again?"

Only making eye contact for a moment, then staring downward, Kaden nodded.

They made out for a few minutes, then Hunter sat back up. "This is nice. Just the two of us out here. No Jacob or Gabby disturbing us."

Kaden grinned. "Yeah."

"Want to go for a walk and hunt for seashells?"

"Sure."

As they strolled along the shore, they waded into the waves occasionally.

"You didn't actually answer my question earlier," Hunter said. "Are things going okay at home? I don't mean to pry, but I was wondering."

"It's an adjustment. Probably more for Jacob. He's not used to having adult supervision all the time, since our moms worked so much."

"And does Duncan seem like he's doing okay?"

Kaden shrugged. "I guess. I'm certain he misses Chip tons. They talk on the phone a lot. Other than that... well..."

"Well, what?"

"He said something when he first got here. He said he likes me and Jacob."

"That's good, eh?" Hunter asked.

"Yeah. But he said he wouldn't be here if he didn't like us. And I just worry what if... what if he stops liking us?"

"Don't worry, babe. You are extremely likable. Trust me on that." Hunter grabbed hold of Kaden's hand and squeezed it. He held onto it for the rest of their stroll, not even letting go when he picked up shells.

WHEN KADEN GOT HOME, he tried to sneak in unnoticed. Duncan and Jacob were in the spare bedroom that Duncan had converted into an office. He could overhear them chatting.

"So, Duncan," Jacob said, "I'm thinking we should do a TikTok colab."

"A TikTok colab? I don't even have a TikTok."

"That's okay. You don't need one," Jacob said.

"And what will we do exactly?"

"A dance. We'll both dance."

"Oh, okay." Duncan sounded excited. "I took some dance classes in college."

"Wait? What? You actually *can* dance?" Jacob said.

"I'm a gay man. Of course, I can dance."

Jacob groaned. "Shit. Never mind, then."

Duncan's raucous laughter filtered into the kitchen.

Jacob came out of the office and spotted Kaden after he'd gotten a granola bar out of the pantry. "There he is. Oooh, is that the going-steady granola bar? Did Hunter give that to you at the beach?"

"You're hilarious," Kaden deadpanned.

Duncan popped out of his office. "Oh. How did it go? It appears you used sunblock. Good job."

"Yes sir. It went fine."

"Just... fine?" Duncan said.

Jacob circled Kaden, looking him over, pulling at his shirt collar. "No hickeys. That's disappointing. Some sand stuck in sussy places though. But no evidence of excessive beach frolicking or deflowering. Again, disappointing, bro."

Kaden groaned. His voice betrayed his annoyance. "It was loads of fun. Okay? Hunter drove, so that was cool. We found some seashells. And there were no nuclear meltdowns today thanks to Hunter's mom. Some lady brought three border collie puppies to the beach and let us play with them. So yeah. It was fun! Are you satisfied now?"

"No hickeys though," Jacob said, shaking his head. "Tell me you at least made out some. Or that you gave Hunter a hickey?" He nudged his elbow into Kaden's ribs. "Eh, did you? Did you? He looks like his neck would taste good for a dude. Does it?"

"Is that all you think about? God!" Kaden said.

"Shit, bro. I'm not getting any right now. Duncan's not getting any. Am I right? We are living our lives vivaciously through you."

"Vicariously," Duncan corrected.

"Whatever." Jacob threw up his hands and sauntered toward his room, calling back. "So fucking disappointing, bro."

Duncan looked at Kaden. "Should I be reprimanding him for cussing?"

"Nanay used to, but she gave up eventually."

Duncan nodded.

"Sorry I got upset. How was your day?" Kaden asked.

"It was typical, mind-numbing work stuff. Uh, no disasters at any data centers today, again. Thanks for asking."

"Did you really take dance classes?"

"I did, indeed."

Kaden rocked his weight back and forth, avoiding eye contact. "Do you think you could teach me how to dance?"

"Sure. Any particular reason you want to learn? You want to do the TikTok thing?"

"Oh, no. Hunter said that maybe this year, we could go to a school dance together."

Duncan smiled. "I would love to teach you. So, did Hunter do a... what do they call them? A promposal? Did he have a flash-mob on the beach or sing you a song or something cute like that?"

A flash-mob? Seriously? Did anyone do those anymore? He kept that thought to himself. "No. No. And he didn't say prom specifically, just some dance. Apparently, there's more than one during the year."

"Well, we'll get you up to speed on the dance floor. For sure! You'll be a regular John Travolta."

"Who?"

"Did I say John Travolta? I meant, er, BTS? He dances?"

"They. And, yes, they dance," Kaden said, chuckling.

"And they said I'd never be one of the cool kids. Take that Alan Nertlewick and your fancy sunglasses."

"Who is that?"

"Just a guy who would make fun of me in school."

"I know the type," Kaden said. "I know the type."

THE SUN from the beach day had seeped into Kaden's skin, making him sweat beneath the sheets even in the middle of the night. That wasn't the only thing keeping him from sleeping though. His mind raced with memories of earlier that day.

As he stared at the whirring blades of the ceiling fan, barely visible in the darkness, he was still steaming from Jacob's ribbing. Why did Jacob have to be so nosy? It wasn't his business what he and Hunter did or didn't do on the beach, or anywhere else, for that matter.

He let out a breath. Was Jacob really the reason he was angry? Or was it something else? His brother seemed so at ease with expressing affection, whether it was hugging friends and family, or getting with girls. It was possible Jacob was more talk than actual action. Still,

Kaden was sure his brother had at least some sexual experiences. And he'd certainly implied that Hunter and Kaden should be doing more than they had.

What if Jacob was right? What if Hunter wanted to go further? After all, he was a whole year older. And Hunter even had his learner's permit. He was practically grown up. Surely, he must want to do more.

Perhaps Hunter was holding back only because he sensed how uncomfortable it was for Kaden just to take off his shirt. But how much patience would Hunter and his manly body have with his reluctant, prudish, boyish boyfriend before he would give up and look for someone more willing?

Kaden felt his chest tighten and he took a deep breath. He wished he could just forget everything and go to sleep.

27

KADEN

Kaden was seated at the dining table with his iPad displaying his favorite cake recipe. He flipped between his recipe app, web browser, and some Pinterest boards, hunting for solutions to give it a lighter, silkier texture that would make it melt on the tongue.

On his left was Hunter, who had his gaming laptop. But today, he just had the web browser running, helping Kaden search the web for more cake decorating ideas.

To Kaden's right was Gabby, her face buried in her phone. "Here's one that uses more eggs. What do you think?" She showed the screen to Kaden.

"I dunno," Kaden said.

Together, they were on a quest to find the perfect cake recipe and decorations. Now that Unique Mills-Foy had tasted his latest version, Kaden knew he had to go a step further to have any chance of winning the competition. And it wasn't just Unique he had to worry about. There had been a couple of new competitors last year who performed surprisingly well.

Duncan stepped out of his office. "Sorry, I'm late guys. My

conference call ran long. But I'm all done with work today now. So, what are we doing here?" He sat down at the table with the others. "And where's Jacob?"

Gabby groaned at the utterance of Jacob's name.

"Um. We sent him on a side quest," Kaden said. "He was being a distraction, so we tasked him with picking a team name." He wasn't sure that had been a good idea, either. At the top of Jacob's list of team names the previous year were "Evil Cake Council," and "Bakers of Doom."

"Wait," Duncan said. "It's a team competition?"

"Yes. A team of two. Gabby's my partner."

"Kaden does most of the work, obviously, but I'm getting better," she said.

Kaden smiled. "She's indispensable."

"So, what are we doing now?" Duncan asked.

"We're looking at recipes. Seeing if we can discover one that looks better," Kaden said.

"You can tell by looking?"

"Pretty much," Kaden said. "I'd have to try it out, of course. But I'm not seeing anything I like."

After tossing around and rejecting several ideas, Kaden set down his iPad. He tapped his fingers against the table and shook his head. "I just don't see how to improve this." He scowled and rubbed his eyes.

Duncan scratched his chin. "Maybe you need to consider something else. You know that food show with that guy, and that other guy?"

"Huh?" Gabby said.

"On Netflix."

Gabby blinked at him, still befuddled.

"Oh. You mean the one with the guy?" Kaden said. "And the other guy?"

"Yes, that one!"

"What are you even talking about?" Gabby said.

"The one with the Star Wars guy?" Hunter asked.

"Yes," Kaden and Duncan both said.

"And the Korean guy?" Hunter asked.

"Yep," Duncan said.

"My homey." Hunter smiled.

Gabby shook her head. "How did you know what show you guys were talking about? Is this a gay telepathy thing? Do you have telepathy? Because that would explain a lot."

"No, no," Duncan said. "Kaden and Hunter were watching it the other evening and sneaking in kisses when they thought I couldn't see them."

Hunter contorted his lips as he turned away and gazed at the floor.

A rush of heat formed a layer of sweat on Kaden's forehead. He cleared his throat. "Anyway, what about the show?"

"Wait here." Duncan went to the kitchen and opened a cabinet, and took something out, then to the fridge. He brought two items back and placed them on the table: vanilla extract and eggs.

"Okay," Kaden said. "So?"

"What is it the chefs use on those TV shows?"

Kaden shrugged.

"Better ingredients. Look at this." Duncan held up the bottle. "What is it?"

"Vanilla extract?" Kaden said, knitting his brow.

"Wrong! It's *Imitation* Vanilla Extract." Duncan opened the egg carton. "And these are run-of-the-mill eggs. You need real Vanilla Extract or better yet, actual vanilla beans. And these eggs are crap. We should get free range, laid by organic fed chickens. And that Irish butter from grass-fed cows."

"But those cost extra. I've never been able to use those," Kaden said.

"Well, now you will." Duncan placed his hand on top of Kaden's.

"You realize the first prize is only a hundred dollars?" Kaden said.

"Is this about the money, Kaden?" Duncan asked, looking straight into his eyes.

"Um."

"Or is it about more?" Duncan said. "Isn't it about you wanting to be the best you can be at something you love?"

"Yes sir."

"Good. Now, the grocery stores down here suck, but if we shop around or order online, I bet we can find what we need. And if we have to go to Orlando or somewhere to find stuff, then we'll do that. Or I can get my mom or Chip to send us something from Charlotte."

"Really?" Kaden asked.

"Of course," Duncan said. "We should make sure all of your equipment and utensils are good too. Like do you have a decent um, thingy that you twirl the cake around on?"

"Turntable." Kaden said. "It doesn't rotate that smoothly, to be honest."

"We'll get online and order some stuff. Make a list."

"Thanks."

"Just promise me none of you will tell Chip how much of a glutton I've been with practice cakes." Duncan winked.

Jacob emerged from his room. "Okay guys. I got it!"

"You found a *good* team name already?" Gabby said.

Kaden braced himself for whatever horrible name Jacob had picked.

"What? No. I finally figured out how to remember the difference between baking and cooking. Are you ready? You cook cookies, and you bake bacon."

"Nope. Backwards," Gabby said while the others laughed.

"You have got to be fucking kidding me. I give up." He threw up his hands and walked back to his room.

～

THAT WEEKEND, Kaden and Duncan were alone in the house. Jacob and Hunter were attending a swimming summer camp.

Kaden pulled his latest creations from the oven, setting the hot cake pans on a cooling rack. As he removed his oven mitts, he glanced outside and saw Duncan floating around in the pool. The kitchen was hot with the oven going—the pool was too inviting to pass up. He untied his apron, changed into his swimsuit, and joined Duncan.

"Hi," Duncan said, as Kaden floated up beside him. They were using tube floats, and their bodies were mostly underwater.

"Hello."

"Baking going well?"

"Yes sir. I'm waiting for them to cool before I decorate."

"Nice. It's funny, I never realized how much I'd enjoy having a pool in the backyard. I wish I could swim better so I could get exercise in here."

"You're not a good swimmer?"

"No. Never had a pool. I can dog paddle, that's about it. But it's still fun to float around. I can't wait for Chip to come down and enjoy this too."

"Yes sir."

"Kaden, you don't have to call me sir all the time? Just Duncan, or hey you, or whatever."

"Yes sir."

Duncan laughed.

Kaden felt his cheeks warm. "Old habits." He dunked himself under the water, then floated back up, shaking the water off. "So, you miss Chip?"

"More than I can put into words. You miss Hunter?"

"Yes, but it's not the same. Hunter's only gone for two days," Kaden said. "So, do you love Chip?"

"Very much."

"And he loves you back?"

"Apparently, as shocking as that is," Duncan said.

"Why do you say that?"

"I dunno. I'm just surprised sometimes that I'm so lucky to have him."

"I know the feeling. I still don't know what Hunter sees in me."

Duncan looked him in the eye. "God, you really are a clone of me, not just in appearance either."

"Do you... do you ever..." Kaden wondered how deep their similarities went. He wanted to ask Duncan if he also suffered panic attacks, but he couldn't. It was too scary. He changed the subject. "I mean, how do you know if you're in love with someone?"

"Oh. Well." Duncan tilted his head, lost in reflection. "You sure you wouldn't rather hear where babies come from?"

Kaden chuckled. "Sorry. I know it's a weird question. It's okay. Forget I asked."

Duncan scrunched his face. "It's not a weird question. Not at all. And I guess you're only asking because it's relevant to you right now."

"Kinda."

"Have either of you guys said the 'L' word to each other yet?"

"No. Should we have by now?"

Duncan slicked his hair back with the water. "I wouldn't rush that. It's good to think about it though. You should be prepared, in case he says it first, so you know how you want to respond."

"That's why I was wondering. Seems like it could be awkward if one person says it and the other doesn't say it back. Or even hesitates to answer."

"Absolutely. I've been on the wrong end of that before."

"So, is there a way to tell if you're in love?"

Duncan rubbed his nose and exhaled. "I'm really trying to figure out an answer other than, 'You'll just know when it happens.' There's no definite way, but I'll tell you about the first time I fell in love. I was in college and there was this guy I'd been dating for months. One night, we went to dinner and he ordered steak. I was sitting there watching him eat, the cute way he held his knife and fork, and the delicate way he sliced the steak. I said to myself, this is the cutest thing I've ever seen."

Kaden furrowed his brow. "What was so cute about it?"

"That's just it. It was only a guy cutting his steak and eating it. Nothing unusual. So, the next day, Roz asks me how my date went. I mention about how cute he was cutting the food, and she tells me I'm in love. I thought about it, and I was like, damn, she's right."

Kaden leaned his head back on his float. His gaze drifted skyward. "I think I might already be in love then."

"If you think you are, then you probably are. And I haven't gotten any texts from you about protection, yet. I'm not actually trying to encourage you to be, you know, sexually active, but I was a teenage boy myself once. You guys aren't taking risks, are you?"

Kaden squeezed his eyes shut. Not this again. "No sir."

He still wasn't even comfortable taking his shirt off around Hunter. Not to mention any other articles of clothing. Kaden usually turned away when Hunter took off his shirt. His stomach would knot up, turning his insides into a pretzel. His heart would race, and he didn't know if it was a panic attack or something else.

As they drifted around the pool, their floats had separated. Water splashed and Kaden opened his eyes to see Duncan kicking, closing in on him. He stopped alongside.

"Kaden. I'm not sure what's going on in your head right now. You look like you're giving birth. So, I'm not going to bug you about it. But I do want to say this again. If you ever need to talk about anything, we can. Anything. And if not with me, a counselor. Okay?"

"Yes sir."

A couple of days later, they'd acquired the vanilla, butter, and eggs. Kaden wanted to see if those made a difference in the cakes before Duncan spent a bunch of extra money on shipping in more.

Hunter sat at the bar on a stool nearby, timing Kaden and Gabby and making notes. The contest wasn't only about the final product, it also had to be completed within a timeframe.

Kaden wore a beige apron. It belonged to Gabby. She was wearing his old Hello Kitty apron because Kaden had begged her to switch with him. He didn't want Hunter to see him in the Hello Kitty one. Though to his surprise, Hunter had said it looked cute on Gabby.

Kaden eased two round cake pans into the oven. "Now we wait."

"I'm going to the bathroom," Gabby said.

Kaden gazed at Hunter who was attentively looking at him, and had been for some time. "What are you staring at?"

Hunter grinned. "A really cute chef."

Kaden felt heat rise to his cheeks. "You're embarrassing me, you realize?"

"Good." Hunter hopped off the barstool, strode around the kitchen island, and planted a wet kiss on his lips. "I really love watching you bake. I see you one day, working in some high-end restaurant or bakery somewhere."

A grin grew on Kaden's face. "Life goals."

"It's so cool that you already know what you want to do with your life. It's very... what's the word?"

"Practical?"

"Nope. Sexy. It's actually very sexy." Hunter pulled Kaden into a hug, then kissed him again.

Gabby cleared her throat. "Geez. I can't leave you two alone for two minutes."

"Sorry, Gabs," Hunter said. "I can't help it." He sat back down on the barstool.

Duncan came out of his office later. "Mmm. I smell cake. That's making me hungry." He looked Kaden up and down, then Gabby. "We need matching aprons for you."

"We do?" Kaden asked.

"Absolutely. Did Jacob or anyone else come up with a team name?"

"Yes sir. Since we're baking with love, Gabby suggested we call the team 'Love Wins.'"

Duncan smiled at Gabby. "That's awesome on so many levels." He took out his phone and tapped on it for a minute. "Oh wow. Check this out." On his screen was an online shopping app, and he'd searched the phrase 'Love wins apron.' The result was a rainbow patterned apron with the words 'Love Wins' emblazoned on the front. "What do you think?"

Kaden looked at the screen, then looked at Duncan. "It's perfect."

"It is," Gabby said.

"We're ordering two," Duncan said.

"Thank you, but you really don't have to do this. These are fine." Kaden grabbed the edges of his apron and stretched them.

"Nonsense." Duncan tapped a couple of buttons. "Arriving in two days."

Kaden considered breaking his no-hugging rule. And he might have if his existing apron, as well as his hands, weren't covered in flour and other ingredients. "Thank you, sir."

"Yes. Thanks, Mr. Valentyn," Gabby said.

"Nothing's too good for 'Team Love Wins,'" Duncan said, as he headed into his office, "...within reason," he shouted back.

"I like him," Gabby murmured.

Kaden stared after him. Of all the scenarios he'd envisioned after his moms died, he'd never even dared to dream of one as good as this. And that bothered him, because there was a nagging feeling in his gut that this seemed too good to be true.

2 8

DUNCAN

After many weeks of yearning to see him, Duncan picked up Chip from the airport in West Palm and drove him to the house in Port St. Lucie. When they arrived that evening, after some kissing in the foyer, Duncan had a surprise for Chip.

"Follow me, sweetie."

"What's going on?" Chip asked.

Taking his hand, Duncan led Chip out onto the lanai. A tablecloth draped the café table, and it was set with fine dinnerware. A candle glowed in the center.

"What's all this?" Chip said, grinning.

The sun had set, and ceiling fans spun overhead.

"I told you I had a special treat for you."

Jacob sprinted up from the shadows. In his best impression of a pretentious waiter, Jacob spoke. "Gentlemen." He pulled a chair out for Chip, who then sat. Duncan sat as well. "Welcome to the Imperial House of Kaden Restaurant, the finest Chinese restaurant in all of Port St. Lucie, indeed, the entire Treasure Coast. I'm Jacob, and I'll be your waiter tonight." He had a white dinner napkin draped over one arm, and was dressed in a black button-down shirt and long pants, though his brother had been unable to convince him to wear shoes. This was part of a compromise arrangement. If Jacob could go barefoot, he would agree to introduce himself as Jacob, otherwise he would wear shoes, but go by the moniker of Sean Beanfart for the evening.

"Good lord," Chip said. "What is this? Jacob's wearing actual clothes."

"I know, right?" Jacob said, breaking character a moment before returning to pretentious waiter voice. "Would sirs care for some wine?"

"Yes, two glasses of your finest red," Duncan said.

Jacob went inside.

Chip flashed that dimpled smile that made Duncan's heart flutter. "Babe, you didn't have to go to all this trouble."

"Well, it's no trouble at all for me. Seriously, sweetie, thanks to lax child labor law enforcement."

They laughed.

"The boys wanted to do it for you. Well, Kaden did, and he somehow coerced his brother."

"I doubt it took much coercion," Chip said. "I can see in their eyes they really care for you. And they know how much we mean to each other." He placed his hand on Duncan's and his face beamed.

"So, I hope you're up for Crispy Orange Chicken. Kaden remembered how much you liked it last time and wanted to make it again."

"I hope Hunter realizes how lucky he is to have Kaden."

"I think Hunter knows. I'm just not sure Kaden recognizes that Hunter knows."

Chip frowned. "Oh. Has he expressed feelings of inadequacy?"

"Only about every day," Duncan said. "But I keep trying to help him build confidence. And I have a feeling in my gut that it might be working."

"See, you're already getting gut feelings. I knew you had fatherhood instincts, just waiting to hatch out."

It was only Chip's second visit to Florida since Duncan had

moved. They chatted, laughed, and spent a lot of time just staring at each other. Meanwhile, their pretentious waiter kept the wine glasses topped off, and the plates refilled.

Hours later, they were still there, the moon casting a pale light on the pool. The candle flickered, a puddle of wax mounded at the base.

Jacob had cleaned the dinner plates off the table, and Kaden had come out to receive applause for his efforts before going back inside. Duncan ran a finger across the top of his wineglass.

"Sweetie," Duncan said. "I think it's time."

"Time? For what? Bed? Because I may be a little tipsy, but I think I'm up for a little messing around, if that's what you're suggesting."

"Well, now that's tempting, but it's not what I was talking about. I was thinking it's time that you pack up the moving van and get your fine ass down here." Duncan smiled, anticipating Chip's reaction.

"Wow. I wasn't expecting that." Chip looked surprised, but not in a pleasant way. "I was thinking we'd wait until after Christmas, maybe. Figure out a timeframe, then."

"What do you mean? You've been going on about us living together for so long now, and suddenly you're pushing it back?"

Chip took a swig from his wineglass. "Babe." He exhaled. "I don't know how to say this. There's been a change in my situation."

"What? Are you having doubts about us? Shit. Is there someone else? You've met someone."

"No. No. Nothing like that. It's work." Chip set his glass down and folded his hands in front of himself. "They changed their minds about letting me work remote."

Duncan clutched his forehead. "Are you fucking joking? Please tell me this is a joke."

Chip's frown deepened. "No, it's no joke."

Duncan slumped in his chair. "For the love of... Don't they understand they're playing with people's lives here? They can't just flip-flop on this." He'd known Chip's manager for years. She would not get away with this. Duncan fished in his pocket. "Where's my phone? I'm calling Monica right now."

Chip looked at Duncan and winced. "What?"

"You heard me. She told you that you could move. Dammit, she's gonna make good on that." His fingers fumbled, and the phone slipped out of his pocket, hitting the concrete and bouncing. *Too much wine.*

Chip picked up the phone, but clasped it in his hands, resisting Duncan's efforts to take it. Chip groaned. "Don't call Monica. She did nothing wrong."

"What? She said you could move." No sooner had the words come out of his mouth than he felt an uneasy stir on the back of his neck.

"No," Chip said, his head tilted back. Then he lowered his gaze and stared into Duncan's eyes. "I'm sorry, babe. She never said I could move."

Duncan's mouth fell open. "You lied to me?"

"I'm so sorry, babe. I'm so sorry."

"But why?"

"Why?" Chip motioned to inside the house. "That's why. Those boys are why. And well, babe, one day, when you're an old man, I don't want you to look back and regret not coming here, being here, for them. So, in a way, I did it for you as well."

"You should never have lied to me, Chip." Duncan hopped up, staggered, and braced himself against a column.

"Babe, I meant well. I judged that it was the right thing to do. Or at least the best in a bad list of choices."

Duncan shook his head. "It wasn't your decision alone to make. You should have told me the truth. We should have talked about it."

"Babe... I... I don't know what to say."

"I do. I know what to say. Leave. Just leave."

"You don't mean that?"

Duncan closed his teary eyes and nodded. "Leave."

Without saying another word, Chip left.

Duncan took the remainder of the wine to his bedroom and drank himself to sleep.

By the time he rolled over and looked at the bedside clock, it was almost noon.

His phone had a text from Chip. "I'm still in town, at a hotel, if you want to talk." Duncan didn't respond. Instead, he dragged himself out of bed and trudged to the kitchen to get some water.

"Duncan," Kaden said. "Are you okay?"

He replied with a groan.

"I made you guys breakfast, but I had to throw it out. It got cold. I'll be glad to cook it again." Kaden looked toward the bedroom expectantly.

"Um." Duncan blinked a couple of times while chewing on his dry lips. "Is Jacob here?"

"He's in his room."

"Can you get him? But don't yell or make any loud noises." Duncan massaged his temples.

Shortly, the boys were sitting on barstools, giving Duncan their complete attention.

"You look like shit," Jacob said.

"Feel like it too." Duncan dragged his hands over his face while he forced his brain into gear, contemplating what to tell the boys. The truth was off the table—they didn't need to feel guilt about this situation. He gulped half a glass of water, cleared his throat, then continued. "Listen, boys, I want to tell you something. So, first, I want to say how special that was last night, the meal and all. Chip and I loved it. Thank you very much. After the meal, Chip and I had a serious heart-to-heart talk, and we mutually decided that he and I are... well... we're going to go our separate ways."

"What?" Kaden said. "Why?"

"It's for the best, we think. Sometimes, people drift apart. It's not anyone's fault. But you see, that's why we waited to do the whole living together thing, to make sure. And it turned out we weren't quite right for each other."

Kaden sat in stunned silence, one hand plastered against the back of his head, grasping his hair.

"I'm sorry," Jacob finally said. He got up and gave Duncan a quick hug before going back to his room.

Kaden and Duncan sat looking at each other.

"Are you okay?" Kaden asked.

Duncan looked down and nodded. After a moment, he reached out and put his hand on Kaden's shoulder. "I'm fine. I'm fine." He smiled at Kaden with his eyes. "I drank too much wine though. So, I think I'll try to go sleep this hangover off."

No sooner than he'd closed his bedroom door, Duncan collapsed onto the floor, curled into a ball, and sobbed.

29

KADEN

Summer break had come to an end far too soon. Gaming and lazing endlessly with Hunter took a back seat to school work now.

It was fifth period. And for Kaden's tenth grade year, that meant Culinary Arts class. He signed up for this class for several reasons. First, he figured it would be an easy "A," and ten days into the school year, that was proving to be true. More importantly, it was one of his few classes without Jacob. It had been a close call when Jacob realized the class would be full of girls. In the end, he opted against it because of the ribbing he'd receive from the jock boys.

Kaden's elation that Jacob had elected to pass on Culinary Arts was shattered when, on the first day of class, he saw Unique Mills-Foy in the classroom, strutting around like she owned the place.

The students routinely organized into small groups, and the two adversaries made certain to be in separate ones. Today, Kaden was teamed up with three eighth-grade girls and they were making biscuits from scratch.

"It's so cool that a boy is baking," Madison said, her fawning eyes glued to Kaden. Apparently, rumors about Kaden's sexuality had yet to filter down to the eighth graders.

Kaden smiled at her uneasily as he mixed the batter.

From a nearby group, Unique chimed in. "If *she* even is a boy," she said, her tone surly.

Part of Kaden wanted to respond to Unique. To tell her it was perfectly fine for a boy to be into baking; it wasn't necessary for a boy to like sports; that he could wear a Hello Kitty apron if he wanted; that his three favorite colors could be pink, yellow, and a particular shade of pastel green, in that order. And that he could even be a boy who has a crush on a boy, and maybe even be in love with him, and that was okay. More than okay. It was beautiful. Part of him wanted to get up in Unique's face and let her know in no uncertain terms that there wasn't just one way to be a boy. He could be all the things he was and still be a boy, if that's what he wanted. And that *he* got to choose his pronouns.

If he hadn't been sleep-deprived, tossing and turning all night for the week and a half since Duncan and Chip had broken up; if he hadn't fought off two panic attacks earlier in the week and then lost the fight last night, he might very well have given her a piece of his mind, right there in front of the entire Culinary Arts class, biscuits be damned.

But he was barely holding himself together, functioning on autopilot. He'd thrown out the godawful biscuit recipe his teacher had foisted on them and instead was presenting to his fawning young disciples his tried-and-true recipe that he'd perfected since the age of eight.

So, instead of reacting to her barb, he just kept mixing. Unique turned away and Kaden flipped the bird at her. The girls in Kaden's group giggled at that, causing Unique to turn around and glare.

Kaden feigned innocence. Unique huffed and crossed her arms, opening her mouth to say something, but halted when she spotted the teacher making the rounds.

After the teacher had moved on, Unique turned to Kaden again.

"You're going down, Watson-Rivera," she said, certainly deliberately reversing his last names.

"Bring it on, Mills-Foy," Kaden replied, making sure to accentuate her pretentiously absurd silent *s* so much he nearly spat.

That was as close as he would get to being in a confrontation with Unique, or anyone, really. Especially now. He was a good boy, a well-behaved one. He needed to keep that up, because he couldn't afford for Duncan to stop liking him. In this class, he needed an 'A' and solid grades in his other classes so Duncan would have every reason to continue liking him, maybe even to be proud.

It wasn't just Duncan that Kaden needed to keep wanting him. He had to impress Hunter too. Hunter said Kaden was smart. Kaden had never thought of himself as anything more than a little above average intelligence. In most subjects, Jacob did well, barely even trying, but Kaden had to study harder, and take better notes to match his brother, putting more pressure on him to live up to everyone's expectations.

WHEN KADEN GOT HOME from school, he kicked off his shoes, headed straight to his room, dropped his book bag on the floor and collapsed onto the bed without even taking his school uniform off. The house was quiet, with Duncan in his office and Jacob at swim practice.

Exhausted, he fell asleep.

He hadn't closed his door though, and some hours later, Jacob came in.

"Have I told you that you look like shit today?" Jacob said. "Because I know I've told Duncan that at least three times so far, and I don't want you to feel left out."

Kaden was face down, with his feet hanging off the side of the bed. His only reply was a groan.

"What's wrong, bro? You just being your usual lazybones self, or is something going on?"

"I haven't been sleeping well."

Jacob sat on the other side of the bed. "I can see that from the bags under your eyes."

"Oh geez, have I really got bags? Hunter is so gonna dump me."

"No, he's not. You're not nearly as dumpable as I am. Why aren't you sleeping?"

Kaden rolled over face up and gazed at the ceiling. "I'm worried."

"About? Come on. Talk to me."

Kaden cast a glance at his open bedroom door, then back at Jacob.

Jacob rolled his eyes. "You could just ask me to close the door."

"Okay. Close the door."

"Do it yourself, lazybones," Jacob said.

Kaden let out another groan, whinier than the previous one.

"Dios mío." Jacob closed the door, then hopped back onto the bed. "Okay, spill it."

Even with the door closed, Kaden spoke in Filipino, in case Duncan might hear. "This whole situation with Duncan and Chip, what if that happens to me and Hunter? You know how much they loved each other. And then they just decided to break up. Hunter hasn't even said he loves me. He's probably already trying to figure out how to break it off."

"That's crazy talk, bro. He kept asking about you during practice to the point of being annoying. The boy is super into you."

"And Duncan and Chip were into each other. And yet..."

"Dude, that's totally different."

"I don't see how. The whole thing is making me wonder what it even means to be in love. If people split up like that, what's the point? What's the point of any of it?" Kaden looked at Jacob expectantly.

Jacob looked away, then back at Kaden, like he was wrestling with some decision. He exhaled. "I'm going to tell you something, but you can't let Duncan know. Okay?"

"Sure."

"They didn't just mutually decide to break up."

"What?" Kaden propped himself up on his elbows.

"When we did that dinner date on the lanai, after I had brought the dirty dishes in, I went back outside to see if they needed anything. I was a stealth-ninja, hanging in the shadows, so they didn't know I was there."

With anyone else, Kaden couldn't imagine them not knowing they weren't alone, but Jacob was such a presence, when he was actually being quiet, someone who knew him wouldn't have believed he was in the room with them.

Jacob continued. "They were talking, and I heard stuff I shouldn't have."

"What?" Kaden said.

Jacob scrunched his face like he was in pain.

"Jacob, tell me. I promise I won't say anything."

"Okay. So, you know how Chip was planning to move down here and work remotely, like Duncan did? Well, his boss never said he could do that. So Chip can't move and Duncan got upset and told him to leave. That's why he's been moping around. He's heartbroken, I guess. So, see? They didn't stop loving each other. I'm sure Hunter's not going to up and dump you for no reason. You got nothing to worry about, bro. Trust me."

Kaden closed his eyes. "Chip lied? He lied to Duncan?"

"Um. Yeah. But bro, you're not hearing me. They didn't randomly break up. Okay? So, Hunter isn't going to just up and leave you. That's good, right?"

"Why? Why would Chip do that?"

"This conversation is not going the way I wanted it to. I hate when that happens." Jacob ran his hand through his hair. "I guess Chip might've been afraid that Duncan wouldn't have moved here if he knew that he would be basically ending his relationship. That seems to be what makes the most sense. Even as a one hundred percent straight guy, I can tell Chip is a good catch for the Duncster. Am I right?"

Kaden flopped back down. Now it made sense why Duncan was so downcast.

He wondered if Chip had been right. Would Duncan have decided not to come to Florida without him? And what about now? Maybe he wanted to go back. Perhaps he'd had enough of this, anyway. Maybe he and Jacob were already way more trouble than he bargained for. Jacob had brought up all that sex stuff as soon as he got here. Possibly he'd already been thinking about leaving them. And what if the situation with Chip had pushed Duncan over the edge?

Sweat beaded on his forehead, and his heart thumped harder. Each second, faster, getting louder in his ears until it seemed it was going to beat through his ribcage and fly out of his chest. His body tensed, his throat tightened.

"Bro, breathe."

He couldn't.

"Come on, bro. Don't make me mouth-to-mouth you." Jacob put a gentle hand on Kaden's chest. "Pull some air in."

It was almost fifteen minutes later by the time Kaden had climbed back out of the pit. Jacob coached him, held him, wiped his sweat and tears away. And he kept telling Kaden everything was going to be all right.

"You okay now, bro?"

"Sort of," Kaden said, Jacob still cradling him against his chest.

"That one was too scary. I swear you were turning blue," Jacob said. "It was my fault too. I shouldn't have told you that. My bad, dude. I'm so stupid. I should have known."

"It's not your fault. You were trying to help. I'm just... I'm just... broken."

"No, you're not, bro. You're not. You're normal. What you've been through, what I've been through. That's rough buddy."

Kaden listened to his brother's words, but he couldn't force himself to believe he was normal.

30

KADEN

A couple of days had passed since Kaden's last panic attack and his anxiety still festered just beneath the surface.

Today, after school, Kaden rushed home from the bus stop and changed into casual clothes. He had a date. After several days of swim team practice in a row, Hunter finally had a free afternoon and Kaden didn't want to waste any time getting over to see him.

Kaden heard Duncan's voice coming from his office and he listened from outside for a moment. He must be on the phone. Surprisingly, he didn't sound as down as he had been, more agitated, if anything.

Kaden entered, waved, and smiled at him.

Duncan nodded at Kaden and held up one index finger as he chatted. His fingertips reached to his forehead. "Geez, they really charge you when they've got you over a barrel. I guess we have no choice. Tell them to go ahead... Huh? Yeah... Okay dear. Thanks. Love you too."

That sounded like an odd way to end a work call.

Duncan hung up, shaking his head. "Hi. I didn't even know you were home already. Wait. You didn't skip classes, did you?"

"No sir."

"Okay. Good." Duncan sighed.

"Everything okay?"

"Oh, just a crisis with a water heater."

"Ours?"

"No. The one at my house in Charlotte. My niece is house-sitting, and she saw water on the floor of the garage this morning. Two thousand bucks to replace. Just what I need."

"You have a house there?" Kaden asked, trying to hide his shock.

"Yeah. It's not as nice as this one. No pool and it's smaller, but it's cozy."

"Oh. I guess I never thought about what you lived in before. So, your niece is there?"

"Yes. Laura's been staying there since I left. She recently graduated from college and is looking for gainful employment, so it works out great."

"What happens if she finds something in another city?"

Duncan shrugged. "I suppose we'll figure that out when it happens. She's an English Lit major, so it might be a while." He smiled. "Well, I guess I better get back to work unless you need something."

Momentarily, Kaden forgot why he'd come into the room in the first place. He shook his head to jar his memory. "Uh, I was wondering, can I go to Hunter's, please?"

"Sure. You haven't hung out with him in several days, right?"

"Right."

"Well, enjoy."

"Thanks." Kaden figured it was futile, but he had to try once more to get Duncan to open up. "Um, are you doing okay?"

"Oh yeah. I mean, I'm two thousand dollars poorer. But otherwise..."

"Okay." Kaden was so frustrated by Duncan's obstinance that he almost gave up, but tried once again. "It's just you have seemed kind of down for a while now."

"Work's been pretty stressful, is all."

"Ah. If you ever need to vent about anything, I'm better at listening than talking."

Duncan smiled, but all too briefly. "Thanks, Kaden. I'm good for now though. You go have, um, well... fun." He winked, then waggled his eyebrows.

Kaden swallowed, and his cheeks warmed. "Bye."

As his hands gripped the bike's handlebars, pavement passing under his wheels, wind whipping through the strands of hair that flowed out of his helmet, there was only one thing on Kaden's mind: Duncan still owned a house in Charlotte. He hadn't sold it. He'd kept an easy escape route for himself. It wasn't even rented out. He could move back without kicking out his niece. And if she found a job and moved somewhere, what then? Might Duncan feel compelled to move back?

He pushed these thoughts away. Hunter was finally free this afternoon. He had missed him terribly. And he deserved Kaden's undivided attention.

As Kaden turned the last corner, he spotted Hunter outside in his driveway, rolling a trash can to the road. He was wearing faded red basketball shorts, no shirt, his hair wet and messy.

The bike's brakes squealed as Kaden came to a stop a few feet from Hunter. "You copying Jacob now?" he asked, face beaming as he removed his helmet.

"What?"

"Shirtless," Kaden said.

"Ah. Yeah. I just got out of the shower, and my skin was too wet to put the shirt on. Is that a problem, chef?"

Kaden gave him a lopsided grin. "Nope."

Hunter parked the trash bin and glanced up and down the street. He stepped toward the bike, straddling the front tire, facing Kaden, and kissed him while putting a hand on his cheek. The tips of his fingers brushed across the nape of Kaden's neck, making his skin tingle. When Hunter pulled back, his grin was wide. "Come on, let's put the bike up and go inside."

After they entered the foyer, Kaden glanced around. Toys were scattered about, but the house was quiet. "Is Zoey here?"

"Emma took her to the park."

"So, we're alone?"

"Yep."

"Oh."

"Should we hang out in my room?"

Kaden's eyes grew wide. "Okay."

They both kicked off their shoes next to the front door. Then Hunter took his hand and led him to the bedroom, closing the door after they were inside.

The bed was made, with Hunter's school uniform pants and shirt hung over a chair back. The room smelled of Hunter's cologne. The afternoon sun filtered in through the sheer white curtains, transforming his bedroom into a softly lit cocoon.

"So, what do you want to do?" Kaden asked.

"I dunno," Hunter said, but then he backed him against the wall, leaned forward, and kissed him hard.

Kaden laughed as Hunter's lips nipped at his chin and cheeks. "That tickles."

"Really? You ticklish anywhere else?"

Their foreheads pressed together. "Maybe."

"Maybe? I think that means yes."

Kaden laughed and kissed him again. "Your lips are so sweet. I mean, literally."

Hunter chuckled and opened his mouth. Clenched between his teeth was some red candy. "Jolly Rancher."

"Oh."

"Want one?"

"Sure."

Hunter opened a desk drawer and got out a bag of candy. "Flavor?"

"Green apple if you got it."

Hunter took a candy from the bag, still in its plastic wrapper. He dangled it in front of Kaden, but as Kaden reached for it, Hunter moved his hand out of reach, smiling mischievously.

Kaden mock pouted.

Hunter winked while removing the wrapper. Then he motioned like he was going to put it into Kaden's mouth, only to once again move his hand away.

"Why are you being mean to me?"

Hunter smiled, then put the candy into his own mouth. He leaned in.

Kaden loved how Hunter smelled, how the scent of his soap and cologne hung on him. He could smell the candy on Hunter's warm breath, the cherry and sweet apple.

He pressed his lips to Kaden's, placing a hand on the back of his neck. Hunter's tongue pushed the candy into Kaden's mouth, and lingered a moment. The taste of the green apple on Kaden's tongue exploded. Hunter backed up.

"Wow," Kaden said, a sense of awe in his voice. He rolled the candy around in his mouth and stared at Hunter with rapt attention. "You got game boy, so much game." Kaden looked away and his voice got quieter. "And I have no clue what I'm doing."

Hunter gave him a smile, his eyes crinkling around the edges. "I don't know what I'm doing either. I'm just winging it."

"This is you just winging it?" Kaden's eyes grew wide.

"Well, you're a great inspiration."

"I am?" Kaden asked.

"Yep." Hunter stared into Kaden's eyes, his own so deep brown they seemed like chocolate.

Kaden shuddered and let his head fall on Hunter's shoulder. "Oh geez," he said under his breath. He was at a loss as to what to do next.

"You okay?" He kissed Kaden's ear.

"I'm fine."

"You don't sound fine," Hunter said.

"It's embarrassing, that's all."

"What's embarrassing?"

Kaden shook his head, muttering, "I don't know. All of it. You see people in movies, being lovey-dovey, and it's so romantic. And you say you're winging it, but you're such a natural, and perfect, while I feel so awkward." His breath quickened, his heart pounded. The excitement he'd felt earlier vanished.

Hunter kissed his temple. "It's okay. We don't have to kiss or anything like that if you don't want to."

The pounding in Kaden's heart wasn't slowing. Not now. Please! Once before, in the kitchen at his house, somehow, Hunter had unwittingly pulled Kaden out of his nosedive into panic by hugging him. He faced Hunter and stared into those bottomless eyes. "Will you hold me?" he asked.

"Of course."

Kaden gave himself up to Hunter's embrace, breathing in deeply as he worked hard to calm his racing heart and mind. He felt as if he was breaking under the weight of his emotions, about to snap into pieces.

"You're breathing kind of fast," Hunter said, apprehension in his voice.

Kaden pulled away from Hunter. He wanted to lie and say there was nothing wrong. But his throat tightened. The thump of his heart grew louder, faster. He tried to imagine Jacob talking him through the attack. Breathe. Breathe. But he *was* breathing. Fast. Too fast. Too shallow.

What was he supposed to do? Why couldn't he remember? A wave of lightheadedness struck him, sending him staggering against a wall.

"Kaden?" Hunter's voice sounded like it was passing through water. "Kaden!"

He took a step away from the wall, his legs turning to jelly, sending him out of control. Hunter's hands gripped him, stopping his fall.

"What's happening?" Hunter said, his voice echoing in Kaden's head. Hunter lifted him, eased him onto the bed. "Should I call 9-1-1?"

Kaden mouthed "No."

"What then?" Hunter didn't wait for an answer. He disappeared from Kaden's view a moment, then returned, phone in hand. Was he calling 9-1-1, anyway? Please, no. No.

"Dude, there's something wrong with Kaden. His heart is really pounding, and he about fell down."

"Is he having a panic attack?" Jacob's voice blared from the phone's speaker.

"I dunno."

Kaden nodded his head.

"He's nodding."

"Is he holding his breath?" Jacob said.

"No. He's breathing really fast."

"He's hyperventilating. Pinch one of his nostrils closed and make him breathe through his nose."

Hunter obeyed Jacob's instructions.

"Bro," Jacob's voiced blared from the phone. "Slow your breaths. Slow it down, buddy. It's gonna be okay."

Jacob's calming reassurance and Hunter's attentive strokes on his forehead guided Kaden back from the edge. Some minutes later, it was over.

"I'm okay now," Kaden said.

"I'm only a few blocks away," Jacob said, sounding out of breath.

"You don't need to come," Kaden said. "I'm fine now. I'm fine."

"You sure?" Jacob asked.

"Yes."

"Okay. If you need me, call back or text, bro."

After they were off the call, Hunter peered into Kaden's eyes, wiping sweat off his face with the corner of the bedsheet.

Hunter's skin was ashen. "You scared me." His voice trembled.

"I'm sorry. I'm so sorry."

"Kaden—I'm sorry. I feel so bad. I guess I was pushing too much. I just really like you. And I've missed you this week."

"It's not you, or anything you did."

"What then?"

"It's me. I'm just broken. I have these panic attacks. I used to have them and thought I outgrew it, but after the wreck, they started again. I've been hiding it."

Hunter leaned over him and held his shoulder. "Have you talked to a doctor or anything?"

"I've got a therapist. He's helped, and Jacob knows how to calm me down, get me breathing right again. But sometimes, I lose control. Like today, I couldn't even remember what to do."

"Oh."

"I guess I should get up and leave now." Kaden leaned up on his elbows, shaking off a slight wave of dizziness.

"Are you sure?"

"Well. Don't you want me to leave?"

"What?! Why would I want you to go?"

Kaden closed his eyes. "I guess I assumed that..." Tears sprang from the corners of his eyes and slid down his cheeks.

Hunter wiped them. "I only want you to go if you have to."

"You don't want to split up?" Kaden asked.

"What? No. Of course not." He lay next to Kaden, cradling him. "I really, really, really like you, Kaden."

Kaden pressed the heels of his hands against his eyes to wipe the tears out. "I like you too." *More than like. Much more.*

"I'm glad. So, does that mean you're staying?"

"I guess, if you want." Kaden let out a deep breath. "I really expected you'd break up with me."

"You wouldn't dump me for that, would you?"

"No. Never."

"Well, there you go. Kaden, if someone's so shitty that they'd split with you for that, you should consider yourself lucky to be rid of them. You deserve better than that."

Kaden didn't know what to say. Instead of speaking, he turned his head and kissed Hunter's cheek.

Hunter smiled. "Can you and Jacob teach me how I can help you if you have another attack? I got some idea of it today, but I want to be able to help you any way I can."

Kaden swallowed a lump in his throat. "Sure." It never entered his mind that not only would Hunter stay with him after the panic attack, but that he'd actually want to help him.

They lay together for some time.

"Do you need anything to drink?" Hunter eventually said, breaking the silence.

Kaden's mouth was dry. "Water would be good."

Hunter fetched two plastic cups of water. The boys sat on a fluffy rug, both leaning against the bed's footboard. Hunter handed him a cup. Kaden drank half in one go.

"So, these panic attacks? Is there something that triggers them?"

Kaden traced his finger over the rim of the cup. "Basically, it's stress. That's the main thing. When everything is shit, it puts me on edge and anything can push me over."

"Has something got you stressed? I know you said it wasn't me, but I'm not sure I believe that." Hunter chewed on his lower lip.

"The only part of it that has to do with you is that I fear you're going to realize how boring I am and dump me."

Hunter put a hand on his own chest and stared at Kaden, his expression emphatic. "You're not boring. Not at all. If anything, I worry you'll get bored with all my stupid swim practices."

"No. I understand. I miss you, but it's important to you, like baking is to me."

"So, if I'm not stressing you, then who is?"

Kaden opened up. He told Hunter all about Duncan and Chip's breakup and about the fact that Duncan wasn't aware that he and Jacob knew the truth about it; his worries about the fact Duncan still had his house in Charlotte; his fears that Duncan would just abandon him and Jacob; that he didn't know what would happen to him if that occurred.

"How serious do you figure it is?" Hunter asked.

"I dunno. Duncan's mood is up and down, but mostly down. I tried to get him to open up to me about it earlier, but he brushed it off. Honestly, I think it's only a matter of time before he leaves. And if he finds out about my panic attacks, it could be sooner rather than later."

"He doesn't know?"

"Not unless Grandpa told him. And well, see, Grandpa made some notes for Duncan to read. The stuff about my attacks was in there. I think Grandpa didn't tell Duncan ahead of time because he was afraid it would scare him off. And I kinda removed some things from the notes. So, I'm pretty sure he doesn't know."

"Well, he won't find out from me."

"Thanks," Kaden said.

"So, do you really think they would separate you and Jacob?"

"Probably. Jacob's biological grandparents were really fighting hard to get custody of him. In fact, they're probably still scheming to get him, just waiting for something to go wrong. And I'd wind up in foster care or a group home or maybe move to the mountains in North Carolina with Grandpa Bill." He shook his head.

"Well, maybe if Duncan went back to Charlotte, he would take you with him."

"Maybe. I suppose that would be better than the mountains. Still, I barely know Duncan and I'd be so far from Jacob."

"And me."

Kaden looked into Hunter's eyes and nodded. "I knew this was too good to be true."

Hunter took Kaden's hand. "The thought of losing you is tearing me up, but then I think about everything you would lose. Kaden, if you do have to leave, and we're separated, I... I would do all I can to be with you again."

"You would?" Kaden's eyebrows raised.

"Of course. Even if it took time, I wouldn't give up on us. We could always be together in *EoOO*. And maybe we could go to the same college."

"College? But you'll be there a year ahead of me," Kaden said. A year to find some hot college jock and forget that Kaden ever existed. "I wonder if I could take summer classes and graduate a year early."

"Do you think you could?"

"I should look into it."

"For sure," Hunter said.

Kaden sighed. "I'm not sure how the schools are in Charlotte, if that's where I wind up."

"You should check and see," Hunter said. "What if, oh man, what if you guys suggested that you move to Charlotte? Like if you talk to Duncan and say you want to move?"

Kaden stared at the floor. "Wow. I hadn't thought about that. Duncan and Chip would be together again. It would be the four of us, just in Charlotte instead of here."

"Yeah," Hunter said. "You'd still give up a lot though. But if you're losing everything anyway, it might be the best option. Cut your losses, as they say. And then we figure out the whole college thing."

"I'm just not sure if the family court judge would let us do that. The other problem would be trying to convince Duncan that we really prefer to move. He might see through that."

"True. Especially since you'd be leaving me. He'd get suspicious something was up."

"And then there's my brother. Would Jacob even want to move? He's not dating anyone right now, so he's less attached than I am."

Hunter chuckled. "It would give him a whole new population of girls to flirt with."

"He might like that. Even so, I'm not sure I could convince Duncan that I really want to move without him getting suspicious. And he'd probably get really pissed if he realized Jacob overheard that conversation with Chip."

Hunter tilted his head. "Hmm. What if we pretend to break up? That would make it more plausible."

"Maybe. But to make it more convincing, Jacob would have to believe we broke up. He's been pretty good at keeping my panic attacks secret, but that's mainly because Duncan doesn't have any clue. But if we pretended to break up, and you and I were the only ones who know it's not true, it might have a better chance."

"With swim practice, we've had little time together anyway, and it's just going to be worse until the season is over."

"If we did pretend to break up, that could be my supposed reason."

Hunter nodded. "Totally plausible. I think that was what happened to one of Jacob's girlfriends last season."

Kaden finished the water, set the glass aside, and wiped his lips. "This is a lot to think about. As scary as it is, I feel better that maybe this is something to try. I'll have to do some research about Charlotte first though."

Hunter went to his desk and grabbed his laptop. "Let's look."

They spent the next while exploring.

"There's a culinary college there," Hunter said.

"What?"

"Johnson and Wales. Have you heard of it?"

"I have. They had a campus near Miami that I was interested in, but they closed it," Kaden said.

"Well, the Charlotte location is still there."

"That would be great for me, but what about you?"

Hunter clicked around on the website. "They offer several business degrees. I'm sure I'd find something to my liking."

Kaden realized he'd never talked to Hunter about his career aspirations. "Is that what you want?"

"Well, I think so. It's worked out for Dad. Leaves a lot of options open. Could come in handy when you need someone to help you with your Michelin rated restaurant. Eh, chef?"

A wave of warmth swept over Kaden, and he smiled. "Here we are dealing with my panic and anxiety, talking about all this college stuff, and I'm pretty sure you had something other than talking in mind for today. Sorry."

"It's okay, babe. They say the key to a relationship is communicating."

"Babe? What happened to *chef*?"

Hunter grinned and lunged toward him, nuzzling him onto the rug, bracing his neck. "Communicating time is over."

Hunter's face had that look on it again. The look that made Kaden's stomach flip and his heart thump in his throat.

Kaden's face widened into a grin. "What time is it, then?"

"What time do you think it is?"

Kaden opened his mouth to respond, but Hunter cut him off with a smashing of their lips together. The kiss was long and deep. Kaden's hands snaked up Hunter's back and curled around his neck. For a while, Kaden's worries gave way to other emotions.

AFTER HE RETURNED HOME from Hunter's that evening, Kaden rushed to his room to change, trying to avoid bumping into Jacob or Duncan. At Hunter's house, his shirt had gotten wadded up on the bedroom floor and was wrinkled when he put it back on. But before he got another tee put on, Jacob barged in, ignoring the closed door.

He stood, arms folded, staring at Kaden, a smug grin on his face. "So, someone's got an afterglow."

"What are you talking about?" Kaden finished pulling on the tee.

"Did you guys do..." Jacob made a sexual gesture.

"Oh my god. No!"

"Damn. That's too bad. Which one of you is playing hard to get?"

Kaden shook his head. "Do I get all up in your business?"

"No. And it makes me wonder if you really care about me." Jacob turned back to the door and shut it. He looked at Kaden, his expression dour. He continued in Filipino. "So, in all seriousness, are you okay, bro?"

"I guess."

"So, I take it Hunter didn't dump your panicky ass?"

"Nope."

"Good. I told you he's an understanding and loyal guy. You really need to learn to listen to me. So, what triggered this one? Or is that getting too much up in your shit?"

Kaden plopped onto his bed. Jacob sat next to him, putting an arm over his shoulders.

"Duncan has a house in Charlotte," Kaden said. "He has a niece named Laura watching the house for him."

"Fuck. No wonder you freaked. How did we not know that? I assumed he just had an apartment."

Kaden shrugged. "He could up and leave us any time and return to his old life. After I found out about his house, I tried to get Duncan to open up about how he was feeling to see if his mood was any better."

"And?" Jacob asked.

Kaden shrugged. "He likes to talk about stuff less than I do. I guess that's where I get it from. Anyway, he still hasn't shared anything about the whole Chip situation."

"Not with me either."

"I'm more worried than ever," Kaden said. "We've got to figure out how to make him happy."

Jacob frowned and looked away. "I guess this would be a bad time to mention that I got suspended for three days."

"In school or out?"

"Out."

"Fuck!" Kaden said in English, surprising himself, and covering his mouth a moment.

"What's worse, is I've got one of those mental health evaluation things with Harry Balls next week," Jacob said with a defeated look in his eyes.

"Harry Billings."

Jacob waved his hand dismissively. "Whatever. I know they call him a doctor, but the dude is an asshole—keeps asking me to give him details about my sex life. Such a creep. Anyway, the school sends my discipline issues to Grandma and Grandpa Rivera, who I'm sure forward them to the quack doctor. He'll totally grill me on that shit. I know it."

"What did you even do?"

"The usual. Got into an 'altercation' yesterday. I think some people are figuring out you and Hunter are together. Hunter talks about you all the time, bragging about your cooking. After swim practice yesterday, we were hanging out, and a friend of Zeke's came around and said some homophobic shit about you and Hunter. Hunter just left, and he told me to leave, too, but you know me."

Kaden massaged his temples, and a gravelly moan rose from his throat. "So, does Hunter know about this?"

"Nope."

"How bad was the 'altercation', as you call it?"

"I don't call it that, bro. Ms. Middleton does. I call it a battle for righteousness and justice-ness."

"Justice-ness?"

"Whatever. Anyway, no blood spillage this time."

"Does Duncan know?" Kaden grabbed his stuffed manatee, wrapped it in his arms and squeezed tight.

"Yep. We already had the conference call. He was not happy. Of course, he hasn't been happy in a while, so it's hard to tell if I made him less happy, or he'd already hit rock bottom."

When Kaden and Hunter had been scheming about pretending to break up, then trying to get Jacob to want to move to Charlotte, Kaden had only half-heartedly considered going ahead with the idea. But he laid awake half the night thinking about it, his mind racing, imagining all the horrible scenarios if he didn't act. Then he'd convince himself he was overreacting and he should just chill, ride this out and hope for the best. He flip-flopped back and forth.

Desperate for guidance, he turned on the lamp beside his bed, and stared at his favorite family portrait. In it, he and Jacob were eleven, just before the puberty train had wrecked him. But that wasn't the only reason he loved that photo. It was the way Mom and Nanay were clinging onto their sons that warmed him the most.

By morning, he'd made up his mind.

Kaden didn't know if the feeling was reciprocated or not, but his own heart overflowed with love for Hunter. Walking away from that wasn't something he could do voluntarily. He simply didn't have the strength. He would have to take his chances and trust that Duncan cared enough for him and Jacob that he wouldn't leave them.

He hoped he wasn't making a huge mistake.

31

DUNCAN

Duncan tapped his fingers anxiously on his mouse pad. Periodically, he glanced out the window at the tropical plantings around the house, then stared blankly at his computer screen.

Work was slow today. It should have come as a welcome break if only his annoying brain would shut the hell up. Instead, he kept ping-ponging between worrying about Jacob's discipline problems, which were likely to impact the guardianship situation, and his ever-growing desire to speak to Chip. Even though their relationship was over, it should have ended better than the way Duncan had left it.

Chip had reached out via text, and even called a few times. Duncan ignored them all. But his anger had subsided now. And he'd had time to figure out exactly who he was enraged at. And it turned out it wasn't Chip after all.

When his workday finally ended, Duncan retired to his bedroom and closed the door. Phone in hand, he stretched out on the bed and leaned against a mound of pillows. His finger trembled as he tapped on the phone's keyboard.

DUNCAN VALENTYN:

Hi.

CHIP MASTERSON:

Um... Hello?

DUNCAN VALENTYN:

I know this is a surprise.

CHIP MASTERSON:

It is.

DUNCAN VALENTYN:

Can we talk? If you have time?

CHIP MASTERSON:

Okay. Now is good.

Duncan put in his earbuds and called. If he were less of a coward, he would have made a video call, but this was going to be difficult enough without having to look Chip in the eye.

"Hello," Chip said.

"Hi. How are you?"

"I've been better, but I'm hanging in there. You?" Chip's voice sounded as if it had been beaten with a bag of bricks.

"Same," Duncan said flatly. He hesitated, unsure how to proceed. "So, I've got some apologizing I need to do."

"Oh."

"And some crow to eat." Duncan took a breath. "You remember how I got furious about you lying to me? And sent you away late at night? And ghosted you?"

"Um. Yes, I do have a slight recollection of all that."

Duncan stroked his forehead with thumb and index finger. "Well, as you may have guessed, since you apparently know me pretty well, I was more furious at the reason you felt you had to lie to me than the actual lie itself. And I wasn't mad at you as much as I was resentful about the fact that you were right to lie."

"I kind of figured all of that, Duncan." There was empathy in

Chip's voice. God, he missed hearing that from Chip, or anyone, for that matter.

"Did you also guess that I'd eventually recognize all of that and come to a point of self-realization?"

"I hoped so, at least for your sake."

"Well, I did. And I'm sorry I took it out on you. I'm sorry for all of it. I owe you. If I had known it would be the end of our relationship, I seriously doubt I would've moved here. You knew that, and I guess I didn't appreciate having it pushed into my face."

"I was in a tight spot," Chip said, sadness in his voice. "There was nothing I wanted more than to be with you. Selfishly, I wanted you to decide not to go to Florida. But I thought about how you would feel about that at some future time, especially if something dreadful happened to the boys. There was no good answer."

"Nope. We just got dealt a terrible hand."

"So, how are you doing, really?" Chip asked.

"Pretty depressed. Even though I'm trying to hide it from the boys, I'm sure they sense it. I didn't want to lay any kind of guilt trip on them, so I told them you and I mutually decided to end things, that we'd just drifted apart. I get the impression they're not buying that."

"How are the boys?"

"I dunno. Sometimes I think it would have been better if I had stayed in Charlotte. Kaden has bags under his eyes and he's looking absolutely frazzled. I need to figure out what's going on with him. Maybe he's getting bullied. I dunno. He's so closed off. And Jacob got into a fight at school over some homophobic shit that had something to do with Kaden and Hunter. Jacob's suspended and will probably be kicked off the swim team. And he's got a mental health evaluation meeting with some crazy-assed therapist coming up. Which, in itself is probably part of some trap the Riveras have set to get Jacob away from me. I mean, I haven't managed to kill either of the boys, at least not yet. So, that's good, right?"

"Wow. You really are having a trial by fire. And you never

expected to do this alone. I'm sorry. I really wish I could be there for you."

"I know."

"I miss you," Chip said. Duncan could sense the yearning in his voice.

"I miss you too, sweetie." *Sweetie?* Should he have said that? How quickly he'd slipped back into that casual intimacy with Chip. There was a long pause. He shouldn't have said it. Damn!

Finally, Chip spoke. "I'm really glad to hear from you. And I realize it isn't easy for you to say everything you did, apologizing and all. I had confidence that you would eventually though."

"You did?"

"Yep." Chip laughed. "I know you pretty well."

"Obviously."

"I've been looking for jobs down there, babe," Chip said.

Now he said *babe*. Was it intentional or inadvertent? "Really?"

"Don't get excited. The market is still horrible. There are no tech companies there, really. I saw one job that sounded decent, but it was paying about half what I make and they wouldn't even give me a phone interview because I was too far out of their pay range."

"I know," Duncan said. "If I ever get laid off, I'm screwed if I can't find a remote job."

"Of course there are jobs further south. I'd just have to commute three or four hours a day."

"Yeah. I love the location here. It's got a quaint feel. And the house is wonderful. But everything else in my life is shit right now." Duncan let out a nervous laugh.

"It'll get better, I'm sure. Give it time."

"Chip. I know that this is a big ask, especially after ghosting you for so long, but can we be friends... long distance friends? Sometimes, I just need someone to talk to. I realize I'm high maintenance, especially now, so if it's too much to ask, I get it."

"Duncan. I will always be your friend. Always."

"I can't tell you how much that means to me." Duncan wiped his eyes. Should he say the other thing he wanted to? Hell, why not? What was there to lose? "You know I still love you."

"I love you too."

"You didn't have to say that just because I did."

"I said it because it's true, babe."

Duncan let out a breath. "I guess I better let you go now."

"Okay. Take care. And call me if you ever need to talk to a friend."

"Thanks. I will."

They ended the call and Duncan got out of the bed, took a few steps toward the sliding door, then stared out at the pool, as the orange hues of the late afternoon sun cast a golden glow and long shadows.

He sniffed, his cheeks wet with tears—tears that still flowed, unstoppable.

As he stood staring at nothing, a figure surprised him. Kaden appeared on the concrete deck, walking to the entry steps of the pool. Startled, Duncan gasped loud enough to be heard outside.

Kaden whirled around. Their eyes met. Kaden's forehead furrowed and his jaw dropped. As Kaden stared, he bit his lower lip, then walked to the door, tilted his head. He looked at Duncan in the same way one would gaze at a lost puppy.

Duncan turned away and wiped his eyes. There was a knock on the glass door. He ignored it. Another knock, harder, louder.

"Duncan? Let me in."

Duncan turned partly toward the door, but froze.

"Please," Kaden said.

Duncan reached a hand to the lock and flipped it, then walked a few steps away. The door slid open behind him and then closed.

"Duncan. What is it?"

His throat was too tight to speak. He shook his head, unable to meet Kaden's gaze.

A moment later, the teen's thin arms wrapped around him, squeezing tight.

"You miss him, don't you?" Kaden said.

Duncan made a sound that was a reasonable approximation of confirmation.

"Do you still love him?" Kaden asked.

Duncan wrapped his arms around Kaden's slender body and swallowed, willing his throat to let him speak. "Yes."

"And he loves you?"

"Um hm."

Duncan looked down at Kaden's face. His eyes were closed, tears streaming. They held each other for some time before Duncan pulled himself together.

"I thought you don't hug. Isn't that your rule?" Duncan said.

Kaden sniffed. "You looked like you needed it. I decided to make an exception."

"It's appreciated, Kaden. Very much. I feel better already."

"No problem. You and Chip, you didn't just decide to break up, did you?"

Should he admit the truth? Duncan exhaled. "No."

Kaden squeezed tighter. "You could have told us."

"I didn't want to burden you guys."

"I understand." Kaden let him go and stepped back, wiping his eyes.

"Thank you," Duncan said, mussing Kaden's hair. "I guess you should go hop in the pool if you're going to before dinner."

"Yes sir." He turned and walked to the door, then looked back at him. "If you ever need a hug again, let me know. I'll break my rule for you, Duncan."

As he watched Kaden walking away, something clicked in his brain, like a gear that had been jammed up, but suddenly fell into place. A moment of clarity that he knew he'd have to analyze later, but not in this moment. In this moment, he urgently needed to do something though. It had to be now.

"Kaden, wait."

"Yes?" he said, turning back.

"I love you, son."

Growing up, Duncan had rarely heard those words exchanged among his family members. His mother's family had mostly lived in North Carolina. It was odd how many of them stayed inside the state, like mimes trapped in an imaginary box whose borders coincided with the state line. He'd rarely heard any members of her family say these words. He felt loved, nonetheless. That stood in contrast to Roz and her father. They never left the house or hung up the phone without an "I love you." The Valentyn side of his own family was the same way, though he rarely saw them. They all dropped those three words all the time.

Duncan thought back to that conversation with Kaden when they'd talked about romantic love, and the potential hurt of saying "I love you," and not hearing the words echoed back. The realization struck Duncan that all the hesitation he'd had about meeting the boys in the first place had been rooted in a fear that they wouldn't love him. This would be another one-sided love, like the first boy he'd fallen for. Insecurity had paralyzed him all along. Now that he'd inadvertently been emotionally exposed when Kaden saw him crying, he just threw everything wide open, and said the words he should have had the courage to say long ago, regardless of whether he ever heard them back.

Kaden froze, his eyes widened. "You do?"

"I do. Your whole life, I've loved you."

Kaden looked like he was going to fall over. Duncan ran to him and held him. Kaden wrapped his arms around him again, tears flowing, resting his wet face against Duncan's chest. "I love you, too... Dad."

Dad! After having barely composed himself, Duncan lost it again. Through his own tears, he spoke, sniffing. "I should have told you that a long time ago, son. And I need to tell Jacob too. I love you both so much. More than anyone... ever."

Duncan could feel the tension melting out of Kaden's body. When they finally stopped hugging, and Kaden left the room, his son seemed like a different person. It was as if some spell had been cast.

32

KADEN

Kaden swam back and forth through the pool, occasionally submerging before rising to the surface, lap after lap. He swam until he was exhausted, then went to the shallow end and rested partially submerged on the steps, panting. He leaned back, his face cast toward the orange and purple sky of sunset.

I love you, son. The words had echoed in his mind over and over since Duncan had said them. The tension had immediately melted out of his body. He'd nearly collapsed to the floor, as if nothing had suspended his bones but worry. For the first time since he watched Roz take her last breath, a certain tranquility enveloped Kaden that he thought he'd never experience again.

Duncan would not abandon him and Jacob. They were a genuine family now.

Kaden caught his breath, sucking huge gulps of the humid late afternoon air. Recovered, he plunged again into the water, suddenly full of energy, swimming the length of the pool and back, over and over.

But there was an image he couldn't shake: the pain in Duncan's eyes seared into his mind. The pain had been raw, and certainly

Duncan had never meant for anyone to see him so vulnerable, but for an all too brief moment, his heart was there, exposed, naked.

Before Kaden had suffered the profound loss of his mothers, and before he had fallen in love with Hunter, he never could have comprehended how much Duncan needed Chip. His soul yearned for this man who had come into his life. He'd searched for decades to find him, only to see a cruel twist of fate steal him away.

As the water had flowed over his body, with each stroke, Kaden's own needs washed away with the lapping waves, as if his body and spirit were being cleansed. With each stroke, a passion grew in his heart. His mission became clear. He and Hunter must go through with their plan. Duncan and Chip needed each other.

That evening, tucked into his bed, lights turned out, he texted Hunter.

KADEN RIVERA-WATSON:

I need to talk to you

HUNTER GAN:

Can you just text?

KADEN RIVERA-WATSON:

I think we should talk in person

HUNTER GAN:

Is this about what I think it is?

KADEN RIVERA-WATSON:

Probably

HUNTER GAN:

Can you sneak outside?

KADEN RIVERA-WATSON:

Yes

HUNTER GAN:

Meet at OH park?

KADEN RIVERA-WATSON:

Okay

Kaden slid on shorts, a tee and sneakers. Roz and Angie had known better than to give this bedroom to Jacob. It would have been too easy for him to sneak out through the sliding door. So, Kaden got it because they knew he was the good kid, who wasn't likely to be on the prowl at night. They were mostly right, but not tonight. He eased the door open.

The park was a small neighborhood one, with a playground and a boat ramp next to a canal. It wasn't exactly on a direct line between his and Hunter's house, but not far off.

He could walk there if need be, but opted to tiptoe into the garage from the side door and get his bike.

When he got to the park, Hunter was already there, sitting on a bench next to the canal. Nausea arose from the pit of Kaden's stomach.

Despite all of his trepidation, Kaden pushed through the park gate, headed for the bench where Hunter was waiting for him. Hunter's eyes were teary when Kaden approached, but he looked so relieved to see him that the sickening feelings in Kaden's stomach intensified. He wanted to turn around and head home, but he knew he could not.

Kaden got off his bike and walked toward him. As he neared Hunter, he could see Hunter's hands trembling. They embraced and let go of each other. Hunter wiped away his tears.

Frogs, insects and the occasional distant truck or motorcycle disturbed the quiet. They sat on the bench, holding hands.

"How are you?" Hunter asked.

"I'm a mess."

"A hot mess." Hunter offered a faint smile that faded all too soon.

"You?" Kaden asked.

"Same."

Kaden sat, frozen, sensing the anxiety in Hunter's hands.

Hunter broke the silence. "So, what did you need to talk about?"

Kaden exhaled. "I need to try to move to Charlotte."

Hunter squeezed his eyes closed momentarily. "I figured as

much. Is it truly that bad? Do you really think Duncan is ready to abandon you guys?"

Kaden hesitated. "Actually, no."

"What?"

Kaden recounted to Hunter the moment he'd shared with Duncan, seeing him in tears, the pain in his eyes. The hugs. All of it. "He called me *son* and said he loved me."

"Holy shit. Is that the first time he did either of those?"

Kaden nodded. "And I told him I loved him back and called him *Dad*."

Hunter grasped Kaden's hand and kissed his cheek. "I can't imagine what that must have been like for you."

"I know, right? It almost made me sort of low-key cry a little, maybe. Our moms always made sure we had plenty of male role models in our lives. Jacob with his sports, and I did summer camps and scouting for a while. I'm grateful for that. It helped me. But I hadn't realized how special it would feel to actually call someone Dad. It still hasn't sunken in. And as great as that was, the entire conversation was so heartbreaking."

"Yeah?"

"I can't stop thinking of his face, the pain from missing Chip." Kaden's throat tightened. "When Grandpa first told me and Jacob about Duncan, we asked him a million questions. And he told us that once, Duncan was in a horrible relationship with a guy who had substance abuse problems. At the time, I thought Grandpa might be making it up to scare us into not doing drugs. But now, I feel like it must have been true."

"Oh, wow."

"And I think about how long it took Duncan to find someone he wanted to share his life with, then to have him taken from him." Kaden slumped.

"That's rough."

"I can't do it. I can't take that from him. As much as I want us to be together, Duncan deserves it more. He's earned the right to be happy. He's saved me from who knows what by getting custody of us. I owe him this."

Hunter stared into the night. "I agree." He looked Kaden in the eye. "I agree."

"I don't know if the court will let us move, but I have to try."

"I'll do anything I can to help you, though I don't know what that might be. And I promise you this, we'll be together again. I swear it."

Kaden glanced around at the park. "In the time we have left, we might need to keep sneaking out here at night while we still can."

"Yes." Hunter nudged closer to him. "The worst part of this is I care for you more now than ever. That you would do this for Duncan. You're the most romantic and kind-hearted person I've ever met." He leaned in and kissed him. "I'm gonna miss you so much, Kaden."

Kaden wished to tell Hunter that he loved him, but he couldn't. Those three words would merely make parting that much harsher, that much more painful. "I'll miss you too."

Hunter nodded. "I need you to know I'll be thinking about you every day."

Kaden swallowed hard, feeling himself begin to quiver. "You will?"

"Of course." Hunter squeezed his hands harder. "So, how are we going to do this? The fake breakup?"

"I guess we'll blame it on your swim practice."

"Okay. That makes the most sense."

"I'll tell my brother first. I've got to convince him if I can. That's gonna be the trickiest part. Jacob knows me too well."

Kaden and Hunter chatted for a while longer, discussing the finer details of their fake breakup, then kissed goodbye.

THE HOUSE WAS dark when Kaden sneaked back in through the sliding door to his bedroom. When he'd left, the great room TV's surround sound speakers had been booming. Duncan had been watching *Notting Hill* and *Four Weddings and a Funeral* over and over all week. But now, the house was quiet as a whisper.

No sooner than he'd gently closed and locked the slider, he was startled.

"Boo!" Jacob said, turning on a light on Kaden's desk at the same time.

Kaden let loose a string of Filipino expletives. "You could have killed me," he said, clutching his chest.

"Well, that's what you get for sneaking out without telling me. So, getting serious with Hunter, I guess. Two booty calls in one day."

"No," Kaden said.

"Not a booty call? Too bad. What then? Wait! You got a side piece, bro?"

"Oh my god. No. Just stop."

"Wow. Your kind are so touchy." Jacob's smile disappeared, though, and his eyebrows furrowed in concern. He tilted his head as he glared at him. "What's going on?"

Kaden sat on the bed, staring at the floor, steeling himself to lie as convincingly as he could. "Hunter and I decided to just be friends."

Jacob took two steps back. "What? Why?"

Kaden shrugged, still averting Jacob's stare. "He's busy with practice all the time."

"Oh. I've been dumped for that." Jacob sat next to Kaden. "Is that all? He didn't hurt you or anything?" Jacob's body tensed. "I mean, he's my best friend, but I will mess him up if he hurt you, bro. You know that."

"No. Nothing like that. Don't hurt him. And we're still friends, and still gonna hang out and play *EoOO* together."

"Okay. That's cool." Jacob's clenched jaw and fist relaxed. "I thought you guys were totally into each other."

"I think I was merely excited someone was interested in me. And when that wore off, we didn't have much chemistry."

Jacob scrunched his face in a way that made Kaden fear he wasn't buying the lie. He had to sell it better. "You remember when I had that panic attack at his house?" Kaden asked.

"Yeah."

"The reason I got triggered was that I was going to try to tell him that day... to break up. I couldn't go through with it then."

"Oh. That's what that was about." Jacob exhaled. "I'm sorry it didn't work out, bro. I truly am. He's a great guy, but you can't force yourself to feel something, you know?"

"Yep."

"I'm glad I don't have to mess him up for you though. I'm in enough trouble as it is already. Looks like they might kick me off the swim team."

"I heard. And all over a fight for nothing, it turns out."

"No. Not for nothing," Jacob said. "Whether or not you guys are together, nobody should talk that kind of homophobic shit about either of you. I wouldn't change a thing."

Kaden locked eyes with Jacob and stared at him intensely, searching Jacob's face for any sign of doubt or regret, but Jacob didn't flinch. Kaden hoped he was doing as convincing a job of lying as Jacob was.

Jacob looked away first. "How did Hunter take getting dumped? Was he okay?"

"He'll be fine. I don't think he was terribly heartbroken."

Jacob nodded. "I'll have to check in with him tomorrow and see how he's doing. So, not to change the subject or anything, but I had an interesting convo with the bio-dad. And I heard you did too. I'm kind of surprised you didn't tell me about it."

"He said he was going to talk to you; I didn't want to steal his thunder."

"Makes sense," Jacob said, but there was hurt in his voice.

Kaden put a hand on his brother's knee. "I'm gonna be calling him Dad from now on, by the way. Not Duncan, not bio-dad."

Jacob smiled. "I guess I will, too, then. Maybe that will cheer him up. I can't take much more of this moping and him watching these chick flicks every single night. You're gay, so maybe you don't mind it, but damn..."

"Tell me about it."

"So, bro, are you gonna be okay now? Do you feel better about your abandonment fears? I mean, he says he loves us. That's got to count for something."

"I do feel better. But..." Kaden's voice trailed off. He hadn't even planned to tell Jacob that he and Hunter had broken up this soon. He figured he'd stew on it, lying awake all night. But he'd seized this opportunity. Should he go to stage two of the plan already? Would that be too fast? It might make Jacob suspicious.

"But what?"

"Nothing."

"Come on. Talk to me."

Kaden swallowed. "Have you ever thought about moving?"

"Moving? Where?"

"Charlotte."

Jacob's eyes widened. "Wow. Have you thought about it?"

"Yes. A lot. I've even done some research on the city. There's a culinary college there. They have lots of sports stuff in the city too. You might like that."

"I never even thought about it for a second. Are you seriously considering this?"

"I am. I just think about what... Dad... what Dad gave up to be with us. And I kinda feel like this might be a way to give something back to him. To let him know with more than only words that I do love him."

Jacob let his torso fall back on the bed and put his arms behind his head, casting his gaze at the ceiling. "We'd have to give up a lot, bro. Gabby and Hunter. All our friends. That would be rough, buddy."

"It could also be a fresh start, though, especially if you get kicked off the swim team here. And we can always stay in touch with Gabs and Hunter and play *EoOO* together."

Jacob didn't speak. His chest rose and fell as he took several deep breaths. "Dad is such a downer right now. It's kinda depressing to be around him. What about the custody agreement stuff, though? Could we even do it? Grandpa Cesar and Grandma Maya would launch a shit storm if their visitation rights with me were threatened in any way."

"I dunno. We could ask Tamika. See if it would even be possible. Do that before we get Dad's hopes up."

"Yeah. I could call her since I'm on this unplanned school break for three days," Jacob said.

"Speaking of school, since I still have to go tomorrow, I should get some sleep."

After Jacob left, Kaden exhaled. This was moving so fast. He hadn't even planned to start phase one until tomorrow, and here he was, already into phase two. He was doing this. His stomach tightened and churned. He was actually doing this.

He didn't know what scared him more: that the plan would fail, or that it would succeed.

33

KADEN

Kaden was certain Jacob would want to chat with Hunter about their *breakup*. He and Hunter had to have a consistent story if they were going to pull off this ruse. So, early the next morning, before he even arose from bed, Kaden messaged Hunter to let him know about his late-night conversation with Jacob so they would the on the same page.

After arriving home from school, Kaden checked in with Jacob, not only to see how he was coping with his suspension, but also to make sure the sham breakup hadn't been discovered.

Jacob was stretched out on the sofa, remote in hand, wireless headphones on his head, binging *Avatar: The Last Airbender* for the hundredth time. His hair was a mess, even by his standards. He paused the video and pulled the headphones off his ears. "How was school, bro? Did I miss anything?"

"Just a typical day. I'll send you my notes." Kaden strained his neck, looking toward Duncan's office. The door was closed, but he still feared Duncan might hear him. Kaden shoved Jacob's legs out of the way so he could sit next to him. "You thought any about what I spoke to you about last night?" he said in Filipino.

"You mean moving?" Jacob replied in Filipino as well.

Kaden nodded.

"Well, I thought about it some," Jacob said.

"Did you talk to Tamika?"

"Oh, no. I forgot."

Kaden's eyes grew, and he pushed the palm of his hand hard into Jacob's shoulder. "I texted you twenty times to remind you."

Jacob laughed. "You're so gullible, bro. I called her."

"And?"

"I told her about the whole Duncan and Chip situation and about the idea of moving. She wasn't optimistic."

"What? Why?"

Jacob looked at him, then averted his eyes. "Bro, I think I might have really fucked up."

"How? What's going on?"

"My fight may have some bigger impacts than just the suspension. I'll probably get kicked off the swim team, but it gets worse. When I was on the phone with Tamika, she was like, are you in school today? So, I had to tell her about the suspension."

"And?"

"Bro, she went off on me. I never knew you could mix cussing like a sailor and legalese in the same sentence, but damn if she didn't. This whole thing is gonna be reported to Grandpa Cesar's lawyers, and also to that Harry Balls quack."

"Oh god." Kaden sighed. "At least Dad will fight for us. I know he will now. And Tamika's smart. Grandpa Bill always says she's smart."

Jacob shook his head. "That may not be enough. Tamika said this whole guardianship compromise was probably a trap. And it looks like I just sprang it."

"Did she say what might happen?"

"Worst case, they might be able to convince the judge that Duncan's an unfit parent. Then he loses custody of both of us."

Kaden's head collapsed back onto the sofa cushion and he stroked the bridge of his nose. "God. Jacob, you should have just walked away like Hunter said."

"I know that *now*, bro. But it's too late at this point." Jacob put a hand on Kaden's leg. "She said it probably won't be that bad, but it's possible. More likely though, is that I could wind up with Cesar and Maya. And I swear, I will run away if that happens."

Kaden groaned. "You can't do that."

"Well, then I'll just annoy the shit out of them until they beg me to leave."

"You probably annoy them anyway."

Jacob smirked. "Truly."

"Did Tamika say what our chances are?" Kaden asked.

"She started to, but I told her to never tell me the odds."

"Oh my god. Why?"

"You know I can never pass up an opportunity to drop a *Star Wars* quote."

Kaden's jaw clenched. He would have to call Tamika himself. He sat in silence for a minute and took a few deep breaths, though he feared his anger might be the only thing keeping him from sinking into a panic. Finally, he spoke again. "So, assuming we somehow stay in Dad's custody, and that Tamika can get the court to let us move, what are your thoughts about it? Would you want to try it?"

Jacob stared toward Duncan's office. "I dunno. Dad's still being mopey, so I watched some YouTube vids on the city and read the wiki page. I mean, it's a place with stuff. Just like this is a place with stuff." He shrugged. "I worry about missing our friends, bro, and can we make new ones?"

"Well, Gabby and Hunter are great friends," Kaden said, "but my very best friend is you. As long as I've got you, I'm good."

"How can you say that after I possibly screwed us both?"

Kaden half smiled. "Because I know you meant well. Even when you mess up, you do it out of love."

"Ugh. Don't get mushy on me, bro." Jacob turned away. But then he turned back and pulled Kaden into a tight hug. "Let me think about it some more," he said, releasing the hug.

"Fair enough."

"Well, I should do some assignments, I guess." Jacob switched off the TV and headed to his room.

Kaden exhaled, relieved that Jacob hadn't even mentioned the *breakup*. However, he wasn't confident Jacob was as inclined to move to Charlotte as he was. Kaden was certain that Jacob had never fallen in love, despite his string of girlfriends. For Kaden, it was different. He knew the power of true love. He appreciated what Duncan had sacrificed for them. Every fiber of his being empathized.

Jacob couldn't understand that, at least not at this stage in his life. And Jacob would never know how much harder it was for two gay people to find each other. It was easy for Jacob to flirt and ask girls out, because that's what society expected him to do. But Kaden and Duncan were swimming against the stream.

Kaden walked to his room and changed out of his school uniform, then headed to the kitchen to clean some pots and pans.

He and Gabby had planned to have another go at cake-baking practice today. Even though he wasn't in the mood, Kaden hadn't canceled. If his scheme succeeded, he may very well not even be in Florida by the time the contest happened. All their baking practice would be for nothing. But if he was going to make this plan work, Gabby would have to believe the breakup was real. Her visit was his opportunity to see one way or the other.

He also hoped that getting into his *happy place*, the kitchen, might calm him after the bomb Jacob had dropped on him.

Some time later, Gabby slid open the door, sandals flopping off as she entered the kitchen to join him.. "So, how was snooty private school today?"

"The usual. Public school?" Kaden said, slipping his apron on over his head. It was the new one Duncan had gotten him. He handed her the matching apron.

"Same," she said. "Anything new going on?" Her eyes darted about.

Kaden sighed. Jacob must have already told her about the *breakup.* "No," he said.

"Oh, really?" She put her apron on and turned her back to Kaden. He tied her apron strings as he always did.

"Nothing you haven't already heard, apparently." He tied his own apron.

She spun around and glared. "Well, I'm surprised and disappointed I had to hear it from Jacob. Why didn't you tell me?"

Kaden shrugged. He would have a harder time getting a lie past Gabby than he did Jacob. She had an instinctive ability to read him. Navigating this conversation required extreme care. "You know me," he said, getting a mixing bowl out of a cabinet and avoiding letting her see his eyes.

"Well, you could have texted me if you didn't want to talk about it."

"Not much to talk about. We're just better off as friends, that's all." Kaden continued to avoid eye contact, retrieving measuring cups and spoons, along with the ingredients.

"So who dumped who?"

Kaden opened the cupboard where they kept the stand mixer, then beckoned Gabby over. Together, they picked it up and set it on the counter, while he replied. "Nobody dumped anyone. We mutually decided to be friends only."

"Friends, or friends with benefits?" Gabby asked.

"Oh my god. Just friends."

"Is it because you're both the same... how can I say this?"

Kaden glared at her. "If it's something to do with sex position stuff, then you don't need to say it at all."

She rolled her eyes. "Okay, then."

Kaden shook his head. "Geez, you're as bad as my brother."

She waved a dismissive hand at him. "Seriously? That's a low blow, Kaden. So, Hunter is still gay?" Gabby's eyebrows raised.

"What kind of question is that? Of course he is." Kaden got eggs and butter out of the refrigerator.

"Okay. Okay. You don't have to jump all over me."

"You're still low-key crushing on him, aren't you?"

"Well, he's still hot? Can't a girl hope he might be bi?" She eyed him suspiciously. "You're not jelly, are you?"

He looked away. "Why would I be jealous? We're only friends. Now, are we baking a cake today or only gabbing?"

"I don't get it, Kaden. You seemed so obsessed with each other."

He started measuring cake flour and dumping it into the mixing bowl. "I wasn't into Hunter as much as you were. I think I was more excited that someone was actually interested in me. That's never happened to me before. And when that wore off, I realized we didn't have any magic beyond being friends."

"I guess I get it. I was so shipping you guys though. It makes me sad. After all you've been through, I wanted you to be happy. You deserve it."

Kaden stopped fiddling with the cake ingredients and looked her in the eyes, then exhaled. "I am happy." It wasn't entirely a lie. Having to pretend he wasn't in love with Hunter tore and twisted at his gut, but the bond he and his father forged truly lifted his spirits.

Their attention turned to cake-baking, and some time later, Duncan left his office and passed through the kitchen. He stopped and rested a hand on Kaden's shoulder. "Hi Gabby. Son, how's the cake coming?"

"Going good, Dad."

Duncan looked at Gabby. "You and my son are torturing me, making me smell these yummy cakes baking all the time."

She grinned at Duncan, and he headed to his bedroom. Then Gabby arched an eyebrow at Kaden, her mouth hanging open. "Son? Dad? When did this start?"

Kaden gave her a sideways smile. "Yesterday."

She put a hand on his back. "No wonder you're happy."

"Yeah."

"Well," Gabby said, "at least *this* relationship is going well. That's the most important. If one of your relationships had to fail, it's better that it was the one with Hunter. After all, it's not like that probably would have lasted that long anyway, a jock and a nerd. Am I right?"

Kaden felt like a knife had just been stuck into his gut and twisted. He turned away from her, checking his cakes through the oven window to hide his face. He swallowed through a knot in his throat. "For sure." What did she mean, it wouldn't have lasted that long?

"Sometimes you hear about someone marrying a high school sweetheart, but usually, it's old people," she said. "It's very rare these days. Our generation is more practical. Dating around, keeping options open. It's better that way."

Was that true?

Gabby's words weighed heavily on Kaden as reality slowly dawned. If she was right, maybe deep down, he'd known that all along. Was that why he'd concocted this scheme in the first place?

As Kaden took the cake tins out of the oven, he tried to shake the worries from his mind, but they clung to him like his own shadow. It was hard not to wonder if, perhaps, he had had this all along, this fear and insecurity, but that he'd chosen to ignore them on purpose. Maybe, after all he'd been through, his subconscious was trying to save him from worse heartbreak later. This was a self-defense mechanism, like a turtle, drawing its limbs back into the shell.

Had Hunter seen this as well? Was that why he'd agreed to it so easily? Kaden got a sinking feeling. Whose idea was it in the first place, this whole fake breakup? Kaden thought it was his idea, but now he wasn't sure. Had Hunter suggested it? Was Kaden being manipulated? Could this entire scheme be a low-key way for Hunter to dump him without him even realizing it? After witnessing the panic attack, had Hunter decided that Kaden was too high main-tenance?

His heart quickened. Kaden sensed disappointment and betrayal welling up. What if everything that Hunter had said was a lie or an act?

No. This couldn't be true. Could it?

He'd already determined he wouldn't get any sleep tonight from worrying about the custody situation. He didn't need this cloud hanging over him as well.

34

DUNCAN

Duncan concluded another workday and headed to the great room. His sons were playing the elf game, but the sounds of simulated carnage that reverberated through the house all afternoon had mostly quieted.

"Hey, are you guys done with your homework?"

"Yep," Jacob said, not looking up from the computer screen.

Duncan wasn't sure he believed him. At least he was back in school after the three-day suspension, but he was not permitted at swim practice for now, while they decided if he would be allowed to remain on the team.

"Kaden?"

"Yes sir... Dad."

"Okay. Listen, are you guys at a stopping point? I need to chat about something."

"Yeah, we're in the city, selling our loot," Jacob said.

"I've got a business trip. I have to go to Charlotte this weekend."

"Okay. Have fun." Jacob turned back to the game.

"I don't think you understand. I can't leave you guys alone."

"What? Why not?" Jacob asked. "We're fifteen."

"I don't think I can."

"Sure you can, dude. We'll be fine."

Duncan shook his head. "I'm sure you wouldn't starve or anything, but it's more about the court custody agreement." Plus, he wasn't sure he trusted Jacob. He didn't want to come home to a wrecked party house, recalling an incident in his own childhood instigated by his older brother, Matt.

"Could we stay at Gabby's? She's been bugging me to have another sleepover anyway," Kaden asked.

"I don't know if that would work," Duncan said. "I'm thinking more along the lines of seeing if Tamika can stay here."

"Oh."

"There is one other option," Duncan said. "My brother, Matt and his family are going to be in Charlotte visiting our parents for Labor Day weekend. I've checked and there are some cheap flights out of Orlando. Would you like to go to Charlotte with me to meet your aunt and uncle, along with some cousins?"

Kaden's and Jacob's faces lit up as they cast glances at each other.

Jacob looked at Duncan. "I'm in, but I only fly first-class, Duncan."

"Then you're not in," Duncan said.

He groaned. "Dios mío. Fine. I'll pretend I'm a commoner. You're lucky I'm such a dutiful son."

"I'd like to go, but I'll need air sickness pills," Kaden said. "Oh, and gum to help my ears pop. A new travel pillow would be good. I threw up on my old one."

"Okay, we'll hit the store later, but I'll go book our tickets."

THAT EVENING, when Duncan tried to watch *Four Weddings and a Funeral* again, his sons had raised holy hell. They watched one of the *Lord of the Rings* movies instead.

He went to the master bedroom suite and undressed to shower.

He hated this master bathroom. If he ever met the sadistic asshole of a designer who had decided it was a good idea to put four full-length mirrors in a room he walked around naked in, violence was a high probability.

After bathing, he turned the bedroom lights down and settled into the bed to read a cozy mystery.

At least that's how he envisioned he'd spend his time before going to sleep. Three pages in, he'd read the same paragraph five times, his mind drifting to thoughts of Chip.

Late this coming Friday night, assuming the highway gods were kind enough to let them get to Orlando in time to catch the flight, and Jacob didn't get into any fisticuffs with other passengers, and Kaden somehow managed to pull through without puking his guts out, Duncan would be in the same city with Chip for the first time since the night he'd kicked him out, the night Chip's lie was revealed.

That he still loved Chip was not in question, and never had been. Since the reconciliation, they'd kept in touch via text or the occasional voice call, but the conversations were mundane. Despite his desires, Duncan doubted that he would be able to maintain a friendship with him. He suspected they'd gradually contact each other less and less, until one day, he'd realize it had been years. It would be like it was with Roz.

Given that likelihood, he wondered if it would even be worth trying to meet up with Chip this weekend. Maybe he should put the ball in Chip's court.

He set the book down and took his phone off the charger, then called.

"Hey," Chip said.

"I didn't wake you, did I?"

"Nope."

"So, I've got a business trip to Charlotte this weekend. We've got to run a disaster recovery test and, of course, they want to ruin a three-day weekend by doing it then."

"Naturally," Chip said, laughing. "So Cindy's making you come in?"

"She didn't order it, but strongly hinted, and they recently gave me a big raise, so some combination of guilt and duty kinda kicked in."

"Is that why? Really?" Chip asked.

"Well, I know it's a holiday weekend and you've probably got plans already, and it's such short notice, but..."

"I have time on Saturday night," Chip said.

"Saturday? No hot date?"

"Nope. Not much in the dating mood, I guess."

"Me either." Duncan exhaled. "I just wonder if it's a good idea or not. Us meeting up, that is. Are we twisting the knives in our wounds?"

"I'd like to see you, Duncan. I didn't like the way our last in-person encounter ended."

"Same," Duncan said. "I'm not sure of my exact work schedule yet. We're still ironing out the details."

"I'll leave my schedule open. Text me when you learn more."

"Will do."

They talked a while longer, again, keeping it mundane, because anything deeper would hurt too much.

After they hung up, Duncan stared at the picture of Chip on his phone's contact screen: the bright eyes, the toothy grin, and the dimples. Oh, the dimples. Those dimples had gotten him into this predicament in the first place.

He thought back to the day they'd met. It was one of the rare days Duncan had to go into the office. Some vendors were coming in to do presentations. Duncan entered the conference room and saw his boss, Cindy, chatting with someone. Everyone was wearing a mask, but as Duncan approached Cindy, the man she was chatting with took his off for a moment.

"There are those dimples," Cindy said. "God, I remember them."

The man put the mask back on before Duncan got a proper look.

"Oh Duncan," Cindy said. "This is Chip Masterson, from Zotromia Datanetechs. Duncan Valentyn is one of my Disaster Recovery analysts."

"Oh. Nice to meet you."

"Likewise," Chip said.

"Chip and I were in college together, worked on a group project. And he has the cutest dimples," Cindy said, giggling like a schoolgirl.

Even the mask couldn't hide Chip's blushing.

Duncan took a deep breath and held it for a few seconds. He was not the flirty type, especially at work, and after being isolated from human contact for so much of the last two years with the pandemic, even less so. Yet, despite that, and even though he really had no idea who this man was, Duncan couldn't help himself. "Dimples? Really? Let me see."

Chip obliged, cheeks still red. He looked straight into Duncan's eyes, and pulling the mask down, grinned at him.

That's all it took. Duncan was obsessed. After the meeting, Duncan had taken Cindy aside.

"Okay, is Chip on your team, or my team?" Duncan asked. She knew he was referring to his sexual orientation.

"I honestly don't know," Cindy said. "Back in college, I already had a boyfriend, so I just admired the dimples from afar. He's a nice guy though."

That night, Duncan did what any normal person would, who had just become obsessed with a guy whose orientation he couldn't figure out. He cyber-stalked him. Or he tried to. The guy was some kind of freak, with none of the usual social media accounts as far as Duncan could detect. He'd have to be more direct.

Asking Chip to show him his dimples was already well out of Duncan's comfort zone, but he figured, go big or go home. The next morning, he emailed Chip. It was a polite but pointless message, just saying nice to meet you. But he typed a postscript: By the way, you really do have great dimples.

After he'd hit send, he wondered if he could retract the message.

If he turned out to be straight, and they ever came face-to-face again, it would be awkward, but there was no way to retract it. And so, Duncan sat in his chair, tapping his fingers on his mouse pad, not getting any work done.

Half an hour later, a reply came. He took a deep breath before he opened it. "Duncan, it was great meeting you too. Would you like to grab dinner sometime?"

Thus began their rollercoaster ride that had led them to here.

The irony was that they never would have met if Chip's career hadn't taken him across Duncan's path. And yet, now, that same career was keeping them apart. Both men had tied up so much of themselves in their respective careers. As much as Duncan wanted to ask Chip to walk away from it, he couldn't. He didn't have it in himself to even hint to Chip that he give that up for him. It was too much of his life, his identity, his sense of self-worth. Duncan understood that, because he was the same before he'd unexpectedly become a father.

Without saying it to each other, they both knew that it was best if they cut ties, a clean break, get it over with, and work on healing the wounds. But would either of them have the strength to say that out loud?

35

KADEN

The night air felt cool against Kaden's skin as he sped on his bike to the park for another clandestine meeting with Hunter. This rendezvous was later than the last one. The city was quieter. There was a smoky smell in the air as an enormous field of mulch had caught fire some miles away, making the air foggy.

When Kaden reached the park, Hunter was waiting for him in a gazebo.

"There you are," Hunter said, reaching his arms around Kaden before he could even lay his bike down.

Kaden closed his eyes and gave in to the hug. On the ride over, he wondered if Hunter would even try to hug him. And Kaden was so filled with worry and doubt, he hadn't even been sure he wanted a hug from Hunter, anyway. However, now that he was in his embrace, it was like being wrapped in a blanket on a chilly morning.

The hug ended in a kiss.

"I missed you," Hunter said, stepping back, but gripping both of Kaden's hands.

"I missed you too."

"Zoey has been pitching a fit. She keeps asking me where you are so you can make her more mac and cheese."

Kaden smiled. "We're in the gazebo today, I see."

"Yep. Gotta mix it up; keep it fresh."

"This reminds me of *The Sound of Music*," Kaden said.

Hunter grinned. "Well, I am sixteen..."

"Going on seventeen," Kaden said. "It's funny. I'm surprised you even know that movie. It seems kinda, I dunno..."

"Gay?"

"Yes."

"Well," Hunter said, "you know I'm gay, eh?"

"I know, but you don't seem to fit so many of the stereotypes like I do. It throws me when you do fall into one."

"Well, I'm not super into musicals, but I think everyone loves *The Sound of Music*." Hunter glanced around. "In the movie, didn't they dance in the gazebo?"

"Yeah."

"Dance with me, Kaden." Hunter reached out and took one of his hands.

Kaden resisted Hunter's tugging. "I can't dance. I was gonna have Dad teach me, but he hasn't seemed like he'd be in the mood for that lately. And I don't guess we'll get to go to any dances, so it's just as well, I suppose."

"I'll teach you right now."

"Now?"

"Sure. Just a simple slow dance. Before my cousin's wedding, Mom taught me the most basic thing you need to know to dance. It's only eight steps. I had to dance with every aunt and every girl cousin, so I got a bit of practice in." Hunter pulled Kaden to the center of the gazebo.

"I'm gonna step on your feet," Kaden said.

"Even if you do, I'm pretty sure it won't kill me. Now, put your hands here and here, then mirror my steps, doing a little sidestep."

"There's no music," Kaden protested.

Hunter took out his phone, and in a few seconds, John Legend's "Conversations in the Dark" was playing. "No more excuses, chef."

Kaden was surprised at how easily he picked up the simple side steps. The song played on repeat, and Hunter sang along with it softly into Kaden's ear.

After a bit, Hunter added a move to the dance, spinning Kaden under his raised arm.

"I'm dancing the girl's part, aren't I?" Kaden asked, grinning.

"Maybe," Hunter said, winking.

The song had repeated seven or eight times when Hunter said, "Hopefully, I'm not ruining this song too much singing along."

"Not at all. I like your voice."

"You do?" Hunter asked.

"Yeah."

"I enjoy singing it to you, because the words… I feel like if I wrote a song for you, this would be it."

All the lyrics moved Kaden. He closed his eyes and pressed his face into the hollow of Hunter's throat, hiding his tears until he felt them bursting out of his eyes and streaming down his cheeks. Hunter held him and let him cry.

Every word Hunter sang was like a spear, skewering the doubt that Gabby had unwittingly planted in Kaden's heart. It was like he could see it decay. The apprehension fell away, blackened and dead.

"You okay?" Hunter asked.

"I am."

"You sure? It's so hard to tell with you sometimes," Hunter said.

"I am now."

They danced through the song a couple more times, before they took a break, sitting on a bench, Hunter's arm over his shoulder.

"I'm going to Charlotte Friday."

"What? Moving? Already?"

"No. No," Kaden said. "Just visiting. We're meeting one of my uncles and his family. Then coming back Monday."

Hunter exhaled. "You scared me there for a minute."

"Sorry."

"That sounds fun. And the timing is on point."

"Yeah. I guess it'll be good to see if I'd really like to live there. And perhaps Jacob will decide one way or the other. I think he's on the fence right now."

"I haven't heard him mention it at all. I guess he's not wanting to talk to me about it."

"Kind of surprising."

"True," Hunter said. "I think he's better at keeping secrets than he lets on, at least when he wants to."

The other possibility, which Kaden didn't want to talk about, was that Jacob had already unmasked this breakup ruse.

They sat in silence for a while.

"This is so nice," Hunter said. "When we're in college, we'll have to find a place with this same vibe and go to it in the middle of the night like this."

They kissed then—for a long time.

As they said their goodbyes, still unspoken were the three words Kaden most wanted to say to Hunter, the same three words he most wanted to hear roll off Hunter's tongue.

They parted, Kaden unable to muster the will to utter the words nor hearing them pass through Hunter's lips.

When Kaden was at the end of the block, about to turn a corner, he looked behind him. The love of his life was barely visible in the distance. Kaden paused, listening to the night sounds, a chorus of crickets and frogs.

"I love you," Kaden said, the words so quiet even the crickets at his feet couldn't hear them.

36

DUNCAN

After a close call involving Jacob making the mistake of thinking that TSA officers had a sense of humor, and Kaden's stomach turning itself inside out a couple of times during the landing, relief washed over Duncan as he set foot on solid, chewing gum covered, coffee-stained sidewalks.

Kaden coughed as they inhaled the diesel exhaust of an airport shuttle bus. "I think I'm gonna be sick again."

"It's just the polluted air," Duncan said. "Let's get out of here."

Jacob already had his eyes on a group of flight attendants entering a shuttle bus nearby, and with a glimmer in his eye, he said, "You guys go without me. I'm taking that bus."

With some effort, Duncan herded them to their rental car and squeezed all their luggage into the back. The boys had packed way too much stuff for a mere three-day trip.

Soon enough, they pulled up to his parent's house in a neighborhood of late 1950s era homes surrounded by mature trees.

"You grew up here?" Jacob asked as they all got out of the car and unloaded luggage.

"Yeppers. Two parents, four kids, and a St. Bernard, crammed into a four-bedroom, one-and-a-half bath split level. And that's why I used to do sleepovers at Roz's house every chance I could. I was so jealous of her being an only child."

"How many people are here now?" Kaden asked.

"My parents, your uncle and aunt, two or three cousins, plus the three of us."

Kaden slumped. He'd only gotten his glow back from the motion sickness a few minutes earlier, and now he was turning pale again.

"It won't be that bad, son."

"If you say so."

Duncan placed a hand on Kaden's shoulder. "Well, your grandmother got all the ingredients you requested, so you can go be unsociable in the kitchen."

They walked along the weathered concrete sidewalk to the front steps.

"I'm not sure I even want to think about food right now," Kaden said.

Duncan led them inside without knocking. His parents and Matt's family were all crowded into the living room.

"Well, shit, bro," Matt said, looking at Kaden and Jacob. "You really do have sons. My gay little brother helped make babies. How crazy is that? Boys, I'm your uncle, Matt."

"Uncle! I'm Jacob, your favorite nephew."

"Really? You're my favorite nephew?" Matt's eyebrows raised.

Jacob put a patronizing hand on Matt's broad back. "Uncle Matt, I like the words in that sentence, but I'm gonna need you to say it again, this time, less questiony, more statement. Got it?" Jacob stood back from him and clapped his hands. "Okay, places everyone, and... action!"

His body shaking with laughter, Matt did a slow turn toward Duncan and fixed his gaze on him. "You weren't lying about this one."

"Ah, my reputation is worldwide already, apparently. Just as I suspected," Jacob said, giving Matt a bear hug.

Matt reached out to Kaden, both arms wide. "So if he's the bull-shitter, you must be the shy one."

"Kaden doesn't hug," Duncan said.

"Oh. Okay." Matt extended a hand, and they shook.

"Hi sir."

"Sir? Just call me Matt, or Uncle Matt."

"Yes sir."

"Um. That's ah... never mind," Matt said, shaking his head.

They finished introductions and Kaden didn't appear pleased to be among so many strangers in such a small space, slinking into a corner chair and sitting on his hands.

Then, Duncan, only half listening to his brother's braggadocious discussion of his work, noticed his niece and nephew, Ashley and Austin, heading toward Kaden. The twins were almost eighteen.

Decked out in goth styles, they were both sullen and moody, as usual, speaking with drained, monotone voices, as if the entire world could be in flames and their reaction would be... a shrug. Both insisted their names were not Ashley and Austin, but Scarlet and Raven.

"So, you're the gay one?" Scarlet droned as she and her brother flopped onto a loveseat near Kaden.

Kaden nodded as Jacob sat on the arm of his chair.

"Interesting," Raven drawled, his stern face managing a slight upturn. Duncan assumed that was Raven's version of a grin.

Jacob scoffed. "Too bad he's not the good kind of gay."

"He's not?" Scarlet asked.

"Nope."

Her pierced eyebrows raised. "How so?"

"He doesn't have any of the magical gay abilities. For starters, he isn't nearly sassy enough. He can't do ballet, interpretive dance, or sing Broadway tunes. Doesn't do makeup tutorials on YouTube, and as we discovered during the pandemic, he can't even cut and style hair."

Kaden crossed his arms in frustration and shot Jacob an icy glare. "That was your fault! I told you I never did that before."

"Bro, it's supposed to come naturally to your kind. It's magic!" He waved his hands like a wizard casting a spell.

Kaden stared at the floor.

At least they weren't all spending the night in the house. Matt's family would be leaving and coming back in the morning.

Duncan chatted with his family for a few minutes, but as it was already eleven, his brother's family left shortly and went to spend the night at Duncan's house.

By midnight, Duncan was in the den setting up an air mattress for himself, and two sleeping bags for the boys.

Jacob bounded down the stairs. "So, why are we all three sleeping in this basement, Dad?" he asked.

"It's not a basement. It's a den that's partially subterranean."

"Mmmkay, then why are we sleeping in a partially sub-terrarium den?"

"Subterranean," Duncan said.

Jacob raised his eyebrows. "Well, it's pretty humid and musty down here and there's a mushroom growing out of the carpet over there, so it feels like the inside of a terrarium."

"How do you know what that feels like?"

"Dad, let's just say that I've lived an interesting life so far and leave it at that. But I still don't know why we're here, expected to sleep on the floor in a four-bedroom house. Is there a reason we can't have a bedroom or two?"

"Well, Mom and Dad are in the master." Duncan started counting on his fingers. "One guest bedroom is where my father's old hobbies go to die. It's filled with photography equipment, fishing gear, a guitar with amp, and his mountain bike. Another is where my mom's hobbies die, with boxes full of knitting yarn, bolts of fabric and old clothes for quilting. Then there's the painting and pottery-making junk."

"And that leaves one," Jacob said.

"That's the room where they keep all the furniture they took out of the other two spare bedrooms, plus all the rest of the crap they have. And before you ask, yes, I've considered an intervention by one of those hoarder deprogramming groups. So, we're either sleeping on the floor here, or in the backyard."

Jacob groaned. "Fine. But this is the last time I'm living like such a peasant."

Kaden came down the stairs, having finished showering. His hair was wet and matted, and he kept sticking his fingers in his ears and shaking his head.

"Problem?" Duncan asked.

"Just the towel wasn't very absorbent."

"Yeah, Mom bought them from the dollar store and doubtless used too much fabric softener as always."

Jacob had finished unrolling his sleeping bag. "Dad, just an FYI, I sleep in the nude."

"Um. No. You will wear underwear."

"Dude, I can't stifle my junk. I'm a growing boy, and everyone knows that the prime growing time is overnight."

"I've never heard that," Duncan said.

"I saw it on a video for protein shakes," Jacob said. "I'm pretty sure they can't lie on those things."

Duncan made a mental note to teach the boys about critical thinking skills. "I thought from the condom discussion, we ascertained that you're already extra, extra-large anyway, yes?"

"I'm getting there."

"Okay. Then wear gym shorts. No nude sleeping here. It's only for three nights. Your junk will not suffer any lasting harm."

Jacob rolled his eyes and groaned. "Fine. Just remember all these sacrifices I'm making when my birthday and Christmas roll around."

Duncan turned to Kaden. "And you're okay with the no nude sleeping here rule?"

Kaden looked down at his tee and sea turtle pajama bottoms. "I'm more than okay with no nude sleeping anywhere. Can I put my sleeping bag over in the corner, away from Jacob? He's a roller. And I don't need his feet in my face by morning."

"Oh, that's true," Jacob said. "Massive roller. I used to have guardrails on my bed when I was little."

"I think that's called a crib," Duncan said.

"No, this was after the crib. They had me in a hospital bed."

Duncan looked at Kaden for confirmation.

"It's true. He would be on the floor ninety percent of the time by morning. I think he fell on his head a lot."

Jacob mock gut-punched Kaden while Kaden pretended injury.

"Okay," Duncan said.

While Jacob had admitted he rolled around in his sleep, he failed to disclose the volume of his snoring. Between that and the fact that the air mattress deflated three times, Duncan barely slept.

To make matters worse, he had to spend all day Saturday at the office, with a bunch of *real* computer nerds who knew how to do actual work, while all he knew how to do was write disaster recovery plans that never got put into practice due to an appalling lack of disasters. He was pretty sure the *real* nerds had no respect for him at all.

Meanwhile, his sons had been keenly interested in exploring the city. Matt's oldest daughter, Laura, the one house-sitting for Duncan, spent the day driving them around town.

In the evening, after work, Duncan came back to his parents' home and joined his mother on the patio for a glass of wine, while Kaden made dinner.

"It's killing you to have to give up your kitchen, isn't it?"

"Not really," Olivia said. "Kinda nice to have someone else deal with that for once. Besides, I peeked in on him a few times. He seems to know what he's doing. And that breakfast, my lord, those frittatas!"

"He definitely knows what he's doing," Duncan said.

"Speaking of knowing what you're doing, how's parenting going? Seems like you're calling me for advice less and less."

"Parenting is going okay. As you can see, they are still alive, so no repeat of the Goldie Incident or the Myrtle Incident." He waved a hand toward the back corner of the yard, wondering if his turtle's tombstone was still back there somewhere.

Duncan exhaled. "I... I made a breakthrough."

"A breakthrough? For you? Or them?"

"Both, I think. I told them I love them, called them my sons and they've started calling me Dad, at least sometimes."

Olivia put her hand on his, and a warm, knowing smile crossed her face. "I've always believed you could do this. When you came out, the one thing that bothered me was I knew you would have made a great father and figured you'd never get the chance."

"Well, you were the only one who believed that. I didn't even think I had it in me."

"Moms know best," she said, beaming. Then her expression turned earnest. "Any updates on the legal front... with the custody stuff?"

Duncan nodded slowly. "The good news is that the judge who had been handling our case was transferred to another district. So, Tamika says now, we just have to pin our hopes on whoever we get to replace him. She's feeling a certain amount of optimism."

"Well, that's a sign. I'm sure it will all work out."

Duncan flashed a smile momentarily. "I still worry about Kaden though. I feel like there's something going on with him that I can't put my finger on. Roz always said he's a sensitive soul. I think Jacob is too, he just hides it better and seems more resilient."

"Just keep loving them, dear. It will all work out and they'll become the best men they can."

Chef Kaden prepared an extravagant meal of mostly Filipino dishes. Jacob was drafted into being his wait staff again. Although Duncan had always known Kaden would prepare a delectable meal, Jacob's performance tonight was unexpected. Not only was he skilled at handling the dishes, but he had the entire family in stitches with his typical banter.

"Sorry Jacob, but as good a job as you're doing, I'm afraid Kaden is now officially my favorite nephew," Matt said, as Jacob took his empty plate away.

"He should go to culinary school," Eric said, "as a teacher, not a student."

After dinner, Olivia goaded the adults into playing board games while the teens all stared at their phones. Duncan took it as a cue to bail out and go to Chip's apartment.

It was probably a bad idea. He knew that. Even when he'd debated in his mind whether or not he'd go, the answer was always going to be yes.

And it was also a foregone conclusion that he would not be coming home until morning. He texted his sons to let them know not to wait up for him.

"Booty call!" Jacob replied, including some sexually suggestive emojis.

"I'm not even gonna try to deny it," Duncan sent back.

He returned to his parents' the next day, having slept better than he had in months, and more in love with Chip than ever.

Duncan had promised to take his sons to see his house. He wanted to check on it, anyway. While he trusted Laura was taking good care, it wouldn't hurt to make sure, and there were a few minor items he wanted to take back to Florida with them.

"Dad, you're in a good mood today," Kaden said as they rode over in the rental car.

"Afterglow," Jacob said. "I know the feeling."

Duncan tried to ignore the fact that his fifteen-year-old son knew what *afterglow* was like. "It was nice not to sleep on an air mattress."

"Right. That's what it was all about, the air mattress," Jacob scoffed, then chuckled.

When they got to the house, Duncan showed them around. "Nothing special. Just your typical three-bedroom ranch."

"Nice kitchen," Kaden said. "Compact, but easy to maneuver around." He opened and closed drawers, looked at some utensils, and Duncan sensed he was being judged.

"I remodeled it myself, mostly. Well, I put the cabinets together, but that was the hardest part of the renovation. I will never do flat packs again."

The boys insisted on a thorough tour, going through every room, every closet, and chatted amongst themselves in Filipino. Duncan almost felt like he was a real estate agent doing a showing. When they finished, Jacob and Kaden spoke some more.

"Can I ask what you're talking about, guys?" Duncan said.

"Duncan, let's go have a chat," Jacob said, doing his disconcerting TV game show host voice again and putting a patronizing hand on Duncan's shoulder.

They all sat in the great room and Jacob continued, but he dropped the mimicking voice and a look of sincerity spread across his face. "Dad, we've got a question for you. Do you still love Chip?"

Duncan swallowed. He hadn't anticipated having to discuss his deepest emotions after a house tour. He paused before replying. "That's random. I'm not sure how to respond."

"Just tell us the truth," Jacob said. "Please? It's important."

Kaden didn't say anything, but his face echoed Jacob's pleading.

Duncan exhaled. "Yes. I do."

"Is the feeling mutual, to the best of your knowledge?" Jacob asked.

"He says he loves me."

"Excellent. So, the bro here and I have been thinking about something. It just seems that ten thousand miles is a bit much for a booty call with the Chip-meister."

"It's only six hundred, and that isn't the reason for this visit. Well, not the main reason."

Jacob held up a hand. "Whatever! Don't interrupt me when I'm trying to be monogamous."

Kaden grimaced. "He means magnanimous."

"Whatever!" Jacob said. "Dad, let me float an idea here. We like what we've seen of Charlotte. Kaden made Laura take us to Whole

Foods Market, and I swear I thought he was gonna have an orgasm right there in the organic produce section."

Kaden's cheeks reddened.

"And there's a nice aquatic center she showed us too," Jacob continued.

"Don't forget the Johnson and Wales Culinary school," Kaden said.

"Anyway, we're tired of seeing you be Mopey McMope-Face, so we thought maybe we could see about moving here."

Duncan's jaw dropped. "Moving here?"

Jacob nodded. "We checked with Tamika. Now, she said all bets are off if we get another asshole judge—in which case I'll probably run away and join the circus—but assuming we luck out and get the good judge she's hoping for, she could kick things off on the family court side and all that other junk, like selling the house."

Duncan's eyebrows raised. "Are you serious?"

"Absolutely," Jacob said.

"Yes sir."

"Guys, I appreciate what you're doing, but I don't want to uproot your lives."

"Dad," Kaden said. "We want you to be happy. We want us all to be a big, happy family, including Chip. We really like him."

"Plus, we can always use another healer in *Elves of Ora Online*," Jacob added. "And honestly, your ship name is really cool."

"Our ship name?" Duncan said. "I'm afraid to ask what it is."

"Our social media polling shows Chuncan as the winner, edging out Dip, 54% to 46%," Jacob said.

"Oh," Duncan said.

"And we'd be near Grandma Olivia and Grandpa Eric. And your house is pretty sweet. We just think this is for the best," Kaden said.

Duncan tried to hold back his tears, but he failed. "Come here," he said, standing up and extending his arms. They came to him and he embraced his sons so tight he was afraid he might crush them.

"Guys, I don't know if we can make this work, but it means the world to me that you would even consider it."

3 7

KADEN

Kaden wasn't sure he ever wanted to fly again. But airsickness may have only been part of the reason his stomach twisted into knots on the return flight from Charlotte to Orlando. From the moment he and Jacob had suggested the move to Duncan, anxiety stirred in his gut again.

In the three weeks since then, his life had been a living hell. Nothing seemed to make sense anymore, and he felt like his world was crumbling around him. Every day, he was in a constant struggle with himself not to tell the truth about their breakup ruse and carry on with the charade. He was growing more exhausted by the second, but he still held on, somehow keeping himself from spilling the beans.

As if that wasn't enough, the custody issue loomed like a gallows. They all should have known better than to step into the trap the Riveras and their lawyers had set for them with that compromise offer; should have foreseen that Jacob would fall into it head first.

Today, the trap could close on them. Duncan had dropped him and Jacob off at school, then gone directly to Tamika's office to prepare for a court hearing. Duncan promised to text them as soon as he knew something.

Meanwhile, Kaden's mind spun in a dizzying and disorganized whirl, making it impossible for him to focus on anything, least of all his classwork. Every thought was muddled, jumbled in a chaotic mess that he couldn't untangle.

He and Jacob were in the school cafeteria when both of their phones chimed at once. Kaden checked notifications; a message from Duncan. He closed his eyes and took a deep breath before tapping to see it. Just one word: "Victory!"

Then, a series of messages from Duncan followed, one every few seconds.

DUNCAN VALENTYN:

Tamika is a badass! 😄

I'm still your guardian.

Jacob doesn't have to go to any more mental health evaluations with that Harry Billings jerk.

Jacob only has to visit Cesar and Maya if he wants to.

Kaden's face lit up more with each message. Until the last one.

DUNCAN VALENTYN:

Judge says we can move to NC, sons!

It was exactly what he'd been scheming to do. So why did it feel like he'd just had a knife slice through his stomach as he read the words?

Jacob had checked his phone too. "Dios mío. Did you see this, bro? I can't believe it!" He gave Kaden a fist-bump. "I gotta say, I've never been so relieved about anything in my life. Not gonna lie, I thought I'd fucked us all over with that stupid fight. This is so awesome."

Kaden swallowed. "Yep." He forced a shaky smile.

He and Hunter had been sneaking out at night, going to the park several times, pressing their luck on getting caught.

Hunter arrived at their lunch table. "Hey guys."

"Yo," Jacob said. "Looks like it's happening, dude. We're moving."

"Oh." Hunter bit his lip and stared at Kaden, his shoulders slumping.

Kaden expected that Hunter privately wished the court would prohibit the relocation, and he couldn't blame him, because as each anxious day passed, waiting for the answer, Kaden's desire for that grew as well.

"This is my chance for a new start," Jacob said. "If we move soon enough, I might be able to get back in the pool before the season is out."

Jacob's fight with Zeke's friend had ultimately resulted in his suspension for the remainder of the season. There was a chance he might make it onto the swim team in Charlotte. And Duncan assured the boys that the school in Charlotte was more diverse than Aldenbrook Academy. The change might truly be a blessing for Jacob.

That afternoon, when Kaden was in Culinary Arts class, Unique Mills-Foy came up to him, a smug smile plastered on her face.

"I hear you're moving, Watson-Rivera," she said, reversing his last names as always.

Kaden wondered if the entire school already knew. How did these rumors spread so fast?

"Too bad," Unique continued. "I was looking forward to beating you for a fourth year in a row." Kaden half expected to hear an evil villain laugh come out of her mouth.

He wanted to give some pithy reply, but his brain had nothing for him. He just stared at her blankly until she walked away.

At dinner that night, Duncan talked to them about a timeline for the move.

"Tamika says the real estate market is cooling off fast with these higher interest rates," Duncan said. "We'll need to list the house right away and hope for the best."

"I'm gonna miss this place," Jacob said.

"Yeah," Duncan said. "It's grown on me. But anyway, your fall break is coming up, and we should visit Charlotte again and take care of the school enrollment and get some of my furniture out so we'll have room for your stuff."

"Sounds good," Jacob said.

Kaden nodded.

THAT NIGHT, he and Hunter met at the park again. It was empty as usual this time of night. They strolled along a path by the canal, the sounds of crickets and frogs echoing along the banks.

"When we visit our new school, I'm going to ask them if there's a way to graduate a year early," Kaden said.

"Cool. Then we'll be together again in just two years."

Two years. It seemed like such a long time to Kaden. And much could happen in those years.

"The Johnson and Wales campus is nice," Kaden said. "Once we move, you'll have to see if you can visit and we can tour."

"Yeah. If I pass my test and get my license, maybe I can drive up myself. I can't wait to drive you around, just the two of us, no Mom." Hunter's test was coming up just before fall break.

"That would be awesome."

They strolled in silence for some time, hand-in-hand.

"I'm nervous about all this," Kaden said. He tightened his grip on Hunter's hand.

"It's going to be okay, chef." He halted and spun Kaden toward him, planted a kiss on his lips. Then Hunter stood there, staring into Kaden's eyes, his mouth hanging open, as if something were on the tip of his tongue, but he didn't speak.

Kaden wanted to ask him if he had something to say, but was afraid it might not be the words he longed to hear. Eventually, Hunter closed his mouth and smiled. He turned, and they resumed walking.

"I keep hoping that I'll be more comfortable with this over time, but the opposite is happening," Kaden said.

Hunter halted again, took him into his arms, and held him against his chest. He started singing a song to him, but Kaden couldn't understand the words. It was soothing nonetheless.

Finally, Kaden's curiosity had to be satisfied. "What is that song, Hunter? It's so pretty."

"It's something my grandmother used to sing to me."

"I didn't think you knew Korean."

"I don't," Hunter said, laughing. "I have no idea what it means, and I'm probably mangling the pronunciation."

Kaden pushed his face against Hunter's chest again. "Keep singing it, please."

And he did.

HUNTER PASSED his driver's license exam on the first try, but there hadn't been time for them to hang out since then. Kaden and Jacob had school assignments to complete and packing to do for their road trip to Charlotte.

As Duncan's SUV backed out of their driveway, Kaden stared forlornly at the 'For Sale' sign in the yard, wondering if it might have a 'SOLD' sticker on it by the time they got back here.

Kaden was thankful they were driving for this visit. His stomach was gnarled enough without adding airsickness to the mix. What had started as a frivolous idea at first, pretending to break up, had evolved into an elaborate scheme. Then it lurched into motion, as if set off by the fall of a single domino, and was now rolling along like a runaway locomotive, unstoppable, completely out of his control. All Kaden could do at this point was watch it unfold, and hope it didn't turn into a train crash.

While Duncan drove, Jacob had his face buried in his phone. Kaden sat in the backseat behind Jacob. If he stared at his phone screen in the car, he'd surely vomit, so he listened to a *Star Wars* audio book, then baking podcasts for hours on end to distract himself.

"Oh wow," Jacob said. "Zeke came out."

"Zeke?" Duncan said. "The guy you got into a fight with?"

"No. That was Zeke's friend," Jacob said.

Kaden paused his audio and pulled an AirPod out of his ear. "Wait. What are you guys talking about? Who did what?"

"Zeke, on the swim team, he came out, bro."

"Came out? Out of what? His swimsuit?" Kaden asked.

Jacob turned to him and rolled his eyes. "Came out as gay."

"How do you know?"

"Hunter texted me."

Why hadn't Hunter texted him? Kaden's chest tightened.

Kaden thought he'd met Zeke once or twice, but he wasn't sure which boy he was. He hoped it wasn't the handsome boy he was thinking of. Please don't let it be him.

"Zeke? Which one is he?"

Jacob pulled up a social media profile and showed Zeke's picture to Kaden. It was him! Zeke had a gorgeous toothy smile and inviting eyes. Kaden swiped the photo to the side to look at others: One of him surfing, another in his skimpy swimsuit. It was just one thirst-trappy photo after another. Kaden could feel the blood draining out of his head with each swipe of his finger. The profile listed his age as seventeen. His muscles were even bigger than Hunter's.

One of the photos showed his shoulder tattoo. A tattoo? Kaden couldn't compete with that. Zeke wasn't even eighteen yet. How could he have a tattoo? Was that even legal? It occurred to him that perhaps he could get Zeke arrested. Or would that make him that much more desirable to Hunter? He could envision Hunter faithfully visiting him in prison, the two figuring out it was Kaden who was the rat, then plotting a painful revenge once he was released!

There was no way around it. This was an unmitigated disaster. Kaden handed the phone back to his brother as a wave of nausea flowed over him, only partly caused by motion sickness.

"You know," Jacob said, "if he quits hanging out with jerks, Zeke might be a good match for Hunter. They have so much in common. Though I'm not a fan of their ship name possibilities. Huke? Zenter?" He made a face.

Kaden slumped back into his seat and closed his eyes. That any of the older boys on the swim team came out was bad enough, but there was no way he could compete with someone like Zeke, the dream jock who also happened to surf. Surely, Hunter had already seen Zeke naked in the locker room, probably lusted after every inch of him. Now, he was out and attainable.

Kaden's worst fear had come to pass, and far sooner than he'd expected. He'd been fooling himself to think that he could finish school a year early and go to college with Hunter. He hadn't even moved away yet, and already he may as well give up.

In his heart, he'd always known that having a boyfriend like Hunter was too good to be true. Kaden had just been lucky that the pickings were slim, with only one boy at the school who was officially out. Hunter could have just as easily been dating that boy, but Kaden was more convenient, someone he already knew as a friend. Someone rumored to be gay, most likely thanks to Jacob and his unfiltered, loud mouth.

Later, they stopped at a rest area. As Kaden paced around to stretch his legs, he had his phone out, texting Hunter.

KADEN RIVERA-WATSON:

Hey. How's it going?

HUNTER GAN:

Good. You? Trip going okay? No car sickness?

KADEN RIVERA-WATSON:

So far, so good. Just can't look at my phone on the road. Anything new going on?

HUNTER GAN:

Not really. Mom and Dad said they have a surprise for me later. So we'll see

KADEN RIVERA-WATSON:

Cool. Any other surprises? Besides that?

HUNTER GAN:

Nope

KADEN RIVERA-WATSON:

Okay. Got to go now. Laters

After texting Jacob about Zeke coming out, why wouldn't Hunter have mentioned it? He gave him every opportunity. It seemed like something to chat about, unless Hunter was hiding something.

Of course, it could just be that he hadn't mentioned it because Kaden didn't know Zeke. Maybe he was just overthinking it. Hadn't his moms said he was prone to overthinking?

When they were back on the road, Kaden played his podcasts again, but he couldn't focus on the words. He finally stopped it and just stared mindlessly out the window for hours.

"Holy shit!" Jacob said, startling Kaden.

"Inside voice," Duncan said. "Wow. I'm so turning into my father."

"Sorry. Bro, look! Hunter's parents gave him a car, a 2018 Mustang convertible. That is savage." Jacob handed his phone to Kaden.

There he was, in the driver's seat of a white Mustang with the top down, hands on the steering wheel, beaming, his teeth shining as white as the car. But he wasn't alone. Sitting in the passenger seat, with a smile as huge as Hunter's, wearing a tank top, exactly like the one Hunter wore, was none other than the newly out hunk, Zeke.

Kaden's grip on the phone weakened and it began to slip from his fingers. He caught it, and handed it back to Jacob, then closed his eyes, holding back tears. "Good for him," he said, his voice trembling.

It was hours later before Hunter could be bothered to text Kaden about his gift. He sent photos of the car, some with him in it, some beside it. Hunter didn't send any pictures with Zeke in them.

Kaden tried to push all this out of his head by reminding himself of everything he'd been blessed with. He wouldn't be put into foster care or a group home. He was going to reside in a big city with the brother he loved more than any other person in the world. He'd be living with his father, whom he loved a lot already and was loving more every day. And surely, he'd grow to love Chip too.

When they sold their house in Port St. Lucie, the money from it would be added to his and Jacob's trust funds. Not only could Kaden go to Johnson and Wales for their culinary program, but after he graduated, there might be money enough left for him to study in France or Switzerland. Duncan and Chip would be together, and Jacob would get his fresh start.

His family would get all of that, and in exchange, all he had to do was give up the boy he loved with all his heart. And now, it seemed he'd lost the boy, anyway. Even if he were staying in Port St. Lucie, he couldn't compete with Zeke.

THEY REACHED Charlotte by evening and spent the night in Duncan's house. No, not just Duncan's house. Soon enough, they would move and it would be *their* house. Cousin Laura had Chinese food waiting for them from Duncan's favorite restaurant.

Kaden had no appetite, but tasted it anyway. He had to admit it was the best Kung Po Chicken he'd ever had. It got cold on his plate as the others ate every bite of theirs.

"You okay?" Duncan asked him.

"I think I just got a little queasy in the car. I'll save it for later if I get hungry."

It was unseasonably chilly that night. Kaden volunteered to sleep on the sofa and Duncan turned on the gas logs in the fireplace. The flickering flames cast an orange glow onto Kaden's body as he laid there, unable to sleep, forcing himself to breathe in a steady rhythm, pushing the panic beneath the surface with every ounce of strength he had.

He felt like he was the walking dead the next day as Duncan took the boys to see a guidance counselor at the public high school.

Kaden paid little attention to the discussions, but near the end, the counselor asked them if they had any questions.

Jacob spoke first, and he snapped into his trademark quiz show host mimicking voice. "Stevo... can I call you Stevo?"

The counselor raised one eyebrow. "That's not even close to my name, but if it makes you happy."

"Good. Because you look like a Stevo," Jacob said, pointing an index finger at the man as he spoke. "As you may have noticed, I'm a fellow person of color. The dadster here says this school is diverse. Is that true?"

"The student body is a majority minority."

"Sweet." Jacob put a hand on Kaden's shoulder. "And Stevo, how is it for queer kids like my bro?"

The counselor looked at Kaden. "We have quite a few openly LGBTQ+ students and some teachers as well. Plus, we have a zero-tolerance policy when it comes to bullying."

"That is acceptable, Stevo," Jacob said.

"Kaden, do you have any questions or concerns?" the counselor asked.

"What would I have to do if I wanted to graduate a year early?" Kaden asked. After seeing that picture of Zeke in Hunter's car, Kaden was certain it didn't matter anymore that he entered college at the same time as Hunter, so he wasn't even sure why he asked at this point.

Duncan looked at him curiously. "Why would you want to do that?"

Kaden blurted out the first thing that popped into his head. "Well, I'm not getting any younger."

Duncan laughed. "You're only fifteen, but okay."

The guidance counselor smiled. "We can figure that out once we get your transcripts, Kaden, and see if it's possible."

"*If* it's possible?"

"We'd have to see if you have the credits to make it feasible to take enough summer classes to make it a year early."

"Oh, okay." Kaden wasn't hopeful, but then again, it didn't matter, anyway. The picture of Hunter and Zeke in the car, smiling, filled his head. Was he taking Zeke to the dog beach? Were they sneaking out to the park? Dancing in the gazebo?

THAT NIGHT, Jacob took the sofa, and Kaden bunked in the bedroom. It was better this way. He figured he could just close the door and sob in the darkness. But before he turned the lights out, Jacob popped in to grab some clothes out of his luggage.

"Bro, what was up with you wanting to graduate a year early?" Jacob was speaking in Filipino. Obviously, he'd picked up on the fact that Kaden was hiding something and figured he'd be more likely to get a straight answer if it was just between the two of them.

Kaden shrugged and responded in Filipino as well. "I dunno."

Jacob raised an eyebrow. "Are you tired of being in classes with me? Is that it?"

The question caught him by surprise. It wasn't the reason, but it also wasn't untrue. Part of him wanted to be out of Jacob's shadow. Born so close together, they had a bond similar to twins in some ways. However, in many situations, Kaden felt like a little brother, being protected and defended by a big brother. He supposed there were many gay kids who would have loved to have a champion like Jacob. But Kaden only saw the negatives, perhaps taking for granted all the benefits of having his loving brother by his side. Kaden's hesitation to respond was response enough.

"That *is* it." Jacob's face fell and he looked hurt.

Kaden's lips pressed together tightly as he tried to find the words he wanted to say. "No."

Jacob made a buzzing sound like time running out. "You took too long to answer." His expression betrayed his worry that Kaden was hiding something from him.

Kaden's chest tightened and he looked away, unable to meet his brother's gaze. "I just... I just... I don't know how to say it."

"I know I'm too much, bro. I get it. But I don't want anyone hurting you."

"Jacob. You know I love you more than anyone. But sometimes, I feel so small and helpless. I need to be able to handle things myself. But I can't. Not yet. I still need you by my side. And I know that, especially with us moving to a new school."

"Then why did you want to graduate a year early?"

Finally, he thought of something to say. "I guess I was excited about the culinary school."

"Ohhh." A smile tugged at Jacob's face and some of the worry softened in his eyes. He seemed satisfied with that answer for now, and Kaden was thankful for that. He wasn't sure he could lie his way out of any more questions tonight.

"I'm going to wait to graduate though," Kaden said. There was no reason to rush school now. No reason at all.

38

KADEN

Kaden had fallen into a fitful sleep, his exhaustion and despair dragging him down into the depths of darkness.

As the morning sun shone through a window shade, he awoke to boisterous laughter filtering in from the great room. There was Jacob's voice, followed by the familiar chuckles of Duncan and Chip, as well as his cousin Laura's giggles. They sounded like they were having loads of fun that he was missing out on. He was in no mood to laugh though.

A pleasing aroma of sizzling bacon wafted into the room, yet he still couldn't find the willpower to raise his body up. He lay motionless in bed, his gaze fixed on the shadowy white ceiling. His weariness was unrelenting.

He looked at his phone. His eyes widened in shock as he read the time; it was almost ten, and yet not a single text or call from Hunter. Out of sight, out of mind.

It was over. He was nothing to Hunter now but a memory.

He should have known at the very beginning. Actually, maybe he did.

From the first moment that Hunter's leg touched his, on that day he flirted with Kaden, maybe he'd known instantly what Hunter was up to! And hastily buried that knowledge deep inside himself. A part of him had always realized that this heartache would be the inevitable end and had tried to shield him from yet more rejection. Kaden ground his teeth as he came to realize that it was Jacob and Gabby who had thwarted him, refusing to let him hide in his protective cocoon of ignorant bliss, telling him that Hunter was flirting with him, giving him a false hope that he could find happiness with someone like Hunter, pushing him down this path toward utter destruction.

Kaden's heart began to pound in his chest like a war drum. A single bead of sweat raced down his forehead, while his hands succumbed to the icy grip of panic. He clenched the sheets with a desperate force, as if he could claw back control if he just held tight enough. But it wasn't enough. His knuckles turned white from his grasp, and no matter how hard he tried, he couldn't breathe. Panic had gripped him.

Rivulets of perspiration cascaded down his body. The ceiling was a blank white canvas, devoid of anything to help him find his way back. His seashell, the treasured talisman that had provided solace and comfort in the past, the one he could ground himself with, was on his nightstand, six hundred miles away.

A knock at the door. "Bro." The door opened. "Hey lazybones, you..." Jacob's voice faded and he closed the door back. A second later, he was at the side of the bed, stroking Kaden's forehead. "Breathe bro," he whispered. "Breathe."

Some time passed. Kaden still hadn't taken a breath. "Bro, you've got to take a breath. Come on. Just one deep one for me. I'm not liking your skin color. Come on."

But he couldn't do it.

"Don't make me mouth-to-mouth you, bro," Jacob said. He pinched Kaden's nose closed, took in a deep breath. Was he really going to do it? Kaden was pretty sure this wasn't recommended for this situation. He forced Jacob's hand away, then sucked in a breath.

He held it for a moment. As Jacob backed away grinning, Kaden exhaled.

"Awesome, bro. Breathe another one. I know you can."

Kaden inhaled a tentative, shallow breath. Held it a moment, then released. Then another, slightly deeper.

"That's it, bro," Jacob whispered. "Keep going. Come back to me."

After a few more minutes, Kaden's heart had slowed, his breathing returned to normal. His skin was cold and wet, but he had emerged from the depths.

Another knock at the closed door. Duncan spoke from outside it. "Hey guys, are you okay in there?"

"Yes, Dad," Jacob said. "We'll be out in a few minutes."

"Okay."

"Bro," Jacob whispered. "What's going on? What happened?"

"Nothing. Just a random panic."

Jacob looked at him sideways. "That's sussy. In fact, you've seemed off for a while now. You're hiding something. I know you are, bro."

"No, I'm not." Kaden closed his eyes.

"Kaden. You've been weirder than usual. Something's up. Tell me, bro. Come on."

"It's nothing."

Jacob's weight pressed down on the mattress and Kaden sensed he was directly over him. "Open your eyes and tell me that. Look me in the eye and tell me."

Kaden took a calming breath and steeled himself to lie. He opened his eyes, but instead of Jacob staring back at him, there was a phone screen in front of his face with Hello Kitty wallpaper staring back at him. The wallpaper was only visible momentarily because Jacob's finger slid up the screen, unlocking it.

Immediately, Jacob hopped up and dashed to a corner of the room. Kaden didn't comprehend for a moment what had happened.

Then it hit him. Jacob tricked him into opening his eyes specifically so he could unlock Kaden's phone.

"What the fuck?" Kaden said. "Give it here."

"Nope." Jacob was frantically scrolling through something, his index finger zipping along the touch screen.

Kaden leaned up and swung his feet onto the floor, but dizziness threw him. The room whirled around. "Give it," he said, grabbing at the sheets to stop the room from spinning.

"Shit, bro. You and Hunter, you got back together."

"No." Kaden tensed his body, squeezing more blood into his head to regain his balance.

"Yes, you did. Don't lie. There are way too many heart emojis in your texts for just friends." He kept scrolling.

"We didn't get back together. Look me in the eye."

Jacob looked at him.

"We didn't get back together," Kaden said. "I swear it." Technically, that was truthful, since they didn't actually end their relationship.

Jacob glanced back and forth between Kaden and the screen several times. Then his eyebrows raised. "You never broke up. You never broke up."

Kaden closed his eyes.

"Shit. You never broke up, did you, bro?"

Kaden collapsed back onto the bed, tears flowing from his eyes.

"I'm telling Dad," Jacob said.

Kaden leaned back up. "Jacob, no. You can't. Not now."

"I have to, bro."

"No, please. I'm begging you." Kaden's voice cracked.

Jacob sat back on the bed and put a gentle hand on Kaden's shoulder. "I'm telling him. He has to know; he just has to. He's making decisions based on lies. Chip did that to him. You saw how that turned out. You gotta tell him the truth."

Jacob left the room and Kaden collapsed back onto the bed. Moments later, Jacob returned, with Duncan right behind him.

"Close the door please, Dad," Jacob said.

"What's going on?" Duncan said, after closing it and sitting on the bed next to Kaden's prostrate body. He stroked Kaden's forehead. "Son, you seem clammy. Are you okay?"

"I'm fine."

"Dad, he's not fine. There are some things he needs to tell you."

"What is it?" Duncan's voice was soothing, but there was apprehension in it.

"Nothing. I'm fine."

Duncan wiped the side of Kaden's face. "Then why all these tears?"

"If you don't tell him, I will," Jacob said.

"I'm fine."

"Dad, Kaden was having a panic attack when I came in to get him. That's why we didn't come back out."

"A panic attack?" Duncan said.

"He's got a history of them."

"Oh. What causes it?"

"Stress," Jacob said. "We've been kinda hiding it from you."

"Why, for God's sake?" Duncan asked, worry creasing his brow.

"We were afraid you'd get scared off."

"Shit," Duncan said. "How could I not know this? I'm so awful at this parenting thing." He ran a hand through his hair. "So awful."

"No," Kaden said. "You're not."

"Son, if I didn't make you feel you could come to me and tell me that, then obviously, I didn't do something right."

"Tell Dad the rest, bro."

"There's nothing else to tell."

Jacob held the phone up. "These text messages say otherwise. Dad, Kaden and Hunter never broke up."

"What?" Duncan turned to Kaden. "Is that true, son?"

Kaden froze. He clamped his lips together.

"Here, you can read the texts yourself." Jacob held the phone toward Duncan.

Duncan shook his head and pushed the phone away. "I'm not reading his texts. Kaden, did you and Hunter break up?"

Kaden exhaled heavily in resignation. His deceit had come to an end. He shook his head.

"Then why did you say you did?"

Kaden shrugged.

"Oh, bloody hell! You did it for me and Chip, didn't you? You've been pretending this whole time. That's it, isn't it?" Duncan stared at the ceiling, putting his hands on his head. "Oh God." He leaned over Kaden, their faces just inches apart. "Son, do you love Hunter?" His voice was a mere whisper, filled with dread and fear.

Kaden shrugged again, unable to tell the truth, yet also unable to lie any longer.

"Son, you know the answer. I know you know the answer. Tell me, please, the truth. Do you love Hunter?"

Kaden gave a shallow nod before erupting into a pained cry. His entire frame quivered in despair. Duncan swept him up in his arms, the pain in his eyes mirroring Kaden's sorrow, his body shuddering as the sobs ricocheted through the air.

39

DUNCAN

When Duncan finally released Kaden from his embrace, Kaden rolled over and buried his face in a pillow, still crying. Through tear-filled eyes, he stared at his son and let out a deep sigh. With a trembling hand, he reached out to stroke Kaden's curly hair, feeling a knot tighten in his chest as he heard more sniffles, each one rending his heart in two. Every breath out of his son was a sorrow-soaked sob.

Duncan was acutely aware of the sacrifices that had been made for him throughout his life. His mother had endured tremendous pain in bringing him into the world and didn't miss a beat in reminding him that he was her most difficult labor of four. His parents had toiled endlessly to provide for their family, yet still made time to show their love at the end of each long day. His eldest brother had passed up a college education to help shoulder some of the family's burden.

Duncan had never experienced a greater display of love and sacrifice in his life than from this boy, who had been robbed of so much this year, and was ready to forego his own chance at happiness to save his hapless father.

Guilt swept over Duncan as he finally recognized the signs he had so readily dismissed. How could he have not known about the panic attacks? He should have done more to uncover the underlying causes of Kaden's struggles.

Not to mention that Kaden had been in such fear of being rejected and abandoned by his own father that he'd felt a need to hide the attacks in the first place. He'd failed Kaden. Truthfully, he'd failed both his sons. He was unfit to be their father.

Duncan took a deep breath, fighting back the sense of helplessness that threatened to overwhelm him. He slowly ran his hands through his tousled hair, looking away. His voice was ragged when he finally spoke. "Jacob, I need a big favor from you."

"Sure, Dad." Jacob's voice was so uncharacteristically soft, Duncan did a double take.

"Go out and keep Chip and Laura entertained for a bit. Don't let on what's happening." It was a tall task, but Duncan had every confidence in Jacob's capacity to sling bullshit.

"On it." Jacob left and closed the door behind.

Duncan dried tears from his eyes and stared at Kaden. "We're going to fix this, son. It's going to be all right."

"It's too late," Kaden said, his reply muffled. "It's too late. I've already lost him."

"Have faith, son."

Kaden slowly raised his head, his red eyes no longer hidden beneath the pillow. His voice shivered as he spoke the words. "Dad, he's moved on already."

Maybe it was too late. Duncan didn't entirely grasp all that had transpired between Kaden and Hunter. But if there was a glimmer of hope, Duncan had to try to fix it. He owed his son that. Duncan's mother had always believed he'd make a good father. Roz and Angie had put their faith in him too. It was time he proved them right.

Mustering all of his courage, he grabbed a tissue and wiped the tears away from his face, preparing himself for the task that lay ahead.

"Son. Are you okay in here for the moment? I've got to go chat with Chip."

"I'm fine."

"I can send Jacob back in if you want company."

"No. I'd rather be alone for now."

Duncan lowered himself slowly over the bed, his eyes searching Kaden's tear-streaked face. He paused, focusing on each feature as if it were a memory he wanted to keep forever. He pressed his lips to his son's forehead and ran his shaking hand over the boy's wet cheek. "I love you, son." His voice cracked as he uttered the words.

"I love you too, Dad."

Duncan trudged to the great room, each step feeling like he was dragging lead weights.

Chip glanced at him, opening his eyes wide and knitting his brow. "Don't take this the wrong way, but you look like you just got hit with a bat. What's going on?"

"I wish it was only that."

"Tell me, babe."

"Let's go outside." Duncan grasped Chip's hand and led him to the backyard. They sat on a wooden swing shaded by a tall oak.

Duncan exhaled. "Kaden and Hunter didn't really break up. They lied about it. Even Jacob didn't know."

"Wow."

"Then Kaden talked Jacob into saying he wanted to move here. They saw how depressed I was. They wanted us to be together."

"Damn." Chip glanced toward the house. "They really love you, Duncan. They love you so much."

"More than I deserve. Way more."

"That's not true." He clutched Duncan's hand.

Chip's hand was warm, and his own was cold and sweaty.

"So, what does this mean?" Chip asked.

Barely holding back tears, Duncan shook his head. "I can't do this to them. I can't do this to Kaden. I was in my twenties before I truly fell in love. He's fifteen. I can't even imagine what it must be like to fall in love at that age."

"I know. The world we grew up in, that just didn't happen to gay boys. Man, the unrequited crushes I had." Chip sighed. "So, you're not moving back to Charlotte, I take it?"

Duncan steeled himself to say the words. "I just can't."

Chip expelled a deep breath and fixed his gaze on the ground. "I understand. I truly do. But it hurts a lot more this time than when I lost you before. And what you're doing for Kaden, it just makes me love you more, which I didn't even think was possible. I'm not sure my heart can survive watching you walk out of my life again." His chest heaved as he clenched his fists. "Fuck. I should just quit my job."

Until Duncan had taken on the role of being a father, there had been nothing that took more priority in his life than keeping his career. Surely Chip had to feel the same. "Sweetie, I would never ask you to do that. It's not just a job. It's your career. Your whole future."

"I know. But it's my choice if I do. Listen babe, I don't know what kind of job I could find in Port St. Lucie, but if I have to pump gas, then that's what I'll do."

Duncan tilted his head. "Sweetie, you know that's not a job anymore, right?"

Chip rolled his eyes. "I'll bag groceries, or be the annoying guy that glares at customers in the self-checkout lines. Whatever. If you're open to letting me move in, and we make that young man in there happy, and not have the boys feel guilty about us being apart, then I'll do it. I want to be with you that much. God, I wish I had just quit when they first told me I couldn't relocate. If I had only known then what I know now."

"What *do* you know now?"

"I can't live without you, babe."

"Really?"

Chip stood, took Duncan's hands and lifted him, and held him close. Closing his eyes, he pressed his lips against Duncan's for a deep kiss. With their foreheads resting against each other, his voice quivering, Chip spoke. "Yes. I need you. I can't let you slip away from me again, no matter what it takes. I don't want to lose you a second time. But..."

"But what?"

Chip stepped back, but held Duncan's hands. "Babe, you never signed up to be financially responsible for those two boys. I feel like now I'm asking you to be responsible for me too. If I can't make enough money down there, I'll be a third person depending on you."

Duncan stared into his eyes. He was right. The prospect of that frightened him. "Sweetie, I need you to do something for me."

"What?"

"Smile," Duncan said.

"Smile?"

Duncan nodded.

"Okay." Chip turned up his mouth, and there they were. Those dimples he couldn't resist.

Duncan pulled Chip to him and they wrapped their arms around each other. He melted into his embrace, enveloped in Chip's warmth and love. He pulled back slightly and brushed his lips over Chip's cheek as he murmured in delight. "I need to see that smile every morning. Let's make this happen."

A FEW MINUTES LATER, Duncan was on the phone with Tamika. "Is the house under contract yet?"

"It's not," she said. "The broker says we're expecting an offer today."

Remembering all the hoops Tamika had jumped through to arrange the move and put the house on the market, Duncan scrunched his face as he spoke. "We've had a change in plans. Can we take it off the market?" He proceeded to explain the situation to her.

"I'll take care of it," Tamika said. "You're lucky the real estate market has slowed so much. A few months ago, it would have sold over a weekend."

"Tamika. I don't say this enough, but thank you. Thank you for everything you've done for me and my sons."

"Duncan, I've known those lovely boys their whole lives. They're like kin to me. And given what's happened to them, you've been their knight in shining armor. So, I want to say thanks to you. Thanks for stepping in when you didn't have to."

40

KADEN

After Kaden's breakdown, Duncan had cut the trip short, even though Kaden insisted there was no reason to rush back home. No reason to alter their plans, any of their plans. They should go ahead and move to Charlotte.

The drive home was nothing short of torture for Kaden; every emotion had been sapped right out of him.

He should have been aching with heartbreak over the whole Hunter situation. And Jacob's trick to access his phone, followed by the betrayal of Kaden's deepest secret and revealing the breakup ruse, should have enraged him. His father's insistence that they weren't going through with the move, and Chip's giving up his career, should have frustrated him.

When Kaden had gotten into the car and taken his phone out to silence it and put it into *Do Not Disturb*, he saw the date on the lock screen, and realized that today was Nanay's birthday, which should have compelled him to yet another round of grieving, just as Mom's had some months earlier.

He should have felt all these emotions, and probably more. But it was as if a hand grenade had gone off in his head and another one in his heart. There was nothing inside him now but numbness and emptiness. So, he'd collapsed into a mindless daze, drifting in and out of sleep.

It wasn't until they neared the house that he was able to rouse himself from his stupor. It was dark by the time Duncan's SUV exited Interstate-95 and turned east onto Crosstown Parkway.

"Almost home," Duncan called out.

Tenaciously, Kaden forced open his eyes and willed himself awake. Willed himself to feel something. Anything!

Kaden felt the hollow in his gut as he accepted the truth; Hunter was gone. The gut-wrenching evidence was undeniable. It all came back to him. Hunter had been the one to suggest the move in the first place. A sudden realization hit Kaden. Not only had Hunter suggested the move, but he'd gotten the idea after what Kaden now referred to as *The Jolly Rancher Panic Attack*. It was the first time Hunter had seen Kaden have a full-blown panic. The day he learned Kaden was seeing a therapist. The timing couldn't be a coincidence.

The idea of the move must have merely been a convenient way for him to be rid of a clingy, prudish, panicky boyfriend that he no longer found pleasure in. Hunter had managed to escape without having to do the distasteful job of dumping Kaden, and with no remorse.

It was almost certain that Hunter had known about Zeke being gay before it was revealed to the rest of the world. It seemed as if they had conspired together to get Kaden out of the way first. And Zeke was more than likely the brains behind the operation, perhaps even plotting to get Jacob kicked off the swim team. All of their plans culminated into one goal: to get rid of both brothers, and be done with them forever.

And at this point, surrendering to Zeke and Hunter's scheming would be for the best. At least Duncan and Chip would find happiness. Jacob could get a fresh start. It was ridiculous to just give up on the move like this. Pointless. Futile.

Best just to move to Charlotte and try to carry on. Then Kaden wouldn't have to go back to Aldenbrook Academy and risk seeing Zeke and Hunter walking the halls hand-in-hand together, stabbing him in the heart and twisting the knife.

The SUV turned the last corner as they approached their home. When the house came into view, Kaden's jaw dropped and he sat up straight, breathing deeply, trying to get a handle on the flood of emotion that hit him. There was a car in the driveway: a white Mustang convertible. The top was down.

What was going on? Why was Hunter here?

Until now, there hadn't been so much as a sliver of doubt in his mind that their relationship was over. But could he have been mistaken? Was it possible that maybe the entire conspiracy theory he'd concocted was all in his stupid, overthinking head?

Kaden whisked his phone out of his pocket. He'd set it to *Do Not Disturb* on the way home, trying to sleep, not wanting to be bothered when he was awake either. And to avoid the temptation to look at it in the car, and get even more nauseated than he already was. His finger slid open the notifications. There were missed calls, unread texts and a voicemail, all from Hunter.

The car turned into the driveway. Kaden was practically out of the door before it even stopped. He ran to the Mustang, but no one was there. A thin scrap of paper rested atop the steering wheel, reading "Out back."

Jacob joined Kaden beside the car. Kaden stared at him expectantly, holding the note in front of him. One side of Jacob's mouth rose into a smirk as he folded his arms, then cast his eyes about, feigning innocence.

"Why is he here?" Kaden's voice quivered.

"What? Bro, why wouldn't he be here?"

"He was with Zeke. Zeke was literally in his car at his house. I saw it on your phone."

"Bro, that was at swim practice. And that was just one of the photos. Didn't you scroll to see the others?"

Kaden looked away and mumbled, "No. I..." His face flushed, and he shifted his weight, refusing to meet his brother's eyes again.

"Like half the swim team all had pics with him in the car. When you get a Mustang Convertible, it does amazing things for your popularity."

"Oh." His mouth pressed into a thin line, his gaze cast downward.

Jacob's voice softened as he spoke, and his eyebrows creased with concern. "Did you think he was with Zeke?" He reached out a hand and rested it gently on his arm.

"Maybe."

"Bro, he is super into you. And he just might be back there waiting for your skinny ass."

Kaden crept around the side of the house, his heart thumping in his chest. As he rounded the corner, he spotted a glimmering light radiating from beyond the privacy fence. His stomach churning with anticipation, Kaden gingerly opened the gate.

The pool was glowing with the flickering of tea candles that surrounded it and cast an ethereal light. A song wafted through the air: John Legend's "Conversations in the Dark." Their song. Kaden scoured the area, desperate to lay eyes upon his beloved Hunter. He finally spotted him sitting alone at the café table, illuminated by candlelight, with a broad grin on his face.

He was dressed to the nines in a crisp navy suit and tie. He stood and held up a sign: *Would you go to prom with me?*

Kaden's body shook as he gazed upon Hunter, not daring to believe this moment was real. His throat was too tight to speak, and his heart raced as he stepped closer to Hunter. He reached up with both hands, cupping Hunter's face, and pressed his lips against his own. Their kiss seemed to last an eternity, until finally Kaden let go, his heart still pounding in his chest.

"Does that mean yes?" Hunter asked.

Wiping his eyes, Kaden stepped back and nodded.

They held each other tight and exchanged kisses again. Then Hunter swept Kaden onto the pool deck, where they grasped hands and swayed in time to the music. The tea lights below flickered dimly, like a thousand tiny stars, as they moved in unison. The rhythm was mesmerizing, and it felt like the night would never end until, finally, they returned to the table.

As they sat, Kaden picked up the cardboard sign. "Isn't it kinda early to be doing a promposal?" he asked.

"Well, I wanted to get you locked in, just in case some other guy on the swim team might get the idea of asking you."

Kaden twisted his lips. "I kinda freaked out about the whole Zeke coming out thing. And then I saw that picture of him in your car. You looked so happy with him."

Hunter raised his eyebrows. "I was happy. But it had nothing to do with Zeke, and everything to do with Mom and Dad getting me a convertible."

"Oh."

Reaching across the table top, he took Kaden's hand in his. "Speaking of Zeke, he apologized for his friend talking shit about us and starting the whole fight with Jacob thing. Zeke blames himself for it. He was struggling with his sexuality and he thinks he said stuff that triggered it all. He's going to talk to Ms. Middleton on Monday to explain it to her and see if she'll lift Jacob's suspension."

"Oh, wow!"

"He's a good guy. I think he might even become a friend. But only a friend."

"Oh."

"Did you have doubts about us?" Hunter asked, appearing hurt.

Kaden swallowed. "Maybe."

A smile tugged at Hunter's cheek. "I guess I understand. This whole move business has been tough. On both of us. You won't believe how loud I screamed when Jacob texted me that you were staying here."

Kaden smiled. "I wish I'd heard that."

"I'm surprised you didn't. You're okay now?"

"I am."

"And we're okay?"

"Yes." Kaden smiled a moment, then gazed out at the pool deck. "This is nice. Very romantic," he said, changing the subject.

"Full disclosure; Gabby helped me set these up and light them all. But it was my idea."

"It was a good idea," Kaden said.

"I don't know about you, but I could use a milkshake to cool off. I know you've spent all day in a car, but if you are up for it, maybe we could ride over to the Dairy Queen?"

"I dunno. I'm not sure I should go riding around in some boy's car late at night. He might get fresh with me or something."

Hunter laughed. "Look at you, being flirty."

"What? Oh my god. Was that flirty?"

"It was, chef. Very flirty."

"Wow."

"Come on, let's go," Hunter said.

"I feel underdressed next to you."

Hunter started to take off his tie. Kaden stopped him with a gentle hand and smiled. "No, leave it on. It's sexy. Let's go."

Every movement of their feet sent a pulse of pleasure through him as they made their way to the car.

Hunter opened the car door with an exaggerated bow. Kaden squealed and quickly scrambled his lanky body into the passenger seat. Hunter leaned in close. Kaden's heart raced with anticipation as Hunter softly planted a passionate kiss on his lips before hopping into the driver's seat.

Then someone cleared his throat. It was Duncan, coming out the front door of the house. "Boys. Going somewhere?"

Kaden's cheeks flushed. Had Dad seen the kiss?

"Oh, Mr. Valentyn, sir, could I take Kaden for a ride?"

"It's kinda late, but I think I can make an exception under the circumstances. You be safe though, young man. No hot-rodding," Duncan said, shaking his finger. Then almost to himself. "I am so turning into my father."

"I promise, sir."

The wind whipped their hair. They giggled, listened to music, and held hands at every stoplight. Kaden snuggled next to him and laughed when he stole a kiss during one particularly long wait for the light to change. Hunter bought them chocolate shakes and fries. They rode around until after midnight.

As Hunter brought him to the doorstep, the moment became suspended in time. Every movement, every breath, felt like an eternity of bliss. Neither boy wanted to disentangle. They lingered, their lips parted, and offered one last kiss before the night consumed them. Kaden felt the three words poised on his tongue's edge, itching to be spoken. Hunter's gaze seemed to hold the same desire, a plea for them to be uttered. But the boys remained silent, never confessing what lay hidden in their hearts.

"Good night, Kaden. Sleep well."

"You too."

Kaden did sleep well that night, snuggled in his own bed, wearing his sea turtle pajama bottoms, hugging his stuffed manatee, pretending it was Hunter instead.

He was home. In his heart, this was truly home.

41

DUNCAN

There was a loud rumble of a truck engine outside the house. Duncan ran to the front window and peeked out like a kid who'd heard the ice cream man. A rented box truck was coming to a halt in front of the house, its brake squealing.

"He's here!" Duncan said. He ran out to the front yard. Jacob and Hunter followed behind. A moment later, Kaden and Gabby, clad in aprons, joined them.

The truck door opened and Chip hopped out, ran to Duncan and they embraced, then kissed. "Babe. I made it."

"Damn, you look so hot getting out of a truck like that," Duncan said. "So butch."

Soon, they had the back of the truck open, revealing piles of boxes, a mountain bike, and a desk.

"Okay, guys. We've got to get this truck unloaded so he can turn it in," Duncan said.

"Seriously, Duncan," Jacob said, "I feel like a commoner yet again. This nonsense has got to stop."

"Come on," Hunter said, patting Jacob's shoulder. "It won't be that bad."

"You guys have fun," Kaden said. "We'll be in the kitchen." He and Gabby disappeared back into the house.

"Okay, I get that Gabby isn't helping, but how did Kaden get out of unloading duty?" Chip asked.

Duncan shrugged. "He's not really cut out for this, and you don't want him dropping your things, do you?" Aside from that, Duncan had a more important task for Kaden and Gabby that he didn't want to let out of the bag yet.

They began hauling boxes inside the house.

Jacob grabbed one that had about ten different labels on it that all said 'FRAGILE,' but he was handling it as if it were just a bag of trash, rattling and banging along with it.

"Jacob!" Chip said. "Be careful with that one. It's got my work computer in it."

"Dios mío. How am I supposed to know to be careful with it?"

Chip raised his eyebrows and ran his fingers over a few of the labels before taking the box from Jacob.

Duncan had just walked outside. "Did I hear you say *work computer*? Didn't you quit?"

Chip smiled. "I did quit. I marched into Monica's office and handed her my resignation letter, and watched her completely freak out."

"Holy hell. Honestly?"

"Yep," Chip said. "I told her why I was leaving. The whole thing, even about Kaden and Hunter. It brought her to tears. She made a few phone calls and next thing I know, they're letting me work remote. She couldn't let me go—figured she'd rather have me six hundred miles away than not at all."

"Oh sweetie. Why didn't you tell me?"

"I wanted to surprise you."

They continued to unload the truck and when they were done, sweat dripping from his every pore, Duncan said, "Anyone up for a dip in the pool to cool off?"

"Sounds like a plan," Chip said.

Soon, all of them were relaxing in the pool except for Kaden, who was busy in the kitchen.

Jacob was swimming back and forth, but the others, including Gabby, were just wading, lazily dipping their bodies in the refreshing water. Hunter and Gabby drifted over to Chip and Duncan. Hunter's brows furrowed as he glanced between them, then he cleared his throat but remained silent.

"Duncan," Hunter finally spoke, his voice barely audible over the sounds of running water in the pool. He shifted his gaze between the two men, his brows knitting together into a single line of worry. "And Mr. Masterson."

Chip smiled. "Just call me Chip, please."

Despite Chip's casual tone, Hunter still seemed tense, his eyes widening and his skin paling as he released a shaky exhale. "Okay. Thanks. I've been wanting to tell you both how thankful I am that you brought Kaden and Jacob back. I needed to say that, in case it's not obvious."

Gabby blinked back a tear as she looked between them both, her lips forming a grateful smile. "Me too," she said softly, her voice pained as she continued, "They're like brothers to me. I was so down when I learned they were moving. Jacob kept saying we'd still be friends gaming together, but it's not the same. So, thank you both."

Chip let out a breath. "I'm glad things worked out this way. And I really wish we all didn't have to live through the drama we did, especially since it turned out my employer finally came to their senses. At least we got through it, though, right?"

"Yes," Hunter said.

"And I feel like these trials have brought us all closer together," Duncan added.

The others nodded.

Eventually, Kaden came outside and looked at Duncan, his eyes sparkling like stars. Everything must be ready.

Duncan winked at Kaden and gave a slight nod.

Kaden smiled and winked back. "Any of you hungry?"

"Sure," Chip said.

After drying off, they proceeded inside to the great room.

"What's on the table, chef?" Chip asked. "I hope it's your Crispy Orange Chicken. Been craving that."

"Nope," Kaden said. "Something better." He pointed to a cake on the dining table.

Chip looked at the red lettering Kaden had piped on the white cake: *Welcome Home Future Stepdad.*

"What the hell? Future? What?" Chip turned around to look at Duncan, but when he did, he had to gaze down because Duncan had dropped to one knee and was holding a felt covered box out toward Chip.

"Sweetie," Duncan said, "I know we said we should take things slow, but, well, when you know, you know. So, would you marry me?"

Chip's eyes filled with tears. Gabby and the boys all stared at the two grown men with wide eyes. "Of course I will, babe."

They kissed and hugged, then Gabby, Hunter, and Jacob joined in for a group hug. Eventually, they all backed away from Chip. Kaden was standing alone at the table.

Chip smiled at him. "Can I hug my other future stepson?" he asked Kaden.

Kaden smiled back, strolled toward Chip, then wrapped his arms around him in a tight embrace.

42

KADEN

Kaden awoke early, at least early for him, and headed to the kitchen to check all of his supplies one last time. Today was the day, his chance to try once more to win the junior baking competition.

When Kaden had thought he'd miss the competition by moving to Charlotte, he and Gabby had quit practicing. But when he returned, and they'd gotten Chip settled in, he resumed in earnest.

Hunter was still in the middle of swim season, so he couldn't help much, but Kaden and Gabby got back into their rhythm, dividing up the tasks, getting more efficient each time. Playing *Elves of Ora Online* had taught them teamwork skills they'd been able to apply in the kitchen as well.

He'd refined the recipe as much as he was going to, picked out the best sources for each ingredient. Kaden wondered how much money his dad had spent on everything. It had to be at least a couple of thousand dollars by now.

Kaden had taken a great pleasure in letting Unique Mills-Foy know that he, in fact, wasn't moving away and would be happy to once again face her on the floor of the MidFlorida Event Center.

If he could finish ahead of her, even if he didn't win, he would consider that a victory. But there was something more important that motivated Kaden. Some of his fondest memories were the time he spent in the kitchen with Nanay, learning from her, and seeing Mom's and Jacob's faces light up when he'd made a delicious meal. Even if he didn't win, he still wanted to do well enough to honor his moms.

Hunter had a swim meet today and promised he'd come as soon as it was over. But Duncan, Jacob and Chip were going to watch the competition. Kaden loaded his boxes into the SUV, then they all drove to the venue.

"I know watching people cook is gonna be boring," Jacob said, helping Kaden get the boxes out of the car. "But I really wanna see Unique taken down. That would be the *icing on the cake*. Am I right?" He smirked and wiggled his eyebrows.

Kaden and Gabby sighed at Jacob before heading off to the contestants' entrance.

"Hold up," a woman in a nurse's uniform said. "Temperature check."

She pointed the thermometer at his head and after a beep sounded, she waved Kaden through.

Gabby was next. "Normally, I don't let anyone take my temperature without buying me dinner first." She giggled nervously, but the nurse's face was stoic.

The thermometer beeped, and Gabby stepped forward.

"Stop," the nurse said. "Too high. You can't go in."

"Huh?" Gabby said.

She showed the thermometer to Gabby. "You're running a fever."

"But I don't feel sick at all. I'm fine. I just read high sometimes."

"It's true," Kaden said. "Her Mom always says she's hot-blooded."

Gabby turned to him, her face turning redder than the thermometer reading. "That's not what Mom means by that."

"I'm sorry, young lady, but you can't go in."

Gabby closed her eyes. "Oh my god. I had spicy food for lunch. It made my face sweat. That's all it is."

"I'm sorry, but you can't compete today—competition rules. If you can get a COVID test real quick and show me it's negative, and your temperature goes down some... maybe."

"That'll take forever."

"This can't be happening," Kaden said. He then proceeded to express his frustrations in a colorful array of Spanish cuss words.

The nurse's eyebrows raised.

"What can we do?" Gabby asked.

Kaden closed his eyes. "I can't believe I'm suggesting this, but I think we need to see if Jacob can sub."

Gabby looked at him incredulously. "Jacob? Your brother, Jacob?"

"Yep."

"Are you sure? Wouldn't it be better by yourself?"

Kaden shrugged. "I can try to see if he's helpful and make him go away if not."

"I'll text him," Gabby said. "You get set up. I'll talk him through some things outside, then I'll make sure he's inside by the start time."

Kaden checked his phone's clock. He had half an hour. Maybe he could simplify his design and adjust the timing of some tasks. As he was checking to see what time it was, a notification popped up. Hunter had won his heat and was a finalist. He'd never done that well before. Kaden practically felt the victory himself and couldn't help but do a celebratory double-tap on the text message before going back to work.

He was proud of Hunter, but that meant he wouldn't be able to leave early and come here to watch.

Kaden set up on the event floor. There were ten stations for the teams. Chairs were arranged for people who wanted to watch from a distance.

The baking contest took place as part of an annual cooking and baking related trade show. The rest of the hall was abuzz with vendor booths for any and everything related to cooking, from high-end appliances on one hand, to questionable gadgets you'd see advertised on infomercials on the other.

With the competition beginning in under five minutes, Kaden kept glancing at the contestant entrance, hoping to see Jacob enter.

He scanned the audience and saw Duncan and Chip settling into seats, with Jacob right behind them. Kaden's eyes widened. He gestured at Jacob to get up there, and silently mouthed, "What the fuck?"

Jacob smiled and pointed a finger toward the side entrance.

Kaden spun around and there, haloed in the light like an angel, hair dripping wet, wearing a T-shirt, athletic shorts and swim sandals, was the most beautiful boy in the world. Kaden's heart raced like a hummingbird on steroids.

Beaming, he hustled to Kaden's station, the scent of chlorine wafting off his body. "Hi chef. You ready to do this?"

They hugged, and as much as Kaden wanted to kiss him, he was too self-conscious to do it so publicly. "What are you doing here? You didn't finish already?"

"I bailed out."

"But you were a finalist," Kaden said.

Hunter shrugged.

"Aren't your teammates mad that you left?"

Hunter laughed. "I lied and said I had food poisoning. Not something you want to have in a swimming pool if you catch my drift. They were so relieved I decided to leave before anything catastrophic happened. I'm sure they're thanking me by now!"

Kaden giggled. "You didn't have to do this. Honestly."

"Kaden, I wanted to do it. Besides, you and I both know Jacob would be more of a distraction than a help. He'd be like the lifeguard who can't swim."

"Probably." Kaden nodded, but knew Jacob had been the one who contacted Hunter. He owed his brother for that.

"So, what's the game plan?" Hunter said, taking one of the "Love

Wins" aprons and putting it on. He struggled to tie it himself, so Kaden did it for him.

Hunter had seen Kaden and Gabby in action many times, and had helped them make notes on procedures, but had never actually done much of the work. "I hope you were paying attention during the practices," Kaden said.

"I was, but I was paying more attention to you than to what you were doing. Just tell me what to do, chef."

Kaden smiled. "You got it, *chef.*"

"What is this?" A voice came from behind Kaden. He turned. It was Unique Mills-Foy, hands on her hips. "What are you doing here with this gay loser?" she asked Hunter.

"Oh, nothing other than attempting a hostile takeover of your baking contest domination! Just give me a few minutes and I'll have you out of the business for good!" Hunter replied.

She glared at them, then marched back to her station.

"She's in my history class this year," Hunter said. "That girl does not shut up with her bragging and trashing other people."

"Tell me about it."

Kaden had just finished explaining a few things to Hunter when the emcee spoke.

"Ladies and gentlemen. Welcome to the MidFlorida Event Center Junior Baking Competition. Today, over the next three hours, ten teams will vie for the grand prize. Which team will take home the blue ribbon?"

He thanked all the event's sponsors and introduced this year's judges. One was TV24 news anchor Dell Lorian-St. Pierre. Another was Salvador Rios, an awesome cake maker who Kaden followed on social media.

When the third judge was announced, Kaden cringed. It was City Councilwoman Karen E. McCaron-Rostro. He didn't follow local politics much, but he knew who she was. His moms had loathed her. She was infamous for being homophobic and opposed to anything that could be construed as LGBTQ+ affirming.

Kaden glanced at his and Hunter's brightly colored, rainbow patterned aprons with the words "Love Wins" emblazoned on the fronts. He sighed. Before he'd even measured one cup of cake flour, Kaden knew she wouldn't be voting to give him and Hunter a blue ribbon.

He didn't tell Hunter, though, not wanting him to know that they were already fighting an uphill battle after he'd given up so much just to be here.

The clock started, and the boys set to work, with Kaden talking Hunter through tasks, even while he proceeded with his own. They fell behind the planned timeline within the first half hour.

Occasionally, the judges would pass along the line of baking stations, watching each team for a moment, then moving on. The councilwoman never made eye contact with Hunter or Kaden, just poked out her lower lip at them.

"I don't think she likes us," Hunter said.

"Yeah."

"The news anchor lady seems pleasant, though, but that may just be the Botox."

Later, Salvador Rios came by again, this time while Kaden was making decorations for the top of the cake. He was carving a pair of lovebirds out of modeling chocolate. The feathers on one were auburn, the color of Roz's hair. The other was a shade of purple that had been Angie's most frequent tint.

"Impressive, young man," Mr. Rios said.

Kaden responded in Spanish. "Thank you, sir. It's quite an honor to hear that from you. I've long admired your work."

Mr. Rios raised his eyebrows and smiled.

Hunter whispered to Kaden after Mr. Rios had moved on. "I don't know what you said to him, but he seemed impressed."

"Doesn't hurt to butter the judges up."

"And do it in their first language too. You're wicked good at this, chef," Hunter said, beaming. "I know this isn't how either of us planned this day to go, but I have to say, it's cool to see you in action here." He stared at the lovebirds and stroked his chin. "Chef? Are those Roz and Angie's hair colors?"

Even after all their practices, Gabby had never made that connection. "When we are done here, I want to kiss you so bad."

Kaden had finished baking the cakes and put them into the freezer to chill before decorating. He went to check on them so they didn't freeze, but they were still warm. Something was wrong. They should be chilled by now. Then he opened the refrigerator door, and the light didn't cut on. He let loose a string of Filipino curse words as he went to the back and saw it had been unplugged.

"Unique Mills-Foy," he hissed as he plugged it back in and heard the compressor kick on. He spoke to Hunter. "Someone unplugged the refrigerator."

"What?"

"I know it was plugged in earlier. Absolutely, someone had to have unplugged it."

Hunter's eyes drifted toward Unique's station, and his face turned to a scowl. "Sabotage."

"Hunter, I need you to do something."

"Revenge?" Hunter said, wiggling his eyebrows.

"No. I won't sink to her level. Just go to all the other teams and tell them to make sure their fridges are plugged in."

A smile came across Hunter's face. "I would kiss you so hard if we had the time." He ran down the line, telling the other contestants. Hunter returned a minute later.

"Unique's face looked a bit embarrassed when I told her to check her fridge. She must have known she got caught."

"Wow. Sabotage is low, even for her," Kaden said.

After a while, Kaden had made up some of the lost time because the drip icing came out right the first time, and he'd gotten into the zone doing the piping work. Also, Hunter was doing a better job than Kaden would have ever expected.

But the last few minutes were going to be tight. Kaden had saved some caramel decoration work for near the end since the Florida heat and humidity would take a toll on them, even in this climate-controlled space. The later he made these decorations, the better the chance they'd be intact for the judging.

The stress was mounting. Kaden had made a couple of stupid but recoverable mistakes already, and now he had little time at all to get the caramel made. His hands were shaking. The caramel was almost ready to work with, but he glanced away from it for a few seconds to check something else, and when he looked back at the pot, it had crystallized. "Shit."

He dumped that batch and started again. On his next attempt, the pot was too hot, and it burned. Time was almost out. His heart was racing. No, not now. Not a panic attack now.

"You okay, chef?" Hunter said, concern in his eyes.

Kaden's eyes grew wide, and he shook his head.

"Kaden." Hunter put a hand on each of Kaden's cheeks and looked him in the eye. "Kaden. Kaden. Take a deep breath." His voice was calm. "Listen to me. It's going to be all right. No matter whether we win or lose, I still love you."

And there it was, the 'L' bomb dropped. After a moment, Hunter cast his eyes to the side, biting his lips. "Uh."

Kaden's eyes widened and his mouth went limp. By his estimate, he'd run several hundred thousand different "I love you" scenarios in his head, and replayed them millions of times each, imagining situations where Hunter said it first and he responded, or the other way around. In some, they were strolling on a beach. Or they might be at a school dance. He had even dreamed up ever so slightly unrealistic ones where they'd summited Mount Fuji together, Kaden, having twisted his ankle, being carried the last thousand feet in Hunter's arms; or Hunter winning a gold medal at the Olympics, pointing at Kaden from the medal receiving platform, mouthing the three words. But none of them involved him on the verge of a panic attack in the middle of a junior cake-baking competition.

And now was the worst possible time for him to have to respond. Thirty-seven percent of his brain was freaking out about the batch of burned caramel; forty-eight percent was trying to figure out how to avoid having a panic attack in the middle of the MidFlorida Event Center; thirteen and nine-tenths percent had just been vaporized by the 'L' bomb; one percent was devoted to telling himself to just breathe. That left him about eighteen brain cells to process this.

Kaden just stood there, feeling his face melt.

Hunter swallowed. "Wow. I just said that, didn't I?"

"You love me?"

A smile crossed Hunter's lips. "Maybe."

"I love you, too... maybe," Kaden said.

Hunter gave him a quick hug. "Okay, chef. You got this. Third time's the charm."

And it was. The three words had vanquished the panic that had nearly swept him into the abyss again. Kaden was in such a state of euphoria that his body went through the motions like some robot whose only function in the world was to make caramel. It turned out perfect, and Kaden, beaming partly from the caramel success, but mostly from the three words he had wanted to hear for so long, weaved stringy strands of hot caramel into a bird nest and placed it atop the cake, then set two love birds made of modeling chocolate in the nest.

That was it. The cake was done. His station looked like a bomb had gone off with flour, sugar, and chunks of fondant scattered on every surface, aprons covered with all that, and chocolate too. But the cake stood like a bastion in a storm, proud and tall. Gorgeous.

Less than a minute later, the emcee announced that time was up, and all bakers must take their hands off their creations and step away from their stations.

Two photographers swooped in and took photos of all the cakes. A TV station had a cameraman video them as well.

Meanwhile, the judges came down the line, examining and tasting each one, talking to the bakers, asking about flavors and ingredients but giving away nothing in their reactions. They left for some time to deliberate. A while later, it seemed forever, the emcee took a microphone in hand, clicked it on and tapped it to make sure it worked.

Kaden and Hunter stood side-by-side, holding hands. Hunter's hand was warm compared to his.

The emcee was handed three envelopes.

Kaden's grip tightened, the skin on his fingers turning white.

"Ladies and gentlemen, without further ado, the winners of our competition," the announcer started, sounding like those emcees at monster truck events, "But first, a big thank you to our sponsor, Whippanetix Stand Mixers. Whippanetix, the science of mixing."

He opened the first envelope. "Taking home the yellow, third place ribbon is... Team Frosting Goddesses."

They were a new team who'd never competed here before. It surprised Kaden they did so well. A round of applause echoed through the hall.

Every other time Kaden had entered the contest, when second-place was announced, his team's name was called. He waited, his heart racing, squeezing Hunter's hand even tighter. He closed his eyes, hoping to hear second-place go to Unique's team, named Caketastic.

"The second-place red ribbon goes to... Team Cake Makes Every-thing Batter." Another round of applause.

Kaden's eyes popped open, his breath caught. It was all or nothing now. They were getting a blue ribbon or walking out with nothing but dirty aprons and each other. Probably, nothing. He couldn't dare to dream that Unique would go from first place in the previous years, to not even finishing in the top three.

Hunter turned to Kaden. "Remember, chef, I love you, either way."

"I love you too."

"And now, ladies and gentlemen, the moment you've been waiting for. The first place winner is... Team Love Wins!"

Tears of joy flowed from Kaden's eyes. He gazed at Hunter, and his face was wet too.

"We did it," Hunter said. "Hell yeah! We did it!"

"Yep."

"I want to kiss you so bad right now," Hunter said, raising his voice over the din.

"Here, in front of everyone?" Kaden asked.

"Yes. A hell of a way to come out, eh?"

Kaden had resisted kissing Hunter at the start of the competition, hesitant about such a public display. That was before the three words he'd yearned to hear though. He stared into Hunter's eyes, warm eyes, loving eyes. "It certainly would be." His voice was lyrical.

"Can I kiss you, chef?" A bright blush tinted Hunter's cheeks.

"Yes, chef," Kaden said.

With the crowd still cheering them, they faced each other. Hunter cupped Kaden's cheeks, and they pressed their lips together.

They held the kiss until Jacob, beaming with pride, rushed forward and grabbed onto them both and kissed their cheeks. Only steps behind him, Duncan shouted joyously, and Chip bubbled over with enthusiasm as they threw themselves around the couple, wrapping them in an intense, exuberant hug.

Somehow, the emcee got the blue ribbon into Kaden's hand.

Before he knew what was happening, Jacob and Hunter had lifted Kaden into the air, carrying him on their shoulders.

Held above the crowd, Kaden glimpsed Unique Mills-Foy's dour face, lower lip poked out, arms folded. They locked eyes for a moment, then she turned in a huff and walked away.

Chip snapped a photo of Kaden, smiling, holding the ribbon proudly. And that photo would be the first one of himself that Kaden ever posted on social media. But it wasn't to be the only one.

A slew of other posts followed: Kaden and Hunter in his car, holding hands; Kaden and Hunter sitting on the beach, a heart drawn in the sand, their initials inside; Kaden, Hunter, Jacob and Gabby playing with the emotional support dog Chip and Duncan got Kaden for Christmas; Hunter and Kaden, in their prom tuxes, kissing; numerous pictures from Chip and Duncan's wedding.

Then there was the photo of Kaden and Hunter, holding their silver plaque from YouTube, congratulating them for their 100,000 subscribers on the *Chef Kaden and Hunter Baking Channel*.

One of Kaden's favorite photos was of him in front of the courthouse, along with Jacob, just after Chip and Duncan completed their adoption process, holding the birth certificate with his new name: Kaden Duncan Rivera-Watson-Valentyn-Masterson. He insisted he wasn't leaving any of the names out.

There was also a selfie of Kaden and Hunter, in the park gazebo, late at night, because even though they didn't have to sneak out in the middle of the night to see each other anymore, sometimes they still did anyway and slow-danced in the dark.

EPILOGUE

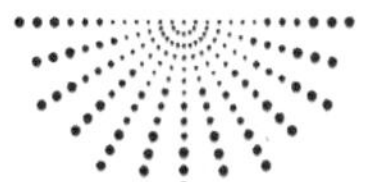

A COUPLE OF YEARS EARLIER...

Roz decked herself out in what she called her hazmat outfit; some well-worn jeans with holes the size of planets; a thick t-shirt that had once sported a picture of a cat next to a teddy bear, with the caption, "I licked it, so it's mine," but the graphics had faded to a ghost of their former glory; on one arm, a thick, bright green rubber glove up to her elbow. Over her eyes, safety goggles, and topped off with a hairnet. Beside her, Angie was decked out in comparable attire.

It was that dreaded time of year when they had to wield their scrub brushes like gallant knights in shining armor, to tackle a deep-clean of the boys' bathroom.

"Ready?" Angie asked.

"Yep." They did rock-paper-scissors on a three count. Angie's rock, lost to Roz's paper. Angie would have to take the dreaded *first crack* at it.

"Okay," Angie said. "I'm going in. If I'm not back in fifteen, you better come to my rescue."

"I will, girl."

Angie shot her a skeptical eyebrow raise.

Roz crossed her heart. "I promise. Last year was a fluke."

"Right." Angie's voiced dripped with sarcasm. She made a show of taking a deep breath before rushing into the bathroom like a soldier taking a beach.

Meanwhile, Roz finished putting her gloves on, readying herself for the second wave. Right when she snapped the second glove on, the silly doorbell chime rang through the house. Perfect timing!

Jacob had invited his friend Hunter over today after school. Her sons had been gaming online with him during the lockdown, and he was finally coming over for a visit for the first time. But the boys weren't home from school yet.

Grumbling, she headed to the front door. When she opened it, there stood a teenage boy, his feet together, hands tucked into the pockets of his athletic shorts, eyes shyly shifting, then he looked at her. His eyebrows raised. "Uh, sorry. I think I have the wrong house."

"Actually, I think you have the right house."

"Ms. Rivera-Watson?"

"You must be Hunter." He nodded at her, then looked off to the side. She couldn't help but crack a smile. This kid was almost as shy as Kaden, and just as adorable. "Well, I'm the odd one out. It's Watson-Rivera. The others are all Rivera-Watson. But just call me Roz."

"Oh, okay. Sorry. Is Jacob here?"

"The boys have been unavoidably delayed. Their carpool had a flat tire. But they should be along shortly."

"I'll come back later, then."

"Nonsense. Come on in and have a seat. But take off the shoes. My wife absolutely hates street shoes inside."

"My mom's the same way." He kicked off his swim sandals with a flourish, adding them to the already messy pile of Jacob's shoes that should have been in his room, but of course, weren't.

"I apologize for my attire." She held up her glove-clad arms. "I swear I'm not a mad scientist or a serial killer. It's bathroom cleaning day."

"Oh." He grinned as he timidly padded into the great room, lugging a nice Tumi bag, his eyes taking in the new surroundings.

Roz pulled off the gloves while making small talk, and offered him some cookies Kaden had made, not bothering to correct him when he assumed she had baked them.

"Jacob said you're the only other Asian on the swim team?"

"Yes. My grandparents all came from Korea."

"Are you one of those multilingual people I'm so jealous of?"

He laughed. "No. Just English for me."

"If the boys speak other languages around you, just slap them. I told them it's rude, but they do it anyway."

"Okay." Smiling, Hunter relaxed back into the sofa cushions.

"So, how does it feel to be back in actual, non-virtual school now?"

"Good. I missed being in the classroom, seeing my friends, and of course, the swim team."

Roz groaned inwardly. So, he was one of *those* kinds of kids, the weird, annoying ones who actually enjoyed school. Probably up at the crack of dawn, like Jacob and Angie too.

"So, you play *Elves of Ora Online* with the boys?"

Hunter nodded. "Yes." He fidgeted on the sofa as Roz struggled to get her rubber gloves back on.

"Believe it or not, I used to play *Resident Evil 4* back in the day," she said with a hint of pride. That only made him fidget more.

Angie emerged from the bathroom, grumbling, and walked over to stand near the sofa. "Oh, I thought I heard the doorbell. You must be Hunter."

Confronted with a second mad scientist-serial killer, Hunter swallowed hard.

The front door swung open, and Jacob bounded in. "Mom, Nanay, we're home." He was clad in nothing but boxer shorts, dirt, grease, and what appeared to be dried blood.

"I gave birth to that," Angie muttered.

"What the hell?" Roz said as she looked him over, hands on her hips. "Did you take up kickboxing and forget to tell us?"

"Nay, something even more impressive. I changed a tire. I'm officially a man." Jacob was beaming ear-to-ear.

"In your underwear?"

"Of course. Mom, look at me. Would you want all this shit to be on my school uniform?"

Roz exhaled. "I guess not."

"Looks like I picked a good day to actually wear underwear, for once."

"Too much information," Roz said. "How much blood did you lose in the battle?"

Jacob held up his arms for inspection, some gashes still oozing. "The exact volume hasn't been determined yet, but I'm still mostly conscious, so I wager no more than two gallons."

Hunter got up from the sofa and came over.

"Hunter!" Jacob approached for a hug, but was stopped by a firm hand blocking him.

"No offense, dude, but not right now," Hunter said with a wry smile. Oddly, the sight of his bloody best friend seemed to have set Hunter at ease finally.

"Oh. Yeah. Sorry. My bad. Obviously, I need to hop in the shower and bandage a few wounds before I can play. Speaking of... Mom, where's the duct tape?"

Before Roz could open her mouth to explain to Jacob that he wouldn't be wasting her good duct tape on himself, Kaden came in the front door. At least he was still fully clothed. Not a surprise. But the kid was barely mobile, his back bent at an odd angle, legs nearly buckling. He had his own book bag on one shoulder, Jacob's on the other. His left arm clutched Jacob's school uniform, while the right hand held Jacob's smelly shoes out away from him, as if they were some sort of toxic waste. He immediately dropped the shoes and uniform onto the floor.

And then, something happened. Something electric, even magical. In that exact instant, Roz felt it to her core. Kaden's eyes transfixed on Hunter. She knew that look. The aggravation that had been plastered all over his face when he had come in the door melted away in seconds, replaced by what in her mind she referred to as his Bambi-face. Uh oh. This poor boy was about to take another one-way trip to Heartbreak City.

Kaden's eyes remained fixed on Hunter's. "Sanyangkkun," he murmured, his voice filled with awe and wonder.

"Kaden Duncan Rivera-Watson! Speak English. That's just rude."

Kaden ignored her, not flinching or acknowledging her scolding even the tiniest bit. The boy was so far gone, she might just as well have been yelling at him from Pluto.

"Mom," Jacob said, "that's Hunter's gaming name. It's Korean for hunter. Pretty sick, yeah?"

"Oh." Roz felt a flash of heat in her cheeks. She was about to apologize to Hunter, but then she saw the expression on Hunter's face. His eyebrows were raised, head half tilted, lips ever so slightly parted. *Bambi-face!*

"Kadenator," Hunter said, his voice filled with the same sense of awe as Kaden's.

Well, now. That was an interesting turn. Roz stroked her chin with gloved fingers. An interesting and unexpected turn, indeed. How had she missed that? Maybe her gaydar wasn't as sharp now after being locked down for so long. If she was reading the room correctly, the magic between these two was mutual.

Beside her, Roz heard a quiet "Hmmm," from her wife. She looked at her. They exchanged a knowing gaze and smiled. They'd both seen it. Turning back to the smitten boys, she felt a sense of warmth well up within.

To this day, Roz remembered that giddy feeling. It took her back to a frat party, where she'd looked across a room and saw a blue-haired girl who looked like a goddess.

As she witnessed these two boys stare unblinkingly at each other, she fought the urge to pipe up and say, "Why don't you just make out already!"

Oblivious to the magic happening before his eyes, Jacob interrupted. "Bro! Why did you drop my shit on the floor?"

Kaden jolted, his eyes finally blinking. "Why does your bag weigh fifty pounds? And I'm not your personal valet."

"Hey, I'm dealing with significant blood loss here, dude."

Hunter sat back down, but kept Kaden in his line of sight.

Angie grabbed Jacob by the shoulder and took him outside to the garden hose to get him cleaned up.

Meanwhile, Hunter and Kaden had both gone into shy mode, casting furtive glances, trying not to get caught staring. Oh, well. Two shy ones. It might take some time, but Roz had a good feeling about this one.

~

THE END

THANK YOU

If you are reading this, I presume you completed the novel. You have my most sincere appreciation. I hope you enjoyed it. If you did, I have a favor to ask: Please tell others who may be interested, share on your socials, and remember, *Crunchy Orange Chicken* would make a great gift!

Finally, I want to mention that one of the best things fans can do for authors they like is to write honest book reviews on popular platforms such as websites where the book is sold.

ACKNOWLEDGMENTS

So many kind souls have aided me in my journey to completing this novel.

First, I must thank Drew, the love of my life, for his patience and for being the first reader of this novel. I also wish to thank those other early readers: Vicki F, Kim L, Rebecca B, Larry G, Alison G, and Debbie H. I truly appreciate the efforts of Betsy Thorpe, my editor, for bringing her decades of experience to this endeavor and making me a better writer.

A big thank you goes to the Morningside Writing Group. Your feedback every week helped shape this novel. I especially want to acknowledge Peter H and Gene H for carrying the torch for the group for over twenty years and I am honored by your trust in me to take the torch for the next generation of writers.

Finally, I want to acknowledge the global community of writers who selflessly help other writers through social media, webinars and conferences.

ALSO BY TREY LARI

Shuttered Hearts

ABOUT THE AUTHOR

After spending most of his life in North Carolina doing I.T. work that seemingly made no difference to anything, Trey Lari now lives in a typical Port St. Lucie, Florida home with the love of his life, Drew. When he's not writing, he can be found wandering beaches on Hutchinson Island, floating in the pool, or hanging out in bakeries or libraries with other writers.

Learn more: TreyLari.com

www.ingramcontent.com/pod-product-compliance
Lightning Source LLC
Chambersburg PA
CBHW051131130726
47988CB00005B/1792